Adam Roberts

THE DEATH OF SIR MARTIN MALPRELATE

DATURA

DATURA BOOKS
An imprint of Watkins Media Ltd

Unit 11, Shepperton House
89 Shepperton Road
London N1 3DF
UK

daturabooks.com
twitter.com/daturabooks
Change begets change. Nothing propagates so fast.

A Datura Books paperback original, 2023

Cover by Alice Coleman
Edited by Simon Spanton Walker and Andrew Hook.

Set in Meridien

ISBN 978 1 91552 302 0
Ebook ISBN 978 1 91552 308 2

Printed and bound in the United Kingdom by TJ Books Ltd.

9 8 7 6 5 4 3 2 1

MIX
Paper from
responsible sources
FSC
www.fsc.org   FSC® C013056

CONTENTS

Revolutions are the locomotives of history.
[Karl Marx, *Die Klassenkämpfe in Frankreich,* ch 3]

In 1848, revolution swept across Europe from Italy to Denmark, from Poland to Spain: more than fifty states were affected. The only major European nation not to undergo a revolution was Britain.

This was not because there was any lack of revolutionary fervour: early in the year there were protests and bread riots in Manchester, Glasgow, and Dublin and a huge gathering was held on Kennington Common, London, organised by the Chartists. Attempts were made by this crowd of protestors to march across the bridges of the Thames in order to present a petition to Parliament – many believed this 'presentation' was the pretext for an uprising, a sacking of Parliament and the establishment of a new revolutionary government. Many thousands of special constables were recruited by the city to contain the gathering, but in the event the crowd's passage across Westminster Bridge was prevented by a small number of police officers who managed to repel the throng despite being massively outnumbered. The petition was delivered to MPs but riot and revolution was avoided.

Chapter 1
THE DEMONIC LOCOMOTIVE

1

The story of the death of Sir Martin Malprelate acquired, from its earliest telling, a phantasmagorical quality, shrouding the violence of the assault in an embellishment of diabolic spectres and uncanny mystery. Strip it down to the bare facts and what did we have? One old man, beaten to death, on a night of freezing fogs, in November. A tale deplorable in itself, and deplorably common in this age of ours – concerning which, pressed between iron and stone, I do not need to elaborate.

The story of this killing became tangled up with the story of the railway the man himself was building: or say rather, the railway he was *forcing through* the material tissue of London, into its very heart. Nor was Sir Martin possessed of friends to decry his posthumous fabulation. An unbenevolent man, grasping, assertive, an individual who put his enormous wealth into the service of only that wealth's further augmentation. A miser, a skinflint, wealthy but sour, selfish and solitary.

No-one could gainsay his *energy*, of course, even in his eighth decade alive. He was often to be seen, stalking along the London streets (for he rarely travelled by carriage, and never rode the locomotives he was so instrumental in bringing into the town), his walking stick rapping a lively tattoo on the pavement. He possessed a head of superior size, whose mottled baldness gave it the appearance of an egg of one of the rarer birds. Sir Martin's nose was sharp as a thorn, and his eyes large and always in motion. His mouth, however, rarely moved from a thin, spirit-level slit across the narrows of his lower face, and on those rare occasions when it curled into a smile it was nothing warming.

His heart was not altogether hardened, it must be said. There was softness in that organ, sensitivity and feeling: but it expended itself upon the animal kingdom, rather than the tribes of his fellow humans. He who could look without a quiver on a suffering man, a begging creditor, a man ruined and expelled, could not stand to see a horse beaten. He hoarded his money and was as sharp at interest and accumulation as any in London, yet he patronized the new London Zoological Gardens with remarkable generosity.

Malprelate had, some decades earlier, made much money from the buying and selling of stock. Since nobody exactly knew his provenance or family, rumour filled the gap with lurid conjecture. His first notability came just at that time the Stock Exchange moved premises, from a Coffee House in Threadneedle Street to the purpose-built edifice in Capel Court and Shorter's Court. Rumour, that cackling bird, says that Martin, perhaps still too poor, or perhaps simply disinclined to furnish such financial stringencies, evaded the requirements by a combination of bribery and blackmail. That is to say: he did not act in the manner of a gentleman.

Three years later he was worth £70,000.

From here, his tireless energy of acquisition, combined with a perfect and merciless rigidity when it came to calling-in debts, propelled Sir Martin to greater and greater wealth. He bought himself a fine Mayfair house, though the outward ostentation of its marble façade was not matched by the disorder and Gothic excesses reputed to prevail in the interior. Judicious dispensation of funds bought him the use of a number of Members of Parliament, as well as a change of surname and soon after a baronetage. He dealt stocks, and he lent money. He bought and sold property. When the railways first came he saw immediately the fiduciary possibilities in the developments they would necessitate. He created the Middlemarch Grand Congruence Railway Company and prosecuted the acquisition of land necessary for its construction with vigour and without ruth.

To Camden, north of Regent Park – in which locality he was fated to die his bizarre and mysterious death – Sir Martin was an earthquake. Where residents were prepared to sell their land to him, he drove down the price with a specie of bullying negotiation he had perfected over many years. Where residents were reluctant to sell, he used his Parliamentary influence to have Acts passed that compelled the sale, and when these were challenged in the courts he did not scruple to have ruffians harass and intimidate the litigants. If that did not discourage them, he would deliver discrete bribes to the sitting judges.

In his last weeks alive he was often seen in that neighbourhood stomping up and down, surveying the ruin he had made: houses dismantled, streets torn open after the manner of a butcher operating upon a carcass. Enormous heaps of red London clay had been thrown up beside new trenches. In amongst this chaos of carts coming and going – past stacks of iron rails rusting purple in the rain – marching past half-built bridges like a bishop's crook rendered gigantic in stone – glancing down thoroughfares that were wholly impassable, stalking his way past the Babel towers of chimneys and fragments of unfinished walls and wildernesses of bricks, Sir Martin went. He looked into every detail of the works personally. He rebuked and chivvied the labourers. He snarled at the residents when they came out to complain.

The night he died he attended a resident's committee, held in the meeting room of a local inn and attended by a great many such irate Camdenites. Sir Martin plocked-in as the clock struck the hour – for he was always a precisely punctual man – attended only by his personal secretary, Aster. For a full hour Sir Martin took questions; or, rather, batted questions away, flourished his walking stick. He snarled and sneered. He insulted the character and manhood of the Camden residents, and mocked them for opposition to progress.

At the end of this meeting Sir Martin blankly refused to leave until he could walk out as the very last man. And so he sat himself on a chair, with his legs wide and his hands resting on his walking stick between them, staring directly ahead as, one by one, local individuals approached him, some pouring contumely furiously upon him, others begging and pleading piteously, but all washing like waves against the implacable and immoveable rock of Sir Martin, seated.

Eventually everyone else left, and Sir Martin remained alone in the hall, save for Aster. He remained for a time in that room serenaded by the hissing of the gas lighting. Then he stood up, told Aster to return to Mayfair and wait for him there, and strode out for one last survey of the on-going works.

Work continued long after sunset, lit by tapers that struggled to push their light through the chilly integuments of winter fog that wrapped themselves around every torch and every person. Workmen swung their picks and hoisted their shovels. They moved barrows full of dirt one way, or brought barrows full of bricks the other. And past them all Sir Martin stomped, stopping from time to time to criticize the energy, or the expertise, of this or that man. They all knew him, and they all knew better than to answer back. A man with a suitcase – perhaps a doctor, carrying a surgeon's bag – stopped on his way along the Camden streets to look down upon the old man walking the valley his men and money had made.

Now it was that Sir Martin approached his last moments alive.

He walked (the witnesses were all clear about this) alone, leaving the better-lit portion of the works to make his way down the corridor of opened land that his company had driven through the midst of what had once been houses and gardens, shops and workshops, schools and churches. Those domiciles spared by the destruction looked on mournfully from either side at the tongue of naked territory separating them.

Sir Martin walked on. The fog swirled as high as his waist, and the three-quarters moon cast a leper-white light upon the bank of mist, reflecting itself back upon his upper body and visage and giving him a spectral, uncanny appearance.

Then, one of two things happened.

If you live in the world of facts, you will believe a mob of disaffected men rushed Sir Martin and beat him down – perhaps angry Camdenites, perhaps workers aggrieved at his exacting and punitive employment, perhaps friends of one of the many labourers who had lost their lives in the oft dangerous work of building this railway line. Or perhaps some other group: anarchists, Reform radicals, foreigners. The police, who are constrained to investigate crime under the rubric of possibility and logical coherence, and who are now going from house to house, from worker's tent to tent asking questions: – they speculate that the attack was the result of some anarchist group, desperate men inspired by the dangerous ideas seeping through from the European mainland. For in this year of eighteen hundred and fortyeight, revolution is raging like wildfire everywhere across the Continent. These men gathered (so the police speculate) waiting for their moment – then came running down the corridor of land whooping and yelling, lanterns swinging, cudgels at the ready.

But not every individual is constrained by possibility and logic. For some a wilder and terrifying truth lies behind Sir Martin's death. And among such people we will find, if we enquire, the actual bystanders who witnessed the death.

For *they* say that they saw no mob of angry men. It was a train, they say they saw: a great spectral locomotive, gleaming pale green and with one headlight to the fore shining a hellish red as it ploughed through the fog. Those who actually witnessed the death swore, and could not be persuaded to forswear, that this great rolling engine appeared as if from nowhere – that its wheels rang suddenly and melodiously upon steel rails like a great bell – though no rails had, at that time, been laid – that tonguing horns of red sparked from its firebox as its driver (no human creature) tossed-in shovelful after shovelful of hellblack coal – a fiery devil-train, thundering along by its own glare of light and lurid smoke.

The police, belonging to this other world, this realm of possibility and logic and material reality, pressed these witnesses to change their testimony. They would not. The witnesses were only relating, they insisted, what they saw.

And Sir Martin saw it as well! For he turned, and loosed a shout of pure terror – saw the red eye of the metal devil, bleared and in the mist, close upon him – and an instant later he was beaten down, caught up, and whirled away upon a jagged mill that spun him round and round, and struck him limb from limb, and licked his stream of life up with its fiery heat, and cast his mutilated fragments in the foggy air.

And then, say these witnesses, the train hurtled away, off into the night.

"But," says Detective Inspector Bucket, his hands behind his back, and his head slightly to one side. "Where did it go *to*, this train you say you saw?"

His interlocutors do not wish to name the place towards

which, they believed, it was travelling. Some of them shuddered in superstitious horror.

"The ground *had* been cleared," said the Inspector. "Preparatory for the laying of railway track. But I walked there this very morning, and examined it under the bright light of a morning sun. No track has as yet been laid in that space. How could a locomotive proceed over the ground without rails?"

"No ordinary locomotive," growled Foreman Williams. "An infernal, a spectral train."

"Spectral enough to float impressionless over the red clay of north London," noted the Inspector, "and yet substantial enough to break Sir Martin Malprelate's body and crush out his life?"

The witnesses will not be talked round. They saw what they saw. "It went whence it came," Foreman Williams insisted, "and it dragged that fellow's soul down with it as it passed."

2

So: Sir Martin dies, as we all must die, and is laid – his bruises and cuts amended by the mortuary make-up and stitching – in the sepulchre he had himself purchased for his mortal remains some years before – a great granite cube situated in the grounds of his country house in Barsetshire, looking like nothing so much as a gigantic cash-box, its curlicues and stony ornamentations like padlocks, and the Malprelate coat of arms, only recently acquired, brazen above the sealed-up entranceway.

But if those who killed him hoped that their desperate and violent actions would in some way impede the progress of the London and Middlemarch Grand Congruence Railway Company, they soon found themselves mistaken.

The Company is more than its founder and chief shareholder. It is a board of stony-faced directors, and a number of brass-buttoned shareholders, and a sheaf of parliamentary orders, and a huge, waiting population of future-travellers. Its momentum is not to be checked by the departure of its founder.

Still, it was considered not conducive to the efficient working of the LMGCR that any mystery, or worse any scandal, or worse still any *supernatural* scandal, be associated with the death of its founder. The stony-faced directors, and the fattest and most dignified of the brass-buttoned shareholders, speak to the Police Inspector regarding his investigation and are not reassured. Prominent among them is the aquiline Sir Persimmon Hawk, hard-eyed and harder-nosed, glowering down from his central seat. They say that Sir Persimmon had been the closest Sir Martin Malprelate came to a human friend – since Sir Martin's former ally on the 'Change, Ebeneezer Scrooge, had undergone his conversion experience (Methodism, is the rumour) and abandoned his efficiencies of money-making for depravities of charitable action and money-dispersing. After that, Sir Martin had walked the chambers of the 'Change, conversing with none, bidding good day to none, and even the directors of his railway company had been as strangers to him. Except Sir Percy, it is said. Approach him – and few have the courage to engage so formidable an individual in idle conversation – and he would deny it. "Martin cared for animals," he would say. "He cared for all animals except one: the human animal. I was not his friend, for human friends were not among his requisites. And now he is dead."

"A tragedy," replied Inspector Bucket.

"His testamentary situation," said Sir Persimmon, "is uncertain. As to which of the several wills that appear to exist are the final item, and to whom his wealth – including his majority shareholding in the London and Middlemarch –

will revert. The London Zoological Gardens, it seems," (the expression on Sir Persimmon's face was such as to express his disdain for such waste of money) "will inherit much. But until the will has worked its way through Chancery, the shares are frozen. Leaving me the leading voting shareholder in the company."

"So I understand, sir," said Inspector Bucket.

"As such, I say: this terrible crime must not be permitted to interfere with, or in any way interrupt, the development of this line. It is good," Sir Persimmon Hawk said, as the other directors bowed their heads, and listened, "that the official line, soon to be confirmed by the coroner, speaks only of common assault, and repudiates the motion of any demonic locomotive. It is necessary for the continuing progress of the line, and the profitability of this company, that the matter be disposed of quickly and put behind us."

"It is a likely explanation of the violence of the death," Inspector Bucket replied.

Sir Percy's expression hardened. "But it is *not* good," he went on, "that the police have proceeded no further in their investigations than this. Luddites or revolutionaries, angry locals or organized criminals – *who* attacked Sir Martin? And why?"

"Our investigations continue, gentlemen," the Inspector said, and took his leave.

At this point, the suggestion came from one of the grave-faced directors to one of the brass-buttoned shareholders, or perhaps the other way around, that Bryde be relieved of his present duties designing improvements to the functioning of the engines and couplings, and instead be deputized by the Company to pursue investigation.

And so they came to Bryde, in his small back-office, a room not very conveniently accessible from the magnificent marble frontage of the LMGCR main building. He was there with his engineering diagrams and sketches, his angled drawing board, and his small iron stove to keep out the worst of the November chill. In they came, two of them, brassy not only in the buttonage, grave in more than just their funereally black frock-coats – sounding, and death-oriented.

Would Mr Bryde be so good as to undertake his own private investigation into the tragic and mysterious death of Sir Martin?

Bryde put his head to one side.

"Mr Bryde," said the grave-faced director on the left. "Your reputation precedes you. The work you did last year, scrupulously unpicking the tangled threads of the Barsetshire Sabotage mystery – the one with the eagle – was most greatly appreciated."

"Of course," said the grave-faced director on the right. "Expenses will be reimbursed by the company. And as before, and upon the satisfactory termination of the investigation of the mystery, an honorarium would..."

Bryde put his hands together. "Gentlemen," he said. "In a case such as this, it is not a matter of financial emolument. It is a question of establishing – by God's grace – that the *material* nature of the crime, horrible though it surely was, ought from the first to drive out thoughts of fables and hell-fire. For that reason alone, I would be honoured to investigate."

They thank him, and shake his hand, and the grave-faced director on the left hands him a letter signed by the board relieving him of his regular company duties for the duration of the investigation. But his mind is already elsewhere: sorting methodically through the many threads and geegaws and items that the bird rumour has gathered in her nest. Every employee in the company has, naturally, been talking about Sir Martin's death and nothing else, since it happened. Speculation built upon dubious reportage, hypothecations and pronounced certainties fly here and there, and Bryde has heard all of them. Most are worthless, he knows. But there may be some that merit his closer investigation.

3

"You must understand," said Enoch Ninecroft, "Sir Martin Malprelate was *such* a man – such a man as is known in all the city from north to south, from west to east. With *such* a man – you mark what I mean when I call a man such? – with *such* a man few mourn his passing. The poet said that the death of every man diminished him, but when Sir Martin was struck down, and the news first reached the 'Change, I may report, sir, a cheer echoed round the building."

They were in the snug of the *Saint George and Dragon*, and Bryde had just finished writing in his notebook the cost, to the last precise ha'penny, of the bowl of punch with which the establishment had supplied their table, so as to be able to claim the expense of it back from the company.

Snug is a snug sort of word, compact and comfortably in-folded but in the *George* (whose proprietor was indeed called George) *and Dragon* (whose innkeeper's wife indeed had a reputation for ferocity) the "Snug" but poorly embodied the qualities such a word ought to body-forth. The walls were grimly coloured, the timbers tar-black, the light from hissing gas-lamps at once too bright to look at and insufficient to drive the shadows from the corners of the space. The lack of a fire in the fireplace meant nothing prevented the tendrils of mist sneaking in from outside.

Both men sat with their coats buttoned-up and their hats still on. There *was* a fire, in the main saloon, and Bryde had suggested they take their seats in there – but Ninecroft was strangely averse to the flames in the fireplace, and so they had moved into this adjoining area. Bryde thought perhaps he wanted privacy. The truth was otherwise.

Still: at least the punch was steaming hot.

"*You* did not cheer?" asked Bryde. "To hear of Sir Martin's death?"

Ninecroft shook his head. "I was perhaps the only man in London truly sorry to hear of his demise. Though this was from no fellowship on my behalf, I assure you."

"Why, then?"

"My father, sir, was in the Marshalsea. I despaired of his release – to think of his gentle heart, breaking under the duress of imprisonment! – of his grey hairs in such a place! Every night I feared he would lie down on the narrow bed of his cell and never wake again."

"And the debt for which he had been incarcerated?"

"It was a note drawn on his name, a sum borrowed from Sir Martin Malprelate. Sir, you must understand – I am not wealthy. From my salary, such as it is, I support my wife and our children – and my father too. I had nothing of value that Sir Martin Malprelate might covet, save only the domestic happiness of a loving wife and family. But I do believe nothing so humane could stir the iron rail heart of that man."

"And yet there *was* a thing he wanted?"

"My house. The row had been purchased, by Parliamentary order, and all my neighbours ejected – but my lease was a separate entailment upon the land which, it so happened, construed a proprietary estoppel. Sir Martin needed the whole plot to drive his railway through and only my house stood in his way. Believe me, Mr Bryde, I did not *desire* to stay in this neighbourhood: Malprelate's workmen had demolished each of the adjoining properties, working to maximise the din, at night, seeking to drive us out by sheer annoyance. But we had nowhere else to go! And we could hardly sell the property on the open market, for a fair price, sir: for who would purchase a house in such a position? Who other than that grindstone of a man, for a knock-down. On a day, Sir Martin sent his secretary – the loathsome Aster, more snake than man – to threaten my children. On another day Sir Martin came himself, rapping at my door with his walking stick and, when I would not open, bellowing through the letter box that he *would* drive the railway directly past my dwelling, and that more smoke and soot would pour *down* my chimney to poison my air than would emerge from it."

"He did offer to purchase the house himself?"

"For a derisory sum, sir. Such was his way. But I must take the amount and with it purchase a new house, must I not?"

Bryde nodded.

"Perhaps I am a stubborn man, Mr Bryde. I had nowhere else to go. And so I resisted, and refrained from answering the old miser in kind. Until my dear father was placed under restraint!"

"You could not raise the funds to clear his debt?"

"No, sir, no. Alas no. There was only one way. I must go to Sir Martin Malprelate's mansion in Brook Street, and make obeisance, and offer him my house – my family's home – in the hope he would accept it and so return to me the promissory note that kept my aged father penned in the Marshalsea."

"And so you went," said Bryde.

"Sir," said Enoch Ninecroft, drawing himself up, "it was a bitter draught for me to drink, but I downed it. I swallowed it whole. I called at Sir Martin's mansion and was announced. Mayfair is a place of fine houses, Mr Bryde, and from the outside Sir Martin's is of its place. But inside it is a miser's cave – each room crazy with heaped-up rubbish and treasure indifferently intermixed. Cats running wild in great packs. Birds nesting in the chandeliers and their waste layering its noisome paint upon the floor beneath."

"Were there no domestics, to clean and care for the place?"

"Sir Martin keeps, kept I should say, but two: one retainer, a twist-faced old goon in livery, and one old crone as maid-of-all-works, to cook but not to clean, for nothing there *was* clean, in that whole mansion. And he the richest man in London, they say!"

"They say," Bryde agreed.

"I could not call during daylight, for I could not absent myself from work. By the early evening when I arrived it was already dark. This was November, a few days before Sir Martin's death – you'll remember how cold was the weather. I was kept waiting in the hallway, rubbing and pressing my hands and shivering, with no company but the spiders who were busy adding more cloth to the great swags of cobweb that hung from the ceiling, peering at myself in the hall's one great mirror, its glass spotted like a pard. The dust was on the marble floor so thick, it looked like velvet, save only the tracks scraped clear by the passage of feet, and two ha'penny candles standing in silver candlesticks on either side of the door were the only illumination.

"Eventually Sir Martin's secretary, Aster, came and asked me whether I had brought the deeds to my house with me. 'For if you have not them about you,' he sneered, 'you but waste our time, and Sir Martin is never pleased with the useless expenditure of time.' I assured him I had the document on my person. With a grin that would befit a tiger, he told me to step through.

"We passed through an unlit chamber in which a narrow way was passable between two banks of piled-up furniture and junk, fitter for a warehouse than a fine mansion in Mayfair – and through to a room lit only by the red gleam of a fire. Though he was called a miser by many, Sir Martin did not altogether stint his creature comforts, though they were such as would gratify a humbler man than he: meat and ale and an open fire. And there he sat, in the glow of the fire, his familiar beside him."

Bryde asked: "His familiar?"

"O, sir! I thought it a devil, upon my faith! Though it was but a bear."

"A bear?"

"It looked like no bear you ever saw – small in stature, no taller than a ten year-old child, and with its fur mostly gone. It had been brought to the country from far away for the baiting, but had proved but poor entertainment in that. Not violent enough they say, not big enough either, or so I have heard. It had been mauled, had lost its claws, and one eye – and then, for the quirk of it, Sir Martin had bought it and kept it in his home. He had his freak for the animal kingdom, as perhaps you know. Would that some such kindness had been his where his fellow men and women were concerned! The bear sat beside him as a loyal dog might, though its scars looked like snakes upon its black skin, and his one eye glared with pure malevolence. Sir Martin would scratch its ears and sometimes feed it morsels of meat, and both he and his pet watched me come in."

"'You have the deeds, sir?' he barked at me. 'I have, Sir Martin,' I replied, in as courteous a tone as I could manage. 'Well you have led me the merry dance, young man,' he growled at me. 'Will you have the good sense to apologise?' I confess, Mr Bryde, that a spurt of manly feeling rose up in my breast at his words. 'You must forgive *me*, Sir Martin,' I said, 'if I abstain from apologizing to a man who designs to seize my only home, and to cast my family on the streets like beggars.' 'Tush,' he said. 'Beggars? You are employed, I believe, as a clerk? Gainful employment makes no beggar.' And all through this exchange, the bear was watching me. I'll not lie Mr Bryde: I had fortified my courage on the way to Mayfair, at a potshop, where I had drunk more than one glass of brandy, and the spirits were toying with my senses. I could not *look* at Sir Martin – for my eye was captured by his pet, his familiar. And as I looked at the bear, the bear looked at me. Its one eye, black and glinting red in the firelight, stared *through* me, sir. I trembled. I am not ashamed to admit it. 'Let us have the deeds, then,' cried Sir Martin. 'Let me cast my eye on them, and ensure they are legal and tight.' I passed the papers to Aster, and Aster carried them to his master. The bear ignored the secretary, all the time keeping his eyes on me. O, but then it roused itself, and stood up – it stood on its hind feet and opened its mouth to show its teeth. I shook where I stood sir, I'll confess it! I might have been seeing a demon rising from hell.

"'In return for these deeds, you require *this* promissory,' said Sir Martin, holding out a folded parchment, but not putting it within reach of my hand. '*This* very document?' 'It will release my father from debtor's goal, sir,' I replied, though my voice quavered, and I could not take my eye from the bear. 'It is my only desire, Sir Martin, that he be quit of the debt to you and free to rejoin his family.' 'Go to, go to,' Sir Martin replied. 'I'll part with the promissory, in return for the house.' But he put the parchment back in the breast of his housecoat. 'Sir,' I addressed him, though my heart was thumping. The bear took a step and another step, walking with its toes turned inward the way bears do, and coming towards me. I could not help but recoil, stepping back towards the door. He had his pet on a leash, like a dog, with a studded collar around its muscular neck, but he was not holding the other end of the rein, so it seemed to me there was nothing to stop this beast launching itself at me. I thought of its feet, Mr Bryde! Its teeth! Its malevolent eye!

"I said: 'Sir Martin, I would be most obliged if you would pass the promissory note over to me, as per our agreement.' 'You seem eager to be *gone* Ninecroft,' he said, grinning a most unkind grin. And again the bear took a step towards me and again I flinched. 'Sir Martin,' I repeated, though my voice was high and my 'm's multiplied like pebbles in my mouth. 'I must beg of you, to let me have the document.'

'I'll have it sent over to your office,' he said. 'Tomorrow – or the next day.' 'But I cannot release my father from prison without it, sir!' I pleaded. 'I must have it.' 'Oh m-m-m-must you?' he mocked. 'Then you shall – tomorrow. Or the next day. I am not in a giving mood this very moment. Tomorrow, I say. Aster, see the gentleman out.'

"You'll think me, perhaps, a coward, but I was so eager to leave that hideous room, and the open malice of that man, and especially that devil-shaped bear, that I fairly ran back through the building to the front door. I was outside again before I knew it."

The memory of the occasion had brought sweat to Ninecroft's brow, despite the chill of that room, and he mopped it with a handkerchief.

"I am not here to impute blame, Mr Ninecroft," Bryde assured him. "I am only trying to understand."

"Understand, then, that I was now, functionally, homeless. Understand that I had surrendered my house not for the note itself, which would have freed my father, but only for that terrible old man's *word* that he would deliver the note to me at some future date. Could I trust his word? Would *you*? But what could I do? I went to work, and spent the next day in an agony of anticipation – but the note did not come. The day after went the same way. On the third morning, I heard the news of Sir Martin's death. Terrible!"

"Terrible," agreed Bryde.

"Malprelate, dead," sobbed Ninecroft. "And my prospects with him! Now, on receiving the news, Mr Bryde, I did something I had never done before: I requested of my supervisor to leave the office – the other clerks were agog – and I fled through town until I came to the Mayfair house. How desperately I desired that note! And, I told myself, Sir Martin had *promised* it to me! So I went to the house. To see it in daylight, and with a great many people coming and going, was to find it looking like any other house, and not an antechamber of hell after all. Just a normal house! But I needed the note. I went to the door and requested assistance – there was a police officer standing in the doorway, and he summoned an inspector—Inspector Bucket—who listened to my pleas. I was permitted inside and was taken through to Sir Martin's study – a great desk, locked, and many boxes. With every step I was in fear of encountering the old man's familiar, but the bear was nowhere to be seen, and I was too trembling and anxious to ask after it. My only thought was to reclaim the note I had been promised. Mr Bucket accompanied me.

"In the study sat Aster and another gentleman – this was Mr Wittiterly, whom I later discovered to be a financial officer for Sir Martin's great railway company, the Middlemarch and London line. Not knowing this individual, I addressed myself to Aster, begging him to let me have the note that would release my father. He affected not to know what I was talking about, and waved his hand at me insolently, to dismiss me from his sight. Oh, Mr Bryde, how my poor heart fluttered! I reminded him of the meeting at which we both had been present, only two nights since, but he only smoked his cigar with insolent disregard and looked past me. It was Mr Wittiterly, a man not so heartless as his colleague, who intervened. 'Come Aster,' he said. 'You yourself told me of this when we lodged the deeds to that house – *this* gentleman's house, I take it. When I asked you how you had finally been able to extract those deeds, you told me you had exchanged them for a promissory note attendant on an old man in debtor's gaol.' 'Why yes,' Aster drawled. 'It had slipped my mind, but now that you say so, Wittiterly, there was something of the sort, some scrap of paper or other.'

"I asked if I might search the desk for the document, and Aster scoffed: 'a nobody like *you*?' he drawled. 'Rummaging through the late Sir Martin's private papers? Certainly not.' But Mr Wittiterly took pity upon me. 'I give you my word,

Mr Ninecroft, in the hearing of Inspector Bucket here, that I shall retrieve the document and bring it to you.' I gave him my card and described the nature of the document itself and returned to my workplace. My wage was docked for this absence, sir, and without the promissory note in my hand I was anxious – terribly anxious. But at the same time I could feel the flickering of hope in my breast, that perhaps my ordeal would soon be over. Mr Wittiterly was surely a gentleman, and surely the Inspector would see right done.

"Alas – Wittiterly came in person to tell me that he had searched the desk and all the boxes in Sir Martin's study and had not found the promissory note. I wept, sir, I will not deny it. 'Mr Ninecroft,' he said to me: 'I apologise. I gave you my word, and would not break my world for all China's tea, but truly I have tried every effort and searched every possible place. I have consulted the clerks – the deeds to your house were indeed received, and have been lodged – but the last anybody saw of the promissory note was Sir Martin putting in in the pocket of his housecoat.' 'And it is not there now?' 'No sir.' 'You *do* believe,' I urged, 'that I passed the deeds to Sir Martin and that assured me he would give me the note?' 'I do,' he replied. 'But there is nothing can be done – without the note itself in your hands, the debt stands and I am afraid your father must remain in prison.' 'Could you at least return me the deeds of my house? I may yet be able to sell it and – 'The demolition order has already gone out. An eviction notice has been pasted to your door. It is too late.'

"The darkest of days, Mr Bryde! When I left work that evening, it was to find my wife and our children sitting in the street, with our few sticks of furniture discarded on the pavement. I was able to rent a single room by pawning my overcoat, and by borrowing a small sum against my end-of-month salary: an incommodious and unsanitary room it was, but at least a roof over our heads. The following morning, before going to work, I called by the police station at the Scots yard and spoke again to the inspector. Such lurid stories were circulating as to the manner of Sir Martin's death I could hardly credit them. But the police were considering foul play and had explored – the inspector assured me – the house in detail. Gone through every room, top to bottom! There was no sign of the promissory note – of *my* promissory note – the key to my father's prison! But without it, how could we rescue my poor beloved sire? The police inspector made me rehearse all the details of my meeting. He was, he said, sympathetic – although I felt, also, that he judged me for having left the Mayfair house without holding the precious parchment in my hands. It is true! I was weak and fearful. I drank, Mr Bryde, and it lowered me."

Ninecroft put his head in his hands.

"Please continue with your account," Bryde prompted.

"The next portion of my narrative is the hardest to credit," said Ninecroft, in a low voice. "And yet I must relate it. You must understand: all hope seemed lost. After work I repaired not to my wife and children, but to a private club in Covent Garden where the brandy is…" He broke off.

Bryde waited, but Ninecroft had stalled.

"*Was* it Covent Garden, Mr Ninecroft?" Bryde prompted, gently.

Ninecroft shook his head.

"Was it," Bryde went on, giving voice to his intuition, "perhaps – Limehouse?"

At this Ninecroft looked up. "It was!" he said.

"And *was* it brandy?"

"Opium," croaked Ninecroft, as if the confession rasped his throat. He put his head in his hands. "It began," he went on, in an uncertain voice, "some years ago, when I was troubled with a raging tooth. That was when I first tasted this cursed drug. But the tooth has long since been extracted and yet – I continue to rely upon – "He stopped.

Bryde waited patiently, judging the time, and then prompted him: "Go on, Mr Ninecroft, with your account."

The hands dropped away, and there was a glare of what seemed, almost, like defiance in Ninecroft's eyes. "Yet I will swear to it," he said. "You will not believe me, but I will *swear* to it! Believe me, Mr Bryde, my shame at my opium-eating is quite as large as your quite proper disgust – and yet I will swear to it! It is the truth, the truth as witnessed by God himself."

"Go on," said Bryde, quietly.

"I visited my usual establishment, in Limehouse as you say, and lay myself on my usual low cot to breathe in the drug," said Ninecroft. "But where, usually, it brings me relief, a semi-somnolent release from my cares, this time the effect was quite different. Whether the scoundrel who runs the den gave me inferior opium, or perhaps included in the gum some extraneous chemical ingredient, I do not know. In the usual way of things I would lie, blearily content, upon my cot half awake and half asleep. But that night! *That* night I plunged – positively plunged, Mr Bryde – as if the bed were a trap-door that opened. I fell into a dark place. I sank, time out of mind. I thought at first that I had been slain, and buried in the ground, so dark and silent it was. And then I saw a glow."

"A glow," Bryde repeated.

"Red as blood, not like regular firelight. Yet it was the glow of fire. It crept at the edges of my vision, and when I turned my head to look upon it, suddenly it was all upon me – all around me – the light rushed me, hurtled in upon me. I was again in that dreadful chamber, and the firelight was again flickering malevolently – and there was Sir Martin Malprelate again, grinning at me. His secretary was not there, nor was that ghastly familiar ape of Sir Martin's, the hairless bear – and yet Sir Martin, dead, *was* attended, by three devils, each grinning like their master, or perhaps he was their prisoner, I know not. One devil was red, one green and one black as coal, and all were covered with steel scales and each had one horn coming out of its broad forehead like a smokestack. The fireplace was no domestic hearth, but a great iron belly with a red-hot iron door hanging open from it, and inside the coke that burned was a pile of coals each one shaped like a human skull, bursting red-hot and the eyeholes white-hot and terror-struck. And the walls of the chamber were of iron, and I could hear a great roaring and howling just beyond the limit of those black walls

"'Are you come to *beg of me again*, you son of a tomb-whistle?' called mocking Martin Malprelate, and his voice, harsh enough in life, had a new quality of harshness in death, like metal grinding on metal. As he laughed so the devils there laughed too, a sound like jackdaws cackling. 'I am surprised you have the courage! Or perhaps did you not have the choice?'

"Some thread of courage in the fluttering and torn rags of my spirit ventured me to say: 'I am come for the promissory note, Sir Martin, which you owe me.'

"When I said so the noise of the hell-gale beyond the room swelled and shrieked, and the whole iron chamber shook and bucked. It was hot, hadean hot in that space, and the scalding coals moaned and howled as they burned, and yet I *knew*, I was touched by, the knowledge that the gales outside that space were colder than the polar wastes, freezing and violent and terrible, and when Sir Martin's three devil men advanced at me I feared that they would hurl me out into that emptiness. But they came only so far, and then they held back, though they grinned, and their smiles were even more fearfully contorted than before, and their laugh passed into such wild sounds as made my very fingernails grow blue and chilled the marrow in my bones.

"'So, my bold clerk,' said Sir Martin. 'You want this chit? For why?' 'Sir Martin,' I told him, 'you know why very well – because with it I can release my father from the Marshalsea Prison, and *without* it he will rot there until he dies, which eventuality will come to him only too soon if he stays. He is, Sir Martin, a decent and virtuous old man, as good a father as anyone might wish, and his white hairs and mild face merit not this incarceration. It was a hard bargain you drove, when alive,' (I choked a moment of this phrase, but out it came: *when you were alive*) 'before you agreed to relinquish the note – I gave over to you, and so to your heirs, my only house. But houseless though I be, I would rather beg on the streets if that my father was with me, than continue living under a roof with him in gaol.' 'Very filial, I daresay, oh most very commendable, I daresay,' growled Sir Martin.

"He reached into his jacket pocket with his right hand and brought out a slip of folded paper. But with his *left* he reached into another pocket and withdrew a piece of black bread, rough edged as if torn from a loaf. 'I am sure you are hungry,' he said. 'And you must sup with us, even if it be just a piece of dry bread. You see, I have supped *full* down here, and it is unlucky for a full man and a starving man to strike a deal between them. Come!' He held out the crust. Mr Bryde, my blood ran cold. But as my hands shook in fear I shook my head in refusal. Perhaps I am an idiot, Mr Bryde, but I am not a fool. 'I will take the paper, sir, but not the bread.' Sir Martin's face glowed red as he frowned at my words. But he did not withdraw the chit as I reached for it and he permitted me to draw it away. It was, I saw, as I unfolded it, not the promissory note – not that precious paper. O, my heart clenched with disappointment! It was, rather, a communication addressed to the secretary Aster, and it consisted of one word only: BRUINSTACK.

"I looked up from reading this mysterious moniker to see the three devils advancing upon me again, faster this time. 'Ye must come again,' Sir Martin was saying, as he tucked the untouched bread back in his jacket pocket. 'I insist upon it – insist upon it, I say. My hospitality will extend to you one twelvemonth from now.' 'I would not wish to impose upon your good nature, Sir Martin,' I replied, somewhat high-pitched and gabbling, for as the devils closed me down and I felt the heat emanating from their scaled skin, terror clutched at my heart. 'No imposition at all my lad,' Sir Martin boomed. 'I insist upon it!'

"And with that the claws of the demons were about my arms and legs, and I was hauled – hauled, sir – through a gap in the black iron wall of that cabin, or through the wall itself, I know not. All I knew was that I was plunged in freezing blackness, and that my ears were filled with the appalling scream of the wind, and the hellish loco, black as sin, blurred away through the blizzard as I tumbled into endless snow and ice. In that moment, Mr Bryde, I assure you I believed I would never again see my wife's sweet face, never again clasp my children to my breast, never again hear my father's voice. It seemed to me in that moment that the howling gale was all the universe, and that any comfort or love I had known was a tiny bubble, blown far away by the hurricane – that I would subsist through eternity as a leaf blown in the deafening midnight storm. Yet I clutched the note, with its unfathomable word, tight in my hand! It wriggled and struggled as I tumbled through the air, as though alive and eager to escape, flapping like a miniature flag. But I clutched it! I knew not, but perhaps, perhaps I told myself – perhaps this was the passport that would indeed free my poor father from his torment.

"But O! The horror of being the plaything of that blind storm! I was buffeted through the dark, tipped end over end, and then, with no warning, I landed with a thump. Landed!

"But where? It was long before I even dared open my eyes, sir. And when I did it was to see great ebon columns, that resolved themselves when I looked again to trunks of trees.

"I sat up. I was lying in the graveyard of St Anne's Church, Limehouse. There was a fretful morning fog on the grass and upon the gravestones around me, and away to my left a horse, saddled, its reins dangling, was feeding quietly beside a granite block over which an angel wept in stone. I looked past this beast and saw its rider, or so I assumed: a fellow, dressed as a gentleman, but slumped asleep in the church entrance, clutching an empty bottle to his breast as a mother might clutch a baby.

I was shivering, for the morning was cold – though this earthly cold was as nothing compared to the horror of ice and noise and darkness out of which I had been ejected. And the most important thing of all was: I still had the note!"

"It was in your hand?" Bryde asked.

"Clutched tight," Ninecroft confirmed. "I stared at it, I will confess. I could scarcely believe it. But then I thought of my dear old father – for whom every moment was precious, and to whom every day incarcerated in the Marshalsea was perhaps deadly – and it prompted me to leap to my feet. I *ran*, Mr Bryde. I ran clean across London, through the streets as the shops were opening their shutters, I ran past workers trudging into their manufactories. I ran and ran all the way to Mayfair. And there was the house of the dead man, with a Constable posted outside. I rushed through the front door, with the policeman crying stop, and stop, and I ran directly into the Inspector. He it was who summoned the secretary Aster, since the note was addressed to that gentleman. Aster came eventually, with ill grace, and his collar badly buttoned-on. But he came. I was waiting, sat on a chair and holding a mug of coffee in both hands, that had been kindly supplied to me. The inspector was astute. All that I had seen was but a dream, he told me, and I almost believed him. The note of paper was not dredged from hell, he said, but scribbled by me, perhaps while still dormant. Such things were not unknown, he assured me. But though I nodded, and agreed with him, in my heart I knew the truth.

"When Aster read the note he twitched, like one seized with sudden pain. 'Does this word, *Bruinstack*, does it have any meaning to you, Mr Aster?' asked the Inspector. The look that foul man bestowed on the police officer was such that might have caused a less disciplined individual to strike him for its insolence. But he replied to the question he had been asked: 'yes, I know it.'

"'To what does it refer, sir?'

"At this Aster hesitated, but he spoke up eventually. 'My former employer was in many ways a sentimental fellow, where animals were concerned – not for human beings, but for dumb beasts. He kept a sort of pet – a near hairless bear he had rescued from a baiting pit, or circus, or some such place. A ghastly brute, but Sir Martin doted upon it.'

"'I saw that bear!' I told them. 'The night I came to exchange my house for my father's freedom. I saw it. Where is it?'

"'Missing,' returned Aster, without looking at me. 'It seems to have absconded as soon as its master departed this mortal coil. Run off – back to the circus, perhaps. Or the baiting pit!'

"'And,' the Inspector pressed. 'This *Bruinstack*?'

"'This house,' said Aster, 'is large. It has many fireplaces, and many chimneys, some of which link together in a vertical maze, others of which pursue their own way through the brickwork. The 'Bruinstack' was Sir Martin's phrase for a shaft running up out of the dining room – we called it the *dining room*, though we never dined there, and as for the room itself, well, 'tis full of lumber. Into this space his pet bear would sometimes retreat. There is a wide, old fireplace full of dust, and the flue rising first vertically and then angling at a slant towards the roof. It was wide enough for the beast to hide itself inside.'"

Bryde took this account in. "And what happened next?" he asked. "Did you, or rather the inspector, search this flue?"

Ninecroft nodded hard: "It was searched as soon as I uttered the name. The inspector had a lamp brought up, and a constable squeezed himself into the shaft. It seems that, through many years of non-use, bricks had fallen away. A few yards up the chimney stack there was a kind of den, a chamber. Inside the constable found the dead carcass of the old bear, and a great many items the creature had taken from the house and hidden there: bric-a-brac and humdrumiana, but also silver candlesticks and valuable treasures. But also – there was my promissory note! The constable brought out, and I kissed the paper, dusty and grimed though it was. Sir Martin had endorsed it and his signature scrawled into a knot of inked lines, as if he had been seized with some dolorous pang as he wrote – of physical pain? Or conscience? I do not know."

"But you had the promissory note!"

"And that very day, to the astonishment of the gaolers, and the greater astonishment of my family, I was able to obtain the release, from the Marshalsea, of my beloved father. Oh, Mr Bryde, I cannot tell you the joy!"

"But your house?"

"Gone, alas," said Ninecroft. "But the love of family is more than the binding of bricks by mortar. Supplying the Marshalsea with the funds to ensure my father was fed and clothed, at the rates they insist upon and which cannot be gainsaid, had not been an impossible burden on my small salary. Absent that, and with some constraint upon our expenditure, and with my eldest daughter working at a Fowler's emporium sewing up damaged nets and making other repairs, we have enough. We are renting at the moment, sir: tight lodgings, but happy."

"And your – forgive me, but – opium?"

Ninecroft's brow darkened. "A blot upon my escutcheon, Mr Bryde. One that will never be expunged. But not, at present, a drain upon my finances."

"I congratulate you for resisting the allure of that terrible drug! And I have only one further question, if you'll forgive me: a question concerning – the note?"

"The promissory note?"

"No, the other one. The one you carried hither from – from that other place."

"Secretary Aster returned it to me, Mr Bryde. But I wanted it not. Consider only whence it had come into my hand! What sane man would wish to hold on to such a thing?"

"What did you do?"

"On this day there was a fire burning in the grate at the Mayfair house, for the morning was characteristically bitter, and I tossed *that* note into the grate."

"So it is destroyed?"

"It did not burn – it did not catch light. Rather it stuck, for a while, under one of the logs, and gleamed green with the heat. But then some parcel of hot air dislodged it and it flew, unconsumed, up the chimney. For all I know it is floating about the atmosphere to this day. Or perhaps it returned to that infernal realm whence it came. I care not! All that matters to me is that my family is whole again."

Bryde shook the fellow's hand. "I thank you," he said, "for your candour here, Mr Ninecroft."

Chapter 2

THE KING OF CARTS

1

Mr Bryde was conscious of the difficulties of his task. To resolve the murder of Sir Martin meant more than simply identifying a murderer. It meant untangling the strange manner of the death itself – an actual locomotive, running on rails that were then removed? A spectral apparition? (But if spectral, how did it interact with Sir Martin's flesh?) Some manner of contrivance murderously kitted-up, for the occasion, by a mob of angry men, much as a guy might be wheeled through the streets on Bonfire Night?

And then there was the question of motive. Of the many possible reasons a malefactor or malefactors might own for committing such a crime, what was the *true* motive here? Revenge? Greed? Revolution?

Bryde walked the streets of North London. He spoke with his various people, acquaintances and familiar faces: postboys and crossing-sweepers, pallet-men and lamplighters, men trudging to work and returning, women on errands through the streets.

The one thing to which Bryde cleaved, a conviction which his febrile interview with Ninecroft had not shaken, was that the murder must have a *rational* explanation. There must be some commonsense, material narrative that explained how the tycoon had met his end; and all stories of ghosts and goblins, of devils and demons, were to be dismissed. It is not that Bryde harboured atheistical beliefs, for he was as conventional a churchgoer as any. It was only that his experience as a designer and engineer disposed him to believe that God and the Adversary, though they watched the drama of the world from their respective thrones with interest, took no day-to-day part in how the complex mechanism worked through its motions. It had been made, in its astounding scale and intricacy, as a huge machine, and set alive, and now it worked according to the laws of Newton and Humphrey Davy.

As a rational man, Bryde did not condescend to the people who talked of Hellish locomotives driven by Beelzebubs. Superstition was a, though perhaps understandable, manifestly *atavistic* desire of the uneducated to make sense of the world. As for Ninecroft's narrative: opium had hallucinogenic properties, as was well known. The only part of *that* story that couldn't be reframed in commonsense and materialist terms was the note with which Ninecroft had woken, upon which was written "Bruinstack", and which wouldn't burn. As to that, Bryde could at least hypothesize: for presumably Ninecroft had written the word himself upon the paper whilst opiated, and then forgotten about it. Perhaps the word had been spoken by Sir Martin during that last conversation, and had stayed in the recesses of Ninecroft's mind without him quite realizing it. His long-term addiction to the smoke of the poppy had surely rendered the fellow's consciousness as full of holes as a colander. And any ordinary piece of paper, cast upon the open fireplace, might be borne aloft without quite catching fire.

What Ninecroft's story confirmed – as did, in its way, the fantastical narrative of the diabolic locomotive – was not their material specifics, but only Sir Martin's reputation in the world as a whole. It spoke to a situation where people considered him so wicked that any and all other manifestations of wickedness clustered around him in their minds. Something similar had happened with his erstwhile fellow money-man, Scrooge. His alteration in manner had been so pronounced that all manner of strange stories, goblins and ghosts and devils, were passed from mouth to ear all over town to explain it. The reality, Bryde believed, was simpler. People do sometimes reassess their life choices, after all. The wicked have been known to pass along the Tarsus Road and convert. Even the devil might repent.

Bryde strolled the streets of Camden. He made his way across to the works, the site of Sir Martin's demise. Work had recommenced in the space opened up. Workmen with handcarts brought gravel and shingles. Others carried railway sleeper spars across their shoulders, their arms hooked round the beam like men walking the stations of the cross. Picks and sledgehammers swung and clattered. Tubs of boiling tar steamed like puddings being cooked. Bryde stood behind a low fence of splintery wood and watched the work proceeding.

This was the very spot where Sir Martin had died. Now it was being dug over, laid with broken stones and rolled. Further back, men pressed spaced blocks of wood, each one hefty as the crossbar of a Christ's cross. The idle fancy crossed Bryde's mind, of the dead man's spirit pinned by this wood, as they say vampyres are in their graves, lying unquiet as the locomotives rolled over and over forever. He was not a superstitious man, but something in this made him shudder. But after all: why should Sir Martin's ghost lie quiet?

Of course, the London and Middlemarch Grand Congruence Railway Company was not one man. A million pounds sterling had been raised in stock, and such a quantity of money possessed a momentum that was not to be prevented by a single death, even of so important a figure as Martin Malprelate.

Bryde introduced himself at the worker's gate and was granted entrance. Down the path, stepping aside to permit a workman passage as he wheeled a barrow full of dirt up. Bryde walked the unlaid stretch of ground. He examined the space where Sir Martin had died. The northwest reaches of this stretch of dirt had been spread with gravel and laid with sleepers ready for the iron rails, but to the south and east the ground was much as it had it been on the night of the killing. Bryde walked slowly, stooped forward, for evidence of – something, anything, he did not know what. Cart tracks? Wheel lines? Evidence, perhaps, that rails had been laid and removed?

It was just mud.

There was no evidence that there had been rails laid and then removed, improbable as that hypothesis had always been. Had it been performed, Bryde told himself, the ground would have been very greatly disturbed and some indication would remain. But the ground over which he now walked did not support the simpler theory either: for a cart, weighted with train-like paraphernalia, horseless and therefore pushed by a great many men in order to achieve a killing velocity, would surely have left the imprints of its wheels, and of the footprints of men. But there was nothing. The pages of this levelled mud were blank.

"Friend," Bryde called, to a working man who was bringing down a barrow of gravel. "Has this area been raked over?"

"Raked over, sir?"

"This stretch, where I'm standing, and going south. Has it been raked over, or smoothed? Since Sir Martin Malprelate's death?"

"This *is* the land on which Sir Martin was standing when the Demon Train struck him down," said the man, setting the barrow down and wiping his brow on the underside of his forearm. "No, sir. Workmen are not over-eager to loiter there, sir, I can tell you. As we work, we settle the ground for the small stones, but we haven't touched *that* ground, sir, not since the evil one snatched away the old man's soul."

"The evil one? You're sure it was he?"

"Whom else, sir?"

"Did you see it happen?"

"Not I, sir. That was a depot night for me. But Pat saw it – the name is short for Patience, sir, not Patrick – he was working on the fence, up yonder. Pat? Pat!"

Pat came down, a wide-faced man with a forked scar on his big left cheek that made it look as though that side of his head was pieced together from three components that didn't quite fit. "Sir?"

Bryde introduced himself and explained his business. "You saw the moment of death?"

"Can't unsee it, sir," growled Pat, sounding as though lava were gurgling in his throat. "I pray to the lord Jesus Christ every night to relieve me of the vision, but it haunts – haunts, sir."

"It *was* a train?"

"I should think I know a train when I see one," said Pat.

"What I mean, good fellow, is to ask, might it have been a cart or carriage?"

"Cart?" retorted Pat, as if nothing could affront him more than such a suggestion, until he added *"carriage*?" and it became clear that a greater affront was indeed possible.

"You grasp the purport of my question," Bryde pressed. "I look at this ground, this very ground here, which your comrade assures me has been left untouched since that night. How *can* a train have passed down here? Without sleepers or rails? How can it have left no track?"

"No mortal train," said Pat. "I know what I saw."

"Perhaps a carriage might be tricked out to resemble a train," Bryde offered.

"As if I wouldn't know the difference!" scoffed Pat.

The other workman put in: "Besides, to what *end*, sir, if you'll pardon my reply? Who would set up a cart to look like a train? Why?"

"It is a good question," Bryde conceded. "But I am only trying to make sense of the evidence."

"That's not it, sir," said Pat. "For wouldn't a cart of such a size – for it was a colossus, that I saw – leave tracks? Wouldn't it spin its wheels? Hooves and tracks? There were no horses, that I am sure. It was a locomotive of a size I ain't have never seen, in *all* of my born days. It was big as the A-warehouse up at depot, which is bigger than any barn. Big as the ware'us, mind: not big as any of the locomotives within the ware'us. And it moved faster than any locomotive I've ever seen, shining with a grinning light. I'll tell you something more, Mr Bryde sir: *it flew*."

"You mean, it was rapid?"

"I mean it floated above the ground. Oh it had wheels, sir, as a locomotive must – but they did not touch the ground."

This was more than Bryde could believe. "Come, my friend," he remonstrated. "There was a fog that night – several feet deep of mist blanketing the ground. How can you know whether the train touched the ground or not?"

"*Because* the fog was there, sir," said Pat. "I saw the wheels of the locomotive running over the top of the fog. It left no trace on the ground, as you have seen sir, because it hurtled through the air, as Satan's sled flies across the moon on the witches' sabbath."

Bryde thanked the man with a shilling for his time, and made his way up the chopsticking path out of the works, pondering this bizarre information.

There was one more bizarreness to encounter, before his day's investigating was complete. As he climbed the shallow rise, to reach again the High Camden Street, Bryde noticed a man watching him.

There was no mistaking it: as Bryde moved, the man

moved his head to follow his movements. As Bryde stood at the top, the man stared frankly at him. He was muffled up against the late November cold: a thick overcoat, a scarf wrapped about his lower face, and the space beneath his felt hat occupied by spectacles of violet-coloured glass. With his face thuswise wholly hidden it was not possible for Bryde to see whom this person might be, or to see if he might recognize the fellow.

He stepped across to him. "Good day, sir," he said. "You are, I think, observing me?"

"I am," the man replied.

"I must ask you: why?"

"You know, I believe, Sir Persimmon Hawk?" The man's voice was somewhat muffled by the scarf so tightly wrapped around his face, but even with this softening his speech possessed a grating, unpleasant quality.

"I know of him and have met him, precisely, once," said Bryde. "He is a managing director of the company that employs me."

"He is," said the stranger, with an odd pause, "a friend of mine."

"I congratulate you on the honour," Bryde returned. "My understanding is that he is not a man to dispose his friendship to many, or with facility, which means you are one of a select and favoured group. Might I ask your name?"

"Griffin," said the man, adding, "like the fabled *bird*, you know."

"And what does Sir Persimmon have to do with you undertaking this surveillance upon me?"

"Oh," Griffin drawled, insolently. "He asked me, you know."

"Sir Persimmon asked you to watch me?"

"To check-up, I think. To make sure you were indeed undertaking the work with which he had tasked you. To be sure things were hurrying along. He's keen to wrap up the matter, you know. Speed! Speed! That's the logic of the railways, ain't it? Rap-*ee*-do."

Bryde felt his grip on his temper begin to loosen. "It is hard to see this as anything other than an insult, Mr Griffin," he said. "Am I not trusted to undertake my commission? Must spies be set to dog my footsteps?"

"Not spies, dear fellow," said Griffin, adjusting his scarf, which was beginning to slip. "Just the one spy. Only me. But don't take on, so. I'm no hireling. It is a favour. Sir Percy and I are engaged in a certain endeavour – a certain *technical* endeavour together. That's all." He touched the brim of his hat. "Good day, Mr Bryde."

Griffin walked jauntily away before the astonished Bryde could reply. His astonishment reflected, in part, the sheer brazen rudeness of the man, his manner, his words. But there was another thing too, more startling yet. As he had adjusted his scarf he had, only for a moment, revealed a patch of his naked face. And it wasn't there. A portion of jaw, simply missing, opening sight into a shadowy cavern. The man was deformed – phossy-jaw perhaps, a war wound perhaps – and that was why he covered his face.

2

There was more to this mystery than Bryde could unravel, alone and unaided, and it was to that end he called upon his friend Vavasour Holmes. Of all the people currently in London, none had a greater intellectual capacity when it came to the solution of riddles, the unpicking of puzzles, the pathmaking through briar-patches.

Holmes' family were Hampshire people, squires of longstanding, but young Vavasour had taken rooms in London and was as often to be found in the metropolis as in the countryside. He pursued certain interests for which the

British Library, and the laboratories of the new University College, were needful.

"Bryde," Holmes exclaimed, as the engineer knocked upon his door. "What a capital surprise. How do you do, my friend?"

"Not imposing, I hope?" Bryde asked, making to put his hat down on a table and then stopping. Holmes's rooms were crowded with myriad objects, books piled in heaps, scientific reports and vials, an articulated skeleton, boxes and samples and equipment. The small table by the door was occupied by a boxy device made of metal spikes and coils. "A galvanic pile," said Holmes, proudly, coming over and taking the hat from Bryde's hand. "I'm rather proud of it." He tossed the hat, more or less carelessly, onto a heap of papers by the fireplace: charts, blueprints and other publications. "Move those boxes from that easy chair and sit yourself down."

The boxes were half a dozen small, sealed cardboard containers, all of which, according to the stickers posted on their outsides, contained lenses and other glassware. Unsure where to put them, Bryde put them down carefully upon the rug beside the chair.

Holmes himself, seated opposite, was filling his pipe, his long legs stretched straight down at an angle of thirty-five degrees from the horizontal.

"I should say that Gwendolin is on her way here this very day."

"My dear fellow," said Bryde, standing up. "You should have said! I really can't intrude on a reunion of man and wife – "

"Sit down, sit down," said Holmes, gesturing with the stem of his pipe. "She'll be half an hour yet. Plenty of time! Besides I was with her only last week: it's hardly a reunion! She's just coming up into town to do a little shopping. *Do* sit down, Bryde. Will you have a drink?" Holmes did not offer his friend any tobacco, for he knew that, though Bryde was himself a smoker, his more refined palate revolted against the rough shag that Holmes himself favoured.

"Nothing to drink, thank you," said Bryde, re-seating himself, a little tentatively. "I only wanted to – as the phrase goes – pick through your brains. The company has asked me to investigate the recent, strange death of Sir Martin Malprelate."

"Oh yes!" said Holmes, animatedly. "I have of course been reading about it in the newspapers. Even granted the tendency of the press to exaggerate and melodramatize, it is a most striking and unusual case. Are you working with the police?"

"In parallel to them," said Bryde. "Sir Martin was, it seems, a man with many enemies. My challenge is in narrowing down the list of possible suspects; for such a list might otherwise stretch out to encompass the whole of London town, and possibly beyond."

"A hard and grinding fellow, it seems, this Malprelate," said Holmes, drawing a deep mass of smoke into his lungs and exhaling it vigorously.

"I was wondering how *you* might go about..." Bryde began. But Holmes interrupted him.

"Oh no, my friend, I've no time to get involved. No time! I won't deny that raptor adventure was diverting, but my researches here are at a *crucial* juncture. Busy busy! You see, with the application of a galvanic current, it proves possible to..."

"Forgive me, Vavasour," said Bryde. "I don't mean to cut you off. But, if we only have a short time, until your lady wife arrives... Please don't misunderstand me: I am not here to *recruit* you to the case. Naturally I understand how busy you are. But to be honest, my friend: I find our conversations on these mysteries to be so wonderfully clarifying."

"Very glad to hear it," said Holmes. "So yes, I see your task. A matter of narrowing the rogues' gallery down to a manageable number, what? Well there's an obvious way to begin."

"There is?"

"Let us say: the King of Carts."

"Let us say what?"

"Let us say: the man had many enemies. So I make this proposition: we divide this population into two groups: his *personal* enemies and his *collective* enemies. In the former group are to be found individuals with a personal grudge against the man. In the latter, people who object, as we might say, to the Malprelate project – to, let us say, the railways he is building, at the cost of ordinary houses and businesses. I suggest that, merely by making this distinction, we have identified the group of the two *more* likely to be responsible and so have triaged your task."

"The second group?"

"Precisely. An individual might, of course, be moved to kill Sir Martin. Reading about the fellow I'm sure several were. But in that case they would act the assassin: shoot him with a firearm, stab him with a dagger, bludgeon him with a club. A woman might put poison in his potation. In each case the purpose would be to rip out the fellow's life. But what happened to this man was far more theatrical than this! A gigantic, seemingly spectral locomotive running him down? This was more than merely killing him. This was making a point."

"And so our task is to identify which groups might want the man dead, and what kind of message this elaborate and complicated mode of murder communicates to the world."

"Precisely so. Think of Ned Ludd, from the eighteen-teens. A few short decades ago. The Luddites smashed up machinery, and sometimes killed manufactory owners. It was no personal animus that motivated such crimes, but a collective anger against the coming of machinery as such. The perpetrators dressed in women's attire and banded together:

a performance of ridicule as well as strength, of disguise as well as intimidation. And so we may ask ourselves: what purpose might this display of ghost-locomotion serve?"

He drew another lungful from his pipe, and expelled a spear of smoke up towards the corner of the room. Bryde coughed a little. The air in the room was growing mistier with tobacco.

"Sir Martin had many business interests," Bryde said. "Of course, as you know, he came to prominence marketing stocks, trades, debts and other forms of legal usury. But were the animus against him motivated by this side of him, a locomotive engine would not be the mode of assassination."

"Indeed not," agreed Holmes. "Consider the place in which the killing happened, and the prominence of Malprelate himself as an, as it were, *figurehead* of the new motile-machinery that is presently rending London, ripping through its ancient suburbs and filling its skies with smoke. Is it likely that one group, or another, antagonistic to the coming of the railways might have staged this death? A warning to other railway magnates – a display for the people of the city – a statement that Saturn will devour its young!"

"The King of Carts," said Bryde. "Yes, I see. Thank you, Holmes!"

"There is one more question to consider," Holmes added. "Though – as a rational man, and an engineer, you may believe it already settled. You consider the locomotive that struck Malprelate down to be a… *material* object?"

"That is surely the more likely hypothesis," said Bryde. "More likely than that it was, as the populace excitedly exclaim, a train-engine driven out of Hell by demonic drivers for the purpose of collecting Malprelate to the nether world!"

"I would not be so hasty to dismiss the possibility. There are other forms of the immaterial. Perhaps it was a mere hallucination, like Banquo's ghost?"

"An hallucination could hardly have beaten Malprelate to death!"

"No, of course, of course. Let us agree Sir Martin died because something solid, not spectral, collided with him. But how to explain the reports of so many that it *was* spectral?"

"You propose an hallucination observed by two dozen independent people, simultaneous? Macbeth *solus* saw Banquo's ghost, my friend – none of the other guests at his feast saw a thing. And is that not what one would expect? Surely hallucinations are the product of a derangement of the *individual* consciousness?"

"Collective hallucinations are not unknown. And what of other possibilities? The ghostly or spectral world," Holmes went on, accompanying his words with his pipe stem as an orchestral conductor uses his baton, "may soon prove amenable to science, just as the material world is. Experiments are being conducted even as we speak concerning the communication of the dead, spirit-writing, and the spectral plane."

"Surely, Holmes!" Bryde cried out. "You don't believe in all that jibberish? I thought you a man of the natural sciences!"

"And so I am. I am not proposing a vulgar superstition of bogeymen and dancing devils. But there *is* something else: an account of the dimensions of our world, width, breadth and height, that encompass also *time* – for no object can exist instantaneously, everything around us must persist in time for their various widths and breadths and heights to figure – and conceivably time as a triple-form iteration, just as space is. Dimensions, you see, Bryde. We know what it is if an object becomes unmoored in space – as a hat is blown off a man's head in a strong gale, and he must go running after it. Might something equivalent not explain the appearance of this machine?"

"But a locomotive must have rails to run along," pointed

out Bryde, who, to be honest, had not quite followed this last lucubration of his friend's. "It cannot run on mud. Go to the place yourself, Holmes, if you don't believe me – there were no rails, no wheel-tracks, nothing at all."

"It is an important consideration," agreed Holmes. "Indeed, indeed. You don't think the rails were perhaps laid down, and then afterwards removed?"

"I don't see how they could have been," said Bryde. "It would have been a vast labour – not just the rails, but the sleepers. And surely, if that *had* happened, the mud would bear the impress of the removed metal roadway? No, no, it is not conceivable."

"I must take your word," said Holmes.

"A locomotive *as such*," said Bryde, "seems to me a plain impossibility. A cart or carriage, on the other hand, might very well roll along the bare ground. And perhaps a cart or carriage could be fitted-up to resemble a train – for that would be in keeping, precisely, with the Luddite performance to which you earlier alluded. It is as I knew it would be," Bryde, went on: "wonderfully clarifying to speak with you, Holmes!"

"I mention the King of Carts," said Holmes, "though I have no notion as to how to locate him."

"It so happens that I do, though, my friend. His path and mine have crossed before. Given my profession – and the fact that I sometimes go out into the world to investigate mysteries – perhaps that news does not surprise you."

"And yet it does! Still, I am glad to hear it. Perhaps a conversation with this King will help resolve the whole mystery."

"I am keen to resolve it, believe me. And my employers are even keener. Do you know they have set a man to watch me?"

"To watch you? You mean – to spy on you?"

"Just so."

"How extraordinary! You are sure of this? It might be merely a curious passer-by, watching you without ulterior motive."

"I confronted the fellow, and he confessed all. Name of Griffin."

Holmes opened his eyes very wide at this. "The devil it is – his name is Griffin, you say? Tall pale fellow?"

"As to pallor I cannot testify," said Bryde. "For he wore his face muffled against the cold with a scarf, and had on spectacles fitted with smoke-tinted glass. I honestly did not see his face at all."

"But it is the *very man*," said Holmes. "I know him by the spectacles. He has some derangement of the retinas, something to do with albinism I believe, and needs the coloured eyeglasses to facilitate his sight. Griffin – you met him!"

"You know him?"

"He is an acquaintance of Sir Persimmon Hawk's. Not exactly a partner, and yet not exactly a friend. I do not *know* him, Griffin I mean, directly, but I have seen him at Sir Percy's. I believe him to be some manner of natural scientist, a chymist perhaps. He is, so far as I know, assisting Sir Percy's own researches."

"He did mention the baronet in speaking to me," said Bryde. "Boasted of his friendship. But this is too striking a coincidence, Holmes! I did not realise you were in Sir Percy's orbit?"

"The galvanic device I mentioned earlier, and which you were too much of a brute to tolerate hearing about – it is part of a larger project, overseen and – frankly – financed by Sir Percy. He has a larger device, for which my galvanic apparatus is key, for which it will be the power source."

"I cannot imagine he is an easy man with whom to work!"

"He is bristly, as these aristocrats so often are. He can be *brusque*, as the French term it. But he is genuine in his interest in scientific advance, and generous with his disbursements to that end. I cannot say for certain what role Mr Griffin plays in the project, for I have hardly exchanged a half dozen words with the man, and Sir Percy is not forthcoming. But Griffin is sometimes there when I call at Sir Percy's townhouse, and I have seen him."

"And now Sir Percy has sent him to spy on me!"

"Extraordinary," conceded Holmes, drawing another large dose of smoke into his body and exhaling it again.

"You do not know what is the matter with his jaw?" Bryde asked.

"Jaw?"

"He was, as I say, muffled against the cold, but when he adjusted his scarf I could detect the briefest glimpse of his face beneath, and there is a portion missing from his chin, or lower cheek. Is it disease, I assume. A wasting disease perhaps."

"I saw him two days ago," said Holmes, puzzled, "and his face was complete. Pale, as I say: painted as a woman paints with white-lead so as to regularize her complexion. I believe it to be some medicinal paste, perhaps painted against the harm the sun's blaze may cause an albinic skin. But his face was certainly all there."

"That's queer," said Bryde. "I was sure I saw..." He shook his head. "It was but a moment. Perhaps I was mistaken in what I saw."

At this point the bell sounded downstairs, and Holmes's landlady could be heard below opening the door. "Gwendolin," said Holmes, leaping to his feet.

Bryde also rose. He recovered his hat from where it had been thrown and turned to see the handsome figure of Mrs Holmes coming into the room.

"Mr Bryde," she said. "How lovely to see you again."

Bryde kissed her gloved hand. "Mrs Holmes," he said.

She was, he noticed, in that happy state of incipient

motherhood that rounded her figure, and with which she glowed.

There was a commotion on the stairway, which resolved itself as a maid brought a perambulator and awkwardly clattered up the steps, into the cluttered room. The noise, and shaking, did not seem to have awoken the baby within.

"Vavasour," said Mrs Holmes, "you really must arrange your town possessions in a more orderly manner. There's hardly space, in all this clutter, to bring the baby inside!"

"And how is my little Mycroft?" Holmes asked, leaning over the perambulator with fatherly affection. "Prospering? Still oligocephalic? Prone to *wind*?"

"I must leave you," said Bryde. "But before I go, please allow me to congratulate you, Mrs Holmes, on what will evidently soon be the new addition to your family?"

Mrs Holmes folded her gloved hands over her bump. "Vavasour believes it will be a son, Mr Bryde," she confided. "Where I feel it will be a daughter. Into that impasse we find ourselves unable to propose a name."

"I really must get out from under your feet – as you say, Mrs Holmes, Vavasour doesn't exactly keep a trim or shipshape apartment. Thank you, though," he said, shaking Holmes's hand. "I believe you have set me on the proper path."

"The King of Carts," said Holmes.

"The King of Carts," agreed Bryde, and went out.

3

He opened the door to his own lodgings. As the lock clucked loudly with the turning of the key he called out, "It is I, Mrs Orbit, returning home" – for if he did not do so, his landlady became alarmed that an intruder was breaking into the property.

He went inside, hung up his coat and hat, and before he could do anything else Mrs Orbit had come bustling down the stairs to ask if he required her to set a fire. She offered to do this whenever Bryde returned, no matter the weather.

"There will be no need, Mrs Orbit, thank you. I leave this afternoon by train and won't be back until tomorrow."

At this Mrs Orbit shook her head very hard and fast, such that her large, stiff hat of lacquered blue could not keep up, her head moved independently within its ambit. "I don't hold with *trains*, Mr Bryde, which likewise you know, though I don't consider you to *be* trains you understand, your mode of employment notwithstanding."

"No Mrs Orbit," he replied. "That's quite alright, Mrs Orbit."

"Too fast and far too fiery," the landlady continued. "Not *your* employment, which I understand be located respectable and stationary behind a desk in an office. But actually to travel by such beasts? Did you hear, Mr Bryde, and Lord forgive me for the gossip of it, what happened to that big London financier? Sir Martin was his name, and he was who put all his money into the railways only to be knocked down by one of his own trains!" She shook her head again, leaving her hat in its position in space. "A judgement, it was," she said. "A judgement." Abruptly she fixed Bryde with a stern look. "*Where* are you off to on the infernal tumbrel, Mr Bryde?"

"I have business in Essex, Mrs Orbit, but it will only detain me for one night. I shall return tomorrow before midday."

"Does it – "and here Mrs Orbit actually shuddered, her whole body trembling, "does it *under* go?"

"I believe the train does pass through a tunnel, Mrs Orbit, yes. As it approaches Brentwood. My understanding is that the company made a cutting through the Essex hills and have now covered it."

Mrs Orbit shrieked. "I can't bear the *thought* of it!" she

exclaimed. "Not the *thought* of it, ne'rmind the actuality. Just to think of that great engine, scurrying along through a tunnel, like a rat along a sewer pipe. I can't think how you could do it Mr Bryde, to volunteer to sit within the belly of such a beast."

"I shall screw my courage," Bryde told her, solemnly, "to the sticking point."

"Well," Mrs Orbit said, in a doubting voice, "if there truly *is* no better way of getting there, and if it's business that can't be put off..."

"I plan on interviewing the King of Carts."

"Of *Cards*?" Mrs Orbit had exacting opinions where gambling was concerned.

"Carts, drays, tumbrils, Mrs Orbit."

"You wish to speak to a carter?"

"I do."

"To hire a cart?"

"No, Mrs Orbit. Only to ask some questions. You remember I told you: I am looking into the murder of the gentleman you previously mentioned."

Mrs Orbit threw her hands up. "Such a dreadful crime!" she said. "But I shall tell you, and tell you true, I doubt if it went just as the gossip says it went. I doubt if it was truly a spectral locomotive from Hell. God would never permit such a spectre to run through London town."

"I agree, Mrs Orbit," said Bryde. "I believe the murderers to be flesh and blood, men with a grudge against Sir Martin."

"Wicked men! And you believe these carters might be such men?"

"I will see you tomorrow Mrs Orbit. A light luncheon at one pm, if you please, here in my rooms."

"Very good, Mr Bryde," Mrs Orbit replied, though in a voice that suggested she was doubtful a traveller who ventured so perilously as to pass into the belly of a train that itself passed through the innards of the Earth, would ever be seen again.

Bryde put a fresh shirt, his toothpicks and his pipe and tobacco into a leather satchel, redonned his coat and hat, and stepped back out onto the street. It was a chill but bright afternoon and the walk to Shoreditch was enlivening. Sunshine gleamed off the lancet spire of St Leonard's Church, whose bells though presently dumb were liable to break at any moment to peal out their *when I grow rich*. The pavements were busy, and carriages and drays rattled through the streets. Bryde walked past the theatre and then mounted the stairway to the railway station itself. He paid tenpence and collected his ticket: a piece of taupe card, stiff as a mahjong tile.

From the platform he watched as the engine backed its carriages up to the platform. Birds scattered and trilled through the air. The barrel of the locomotive bore on its side a metal crest: "Grand Eastern Counties Railway", the words disposed circularly around a corrugated five-petalled rose.

Bryde took a seat inside his compartment. He was alone. Unfolding the paper from his inside jacket pocket, he read of the ups and down of stocks and money-rates, of the shocks that had passed through the city with the violent murder of so prominent a man as Malprelate, of the speculations and rumours swirling around the death.

Hissing with a goose-like self-importance, the engine stirred and roused its motile power. It disposed several great white bales of smoke into the sky. The train shuddered, eased forward and soon picked up speed. It passed over the viaduct through Spitalfields, high across Wheeler Street and Brick Lane, and on. At the stop at Mile End station another traveler entered Bryde's carriage, tipped his hat, and disappeared behind the paper panels of the *Times*.

Bryde stared through the window as the train proceeded over Globe Lane and then curved round the East London Waterworks at Old Ford. It chugged on, across the Marshes, and as the city fell away there was less for Bryde to observe.

At Ilford the train paused for a long while as the driver and the station master exchanged a series of angry shouts with one another. Whatever the issue between them, it was eventually resolved and once again the mechanical dragon shook itself awake again to grumble onward, across the Great Essex Turnpike and thereafter chundering along to Romford Station, where Bryde's fellow passenger alighted. From here it was a straight run to Warley Lane, Brentwood, though the adverse incline caused the locomotive to cough and strain itself. Forward motion slowed noticeably.

At Brentwood Bryde alighted, found himself a nearby hotel – a new building, varnish still resinously odiferous on all the woodwork – and took a room. He beguiled the evening by strolling about the town, and admired the sunset across the flat land whilst he smoked a cigar. He took an early supper and retired to bed, requesting a very early alarm call. "Up before dawn, sir?" asked the concierge.

"I have an appointment with the King of Carts," said Bryde.

"Oh!" said the concierge. "Needs to be up betimes to snatch any meeting with *him*. Very good, sir."

Bryde slept poorly, as he usually did, waking at odd moments, for an instant startled to find himself not in his usual bed, before recalling where he was and why he was there, and sliding only slowly back into sleep. He had unnerving dreams, some of which had adapted the story he had heard from the clerk Ninecroft, of the diabolical steam locomotive and its devilish crew. Nonsense of course. But how pungent to the imagination!

There was a banging inside his head and it took him a long minute to separate this out from himself and understand that the banging was coming from outside himself – from outside the room. "I am coming," he croaked. "I am awake, you can stop your knocking." From the other side of his bedroom door he heard: "Begging your pardon mister but my gaffer says I ain't at stopping until you *are* at coming out."

"Infernal urchin," Bryde muttered, disentangling himself from his sheets and blanket and shiveringly opening the door. The boy was there with a candle in his hand and a gleam in his eyes. "Only," he said, "cusmers say they *are* awake and then they fall back asleep, and then I catches it, don't I." The lad then opened his eyes very wide and said, with enormous emphasis, "*Good* morning!"

"Yes, yes," said Bryde, pressing the sleep-sand from his eyes with the heel of his hand. "Good morning to you, my lad." When the boy did not withdraw, Bryde said: "I am in my nightshirt, and such small change as I carry is in the pocket of my breeches. I shall tip you when I am dressed, and have come downstairs."

"Only," the boy said, in no way retreating, "cusmers *say* as they'll tip me later and then later comes and the tip has slipped their mind, and *then* I'm tipless."

"Good grief," said Bryde, crossing the room and retrieving tuppence from his breeches.

Later, dressed, huddling by the downstairs fire with a cup of rough-tasting coffee in his hands, Bryde coughed the last of the night mist away.

"It's a precious early start for you, mister," the boy opined, from just outside the saloon.

"I am in need of a lantern, my boy, and I haven't brought one with me. Might I have the benefit of borrowing one of the lanterns of this establishment?"

"Only," said the boy, "seeing as the gaffer ain't awake yet, so it falls to me to lay out," he nodded at this, as if impressed at the professional idiom in which he was expressing himself, "to lay *out* the terms of such a, as we might say, *mister*, rental of sich and sich an item."

Bryde eventually settled for sixpence for the light, and a promise to return it within twenty-four hours. He buttoned his coat and turned up its collar, and stepped out into the darkness.

It was an affrontingly cold predawn. The steam from Bryde's breathing glinted in his lanternlight.

He passed up the unlit High Steet and across a meadow. A pond had trapped a number of stars beneath its surface. The quiet of the night meant that he heard the snorting and huffing of the dray-horses before he saw the carts – a great line of carts, two abreast all along the London road, each one with a carter at the front, swaddled up in coat, greatcoat and overcoat, wrapped about with scarf, sitting stiller than their animals. Bryde reached the roadside and held up his lantern. To his right were cattle – hundreds of beasts, standing as patient as statues in the bluey gloom, waiting to be driven along the London road to Smithfield.

Before him and to his left were the carts.

Seeing the gleam from his lantern, the driver of the nearest cart turned his head. "Early hours for a stroll, stranger," he said.

"I'm looking for the king," said Bryde. He added: "I have an appointment."

"Appointment!" said the carter. "Upon my soul." The reins were slack in his lap, but he lifted them and sent a wave down their leather to indicate the direction Bryde was to go.

Bryde walked along the pike, passing cart after cart after cart. Each cart was piled high with produce: cabbage-lettuce, endive and succory, soil still adhering to their roots. Here were huge bundles of spinach, wraps of sorrel, clusters of artichokes. Here was a cart bearing a heaped hill of cos-lettuce, each one tied round with straws. The light from the lantern touched colours out of the darkness: a sheeny lacquered green of the beans, deep-toned blue-green of the foliage of the kale; stacks of leeks white as shinbones sprouting lime-green at their heads; the jewel-like oranges of the heaped carrots, snowy turnips, all strewn in prodigious quantities in all these carts. White cabbages as compact and round as metal balls, purpled savoys whose great leaves made them look like basins of green bronze, red cabbages which the lantern caught with hue of wine-lees, splotched with dark purple and scarlet.

And here, at the head of the procession, was one cart wider than all the rest: a huge, broad flatbed of ancient timber, carrying perhaps a half ton of potatoes.

"So I have the honour of addressing the King of Carts?" Bryde asked.

The man seated at the front was of unusual and prodigious stature, such that, large though his conveyance was, he did not seem dwarfed by his huge cart. "Mr Bryde, is it?" he asked. There was a rumble in his voice, as of giant cartwheels trundling across metalled roads, and a shudder in his fleshy chest. His eyes flashed in the lanternlight as he glanced down.

"You received my communication," said Bryde. "I am most grateful for the opportunity to meet with you, sir."

"Clamber up," instructed the king. There was plenty of space on the bench beside him. "To Barking," said the king, "before the east starts to lighten. To Whitechapel as the sun rises."

"I shall not presume upon your time for so long," Bryde assured him. "What we have to discuss may be encompassed within a half hour at most."

The King of Carts turned his gigantic head slightly, and, for the first time, took in Bryde's whole countenance with his eye. "The carts wait on no man," he rumbled. He gave a hoick to his reins and called out *up-up*. His team of shires shuffled and strained, and the giant cart began to roll forward.

The carters behind stirred and called to their horses, the ones behind them likewise, and so, motion itself passing as a wave down the entire enormous train, the entire mighty parade of carts began their journey.

"It occurs to me that I might," Bryde observed, "have met you in the Covent Garden, and saved myself the journey out here."

"Busy," growled the king, "at tother. *Here's* where we can talk, if anywhere. Now's when we can talk if anynow."

"Very well," said Bryde, setting the lantern down on the bench beside him.

For a while the king was silent, and Bryde waited. The grind of the wheels against the turnpike surface, and the plodding rocking imparted from the stepping of the drays, and the movement of the cart, generated an almost lulling effect upon Bryde. After his poor night's sleep, the rocking sent him back, in memory, to the cradle. He clapped his hands, and pulled his own beard, to rouse himself.

"Sir," he said. "You have perhaps some intimation of why I am come to speak with you?"

For a long time the King of Carts said nothing. They rumbled on, under the starlight.

"I am here every night, afore dawn," he said, eventually, speaking slowly. "These folk are *my* folk. They bring down all the victuals for the great city yonder – all that its hordes eat, borne into the metropolis aboard *my* people's carts and carriages."

"I comprehend."

"*You* are here," said the king, shortly, "following that much-publicized death in town."

"Sir Martin Malprelate's demise, yes."

"The railway man," said the king.

"He."

"You, Mr Bryde, are a respectable man. Yet you work for the rail-carriage folk."

"I do."

The king shook his massy head. "Do you drive them?"

"The locomotives? No, I work in an office building. I am an engineer."

"Not the locos. The roads. Do you drive *them*?"

"I have nothing to do with that side of the, eh," said
Bryde. "Business." Dawn was starting to melt into dimness
and light. Bryde blanked the lantern at his side and waited
for his eyes to acculturate to the darkness.

"*That's* the damage," said the king. "That's where it is.
This Sir Martin – he was driving a road into the heart of the
smoke?"

"He was. But north and west – not into *this* territory."

"My territory has already been spiked," growled the king.
"That great metal spear, thrust into the flesh all the way up
to Brentwood hills."

Bryde omitted to remind the king that it was on that very
railway that he had, the previous day, made his way into
Essex. His sight was now dark-adapted enough to see the
silk-thin crescent moon, its bulk emptied out into nothing
except a half-circle thread of silver, so slender as almost not
to be there. The stars poured lactically across the sky.

The pole star stared fixedly down, a royal eye of its own.

"Men," said the king, looking again at Bryde with one hard
eye, "have driven carts across the land since there's *been* a
land. Adam put his belongings in a cart drove it out of Eden."

"I am not sure I recall such being specified in the Bible,"
said Bryde, mildly.

The King of Carts was quick to retort: "You want to
tell me he laid metal rails and hurtled out of paradise in a
locomotive? Booming and spitting sparks and hurling smoke
at God's clean sky? No!"

"Such is not scripturally specified, certainly."

"Carts is God's own moveable. Steam trainage belongs to
the other feller, in his cavernous kingdom below, where all
is fire and smoke anyway."

"Many say," Bryde offered, "that railways are roads that
lead into the future. Times change, sir. Perhaps the steam
locomotive and the dray can cohabit?"

"It is not to be," said the king. "This is a fight to the death. The locomotive and its tail is a snake, and it seeks to throttle young Hercules."

"Do you believe the railways can be stopped?" Bryde asked.

"I believe it would be the action of a coward, Mr Bryde, *not* to fight. All my life, my folk have ported victuals into the great city. All my father's life it was the same. And his father."

"But Railways move people," Bryde objected. "If you were king of stagecoaches I might understand why you feel threatened. But cargo of such bulk…"

"Permit me to contradict you, Mr Bryde. Cargo is already being moved by rail. It will increasingly be moved by rail – if we permit it."

"There are many who feel as you do?"

"You mean," growled the king, "others who might act to murder a prominent railwayman? Nay, sir. Do not impute such baseness to us. We do the Lord's work. There's neither fire nor brimstone in *our* passage, sir. Look to the steam-engine men for that."

"I beg you not to misunderstand me, sir," said Bryde. "I have not come to accuse you. That is not my intention."

"What then?"

"Only that I have heard of the letter," said Bryde.

The cart rolled on. For a long time the king said nothing. Looking behind himself, Bryde could see the first faint intimations of dawn in the east, and starting to amass shape and distinctiveness, the great caravan of drays following.

"I did write it. I wrote to her majesty," said the king eventually. "I wrote as one monarch to another. The letter was delivered to her ministers. A copy was delivered to the railwaymen. A copy shall go to the *Times* newspaper when the railwaymen are agreeable."

"You propose a contest?"

"Let the steam-engine men compete with us in open contest, aye. Let them bring in the supplies I stipulate – in the letter – in *their* way, and let us bring 'em in our way. We shall see who does the better job."

"The tortoise and the hare," objected Bryde. "Do you truly hope to bring such a fairy tale into real life?"

"A fair contest," the king insisted. "Let them see how fragile is their panting-puffing beast. How solid and dependable are our carts."

"Even assuming the railway barons agreed to your contest – they could simply fill their carriages with potatoes, drive them into town at top speed and claim victory. A cart such as this – sturdy, certainly, reliable I do not doubt, but not *rapid* – could not compete."

"I do not say," the king said, "that *this* cart, this one upon which you and I are sitting, Mr Bryde, would compete."

"You have another, more rapid cart?" Bryde asked, sharply. He was aware, for the first time, of a kindling in his solar plexus, a sparking sense of excitement as if comprehension was about to dawn; as if he, by understanding one small thing, would start to understand a series of interlinked large things. But the king of carts did not reply. Bryde repeated the question: "Is there some new, velocitous manner of cart, in your tribe, that might challenge the railways for celerity? Is such a thing behind your proposal of competition?"

Instead of answering this question, the King of Carts said: "We run along the roads, the ancient highways. These steam machines must lay their rails before them as they roll, and might as well pull them up behind them after they have gone, for all such startling novelty could ever endure. *We* feed the city! The roads have done so, and the roads will do so in the future."

"I ask because – "Bryde began. But the King of Carts interrupted him.

"Mr Bryde, you have come here to ask me about the

death of this railwayman, this moneyman, Sir Martin. You
have heard something from the streets, from the gossipers,
from the people the police pay to spy and eavesdrop and
pass on what they hear to the authorities. It is what you
have heard that has brought you here, to me. And you ask
me about this man's death! Mr Bryde, I have no words to
communicate to you on this matter. I have no words to say
to you concerning this knight's death – a knight who never
rode a horse, I'll warrant, this Sir Martin! I am sorry you
have been put to the trouble of travelling out here, and of
rising so early as to meet me, but there is nothing I can say
to you will repay that labour. Here – "He put his head back,
ponderously gesturing forward with his chin, and then
dropped said chin to his breast again. "Romford. I'd say you
could step down from the cart here, Mr Bryde, and be on
your way, with no ill-will between us."

Bryde knew better than to press the king on this matter.
He thanked him for his time, and for the ride, and climbed
down from the cart as it rolled into the outskirts of Romford
village.

There Bryde stood, among the dark houses, watching the
King of Carts rolling on, and the procession of his many
subjects rolling after him. The procession, like that queue of
Banquo's observed so bitterly by Macbeth, seemed to stretch
on to the crack of doom. Cart after cart after cart went by.

Bryde found an inn where one window glimmered with
the lit candle behind the pane and knocked at the door. The
maid was surprised to encounter custom so early in the day,
and could do nothing more for Bryde than beg him to sit and
wait for a little, as she continued laying and then lighting
the fire. Only when this was burning was she able to boil-
up a pot of coffee for him. Bryde sat, solitary in that firelit
room, sipping his coffee and smoking his pipe, revolving in
his mind the substance of his conversation with the King.
He had not said *my people have nothing to do with the death of*

this man. He had not said that. *I have nothing I can say to you on this matter*, was quite another thing to pronounce.

But was Bryde any closer to a solution to this great mystery?

After a while the window glass began to glimmer with the coming dawn. Bryde paid and left, walking down a side street and out across a square towards the railway station.

The various properties of Romford were gradually emerging from the gloom and into the dawn, a greenish-grey colour in the chill eastern sky. The sun itself was not up, but solar imminency stained the east horizon a soft grey.

The station master was opening his main entrance as Bryde approached. He waited patiently for the fellow to ready his establishment. *I have nothing I can say to you on this matter*, was what the King of Carts had said. Was this a politician's answer?

As Bryde waited, the sun swelled up over the landscape eastward in a fine watercolour wash of citron and pale orange light. The brickwork of the station building itself assumed delicate shadowy tints: violet, blush-rose, and greenish yellow.

"My dear man, I must make arrangements," Bryde explained to the station master, holding up the lantern he was still carrying, "for this to be returned – taken up the line to the *George* in Brentwood. Perhaps a shilling would cover the cost of delivering it? As for myself I require only a single ticket, into London."

"Of course sir," said the station master. "Of course."

4

Dawn appeared slowly, softly grey in hue, and spreading a watercolour tint over all the world, the awake and the awakening and the sleeping, across the living and the dead. Surging piles of cloud, akin to hurrying waves, assumed their delicate shadowy tints – tender violet, blush-rose, and greenish yellow, all the soft, light hues which at sunrise make the sky look like a canopy of shot silk. And by degrees, as the fires of dawn rose higher and higher at the far end of the Romford Road, the mass of the world, trees and fields, rooftops and bald hills, grew brighter and brighter, emerging more and more distinctly from the blue gloom that clung to the ground.

Bryde breakfasted in the station hostelry, where a yawning innkeeper provided a bowl of coffee and a thickly sawed slice of bread upon which was spread lard sprinkled with sugar. After he had eaten Bryde merely sat, for a while staring out of the window at the colourful changes in the sky. His lack of sleep muddled his head, and he drifted into a state that was neither entirely awake nor exactly asleep.

In this state, sitting, a vision of sorts manifested to Bryde. It was as if he floated over the city, a skylark drifting up in the zenith and looking down. With preternatural focus he could see every detail: London like a shield upon the face of which was drawn the undulating line of the Thames, the encrustation of houses and shops, of factories and churches, graveyards and hardens, two million people fitted snugly together. From his imaginary vantage Bryde could see the radial roadways along which people travelled into and out of town. And here came the army of carters, northeast from the flatlands of Essex, southeast from the orchards and hop fields of Kent, the corrugated farmlands dug out of the downs to the south and southwest, the market gardens north of the city. Gathering long before dawn, their carts loaded with cabbages and leeks, with potatoes and turnips, with tomatoes and lettuce and spring onions, with clanking pails gravid with frothy milk – carts crammed with sacks of flour plump as cushions – carts heaped with coals and charcoal, or stacked high with firewood – carts bringing barrels of beer and barrels of brandy, racks of champagne bottles so excited to be drunk their enthusiasm threatens to explode the dark green glass in which they are penned. Stacks of butter, racks of hams.

Drovers flourished their switches like orchestral conductors, leading the shuffling lines of cattle along the roads in towards the Smithfield shambles; pigs keening and lambs creaking out little bleats. Carts stacked with wood-and-wire boxes inside which chickens clicked and clucked. Every morning it was the same, day in, day out: a vast army of people assembling and loading and driving the city's daily necessities.

But then, his head lolling against the back of his chair, Bryde's vision, or dream, changed. This swarm of humanity, trudging slowly into the heart of the city and returning into the outskirts unladen, faded away. New roads were gouged through the fabric of the city, and ruled with doubled lines of iron. Bryde understood that he was seeing things as the Sybil does, with the future breaking through into the present. Down every one of the new railed roads came giant trains: cyclops-eyed, steam and smoke pouring from their snouts, elbowed-wheels spinning tirelessly, and each train drawing after it a vast caravan of carriages. From his impossible vantage, Bryde was able to look more closely. The chuntering rhythm of the trains rattling over the rails, pressing and releasing the sleepers in sequence as each engine passed over, was augmented with the groaning of the timber. Except it wasn't timber. It was, Bryde could see, a long string of supine human beings, trussed and pinned beneath the iron, their life-breath pressed from their bodies with every roll of their wheel. Now that he had heard it, Bryde couldn't unhear it.

Bryde woke with a start. The innkeeper was clearing away his bowl and plate. Not wholly in the land of the waking, Bryde thanked him and paid.

Outside, revived by the freshness of the dawn air, he made his way to the platform to await the first train into town.

Chapter 3

THE ETERNAL SOUP

1

Bryde called on Inspector John Bucket at Scotland Yard. This was a courtesy, since the Inspector had overall official command of the investigation of the murder of Sir Martin, and Bryde considered it his duty to share what he gleaned in his own researches with the authorities.

To that end he had introduced himself the very day he had himself been charged, by his employers at the London and Middlemarch Grand Congruence Railway Company, with pursuing investigations. Bryde did not need any formal permission from the police to pursue investigations. But Inspector Bucket expressed himself grateful for the call, only requesting that Bryde share anything he considered pertinent or incriminating. "You may investigate," said the Inspector, "and – your reputation preceding you – I am grateful that you are doing so. But you have not the power of arrest, nor the wherewithal to obtain a warrant to that end." The Inspector was a stoutly built, steady-looking, sharp-eyed man in a black suit, early middle-age, with a large, knowing eye and a habit of emphasising his conversation by the air of a corpulent forefinger, which was constantly in juxtaposition with his eyes or nose.

"Indeed not, Inspector," agreed Bryde.

"If – dare I say, *when* – investigations reach that stage, I would be obliged if you would call once more upon me."

"I would be pleased to call more frequently than that," Bryde assured the police inspector.

After that first meeting Bryde had – as we have seen – spoken to the workmen at the site of the killing, and to various others, including the King of Carts himself. So it was that Bryde made good upon this claim, again stepping up into Whitehall Place and through the entrance of Scotland Yard. The Inspector was sent for. He waited at the front desk, watched by an unblinking sergeant.

"Mr Bryde," said Bucket appearing. "Shall we walk? I find Saint James's a conducive environment, when it comes to thinking through complex matters, and it is handy for Scotland Yard."

The two men walked out, and down to Saint George Street, Bucket pulling on black gloves. The day was the last one of November: bright-lit and sharply cold, such that the blueness of the unclouded sky had the freshness of an icy sea. At Story's Gate they stepped into the park and strolled through to the lake. It lacked an hour of noon. Governesses and nurses pushed perambulators, each as large and impressive as an official pavilion, to and fro. Two soldiers walked, arm in arm, smoking, in the direction of Horseguard's Parade.

By the waterside, Bryde related to Bucket the story of his visit. "The King of Carts," said Bucket, nodding. "I have never met his majesty in person, though stories of him of course abound in my profession. You are saying he did not, in his conversation with you, let slip any particular knowledge of Sir Martin's death?"

"No. There was, however, no doubting the genuine sense of grievance, and animosity, between the tribe of carters – if I might so designate them – and the new railwaymen."

"Animosity enough to provoke assassination, you think?"

"My thinking," said Bryde, looking out across the water. A heron, all attentiveness, its neck an S, pointing the blade of its beak at some fish just below the surface. Drakes bobbed down and up, down and up, like pistons in an engine. "My thinking is that we must discount the notion of an actual locomotive. No such machinery could run except on rails, and the murder scene was not provided with such."

"Might they not," asked Bucket, pushing the top of his forefinger from his cheek to the bridge of his nose to dispose of an itch, "have been laid and afterwards taken away?"

"Whilst such a circumstance is not *im*possible," said Bryde, "it would have involved prodigies of labour – a whole team of workmen, hours of laying and hours afterwards of removal. There would have been the sound of hammers on iron, horses bringing in sleepers on carts – and the same, afterwards, taking them away! Shouting and commotion and a mob of people. Surely there would be many witnesses, in the neighbourhood, who would have reported such a bustle?"

"My thoughts precisely," said Bucket, bringing his finger back from the bridge of his nose to his cheek and thereupon removing it from his face.

"Our choice," Bryde continued, "is to believe the witnesses who said they saw a train, or to *dis*believe them. So far as that goes, I feel the balance of probabilities is on the side of believing them. A single witness might be mistaken, or intoxicated, or mendacious; but a dozen, all saying that same thing?"

"As to that," Bucket said, "I may withhold concurrence for the moment. But, pray, go on, Mr Bryde."

"It is a matter of removing impossibilities, as a sculptor chisels away the stone that does not constitute the statue, so revealing the necessary shape within. If an actual locomotive be impossible in this case – which is to say if we, as men of reason, discount the fantastic stories of diabolical steam-

engines rolling straight from Hell Central – then we are left
with: a carriage, or a cart. *Something* struck and killed Sir
Martin, after all. That something must have combined heft
with motility at speed."

"No horses observed," Bucket noted. "By these dozen
witnesses upon whom you place such emphasis, dear sir."

"Indeed. How, then, was the carriage propelled? For
propelled it must have been, somehow. Perhaps it was
pushed, by a group from behind? Say it was decked out in
Roman Candles, Squibs and Waterloo Crackers, all lit to
produce the firework fizz and uncanny light – and say it
carried upon it a group of jeering and yelling ruffians, one
perhaps holding a large lantern to the fore to imitate the
locomotive's forrard lamp – why then the attention of the
bystanders would be distracted away from the rear of the
equipage. Especially since there was a low mist that night,
which would in part have obscured them, even to eyes that
sought them out."

"It would take quite a crew," was Bucket's opinion, "to
get a heavy carriage up to the kind of speed requisite to
break a man's body apart, as Sir Martin's was – and on
such ground. The mud may have been frozen, but it was
pitted and striated. And to deck it all out to most resemble
a locomotive – it's a peck of work, all this. Much bother to
do something any footpad can do with a thrupenny walking
stick with a knob on its end."

"The spectacle, according to my hypothesis, Inspector,"
Bryde returned, "would be *the point*. It was constructed
to make an impact on bystanders, and so that word of
it would spread about the city. A warning, the direr the
better. Let folk claim it as a satanic engine! So much
greater will be the terror struck into the hearts of railway
magnates."

"I do not notice," said the Inspector, drily, "that the
magnates are much cowed."

"This dray being fitted perhaps beforehand – for the coming of Sir Martin has been advertised, and the assassins knew he would be there," said Bryde, in less certain tones, himself beginning to see the insufficiencies in his hypothetical narrative, "it is pushed *after* him, as he walks away into the misty night."

"Your assassins," Bucket said, "are sure he *will* walk there, are they?"

"I suppose so."

"But how *could* they be sure? Malprelate might very well have remained in the well-lit hall, with his secretary, and the iron stove to keep out the chill. He might have departed in a cabriolet and returned to his home as soon as the meeting broke up. *Wouldn't* that, in fact, be by far the more likely thing for him to do?"

"He did not, though. He walked down the path opened by the demolished houses."

"That's so," Bucket agreed. "But my point is to ask: how could your angry carters *know* he would do so? To go to the lengths you suggest, fixing up this cart, gathering a battalion of men, some to sit in the cart and steer it, more to stand behind and push – any one of whom, by the way, might let slip, in his cups, or in hope of the reward now offered, that this is what they were about? To go to such lengths, arranging the carriage with waterloo fireworks, disguising its form – on the *off chance* that your victim would conveniently present himself in an open space such that you can run him down?"

"These are good points, Inspector," said Bryde. "But still: carriage there must have been, for it was seen by so many people – seen and mistook for a locomotive, I concede, but seen. The mistake surely implies a large and rapid carriage. Such a vehicle must have been made to look like a locomotive, for it can hardly have appeared that way by accident. And if it was travelling at speed, *sans* horses, it must have had access to some other motile power. Such is logic."

"Hmm," Bucket replied, tapping his gloved fingertips together. "I concede your point, Mr Bryde, about impossibilities and the needfulness of removing them from our scenarios. But let me propose this to you. *You* have a set of talents, remarkable talents. In your work, these talents are put at the service of engineering and technology, of the making of ingenious and potent machines, designing according to the tolerances of the natural sciences. What you do, Mr Bryde, I never could."

Bryde tipped his head briefly, acknowledging the compliment.

"I have, perhaps, other talents, however," said the Inspector, modestly. "They are to do with human beings, rather than with pistons and flywheels. All the components in a well-made machine will spin and whir and cog together, as the designer has made them. But human beings do not operate, in themselves or together in groups, after such a fashion. An engine is driven by coal-heated steam, propelled at force around the inner vesicles of the mechanism, according to the laws of science. But a murder is propelled by the human heart – by rage, perhaps; or greed; by jealousy or revenge. These do not follow strict engineering laws, Mr Bryde. And my talent, if I may be permitted the point of comparison, is people."

"You doubt the culprits here are carters?"

"My doubts," said Bucket, turning away from the water and indicating the path back to Story's Gate, "relate to *motivation*. I do not deny that Luddite violence has, very often, attempted to thwart advances in technology and alterations in the old order of things, sometimes with murder. And I do not doubt, as is implicit in your hypothesis, that Luddite violence involves a degree of performance – not the quiet assassination of a misliked individual, but the theatre of punishment and therefore of deterrence. But in such a case one might expect there to be a Carters' Proclamation, signed by some pseudonym, pinned to the main entrance of the House of Commons, admitting the blame, or as they would see it claiming the credit, for the action – for why go to such lengths in dressing up your carriage with such fireworks, if not to make what you have done more widely known?"

"I must concede," said Bryde, as they walked, "you make a penetrating point."

"And there is the question of motive. Your conversation with the King revealed a suspicion that the railways will deprive carters of work – "

"More than a suspicion, I would say. He was certain of it."

"Mr Bryde, you have misread my emphasis. It was not on *suspicion* – a word I will very happily swap-about for certainty, if you please – that I meant to lay my stress, but on the future tense: I do not hold it certain that the railways *will* deprive carters of work."

The two walked back out through Story's Gate and followed the pavement round to Whitehall. Hackney carriages chuntered past. A night-soil man's dray plodded, drawing a covered cart. Other pedestrians passed and repassed.

"You mean to say it has not happened yet," Bryde said.

"You yourself rode into London Town with the King of Carts himself," said Bucket, "at the head of a vast caravan of carts. Think only of the size of the procession! Multiply it by the other processions coming in from other compass points. Oh, there may come a time when the railways can compete with this – when they will bring in more produce than do carters – but it is not this day. On this day, the railways transport some numbers of passengers, and nothing more than that. When the railways encroach upon the livelihood of the carters, then I anticipate some manner of Luddite-style protest. But this is many years, or decades away. Perhaps next century. Perhaps never: for a locomotive, though faster, will always be more expensive than a dray-cart or a barge; and speed is no particular virtue in the transmission of cabbages and potatoes."

Bryde could think of nothing better to say to this, than: "Perhaps the King is planning ahead."

Inspector Bucket shook his head. "You have constructed an elaborate machine, by way of explanation, that contains every moving part save human nature," he said. "I might suggest, utilizing my skills, that such is not the motivation for a crime of this kind."

"Who, then, do you suspect?"

"The parties most immediately injured by Martin Malprelate's business were the people of Camden. Those whom Parliamentary papers deprived of their homes, compulsorily purchased. Those whose homes and livelihoods have been sacrificed to this new monster."

"Have you interviewed these people?"

"I and two constables spent yesterday going up and down the site. I spoke to people glad he was dead, and people shocked that such violence had occurred in their parish. I spoke to people gleeful that the death must put an end to the railway line, and others who saw that the line would continue to be built, since the forces behind it are more than one man. These latter have a better understanding of the world. Malprelate was one man, but the real driver of this railway line is money, and money is a hydra with many heads."

"Did you speak to anyone who gave you to believe that a mob of Camdenites was responsible?"

They had returned to the main entrance to Scotland Yard. Bucket shook Bryde's hand. "You may, or may not, wish to return again to talk to those folk, Bryde," he said. "And if, in doing so, you turn-up anything you might consider of interest to my investigation, I trust you will inform me."

"Of course."

Bucket, unbuttoning his black overcoat, turned to go inside the police building, and Bryde caught sight of a brooch, composed of not much diamond and a good deal of setting, worn in his shirt.

2

Sir Persimmon Hawk required the attendance of Bryde. This was not a courtesy; it was a demand.

Bryde, returning to his office, found a sealed envelope on the top of the heap of engineering sketches and blueprints upon his desk. Inside was a message from Sir Persimmon Hawk, insisting that Bryde attend upon him at his earliest convenience, at his club. Bryde put his hat back upon his head and stepped out, walking to Piccadilly and presenting himself at the Termagent Club without delay.

He was brought through to the smoking room. There he found Sir Percy and three other individuals, sat in leather chairs. One Bryde recognized at once – for it was Mr Griffin, the spy, the self-declared "friend" of Sir Percy, whom Holmes knew as a chymical researcher. Here, indoors, he was not muffled up and his face was entirely visible. There was (as Holmes had said) no abscess in the jawline, although his skin (as Holmes had also said) was covered in a white-lead make-up of some kind.

"Ah, Bryde," said the baronet. "I'm glad you're here. Allow me to introduce – Mr James Carker, confidential manager of Dombey and Son." Carker, with a wide smile, nodded, and Bryde returned the gesture.

"Mr Griffin, a fellow research scientist," said Sir Percy.

"We have met," Bryde noted.

"So we have," said Griffin, smiling widely. "Had quite the pleasant conversation, Camden way."

"And *this*," said the baronet, "is Aster."

"You are, I believe, Mr Malprelate's personal secretary," said Bryde. "I am indeed pleased to make your acquaintance."

In contrast to the grinning Carker, Aster looked somber – cast down, indeed. He was dressed in mourning, and the funereal colour of his jacket matched the tint of his eyes. In dolorous tones he spoke: "Mr Bryde, I have heard much, to do with your perspicacity. I trust you have been able to pierce the *fog*, as it were, of this tragical crime?"

"You overpraise me, Sir Percy. Only this morning," Bryde replied, "in conversation with the police, I was reminded of the limitations of my perspicacity."

"Have *they* advanced their investigations?" Sir Persimmon Hawk asked, sharply.

"Not, I fear, to the point of breaking through what Mr Aster so aptly calls the fog," said Bryde.

"Hmph," the baronet breathed out fiercely. "And what do you say, Bryde? How are you with the fog? It's why I have called you here."

"You have called me here, to...?"

"For you to tell me you've *solved* this dreadful business. Sorted it, blown the blamed fog *away*. Have you?"

"I am sorry to report, sir, that such a declaration on my part would be premature."

"Well, hurry! Hurry sir!" Sir Percy undulated his extended hand, in imitation perhaps of an ocean wave hurrying itself towards the shore. "The uncertainty surrounding Sir Martin's demise is harming business. The rumours! The fairy-stories! It erodes confidence – and we must have confidence."

"Oh absolutely," smiled Carker, narrowing his eyes as he looked up at Bryde. "Confidence is everything."

"Naturally the line is going ahead. Our investors must be sure of it! And be sure of the profits they will accrue. We cannot afford to dilate upon this. The sooner the perpetrators of this dastard act are identified and punished, the better. I have impressed upon the police that celerity is needful, very needful. And now, I impress it upon *you*."

"I understand, sir," said Bryde.

"Oh perdition," barked Sir Percy, suddenly. "Hell and damn it! It's him – he's here."

All eyes turned. Coming into the smoking room was a tall, thin-faced man in a velvet green jacket. His face bore a grin of such dimensions it gave his face the look of having suffered some manner of conniption fit or stroke.

"Scrooge," rasped Sir Percy. "Quick – we must go."

"I did not realise he was a member here," said Aster.

"The old Scrooge would never have wasted his money on the membership fees," said Sir Percy. "He was a sensible-headed old fellow – was, though. Hades, he's changed now, and it's – "

"He's seen us," Bryde observed. "He's coming over."

" – unbearable," Sir Percy gasped.

"Sir Persimmon!" Scrooge cried, across the length of the clubroom. "Grace and greeting to you sir! Oh, my dear and valued friend, my commiserations on your loss!"

"Ebeneezer," said Sir Percy, through gritted teeth. "How surprising to see you here."

"I come," said Scrooge, earnestly grasping the baronet's hand, "to spread the word of God, or charity and good living."

"Christ," Carker muttered.

Scrooge heard this. "Yes!" he called out. "Exactly! Precisely so, sir! I do not know your name but you call on the principle of redemption, love and charity and I thank you!"

"This," said Sir Percy, "is Mr Carker, of Dombey's firm."

"Mr Carker," said Scrooge, bending forward with his beakish nose as if to peck the other man, or take a bite from his promethean viscera, "I am most pleased to meet you. For I know Dombey's firm. And know it to be wealthy, most wealthy – and so well placed to donate much wealth to charitable causes!"

"You must excuse me," said Carker, getting to his feet. "I am already late for another appointment." He added, sotto voce, but not so sotto that Scrooge did not hear him: "Fool."

Scrooge misheard, or heard correctly and chose to misunderstand, the syllable. "Full, yes – our bellies, our wallets, our company's coffers – yes sir, Mr Carker, how right you are. We are full whilst our fellow men and women starve! We must luncheon together you and I to discuss how best to disburse Dombey's lavishly over-full pocketbook."

"I can hardly agree to the disbursement of Mr Dombey's own money in his absence!" Carker objected.

"Then he must join us for luncheon as well. *These* gentlemen," Scrooge exclaimed, "I do not know – and yet, sirs, you are my fellow men, and I embrace you! I may not know your names, but I know your souls, and the goodness therein. Happiness and joy and mutual support!" he said, taking hold of Bryde's hand and fixing him with a gaze fierce enough to burn through metal.

"Bryde," said Bryde.

"Make humanity your business, Mr Bryde," said Scrooge and extended his grin even further, pushing the flesh of his cheeks into two brackets framing the wide mouth. "How much of your salary do you give to charity?"

Bryde, nonplussed by the directness of this question, only cleared his throat.

"I press you for an answer, sir," said Scrooge, manically. "We must all do more! We must all *give* more! You sir – "

"Aster," Aster drawled. "Sir Martin Malprelate's former secretary."

"A case in point!" gabbled Scrooge. "How wealthy was Sir Martin, in monetary terms! Yet how poor in the wealth that truly matters – charity! Giving to others!"

"Sir," said Aster, imbuing the word with a degree of

ferocity. "Before you speak ill of a dead man, I must insist that you listen to me when I..."

Intervening to prevent the exchange from deteriorating into mere belligerence, Sir Persimmon Hawk stood up. Mr Griffin, lounging in an easy chair with his legs straight out, watched them all as if enjoying a private joke. "Apologies, Ebeneezer, but we have an appointment for which we cannot be late. We shall have to postpone this conversation to a different time."

"Give!" Scrooge called, as Sir Percy, Aster and Bryde walked away. "Give your money to charity! To charity!"

In the entrance hall of the club, Sir Persimmon stopped, and brushed cigar ash from his waistcoat.

"Well. Well. Soonest, Bryde! Sooner than that! Sooner than now, even! Reverse the passage of time itself and bring me a solution to the mystery *yesterday*!"

"Sir," said Bryde.

"Since you are leaving," said Aster, "I will walk with you."

If Carker possessed a certain feline quality, there was a more ophidian aspect to Aster. He favoured his companion with no smiles, and moved slowly, his stride entailing a degree of sinuosity. He walked, silent, beside Bryde as they descended and passed out into the Piccadilly busy-ness. The autumn sun shone clear and cold, and Aster's shadow slunk beside him along the pavement, aping his motion as if mocking him.

"I hoped to have a conversation with you, Mr Bryde," he said. "I do not know if you have the time at present?"

"I am at your disposal, Mr Aster."

"Would you, perhaps, come with me up to Camden?"

"By all means."

Aster hailed a cabriolet. As they sat inside, rattling along the London streets, Aster sucked the end of his silver-handled cane, not speaking. Bryde waited. The cabriolet paused, to allow a drover to process four ornery cows down and along, and as they waited Aster brought out a small notepad and a pencil. But before he could write anything the cab lurched into motion again, and the motion inside was too jolting to permit any kind of writing.

"Sir Persimmon Hawk's in a hurry," he said, after a while.

"Naturally eager to wrap-up the mystery," was Bryde's opinion.

"He inherited the baronetcy from his brother, Mulberry, you know," said Aster, peering through the window of the carriage. "Died in disgrace, over in France. Killed a chap in a duel and had to flee. But it was more than that. Old Mulberry was up to his hairline in disreputable dealings. People say the same thing of Sir Martin Malprelate, I know, but in the case of old Hawk it was all true."

"I see," Bryde said.

"There's no family money to draw on, so Sir Persimmon is ever hungry for profits. Careful to steer a path away from the more obviously criminal things Sir Mulberry Hawk did in pursuit of pecuniary advantage, of course – but he has accrued vast amounts. Vast amounts in a suspiciously short time. Paid off family debts and set himself up handsomely."

Bryde nodded, unsure what bearing this assessment of Sir Percy Hawk had on the matter in hand.

Suddenly, and with immense feeling, Aster broke out: "That fellow Scrooge was most offensive! Truly he speaks from utter ignorance!"

"You mean his comments concerning your former employer?" asked Bryde.

"Ignorant and insulting! Sir Martin was..." There was a clucking sound, and Bryde, startled, realised that it was proceeding from Aster's throat. The man was crying! His side-whiskers blotted his tears. For a moment Bryde could think of nothing to say. Then Aster sighed. "I know the world thinks as Scrooge does. I know the whole world despises my former master. It is the injustice of this which I cannot swallow."

The carriage jolted, slowed and stopped. The cabbie called down from outside: "Oakley Square, gentlemen."

"One moment," Aster called back. Once more he brought out his tablet. He wrote a few words. This sheet he tore and passed to Bryde. "I request you to visit this address, sir," he said. He was wiping his eyes with a white handkerchief.

"Will you not accompany me?"

"Duty requires me to be elsewhere," said Aster, tucking the handkerchief away, and looking through the window of the cabriolet by way of avoiding Bryde's gaze. "But I trust you will find in the establishment, and in conversation with the mistress thereof, a corrective."

"A corrective to?"

Aster met Bryde's gaze again. "To the universal, it seems, prejudice against my former employer. The world considers him to have been a very devil, a cruel and grasping miser, a foul unchristian monster. I, who was privy to his many dealings, know otherwise, but I was placed under a grave seal of silence, an oath I swore solemnly in his presence, not to talk about such things. I do not believe his death to have released me from this promise."

There was a certain mincing hauteur in Aster's manner, a mode liable to cause others to bristle and take offence at being patronized; but Bryde, meeting his eyes, was struck by something else, a truth of feeling. He was, Bryde saw, genuinely grieved at the death of his master.

"I see," said Bryde.

"You cannot be ignorant of how widely and how savagely Sir Martin is maligned."

"I'm sure your loyalty to your former employer does you credit."

"A good man," said Aster, with abrupt force. "A good man! He was a good man. He had his cranks, I don't deny it. Many great men do. But he was not as he has been painted in the popular imagination. He was a good man. Which entails a question, to somebody positioned as you are, investigating his death, Mr Bryde. There might be many reasons to kill a truly wicked man – many, many. The people such a person had injured might seek revenge; an assassin might be motivated by a sense of justice; his own crimes might embroil him in violence and death. But I put it to you, sir, that a different question arises if the victim, despite slanders and prejudice, was a good man. For whom, we must ask, seeks to murder *a good man*?"

Bryde looked at the paper: *17 Lyme Street, Mrs Castille.* "You do not alight here?"

"I do not. I will pay the cabbie at my destination."

Bryde opened the door and stepped down. "Permit me to contribute a shilling to the joint fare," he said, reaching into his pocket.

"No need! No need!" snapped Aster, angrily. He banged the ceiling with his cane and, as Bryde was in the process of shutting the door, the cabriolet shook into motion and rattled away.

Unsure of his orientation in Camden Town, a portion of London with which he was not very familiar, Bryde was obliged to buy directions from a crossing sweeper at the cost of a ha'penny. He made his way towards, according to the insistent suggestion of his nose, the canal, along Lyme Street. He passed a bird-fancier's, and then a mutton-pie shop whose signage declared it to be a "celebrated" establishment, and then a narrow property that sold tobacco. Number 17, by contrast, was a spacious and inviting property: a double-door opened beneath a sign that said: *Soup Kitchen, All Welcome, 6-7ante m, 6-7post m.* It not being either hour, the establishment within was empty of soup-seekers, but Bryde could see a woman – perhaps Mrs Castille herself – scrubbing clean one of several wooden tables.

He knocked, and the woman admitted him. "I *would* tell ye to come back at six," she wheezed, "but I can see from your attire you're not in need of my soup."

"I come at the prompting of a gentleman called Aster," Bryde said. "You are, perhaps, Mrs Castille?"

"I am her that is she. I know Mr Aster of course. Are you another, also in the employ of Sir Martin, or as I must now tragedize sir, the late departed and demised Sir Martin?"

"Madam, I am not," said Bryde. "Although I am tasked with investigating his death."

"Then ye must sit, and I *shall* serve you some soup. I shall do it! We is still *in rolls*," she added, tucking her scrub-brush into one of the many pockets in her vast apron, "though I do not say for how long we will so remain, rolls-inward speaking."

"Thank you, madam, but I have no appetite for soup at the moment – delicious though, I don't doubt, it is."

"But you must see," insisted Mrs Castille.

Yielding to her insistence, Bryde followed the old woman to the back of the chamber. Every table and bench was spotless and scrubbed, the white plaster on the walls was fresh as a new snowfall, even the soot-stains on the ceiling above the candle-holders had been cleaned to a ghostly greyness. It was in every particular a room of commendable spick-and-spanness. The walls, otherwise bare, were hung with two improving embroidered messages, both of them Bible verses urging humility and thankfulness.

Mrs Castille herself was a small, ample woman, solid rather than flabby. Her voice had a wheeze at its edge, a soupy quality to its articulation as if some of her viands had made its way into her nature, and her eyes did not entirely agree with one another on the best direction in which to look; but she had a kindly smile and a welcoming demeanour. She wore a dress of pale green that had been, perhaps, a richer green once upon a time but which had been exposed to the thinning powers of sunlight over years enough to reduce it from pea-soup to a less verdant chicken-consommé hue. It was a respectable piece of attire, though somewhat patched and resewn. Over her dress she wore a starch-cotton apron so extensive, and pleated, and bepocketed and marked and stained as to constitute, almost, a structure.

"See," she said. "Soup, sir. So!"

Bryde found himself standing in a vestibule or side-chapel of the main room, through which soup-mendicants presumably passed with their bowls. Dominating the space was a huge tureen, in which – despite the hour being equidistant from the morning and evening hours of dispensation – brimming soup bubbled. Its aroma was savoury and tempting, its steam went up as the sacrifices of the ancients were said to go, to delight the nostrils of the gods.

Mrs Castille took up a ladle that was as long as she was herself tall, dipped it into the broth and stirred it.

"This soup," she said, speaking reverently, "was bequeathed me by my sainted mother, back in the reign of the old king. It had been bequeathed her by *her* mother, during the early years of the king afore that."

"The recipe of it," said Bryde, "you mean?"

"No sir! The soup itself. The very soup. Each morning and each evening I serve it up, and when the hour is done I refill what's been taken, add-in new vegetables, scissor-up new mutton, add a shoulder bone perhaps, and pour in the water. And so the soup stays the same, as ever it is consumed, and so my mother did before me, and hers before her. This soup is the same soup as my grandmother first engendered, at the bidding of a gentleman called Albany Fontblank, old even when my grandmother was a young woman, very old when he died. A week after my own sainted mother herself passed on."

"Remarkable," said Bryde, politely.

"There being," said Mrs Castille, looking up from her stirring sharply, "no point of connection between the two demises, of old Mr Fontblank and my mother, behind the simply co-innocence of it."

Bryde, assuming co-incidence, nodded and offered polite commiserations, only afterwards to wonder whether Mrs Castille had not misspoken at all, but had meant exactly what she said.

"And when Mr Fontblank died," he asked, "would I be right in assuming the funding for this establishment also passed away?"

"He was a good soul," said Mrs Castille fervently. "As Jack Jagger will confirm. A good soul!"

Mr Bryde assured her that he had no desire to impugn the virtue of either Mr Fontblank or Mr Jagger, not least because he had no idea who the latter gentleman even was.

"Not a lawyer," Mrs Castille said, as if this cleared the matter up. "But works clerking for one, if you understand me."

Mr Bryde smiled a smile of noncomprehension.

"*He* cast his eye o'er the will," said Mrs Castille, "as a favour for Mrs Thompson, who asked on *my* behalf."

"Mr Fontblank's will?" asked Bryde, beginning to understand.

"Jack Jagger was willing to bet his breakfast muffin on the tightness of the testament," said Mrs Castille, resuming her stirring. "Mr Fontblank assuredly *intended* to keep the kitchen in funds beyond his death and provided for such in his will, bless his memory. But, this world of ours being a vale – you know – "

"Of tears," agreed Bryde.

"– of wickedness, I *was* going to say. The will was contested by some cousins, or second-cousins, or third-cousins – I don't know how high cousinage goes. Perhaps you do, sir?"

"I am no expert on the topic," Bryde confessed.

"You take my meaning, though, in respect of the *distancy* of the relatives," said Mrs Castille, firmly, and stirred for a time with extra relish.

Bryde being forced to admit that he did not entirely take

her meaning, she brought out the ladle, tapped it thrice on the edge of the giant cauldron, and hung it on its hook on the wall behind. "These cousins, remote as Peru though they were, contested the will. It is still being contested, locked in chancery they say. And meanwhilst, and notwithstanding Jack Jaggers's firmness of opinion – for he declared himself willing to wager not just his breakfast muffin, but all his breakfast muffins going forward into his dotage, and he a young man still – the court case grinds, sir. And whilst it grinds, no money is forthcoming."

"I am sorry to hear it, Mrs Castille," said Bryde.

"Into *this* breach," said Mrs Castille, wiping her steamed-up hands upon her apron, "steps – well, I don't and I'm sure need to tell such an one as *you* sir."

"Sir Martin Malprelate? *He* offered to fund the kitchen?"

"The gentleman to his very name. Out of the blue, Mr Bryde! The blue out of which he approached *could not* have been bluer. He stepped into the shop, and introduced himself, and offered to cover the expenses of on-going operation, simple as that. And he was as good as his word – better, for he subvented *more* money than even kindly old Mr Fontblank had done. With his support we are able to send down to the High Street baker's every morning and bring up three dozen superior rolls. I spoke of the rolls, before? You'll recall my rolls from being mentioned at before?"

"Indeed."

"For all these years he has, without fine-fare or flourish, been financing this establishment. And there's nothing like it, Mr Bryde – my people come, some from as far off as Hilldrop and Paddington, for sustenance without which they would assuringly starve to death. He has done this, and sought no credit. No, no, on the contrary he insisted I keep his identity utter in its secrecy, sir. He himself would not come to the kitchen, for fear of being recognised, so instead sending his secretary Mr Aster, whom you erstwhile named. And when, in utter thankfulness I assure *you*, I suggested we put his portrait, engraved in steel and priced at elevenpence, on the wall, he forbad it, forbad it bad and forthright. His charity was to be, as the Good Book says," and here Mrs Castille shut her eyes and spoke, with a new fluency and perfection of pronunciation, "a heed that do not lay your alms before men, to be seen of them, therefore when thou doest thine alms, do not sound a trumpet before thee, as the hypocrites do in the synagogues and in the streets, that they may have glory of men." She opened her eyes again. "Mr Bryde, I know what the world says of Sir Martin, and how poor a reputation he carried about with him. But he did not deserve such malign-drawing. I know he did not. He was a radically *good* man."

On the way back through the main room, Mrs Castille asked after Sir Martin's will, and with a particular concern as to whether the funding for the kitchen was included therewithin. Bryde admitted he had no information on that subject, but hoped that, if Martin Malprelate had been so good as to fund the kitchen in life, he would continue to do so in death.

"Hope is a faithful charity," said Mrs Castille. "Only I have no trust in the willers."

"The testamentary legal establishment, you mean?"

"Oh!" she said. "*Quite.*" And then: "quite, quite." And then: "quite quite quite. They will tangle up the man's wishes, and the money will stop. I pray, Mr Bryde, but I fear it. And what are the odds of another benefactor stepping through the door, as Sir Martin did those many years ago, to supply the lack? Poor odds. Poor odds."

"I am sorry to hear this news, Mrs Castille. What will you do?"

"What will I do?" the mistress-of-soup replied. "What will the kitchen do? Close, I fear. A dreadful circumstance – and the soup itself, centuries old, the truest badge of continuity and history and community, to go cold, and poured in the canal I daresay. What will *I* do? If I don't find employment, sir, I shall starve on the street, alongside my former soup drinkers. I'm too old to be likely for domestic service, and though my soup is – I say it without bad pride, you understand, sir – exceptional, thanks to my sainted grandmother, my other cooking has its limitations."

"I regret that I am not a wealthy man, Mrs Castille," said Bryde, taking his leave with a bow.

"We are cast into the hands of God," Mrs Castille replied, "and must trust to His mercy. But it is the hands of men that must supply the Mammon-stuff, and I fear men as virtuous and kind-hearted as Sir Martin are rare."

3

Bryde walked, once again, through the streets of Camden.

At the corner – what had perhaps once been a crossroads, before the railway had forced its way through – he stopped outside a hatter's. The shop's young man was wiping the windows with a rag, the more transparently to display the bowlers, toppers, sea-side wide-awakes, shooting-caps, and waterproof head-gear for the moors and mountains within. "Good day," said Bryde.

"Seeking a hat, sir?" asked the young man eagerly, casting a disparaging eye on Bryde's rusty headgear.

"Your shop?" Bryde asked.

"No sir," said the young man. "Only my master is often away. There are no funeral hats in stock at the moment, sir, if that's your pleasure," looking at Bryde's black suit, and making an assumption, "on account of my master putting the entirety of that stock upon the heads of his family and taken them off to the Isle of Thanet, where a great aunt is being lowered into the grave. I alone remains, and remains alone in the shop."

"You are left alone to handle the business?"

"Very often, sir. I have all the hats, sir," said the young man, "but no heads to put in em."

"The new railway must be a great annoyance?"

"The works, sir? They add to the variety and gaiety of life, I think. When heads don't present *inside* the shop for coverings, I'll stand in the doorway and watch the work progress."

"A man was killed down there," said Bryde. "You have heard of this?"

"Sir Martin?" said the young man. "Why yes – a great tragedy."

"Did you know him?" Bryde asked, struck by the tone in which the young hatman had spoken.

"He would sometimes call at the shop, sir. Bought a hat more than once. He consulted."

"Consulted?"

"As to the position of the shop. My gaffer and he had a long conversation, to which they did not stint that I might overhear, as I brought them tea and sugar. The line might have come through here, but my gaffer begged it would not, and Sir Martin was happy to concede the point. Not that he didn't offer a handsome sum to buy the place up – had my gaffer been in the retiring mood he could have lived comfortable by the sea on the sum offered. But Sir Martin took the refusal to sell in the best grace, sir."

"I have heard that there was bad feeling," Bryde pressed. "I heard there was compulsory purchase of people's homes."

"I don't know about up or down the parish, sir, but not here! Them houses he bought-up was all slum properties, and the people in 'em only too keen to sell and move elsewhere."

Bryde thanked the young man and walked on. Round the corner he stepped, on a whim, inside the church: a narrow building, the stained glass in the thin windows very ancient and very grubby, the pews huddling together as if for warmth. The air still held the resinous scent of old incense from the morning service. The clerk was at his desk, to the left of the main entrance, and Bryde asked the fellow what he knew of the lamentable death of Sir Martin.

"He was not of our parish," said the clerk. A split in one of his front teeth edged his words with extra sibilance: the word *parish* elongating itself like a snake uncurling. "Lived, as I believe, in a large house in Barsetshire" – expanding the domain of this ancient county by many hissing acres – "but he would call *by* the church, when he was in town, and speak to the curate, and he was most *generous*" – as the clerk was, with the extra "s" he granted the ending of this word – "in terms of charitable donation. We are to repair the roof, and only because of Sir Martin's generosity. Fifty pound! Offered without being pestered for it. It was a terrible *sssad* day," the clerk concluded, "when news of his demise came to usss."

Bryde walked on. He conversed with a boots boy, not yet ten years old and perched like a parrot on his wooden frame, and who remembered Sir Martin's frequent gifts of tuppences with more heart than even the clerk had remembered the church-donation of fifty pounds. "And when it weren't coin," said the lad, "he would stop and gift me a tin of boot black putty, and that was as good as giving me sixpence." The lad shook his head with a worldly wisdom terribly at odds with his tender age: "It's a brutal world, sir, in which such a gentleman is beaten to death with clubs."

"You saw him beaten with clubs?" Bryde asked.

"I he-eard," said the boy, "that a crowd rushed him, and beat him dead."

"But did not see with your own eyes?"

"That late a'night, sir? No. But I he-eard!"

"A crowd of whom?"

"Ruffians," said the lad, knowingly.

"But what would be their motive?"

The boy had no opinion on this, other than that some people are crooked, just as some are straight. Bryde gave him a penny – he had no tuppence in his pocket, and anyway did not wish to seem to compete with the blessed memory of Sir Martin's former generosity – and walked on.

On this second round of Camden interviews, Bryde spoke to various people: people from the town, rather than workmen employed on the building site. From these interviews a very different portrait of the murdered man emerged.

He chatted with an old lady, out walking a pug almost as small as a mouse. Mistress Peggy was her name, and she claimed to be eighty years old, though Bryde gallantly declared such an age hard to credit, looking at her tiny round white face, in the centre of her huge cream-coloured oyster-shell bonnet like a pearl. Mistress Peggy also had stories of Sir Martin's generosity to the parish: "Not that I'm in need of charity *myself*," she said. "But then, you understand, it was not his way to gift money to the wealthy. He was rich himself, and perhaps for that reason he had more than a little contempt for rich folk. For him it was *work* that justified, not faith. The idleness of the wealthy disgusted him. But the poor, who work and work and work and still don't have enough – well *there* he was only too happy to offer money."

Bryde thanked her and walked on. He strolled along the canal for a half mile or so. Barges lay, like elephant seals, along the bank, attached to the land by the tusks of their gangways. From some of these were being unloaded boxes of cabbages, sacks of flour, urns of milk and barrels of beer, boxes, beds, and bundles. Others were bringing in material for the railway. Two men walking the springy gangway with a metal rail linking their shoulders. Another man shoveling gravel out of the hold of his barge into a backed-up cart.

Bryde spoke to carpenters and wharf-men. He spoke to a

dame who ran an infants school through the open-window of her tiny house, her half-dozen charges sitting outside and paying more attention to drawing in the dirt, or clapping out *one-two-three-captain*, or watching the sparrows, than attending to the old woman's croaky lessons. He spoke to an omnibus driver. He spoke to a gravedigger. He spoke to a top-hatted broker, on his way to his home in Islington. Nobody had a bad word for Sir Martin.

As Bryde himself returned home, the question posed by the secretary, Aster, kept returning to him: *there might be many reasons to kill a truly wicked man, but who seeks to murder a good man?*

Chapter 4

THE MADDENED OX

1

Afterwards, Vavasour Holmes regretted sending Bryde a note inviting him to the Zoological Gardens. It is of course uncomfortable to think that, but for such a summons, your friend might still be alive. But Holmes had at least the consolation of thinking that he had only been reacting to Bryde's own enquiry, which itself actually mentioned the gardens. *I have new evidence as to the pertinence of the zoological gardens to the strange affair of Sir Martin's death*, Bryde wrote, *but I do not believe I can quite make sense of it all. I would very much welcome a chance to talk it over with you, if you are free.*

Standing in his parlour, reading the note, just delivered, Holmes thought to himself: what an intriguing thing! How could the Zoological Gardens possibly relate to this business? Holmes immediately wrote a reply.

Dear Bryde – the oddest coincidence! I am this moment about to leave for the very place – I mean the London Zoological Gardens – to meet with Sir Persimmon Hawk, of all people. I am most intrigued by your assertion that the menagerie might have some place in the jig-saw mystery of Sir Martin's lamentable demise. Join me there, I beg of you, as soon as you receive this, and you can explain: I shall be there from eleven. At the entrance, show them my signature, below, for admittance: I am a trustee.

He curlicued *Vavasour Holmes* at the foot of the page, sealed the note and handed it to the boy with instructions to deliver it at once. Then he put on his coat, settled his hat on his cranium, swept up his walking stick and strode out.

Holmes walked with a long stride through Regent's Park. As a man of the natural sciences, Holmes did not like to speculate without evidence, but he could hardly prevent himself from wondering what it was that had led Bryde to the gardens as an element in the mystery.

At the entrance to the gardens themselves, occupying the northernmost tranche of Regent's Park, Holmes showed his ivory ticket and was granted ingress. The gardens themselves, independent of their many zoological attractions, were a delightful promenade, laid out according to the tenets of the most refined taste. At this season the parterres no longer displayed their varicoloured blooms, but it was heartening to see the different creatures in their various spaces, not caged miserably or penned in a caravan as in other menageries.

He passed the two New Holland emus, land birds resembling ostriches, whose inability of flight is compensated for by the great speed with which they can run. Perhaps, Holmes thought to himself, tipping his hat to the birds as he walked by, Bryde believes these avians pulled the carriage that ran Sir Martin down!

Up the garden's central walk he passed the bear enclosure, its low wall augmented with an iron fence. In the middest of this shallow pit the trunk of a tree, like a ship's mast, had been fixed for the beasts to climb. The llamas were not visible, hiding from the cold inside their Gothic House, but a little further along a swart-headed griffon vulture sat preening its purple-black foliage on its perch, and the goats followed Holmes' passage with their heads, chewing nonchalantly.

Sir Persimmon was beside the Monkey House. He had brought the case, which stood on the ground beside him.

The area devoted to monkeys was adorned with a dozen tall poles. The monkeys, attached by slender chains to hoops threaded round the poles, sat on the ground at their bases, or clambered up to the top of them as they pleased.

Sir Percy was not alone. Mr Griffin was with him, wearing a samite veil across his face like a woman, and, behind the fabric, those violet-tinted glasses he always wore.

"Good day, Sir Percy," Holmes said. Hawk returned the greeting with a single finger tapping the underside of the brim of his top hat. "And," Holmes added, "good day to you too, Mr Griffin."

Griffin's tight-lipped smile was wide and predatory, visible behind the thin fabric. He looked down at the case, on the ground beside Sir Percy's legs, and then looked up again.

Holmes took up a position alongside the baronet, and for a minute the three men simply watched the monkeys climbing up and down.

"Simia quam similis turpissima bestia nobis," said Sir Persimmon, shortly. "True, what? Very true."

"Ennius, I believe," said Holmes, not on his securest ground when it came to classical literature – for he was much more a student of the natural sciences. "Or was it Cicero? On the vraisemblance of men and monkeys."

"Up and down all day. Now and again they'll stop to pick fleas off one other." He laughed. "How foolish we all are, Holmes. Foolish to believe we're different to these beasts! Apes, we're apes, running up and down our various poles, collecting ticks from one another's bodies and dining on 'em, as if they were the finest delicacies. Apes and men the same."

"Some might think there are differences as well as similarities, Sir Percy, and to our advantage," Holmes offered, eyeing the large case at the baronet's feet. "Although I concede the similarities are certainly there."

A monkey had approached the two men, coming as far as his chain permitted him, and was now showing them all his teeth. Sir Persimmon repaid the gesture in kind – scowling. "Go on, you brute! Get away!"

"I see," Holmes noted, "that you have brought the device with you?"

At this, the baronet looked down at the case. "I don't like to leave it behind," he said.

"It is surely safe. Your London lodge is secure – you trust your servants." Holmes couldn't help but glance at Griffin when he said this; for, although he knew very little of the fellow, he felt an instinctive distrust whenever he encountered him. Irrational and doubtless unfair: if Sir Percy was happy to admit Griffin to *his* confidence, it would be petulant of Holmes not to do the same.

Griffin's two violet circles of blankness stared, sphinx-like, back at Holmes's glance.

"Yes, yes," said Sir Percy, impatiently. "I've vetted the servants. Nonetheless!"

"You did not bring the case to show to the curator, I trust?"

"Show him *this*? Why on earth would I do such a thing?"

"I only mean to say I am not sure it would be prudent to bring others into this particular secret at *this* stage," Holmes said. Again he glanced at Griffin.

"No, no," the baronet returned, angrily.

"And *is* the curator in a position to help us?"

"Not this week, damn his eyes. It seems *not* – not this week. The shipment *did* come in, but the eel did not survive the trip, it seems."

"A shame," said Holmes. "And when might he expect a new delivery?"

"Another month," said Sir Percy. "The delay is damnable irritating."

"Well, we shall have to concentrate on other aspects of our researches during that time. Ah!" This last was in reaction to Holmes catching sight of Bryde, making his way along the path towards them. "I invited Bryde here, Sir Percy," he said. "You've met him, I believe?"

"Upon my soul," said Griffin. "It is Mr *Bryde*. Large as life and twice as natural."

"He's a company employee," said the baronet.

"Yes of course. Tasked with investigating the terrible end of Sir Martin."

"But what's he doing here?" Sir Persimmon Hawk looked aggrieved. "Oughtn't he to be over in Camden Town, interviewing witnesses or whatnot? What?"

"I was given the job of observing him," said Griffin, in an amused tone, "and yet he now appears to be dogging *me*."

"That's but coincidence, Griffin, I'm sure," said Holmes. Sir Percy did not look convinced.

"If it's all the same to you, Sir Percy," said Griffin, flipping his walking stick up and down, in ninety-degree swishes like a sword, "I'll wait for you in the carriage."

"Very well."

"Shall I take the device with me?" Griffin asked. There was, Holmes thought, something rapacious in his voice.

"No, no, I'll keep my grasp on *that*, thank you very much."

"Toodle-doo, then," said Griffin, and sauntered away. He took a different path than the one along which Bryde was still approaching.

"I've been meaning to ask," Holmes said. "Concerning Mr Griffin's condition. Albinism, is it?"

"Griffin's condition is stranger than that," growled Sir Percy. "But never mind him. What of Bryde? Has he cleared up the investigation yet, or not?"

"I am not sure he has entirely solved it, Sir Percy."

"Then why is he coming here? What? Wasting everyone's time."

"He has included me in his confidences, so far as the investigation is going," said Holmes. "He is good enough to value my deductive powers, and I hope I am of some use in untangling this mystery. As to why he is *here* – he wrote to me this morning that he had discovered some connection between Sir Martin's death and this very garden. He is coming to discuss it with me."

At this, the baronet grew visibly vexed. His brow corrugated and his eyes pinched tight. "Stuff!" he cried, angrily. "Balderdash. How can there be any connection? Connection? Between a zoological garden and a railway company's building site? Nonsense, nonsense."

"They are close to one another," Holmes pointed out, taken aback by the baronet's sudden vehemence. "Geographically, I mean."

"It's *stuff* I tell you!" barked Sir Persimmon. "There's no connection, none at all. I'll give the lie to any man who says there is!"

"It is hard to see," Holmes said, diplomatically, "on what grounds any such connection might operate, I agree. But you can ask him yourself."

"No, no, I'll not intrude on any conversation *you* and *he* may feel you need to have," said the baronet, fiercely. "I'll go."

"Of course," said Holmes, trying to understand where all this brusqueness and anger had come from. "I comprehend that Sir Martin Malprelate was *your* business partner, your friend, which of course makes you eager to discover – "

"Oh, Malprelate didn't do *friendliness*," Sir Percy interrupted. "Not to human beings, what? Animals: now that was a different matter. He'd have had all *these* monkeys round for tea, quick as an egg – you hear that, you apes? *He* would have welcomed you! Not I."

"My point is that *if* Bryde has indeed unearthed a clue that leads to a solution for this bizarre mystery, then you'll of course want to know what it is – this matter touches you more closely than most. Please do not feel you must leave."

Sir Persimmon's demeanour returned to its usual haughty disdain. "Naturally I want to see the blamed business put to bed. Track down the villains, hang 'em high. Naturally. But the zoological gardens having a part to play? Some connection between that murder and these beasts? *Stuff*, I say."

Bryde was almost upon them. "Good day Sir Persimmon," he called out. "And Holmes, how do you do?"

"Hello Bryde. You know Sir Percy, of course," said Holmes.

"Very good to see you again, Sir Persimmon," Bryde returned.

"Holmes and I are colleagues," said the baronet, gruffly. "Workin' on a project, what?"

"There's no need to tantalise," Holmes said, smiling broadly. "As you know, Bryde, I have been working on a particular galvanic device. Sir Persimmon has an interest in it and is financing the work. Nor is he merely a sleeping partner; his interests in new technology are of longstanding."

"Hence," said Sir Percy, picking up his case, "locomotives and such."

"Steam power is capable of great things. But the galvanic powers of the electrical pile promise even greater wonders."

"How very fascinating," said Bryde, politely. "Holmes – might we…"

"We came to fetch an *eel*," boomed Sir Percy.

"I beg your pardon?"

"Electrophorus gymnotiform," said Holmes. "An electrical eel, of great size and, reputedly, prodigious capacity when it comes to generating galvanic shocks. It comes from the rivers of Brazil, and one was to be delivered to the zoological gardens. Sir Persimmon used his influence with the curator and the trustees to have the creature turned over to us. For our ongoing research, you see. We were hoping to study it:

not vivisect it, just examine it, and afterwards return it to the zoo. But, alas, it seems it did not survive its voyage hither. A great shame: by examining the eel and discovering the means by which it creates the electrical potency it carries, I believe we would have been able to advance our project considerably."

"Very interesting, no question. But Holmes," said Bryde, "I was hoping to have a word – "

"Concerning the death of Martin Malprelate, yes," said Holmes. "Whatever you have to say, surely you would not exclude Sir Percy? It concerns him very closely."

"Need to clear this business up," barked Hawk. "For the good of the company. The Middlemarch line!"

Bryde looked strangely at the baronet. "Of course," he said.

"Have ye?"

"Have I cleared it up? I am not sure, Sir Percy – I mean, I am not able, quite yet, wholly to clear the business up, in all its particularities. That's why I wanted to talk to you, Holmes. But I fear my speculations will be too fragmentary and odd to prove of any interest to Sir Persimmon."

"Speculations that the zoo is somehow connected with Malprelate's death?" shouted the baronet, once again of-a-sudden furiously angry. "Pure stuff. Nonsensical stuff."

"I would appreciate it Holmes, by way of canvassing your ratiocinative powers, if you would accompany me into Camden. I would like to show you something. Something, uh – important."

"I'll come too," said Sir Percy. "*If* you don't mind."

Bryde looked awkwardly but could hardly refuse the baronet. "Of course."

And so the three men set off together, Sir Percy picking up his suitcase and clutching it close to his side as he walked.

A white-headed North American eagle watched them warily from the Bird of Prey house. Herons, standing tall on legs like wire, clacked their beaks together.

As they approached the entrance gate and pay hut, Sir Percy snapped: "Well? Out with it, man!"

"Sir?" Bryde replied.

"What *is* it? Ye came to allege some *conspiracy* between the zoological gardens and the people who murdered Malprelate, didn't you? Don't deny it, Holmes already told me."

"Sir Persimmon," said Bryde. "I beg to correct your misapprehension. I make no conspiratorial allegations. I am charged, by the company – the company established by the departed Sir Martin, and of which of course *you* are a director, and presently major shareholder – to investigate the strange circumstances of his death."

The three men were at the gate.

"In the course of these investigations," Bryde continued, "I have been struck by the propinquity – I mean the sheer *physical* closeness – of these gardens behind us, with their various animal denizens, and the scene of Sir Martin's strange death, some few hundreds of yards over there." He gestured past the Outer Circle Road and across Albany Street towards the roofs of Camden Town, just visible.

"Is that all?" scoffed Sir Percy. "Coincidence of *placement*? Pooh pooh, my dear fellow."

"Very truly, Sir Percy," Bryde conceded. "Only that. And I must beg we no longer trespass upon your time. It cannot be that a gentleman such as yourself, with so many pressing duties of business, can have the leisure to wander the streets of Camden this morning?"

Sir Percy glared at Bryde. "You want a private confab with Holmes?"

"Sir Percy," Bryde began.

"No, no. I see where I'm not wanted." Then, hoisting the suitcase he carried so that it fitted under his arm, he barked: "Give over the zoological garden angle, Bryde, is my advice. You're chasing wild geese with that one. But – what? – I'll bid ye both good day. And yes, you speak truly Bryde when you say I have better things to be doing with my time than trudging around Camden."

"Your position remains," Holmes asked, shaking the baronet's free hand, "that Luddites or ruffians rushed Sir Martin at once and beat him to death with clubs?"

"How else? I certainly don't believe nonsense about trains from perdition driven by grinning devils – I don't care what the so-called witnesses say. Witnesses? Geese, rather. The so-called testimony of a gaggle of gin-stupefied nobodies. No, no, this is Reform! It's Reform, I tell you, always lifting its Hydra head, always. It's the same outrages as occurred in '31 – mobs trying to overthrow the established order. All this chaff about demon locomotives is just smoke and mirrors."

"You could well be right, Sir Persimmon," said Bryde.

The baronet did not shake Bryde's hand. "I'll leave you to your peregrinations, gentlemen. Have a care, though, Bryde. These folk are monsters. If they'd bash-in the head of a prince of industry, a knight of the realm, they'd certainly not think twice before battering one such as you."

"Good day Sir Persimmon."

"Good day!"

The baronet stalked off. That the carriage waiting by the front gate belonged to him was evident from the escutcheon on its side. The baronet climbed inside and the coachman shook the reins.

Holmes said: "An irascible fellow, is Sir Percy. But his interest in new technology is genuine I assure you. He knows a surprising amount about galvanism, about electricity we call it now. And his support is most helpful to me in my work."

"He seemed strangely insistent on there being no connection between the zoo and Sir Martin's death," Bryde observed. "Almost aggressively insistent."

"Oh he gets odd crotchets in his head," said Holmes. "He is only a trustee of these gardens because he sees them as a resource he can exploit – as with the galvanic eel we were to collect today. But the fact that he *is* a trustee means that his name is associated with the place. I daresay he took your suggestion of a connection with Sir Martin's death as a personal affront to his dignity. He is only a baronet, after all."

"Holmes!"

"Oh I mean no offense. But in my experience, those higher up the ladder – your Earls and Dukes – are less quick to escry offence, being more secure in their eminence. Still, let's not worry about Sir Percy's cranks. Tell me: what *is* this connection you mentioned in your note? Beyond the physical propinquity, as Sir Percy said, it's a puzzle as to how the two magisterial could possibly be connected."

"I'll tell you," said Bryde. "One thing, though – was that Mr Griffin I saw, departing in a hurry before I arrived?"

"It was. His jawbone whole and hale."

"How strange that he should dash off as I approached. Do you think," Bryde said, "that he wished to *avoid* me?"

"My dear Bryde, why would anyone wish to avoid you! You are capital company."

"He did rather slink away, though."

"First you accuse him of dogging your footsteps. Now you accuse him of avoiding you. Which is it? Come, Bryde – will you tell me *why* you wished to meet, my friend? What is the link between Sir Martin's death and this zoological garden?"

The two men were standing on the paved sideway of Albany Street. A busy street in the midst of the day.

A one-horse gig rattled past, and then came Sir Percy's own carriage, pulled by two horses black as liquorice, driven by a liveried coachman. The blinds in the carriage windows were lowered, so neither Holmes nor Bryde could see Sir Percy inside.

As soon as it passed, Bryde cried out. "There!"

"What!"

"Look, man! Across the road – *there*!"

Holmes looked. On the far side of the street stood a man of late middle age, dressed in workman's clothes and staring back at them. "You mean that fellow? You know him?"

"It's the King of Carts!" cried Bryde. "How is he *here*, now?"

"The king of – wait: you are not expecting to see him?"

"No!"

"It may be nothing nefarious, John. People have many reasons for being in London."

"I must speak to him," said Bryde, and stepped out into the road.

As to what happened next, Holmes – of course – considered and pondered it a good deal in the days and weeks that followed. Scientific training had given him an attentive and retentive eye, very good on specific detail, and his memory was capacious. More, his consciousness was agile, confident, precise, insusceptible to that malady of collectivity whereby other people make us doubt what we have experienced by pressing some other version upon us. He knew what he saw, and was ready to swear to it. Indeed, he did so swear, to the very iota, when the police afterwards took a statement from him.

A bull, stampeding in wrath up the Albany, tossing Bryde with its horns and then dashing away.

Witnesses were certain that it had been a bull. A bull was what was reported more generally, as in the *Illustrated London News*, who covered the death on page 6 near the bottom, on the left, in a single paragraph that began: "an unsupervised and stampeding bullock has caused a fatality on the outskirts of Regent's Park". No illustration was appended to this small news-story.

This is what Holmes saw. There were people about, carts and carriages, but the street was not excessively busy. Sir Persimmon's carriage rumbled away to their right. Two horsemen were coming down from Camden High Street, on their way to exercise their mounts in the park – the noise and commotion of Bryde's death caused these steeds to rear and whinny, though they were well-trained and, the riders insisted, usually docile creatures. Both riders gave statements to the police that they had seen the bull gore and toss Bryde, and then dash off, none knew whither. Holmes, much closer to the incident, was not sure their evidence could be altogether taken as reliable, given the distance from which they observed things.

Still: Holmes' evidence was surely not reliable either, despite his proximity to the death. For what he described was impossible.

Holmes saw a bull. It came out of nowhere, as the popular phrase has it, in a cloud of glittering steam, snorted out of its brazen nostrils. It moved more rapidly than any bovine Holmes had ever seen. Its horns protruded perpendicular to its narrow, hard-looking head, and the one eye Holmes, from his vantage, observed was sulphurously coloured and wicked, gleaming with an inner light. From silence a moment before the air was split by the bull's roar, a deep-throated and thunderous sound, loud enough to make a fellow flinch. The beast's legs were moving so rapidly they were but a blur and – strangest of all – a creature, naked, thin-bodied, shiny-skinned, huge headed and faceless save for a broad and diabolic grin, rode the beast's back. A Hell-bull, ridden by a devilish rider.

How could that be? In the middle of a bright London day? Hell bursting through into our mortal realm.

Just a maddened ox, broken free of its drover, and stampeding the streets.

Then, almost of an instant, came the collision: Bryde had not enough time even to cry out before the bull was on him. He was in the air, his limbs flailing. His top and bottom swapped places, and, just for a moment, Holmes saw his face, inverted, his eyes wide, his mouth open. But the examination by coroner's surgeon afterwards confirmed that the first impact broke his back instantly, and that he was probably dead as he spun through the air, and was certainly dead by the time his body landed, hard, on the street.

The bull ducked its head down immediately prior to striking Bryde, as a bull will do that seeks to toss a victim upon its horns. The creature galloped by and rushed away.

On this latter point, however, Holmes in all conscience could not swear with absolute definiteness; for, naturally, his attention was taken up by his fallen friend. He rushed to the spot where Bryde's body lay. Somewhere, away to his left, a person was screaming in shock. Pedestrians hurried over. A bow-street whistle was blowing.

Holmes looked up. The King of Carts was nowhere to be seen.

2

Bryde's body was placed on a pallet and carried to the nearby Grove Lodge, home to the noted geologist George Bellas Greenough. He happened to be home that day and, hearing the commotion, had come outside to see what the matter was. He himself ordered his servants to bring Bryde through the gates to his villa, although it was evident, as soon as the body was lifted from the ground, that there was no life in it.

Holmes knew Greenough, as one scientist will generally know another, and although they were not intimates they existed in a state of mutual respect and regard. But as he explained what had happened, or tried to, Holmes saw the expression on Greenough's face fix in disbelief. "My dear fellow," he said, "what a terrible shock for you!"

"If by shock," said Holmes, bridling somewhat, "you mean

to derogate the accuracy of my powers of observation – "But he felt immediate shame at this prideful insistence, most especially at such a time. His friend was lying dead, before them!

"Of course not," Greenough said, hurriedly. "Of course not, my dear fellow."

A constable was with them – PC Raymond Dagg was his name – and another metropolitan officer, summoned by the first's whistle, arrived soon after, having run up and down Albany Street in search of the bull.

"You're sure it *was* a bull?" asked Greenough.

"Everyone saw it," said PC Dagg.

"I only ask because we are, here, hard by the Zoological Gardens."

"You think, sir," said Constable Dagg, "that a wild beast such as a lion or rhine-nose-hoss might have escaped?"

"A wild zoological beast, roaming the city?" said the second constable. "Twould be a most se-*he*rious and grave matter."

"Nonsense, good sirs," Holmes interrupted them. "I am a trustee of the gardens and I assure you that there is neither a lion nor a rhinoceros in the menagerie. The most dangerous beasts in the collection are the bears, and none of them have escaped."

"You are sure of that, are you sir?"

"At any rate, I *saw* the incident – I was standing very close – and it was no bear that I saw."

"Bull, then?"

"A bull," Holmes said. "Although a bull of a strange breed. And I saw, or I thought I saw, a boy riding it."

"Riding it?"

"Perhaps I did not," said Holmes.

The second of the two constables ran off to report the incident and fetch a conveyance for moving Bryde's body to the morgue. This, then, was the last moment Holmes saw his friend in the flesh.

For the first time, looking down at that moment upon the broken body that had once been Bryde, Holmes became first aware of actual shock, although presumably he had felt shock from the very moment of the collision. But now he was aware of it. His hands were trembling. He heaved a breath and felt dizziness. Dead! His friend – struck down before his very eyes.

"My dear fellow," said Greenough. "You've of a sudden turned white as bleach."

"It's just – just now struck me," said Holmes, faintly. "The truth of it. Bryde, dead! Might I sit down?"

Greenough took Holmes himself inside his house, sat him down and had a servant fetch a cup of hot sugared tea. For a long quarter-hour Vavasour Holmes simply sat, cradling the sweet liquid, staring into space. Slowly his powers of ratiocination, shattered by the affront they had just received, began to reassemble himself. What he had seen had, perhaps, resembled a compact but powerful and furious bullock. A bullock running the streets of the capital was no impossible thing – cattle were brought in daily in great herds, from all compass points, to Smithfield by Saint Pauls to be butchered to feed the metropolis's appetite. Perhaps an ox might run mad on the outskirts of Regent's Park and trample a man to death. All this was *possible*. And yet Holmes, who saw it, felt he had seen something that was not natural.

Holmes thought to himself: it was not the bull that had been unnatural, but the sheer fact of Bryde's death. Its suddenness.

Dark, dark, dark. They all go into the dark.

"Mr Vavasour Holmes?" A black-suited man, holding his hat before his stomach and leaning forward slightly, was standing before him. "My name is Bucket – I am an officer of the London police."

"Good day, sir," said Holmes, standing up. "You have come because of the death of Mr Bryde."

"Indeed, sir. I am told you witnessed his demise?"

There was something in Bucket's manner that caught Holmes' eye, although he couldn't quite decipher it: some inflection to the professional discretion and attentiveness of the professional police officer. "I did."

"He was your friend?"

"He was."

"I am indeed sorry for so grave a loss, and such a shocking manner of death. Reports are of a maddened bull, trampling Mr Bryde. You saw this animal?"

"I must be scrupulously honest in my reportage, Mr Bucket," said Holmes. "Although I fear my doing so will sound strangely in your ears. I cannot swear that I saw an ox. I am not certain *what* I saw."

Bucket evinced no surprise at this, only nodding slowly. "I must ask, sir: what do you believe you saw, if not an ox?"

For a moment, Holmes held his tongue. "It must be irritating for you to hear this, Mr Bucket," he said eventually, "but I do not know. I do not know what I saw." He thought to himself: *a demon, from hell.* But the mere idea of this was absurd. He was in shock. The shock was unsettling his perception. It had been an ox, nothing more.

"Did you see anything else?" asked Bucket. "Is there anything else you consider pertinent to this death?"

"It was an ordinary moment in time," said Holmes, putting his face into his hands. "He and I were walking, from the London Zoological Gardens towards Camden. He was struck down. That is all."

"You will find me at Scotland Yard, Mr Holmes, if more reoccurs to you," said Button, tipping his head and putting his hat back on.

"Wait," said Holmes. "There *is* a context – for Mr Bryde was investigating the death of Sir Martin Malprelate. He works – he worked – for the Malprelate railway company as a designing engineer and had some reputation for solving problems. The company directors asked him to look into the death and he was doing so. I mention it, Mr Bucket, because he on occasion came to me to discuss the particularities of the mystery. He was good enough to say that my contribution to the matter was useful. This very morning he wrote me a note – I have it, in my rooms – asking to meet with me to discuss some aspect of the mystery."

Mr Bucket looked sharply at him. "What aspect?"

"Something connected with the Zoological Gardens. I do not know the details, precisely, for he was struck down before he could tell me."

"But – the Zoological Gardens? How so?"

"I cannot tell."

Bucket considered this. "Mr Holmes, I must confide in you that I too knew Mr Bryde. I can go further: he and I had also conferred on this very mystery: Sir Martin's strange death."

Holmes nodded.

Bucket bowed. "We will speak further on this matter Mr Holmes. As I say you may find me at Scotland Yard where I await your convenience. For now I must oversee the scene of this crime, and the movement of Bryde's body to the morgue."

"I wish you good day, Mr Bucket."

Holmes got up. He felt dizzy, but that passed. Suddenly he couldn't bear to be in that place, in that house, at that time. He mumbled thanks and farewell to his host and lurched outside.

He walked first to his club, his head filled with what he had seen. He took a brandy to settle his startlement, at least to some extent. Then wrote two notes: one to his wife, informing her of his shocking news, and saying that circumstances meant he must remain in town for the foreseeable future. Then he wrote a briefer scriptum to

Sir Persimmon Hawk, merely relating the news of Bryde's death.

After that, and with a pace slow enough to be funereal, he walked back to his rooms. There was no rain, but the cloud cover had thickened and lowered, such that the peaks of the buildings almost touched the very sky. Holmes was struck, as if never before, by the sheer size of the city: the factual solidness of London's immensity: the miles of housetops and viaducts, the complication of road junctions; streets of low black houses as inanimate as so many rows of coal scuttles, save where at frequent corners, from a gin-shop, there was a flare of light more brutal still than the afternoon dimness. And here, round a corner, a parade of palatial buildings in which the wealthy were waited on by liveried servants, and lights blazed from mullioned windows. Parkland through which the children of the rich rode on ponies, led by the muzzle by a sour-faced retainer, or men with slender legs and handsome whiskers rode tall horses with panache designed to impress the ladies.

Though not yet three o'clock in the afternoon the light inside Holmes's apartment was such that he was obliged to light a candle. This finger of wax, set in its basin, projected a huge shadow wobblingly against the wall. Holmes thought of ghost stories, or the irrational and the gothique. Was he to abandon natural science and logic and sink into mere superstition? Had he really stood, in the daylight of a modern city, and seen a hell-bullock ridden by a veritable demon, crush the life of his friend?

Impossible.

It was not Holmes's habit to sleep in the afternoon, but the shock of the day left him exhausted and he lay upon his bed and closed his eyes.

* * *

3

He woke because his landlady was banging on his bedroom door. "Sir! Sir! Your wife!"

Bleary-eyed, Holmes stumbled up and staggered into the arms of his wife. Behind her the nurse was carrying baby Mycroft. There was a carpetbag deposited on the floor, containing the material for baby's wellbeing. Gwendolin was wearing a low-waisted pale blue Organza gown, the skirts of which puffed-out like the bell of a giant fuchsia.

"My poor darling Vavasour," she cried, embracing him. "Of course when I got your note I came at once. What a horrid, horrid business! You must be shattered."

"It was," Holmes conceded, "somewhat discombobulating."

"Tragic! That poor man – trampled!"

"Killed, at any rate."

"Of course I had to come," Gwendolin said, relinquishing her embrace and arranging herself and her voluminous skirts into the room's easy chair. Nurse took the sleeping baby through to the other room.

"Really my dear," said Holmes, perching himself on the end of the chaise longue. "In your condition I am very sorry to have given you a start. In your condition, indeed, I am far from sure you should have travelled at all!"

"Nonsense. Baby kicked out his legs a little, but only in the excitement of riding the railway, I do believe. And I could not abandon you to undergo your grief in solitude! Horrid enough to be bereaved – but to witness what you witnessed!"

"I'm honestly not sure *what* I witnessed."

The nurse, Mrs Yamp, returned, bearing a clinking, full-laden tray, having found the cupboard in which the tea things were maintained, lit the gas and boiled up the kettle. An individual of considerable personal initiative, clearly. "Thank you, Mrs Yamp," said Gwendolin, smiling.

Mrs Yamp, a woman of few words, bobbed a slow curtsey and withdrew.

"I read the afternoon paper on the train," said Gwendolin, pouring. "It said a wild bull trampled the life out of him. Horrid!"

"Most horrid," said Holmes.

He explained the circumstances: the note he had received from Bryde, their meeting, his insistence that there was some connection – "though he was not able to explain to me what it might be before he was killed" – between the Zoological Garden and the death of Sir Martin Malprelate.

"Gracious!" Gwendolin exclaimed, pausing her teacup before her mouth. "What on earth could the connection be? Vavasour – you don't think he was killed *in order to prevent* you telling him? Did some malevolent actor set the bull upon him?"

"Oh," exclaimed Holmes, who had not, until his wife suggested it, considered this possibility.

"I don't know, darling. I only know that your friend, dear Mr Bryde, was investigating that ghastly killing – of Sir Martin – and told you he had made some manner of breakthrough in his researches. Might the murderers, fearing discovery, have sought to silence his mouth?"

"But – in such a manner?"

"He himself said there was a connection between the railway works where Sir Martin met his end, and the Zoological Gardens. And he was killed outside the latter! Can this be mere coincidence? Can it? And trampled by a wild animal, no less – just as Sir Martin was ...well, we can't say trampled I suppose, since a locomotive runs on wheels and grooves and rails and such. Say he was *run down*, as was poor Mr Bryde. Does all this not suggest a *pattern* to your mind, Vavasour?"

"My dear," Holmes replied, adding more demerara to his tea. "I wonder if the bull I saw was..."

"What, my dear?"

"I do not know. I might almost – "he drew a deep breath – "might almost believe I saw a veritable devil. I might almost consider the stories the populace are telling to be *true*. Mayhap Sir Martin had perpetrated such enormities that the Evil One himself decided to claim him."

Gwendolin put down her teacup. "Husband!" she rebuked. "Will you sacrifice logic and common sense to the merest mumming-show superstition? What, painted devils leaping onto the stage in a firework puff of smoke? Nonsense. You of all people should know that, however bizarre the appearance, there is a real-world solution to the mystery."

Holmes looked at his wife. He too put his teacup down. "Of course you're right, my dear," he said. "I am – I fear, I am a little shattered by what I have seen. It has weakened my apperception, betrayed me into irrationality. You are quite correct to rebuke me for it!"

With a mighty rustling of skirts Gwendolen rose, came across to her husband and embraced his neck. "My poor Vavasour. Such a terrible thing to happen! Such a terrible, terrible thing to witness! You must rest. Come home to the country and pursue relaxation. You can always return to your work at a later date."

"My dear," he said, returning her embrace. "Truly I yearn for home – to rejoin the bosom of my family. But the work – the work is at a delicate stage."

Gwendolin stood upright. "I see."

"Besides – besides I feel sure the cure for my shock, in this terrible business, would be to unpick its knot. To resolve the mystery of these deaths. According to the tenets of logic and reality, as you say, but to resolve them."

"Such is the nature of your mind," said Gwendolin, not without sadness. "And he was your friend. But you must prepare yourself for the possibility that his death was an accident – for such things are not unknown, you know.

Accident means you will not have the satisfaction of a solution, for they are the universe's randomnesses."

"Of course, my dear. But then again..."

"At any rate, baby and I will not abandon you – not until I am sure the initial shock has passed. There is room for us here. It will be cosy, and Mrs Yamp will have to sleep in the parlour, but we shall manage!"

Chapter 5

THE MIDDLEMARCH
SERPENT

1

Day passed into night, and then again into day. The huge
machine that is London shook itself into life again. Convoys
of carts and streams of herded animals poured into the
metropolis from east and north, south and west. Boats and
barges passed, corpuscles along the Thamesian artery. Men
and women, wrapping themselves against the November
chill, left their houses, their wards, their cots, and shuffled to
their various workplaces. Children walked lethargic towards
their education, winding their inward springs as they did
so ready to release them on the racing, gambolling journey
home at the end of the school day. Pie shops and cafés, pubs
and chophouses fired their ovens, laid out their plates and
cups, opened their doors. The sun leaned over the bowl of
the Thames valley and looked down, parting the clouds to
get a better look. All of life hummed and buzzed, turned and
returned. And much of death was there too: lying in tight,
overfilled urban graveyards, crowds of unmoving corpses,
filed away in their respective slots with a tab, hefty in stone,
protruding up to mark their place. This is the realm of *pax
perpetua*, and even the heifers and pigs herded through the

dawn towards Smithfield market and slaughter glance at it, as they stumble past, and recognise the place. Holmes is the heifer, and his long march towards Smithfield is the night, vexed by dreams of his friend's death, and he wakes with a gasp, miserable and yet elated at not – not yet – not quite yet – having been filed in the earthen drawer of the grave. In one dream Sir Percy had appeared to him, forty feet tall, his hat a smokestack from which smoke guffed and stank; and his suitcase, which he was so insistent on carrying around, was of proportionate size. "Wait 'til I open it," this dream-giant sneered at Holmes, "and tuck you away inside!" And Holmes had seen that the case was made of clay and bones, and the catch was a gravestone, and that as it opened a moaning of the many interred emerged.

"My dear Vavasour," coos his wife, embracing him, and he blinks in the light of the morning. "You've been crying! You've been crying in your sleep again!"

"Bad dreams," he tells her. "But not so very bad. On with the day!"

And so the days went on.

Holmes divided his days. The mornings were when he was mentally most acute; after luncheon he tended to lose sharpness of apperception and rapidity of deduction and altered his labour to more repetitive and mechanical matters; but in the morning, with a cup of sweet coffee buzzing inside him, and the stimulating vapours of his pipe tobacco filling his head, his mind moved as smoothly and rapidly as a locomotive.

The work was pressing, and the device was nearing completion, but Holmes decided that solving the mystery of his friend's death (ascertaining whether there *was* a mystery to it, or whether it was merely, as his wife said, a mere accident; and determining what relationship it had, if any, to the strange death of Martin Malprelate) *really* ought to take precedence, even over the work. Sir Percy was impatient for Holmes to conclude his device. And Sir Percy would surely be enraged to discover that Holmes was (as he would surely say) wasting his time on such nonsense. In the baronet's mind the mystery was *already* solved: agitators, reformists, luddites, the rabble, the mob, followers of the demon Anarchy, were responsible. They had clubbed Sir Martin ignominiously to death. All that remained was to apprehend the specific perpetrators and hang them.

As for Bryde's death, Holmes could not believe Sir Percy gave that any thought whatsoever: a mere commoner, trampled in the street, a nothing.

No: better not to let Sir Percy know what he was doing. And so he would continue with the work of assembling the device. But he would do so in the afternoons, leaving the mornings for his consideration of Bryde's death.

Having Gwendolin staying at his apartment, though a comfort in many ways, was also an inconvenience. Little Mycroft was a lusty crier, and was not always satisfied with the cow's milk Mrs Yamp offered him: a rubber teat like a phrygian cap affixed to a stone bottle. On such occasions the crying would go on and on, waking both Holmes and his wife. Gwendolin, a modern and forward-looking woman, had never employed a wet-nurse, and Baby Mycroft's disinclination to pass from maternal suckling to the bottle meant that she was still in a position to nurse him herself. But Holmes could not sleep whilst his wife was up and performing this maternal duty. Only when the baby was belched and settled again could he resume his own rest. Though slumber was elusive, and was thridded-through with bad dreams and anxieties about Bryde's death.

As a result Holmes was often ragged and friable in the mornings. But, taking such restoratives as he could in coffee and tobacco form, he found in his investigations an excuse – he would not have articulated it in quite so stark a manner, of course, but that is what it was – to leave the apartment.

Solve the mystery, Holmes told himself, and thereby banish the nightmares. Solve the mystery and placate Bryde's ghost.

He began as methodically as he could. First: a visit to Scotland Yard, and an interview with Inspector Bucket, who passed on such information as he could concerning the two deaths. In return Holmes gave the policeman a thorough and detailed account of what he had witnessed on the day of Bryde's death, although he was far enough away from the intensity of actual observation to be able to leaven his account with some common sense. "I appreciate that much of what I say strains credulity, and some can perhaps be attributed to shock. My wife is sure Bryde's death is but a terrible accident."

"Sorry though I am for the loss of my friend's life," Bucket said, "I fear your wife is correct."

"In point of fact," Holmes replied, "my wife also pointed out the peculiar pattern at work."

"Pattern?"

Holmes passed Bryde's note across to the Inspector. "This is the communication he sent me on the day of his death. He speaks there of a connection between Sir Martin's killing in Camden, and the Zoological Gardens nearby – although what connection precisely he did not disclose. As Gwendolin – my wife, Inspector – pointed out, both Sir Martin and our friend were *run down*, killed by a collision from, let us say, a locomotive or cart on the one hand, and an ox on the other."

"You accept, now, that it *was* an ox?"

"I cannot altogether accept it. But in all humility I must concede that I do not *know* what it was, and can only concede my fallibility. My point, though, is this: *might* the two deaths be linked? There are such things as co-incidences in the world, but beyond a certain point co-incidence calcifies into connection, surely. Gwendolin speculated that Bryde had been about to unveil the identity of the murderers, and, somehow knowing this, they unleashed the means of his death upon him – to silence him, you see."

"You think such an assassin was dogging Bryde's steps?"

"We saw the King of Carts across the road," said Holmes.

"Yes, you mentioned as such."

"He may be innocent of course. Perhaps it was some other malefactor. Or malefactors."

"And how would they know that Bryde was about to expose them? How would they know he has lighted upon their identity?"

"I do not know."

"More: how could they be sure he had not *already* named them? Named them to you, and to Sir Percy Hawk, with whom he had just been conversing? Surely a malefactor, surveilling Bryde's movements (as they would have had to be doing, in order to unleash this mode of death) would conclude that Bryde had *already* passed on the information to you and Sir Percy in the gardens. Would they not? In which case, why kill only Bryde? Why not all three of you?"

"An uncomfortable speculation!" Holmes declared. "But these are good questions, Inspector, and I concede, questions to which answers are not obvious."

"One further question, then: why orchestrate so elaborate a mode of murder? If, that is, murder is what it was. If we set aside accident, we must have design. But why would any murderer design to kill a person *in such a way*? Think how cumbersome, to transport the ox (though I know you do not concede it was an ox) to the scene and then to carry it away again afterwards! And what is the advantage, to the criminal in such a mode of assassination? Jostle against Bryde in the London crowd and slip a poignard in his ribs, and the deed is done much more easily."

"In such a case," Holmes noted, "there would be no doubt that it *was* a murder."

"True," said Bucket. "But there are many ways of killing in such a way as to make the crime appear only an accident, and few of them are as over-elaborate as the means by which our friend met his end. No, Holmes, surely the balance of probabilities lies on the side of accidental death. A maddened bull cannot be charged with malice aforethought, or murderous intent, after all. And therefore we must posit a disconnection between Bryde's death and Sir Martin's. For say what we may of *that* killing, it was manifestly no accident."

"There was a spy, though," said Holmes.

"There was?"

"A gentleman had been commissioned by Sir Persimmon Hawk to follow and watch Bryde as he went about his business."

Bucket nodded. "I see. To what end?"

"I am not sure. In point of fact, Inspector, I am a little compromised in this regard. I am an associate of Sir Persimmon's with regard to a particular project. Mr Griffin – whom I believe you know? – is another such: a man, I believe, of scientific training and expertise assisting Sir Percy on a particular project upon which I, also, am an adjunct."

"What project?"

"The particulars are not mine to divulge. Suffice to say that it will be electrical."

"Galvanically powered?"

"Just so. The specifics, though, are hardly relevant to the two deaths with which we are presently concerned. It is worth mentioning that it was Griffin who was watching Bryde. You ask, to what end, and I can only convey my hypothesis: Sir Persimmon Hawk is an impatient man, eager that the death of Sir Martin be cleared up as soon as possible that it not interfere with the onward progress of the railway, or interfere, frankly, with the delivery of profit. You yourself, Inspector, are investigating the crime with, I do not doubt, all professionalism and dispatch. That Sir Percy thought to appoint Bryde to undertake his own investigation speaks, perhaps, to a desire to hurry things along."

"My friend Bryde had some reputation at solving mysteries," said Bucket. "He had looked into one or two such cases for his employers before, though never before something so serious as a murder."

"Indeed. So what I would assume is that Sir Percy, doubly- and trebly eager to move the investigation along, asked Mr Griffin to observe Bryde in, as it were, action."

"As Macbeth hires a third murderer to check-up on the other two murderers he has already hired."

"Well," said Holmes, creasing his brow a little. "Yes. Although surely we do not suspect *Sir Percy* of being Macbeth, here? He can surely have had no involvement in the deaths either of Bryde, or of Sir Martin Malprelate. What would be his motive for either crime? I do not say that Sir Martin's death has greatly grieved him, personally, for Sir Percy is not a man much given to sentimentality or personal attachment. But his death has certainly inconvenienced him, involved him in disagreeable and unprofitable brouhaha. And in what way has he benefited?"

"He has become the major shareholder in the Middlemarch and London company."

"Only until probate be effected upon Sir Martin's portion of shares. And besides: Sir Percy's desire is that Sir Martin's murder be cleared-up quickly. He would hardly employ Bryde to that end one day and kill him off on another."

"And you saw him depart the scene," Bucket noted.

"I did." But the precision of apperception which defined Holmes's mind intervened, so he added: "which is to say, I saw his carriage roll down the road and away, before Bryde's demise." The shock of that moment. Blood droplets cascading from his ruined form. The horror. Holmes bit his lower lip and went on: "It was certainly his carriage, for it bore his crest. The blinds were up, so I could not observe the passengers directly, but we must assume they were Sir Percy himself and Mr Griffin."

"Griffin was at the Zoological Gardens with you, that day?"

"He was there with Sir Percy. He left before Bryde arrived – to wait in the carriage, he said."

"He can hardly have had a raging bullock about him, secreted in his pantaloon pockets," said Bucket.

"No," Holmes agreed.

"It's a tangle, no question of that," said the Inspector.

2

Leaving Scotland Yard, Holmes walked out into an icy but bright-lit December morning. The weather was fresh, and the sun struck sparkles out of the frost so beautifully, that Holmes decided not to take a cab, but instead to walk across town.

His next port of call was Bryde's landlady. He had sent a note ahead requesting an interview and proposing a time. He quickened his pace to ensure he was not late.

Mrs Orbit had swapped her large, stiff hat of lacquered blue for a large, stiff hat of mourning black, and was attired in a dusty dress of the same sable hue. Her budget did not, however, run to the purchase of a black handkerchief, and so she flourished a bright white square of cloth on those occasions, which were many, when she was obliged to wipe away her tears. She apologized to Holmes for this dereliction of the strict proprieties of mourning.

"Please, Mrs Orbit, do not mention it," Holmes murmured.

"He was as good a lodger, and as good a man, as – as – "she returned, going tearful once again and drawing out the bright white handkerchief. Once again she apologized:

"black silk is eight shillings a kerchief, or three for a guinea, and even black cotton is four shilling, embroidered edgework extra. But I do feel the disparity of frock and wiper, sir, I regret it, sir." She burst once more into tears.

"It is a sad loss indeed," said Holmes. Then: "Mrs Orbit, there can be no excuse for me intruding upon you during your moment of grief, except for one. You are aware that, in addition to his regular employment, Mr Bryde had been tasked by the Middlemarch Grand Congruence Railway Company to investigate the terrible death of Sir Martin Malprelate."

"My reasoning," said Mrs Orbit, her mind still running on handkerchiefs, "being as how he wasn't family, but only a lodger, and that the mourning I purchased when my late lamented husband departed would suffice. Eight shilling for silk, Mr Holmes. Ninety six pennies. And he was only a lodger. Yet such a lodger! As good a lodger as landlady ever had to deal with. And run down by a maddened ox in the very streets of London!"

Holmes said: "Mr Bryde may not have made you privy to the details of his investigations..."

"Oh, he did not!" exclaimed Mrs Orbit.

"I am sure he did not wish to trouble you."

"I know he spoke to a carter."

"The King of Carts?" Holmes pressed.

"That was the name. Went by train to Essex to see him. Contrary to all nature."

"He mentioned this interview to me, Mrs Orbit. And the strange thing is that we saw this same fellow – or Bryde did – just before he was knocked down, so dreadfully. He was standing on the far side of the street."

"Gracious!"

"Mrs Orbit, do *you* know how to make contact with this fellow? The King of Carts?"

"I sir?" Mrs Orbit looked startled. "No, sir. How should I?"

"Forgive me," said Holmes. "I had understood your late husband had been in the carriage business."

"No sir. He was not. As a young man he was ostler at the *Bull and Mouth*, on the North Road. He came to be elevated in his employ, until he was overseeing the inn's complete stabling. But he was never a carter."

Holmes knew of the *Bull and Mouth* inn – it carried a bas-relief in stone depicting Milo the Cretan Wrestler, who had grappled with, killed and then eaten whole, a huge bull. Beneath the sculpture was a rhyme:

"Milo the Cretonian
An ox slew with his fist,
And ate it up at one meal,
Ye gods, what a glorious twist!"

"I meant no disrespect, Mrs Orbit," Holmes assured the landlady. "I have been misinformed. But you have no sense of the King of Cart's whereabouts?"

"Essex way, that is all I know. Which is all Mr Bryde told me – except that he was going that route by railway, and through a tunnel too. I told him it was unnatural, Mr Holmes, and he ought not. But he went anyway."

"To Brentwood, then?"

"For all I know. Essex has never been my shire."

Holmes made his farewells and departed.

For the first time since he had witnessed his friend struck down, Holmes made his way past Regent's Park. The street was as busy as usual, with nothing to mark that a man had lost his life there. Holmes stood for a while and watched the bustle: the rattle of carriage wheels, the chatter of people. When the hubbub subsided momentarily, he could hear the cry of birds and the chatter of monkeys coming from the Zoological Gardens at his back. What *had* killed Bryde? The more Holmes struggled to recall the details of that day, the hazier they got; for human memory is rubbed a little smoother and more indistinct with every application of recall. Perhaps it had only been an ox, as everybody else said.

There was no mystery, Holmes concluded gloomily. And no man, howsoever clever, can solve a non-mystery.

3

For a week Holmes pursued the same lines of enquiry Bryde had explored before him. Or he tried to: he asked a number of carters and carriage-drivers if they would be so good as to direct him to the habitation of the King of Carts, but all of them rebuffed him, either feigning ignorance, or else more aggressively insisting he depart in a manner suggesting of the manner of knowing the Bible reserves for husband and wives. Not for the likes of a well-dressed gentleman such as *he*, evidently, to be given access to the court of their King. Holmes wondered how Bryde had effected his royal interview. Whichever had been his contacts, however he had arranged it, Holmes found himself unable to duplicate. This was a pity since the King, being present at Bryde's death, was clearly a person of interest.

Holmes spoke to witnesses at the railway works, who were by now grumpy at being so repeatedly quizzed. He asked about, and discovered – as Bryde had done – that Malprelate's misanthropy was compensated for by a love for the animal kingdom that saw him offering charitable donations to lost dog's homes, that he personally kept and tended a number of wounded and hard-used beasts in his own home, including a nearly hairless bear – and that he had made an annual subvention to the London Zoological Gardens. Might this financial donation have been the 'connection' of which Bryde had spoken, before being struck down? Merely that Malprelate, like other wealthy men, donated money? It could hardly explain his murder.

Since Malprelate had, it seemed, bracketed working-class men and women in much the same category as the beasts of the field, Holmes also discovered his charitable donations to the Camden Soup Kitchen, and others. This complicated the reputation of Malprelate as unremittingly wicked, it is true; but Holmes did not go so far as his friend had done before him, and wonder if Sir Martin might, actually, have been a *good* man. His actions in other regards spoke for themselves – loans called-in without so much as a half-hour of extra grace, the hardest contracts drawn up and insisted upon, a pitiless pursuit of money – and where the new railway line was concerned there were assuredly many people whose houses had been purchased compulsorily, lives upended, ancient neighborhoods torn down. Any of the people affected by this, individually or as a group, would have had reason to resent, and therefore to wish to harm, Malprelate.

One such, Holmes knew from talking with Bryde, had been a clerk called Enoch Ninecroft. This gentleman had spoken to Sir Martin the night before his death, and had returned to the dead man's house the day after to retrieve some promissory note, or other document. He was somebody worth following up.

Inspector Bucket, who had also interviewed the clerk, passed along his contact details, but when Holmes went to the lodgings specified Enoch Ninecroft was not there. The landlady was neither helpful, nor well-disposed to her former guest.

"He did livier but he's garnov."

"Gone off? But where?"

"Do I know? I do not. Would like to," said the landlady, fixing Holmes with her one and only eye, an organ that made up for the lack of a partner with an extra intensity of gaze. "Since he owes me rent."

"His father?"

"In Saint Luke's patch."

"In the patch? You mean – the *graveyard*?"

"I don't mean he was elected vicar of the parish, do I," said the woman. She was a stout individual, with a long upper-lip and the aforementioned deficiency in the double-ness of her eyes. Her dress was a kind of accumulation, or sedimentation, of many layers of more or less hole-y, torn or elderly layers of cloth, of which some shabby levels of cotton, a greasy stretch of fustian wear, and an over-layer, perhaps intended as an apron, of corduroy was visible. It was not a stylish or fragrant example of couture. To emphasize her point she clicked her fingers close to Holmes's face.

"Madam," said Holmes, sternly, but she was not a woman to be cowed by a gentleman.

"*Yarse* he died. Your man Ninecroft may well've joined him, by now, orl I know. Not a man to be trusted, I don't mind telling you. Opium! A *terror* for the opium, he was."

"Might I find him, then, at one of the opium shops? I understand they are located Limehouse way."

"You may find him with the devil for orl I care," said the landlady. "Though if yer do track him down, addled as I don't doubt he will be, tell him he owes me seven and three and one farthing."

"He had, I believe, a wife? And two children?"

"They?" At this the woman laughed. "They didn't stick. One quick look, like a sharpshooter, at these ere digs and she clears right out. Ninecroft sometimes torked of her family, Mudford way. I daresay she made her way up there, and better off she'll be, no doubt. He was a bad sort."

"Nonetheless my good woman," Holmes insisted, "I need to speak with him."

"Try Lime'us. Or the poor'us. Try Perdition's gates for all I know. But tell him, if ye see him, seven and three and a farthing."

Holmes made his way down to Limehouse, pondering all the while how a lodger could have run up any kind of bill that culminated in a farthing. Here, deciding the best procedure was to recruit official help, he approached a constable on the beat, mentioned Inspector Bucket's name, intimated (a slight exaggeration of the truth, this) that he had official sanction by way of investigating the murder of the celebrated Sir Martin Malprelate, and requested assistance in searching the opium shops for the man called Enoch Ninecroft. The constable knew the name, as a notorious partaker of the poppy, but asseverated he had not been seen in the locality for a fortnight. He took Holmes to a succession of low, close rooms, some by the docks, others in side-streets: windows curtained with rags such that the light of the day only intermittently steals inside. In some a row of stunted cots contained the slumbering or writhing forms of opium eaters – or, rather, smokers of the dried-up amber made from the poppy. In others a higgled-piggled set of beds, broken-down bedsteads and burst-open mattresses supplied the lying-places of an interchangeable set of bodies in their various stupors. Holmes examined them all, but the constable confirmed that none were Enoch Ninecroft.

As Holmes made his way homeward again, the familiar despair asserted itself. Was there any point in continuing? Every avenue he turned down revealed itself a dead end.

For two days Holmes made further efforts to uncover more evidence. Bucket could not help him with the location of the King of Carts – "his highness," the inspector noted, drily, "is not amenable to the officers of law enforcement bothering him at home". At his club Holmes again met Carker, senior manager at the trading firm of Dombey and Son, whose smile was like opening a box of freshlypolished white knives.

"So sorry to hear of the demise of your friend, Mr Bryde," said Carker, unable to sheathe his smile long enough to give the condolence the air of genuineness. "A tragic loss."

"Indeed. You met him, I believe?"

"He came here – to this very club – to consult with, I believe, Sir Persimmon Hawk. I happened to be on hand on that occasion." He angled his head and smiled an ingratiating smile.

"Mr Carker," said Holmes. "I hope you don't mind me asking. Does Dombey and Son have any interests or *investments* in the railway? Or railways, I suppose I should say?"

"Mr Holmes," said Carker, making a kind of sinuous motion with his body, and widening his smile even further. "You will hardly expect me to divulge the firm's commercial secrets. But I can tell you that we are a longstanding family firm whose trading links are maritime. We have always, the memory of man goeth not to the contrary, been *maritime*. We buy and sell, trade goods of all kinds, from the ports of this great nation, all around the world. Railway lines are not our path."

"You do not – forgive me, I do not intend to solicit confidential information, but I would value the opinion of a knowledgeable and professional man such as yourself – your firm does not consider railways to be a direct competition to your business? As any manner of rivalry to what you do?"

"My dear Mr Holmes," said Carker warmly, as if they had known one another not glancingly but intimately and for years – although his smile lessened somewhat as he spoke – "by no means, by no means. Show me the railway line that can be built from the West Indies to London docks and I'll revise my opinion! But Sir Martin's Middlemarch line – or any railway line currently under construction – is of no concern to our commercial work whatsoever. Indeed, distribution of goods from the ports would be helped by the railways."

"I see."

"On the other hand," Carker continued, "my employer, Mr Dombey, is naturally concerned for the potential disruption to social and civilized order, when any prominent man – any very wealthy man, such as Sir Martin – is attacked, threatened, or as here slain. It is more than a personal tragedy. It is a political danger. It is anarchy," – as he said this word, his smile widened even further – "anarchy. It must be stamped upon, as one would thrust one's heel down upon a perilous serpent's head."

"You are sure, then, that Sir Martin's murderers were…"

"Of course they were! It was a mob of anarchists, Jacobins, political radicals. You see what is happening all across the Continent of Europe? Revolution and disorder and violence. If it were *my* decision, I would send a troop of soldiers through the streets of Camden, knocking down every door and dragging out every malefactor."

"I fear a good many innocent people would be hurt in such an undertaking," Holmes said.

"The greater good, the sanctity of the social order and the protection of wealth – of, eh, property and virtue – would justify any occasional misidentifications. If a dog-pack contains some number of hydrophobic and ravenous beasts, the best course is to cull the entire pack."

"You have a low opinion of the working man, Mr Carker."

Carker's smile could not have been wider or his head would have split. "Not at all. I have the greatest respect for honest labour. The working man is a fine and necessary thing. In his place."

Holmes made his way back to his rooms in a gloomy spirit. It seemed that the consensus was unassailable: Sir Martin Malprelate's death was the result of anarchistic mob violence. Holmes could see a consequence of this conclusion looming out of the mists of futurity: a collective punishment of the poorest people of Camden Town. A new Peterloo for the 1840s. The passage of police – or, perhaps, soldiers –

through the narrow streets of the labouring classes, arresting, beating, slaying those whose guilt was assumed, and assumed to be collective, and moreover assumed to be compounded by the fact that so many workingmen had collaborated in a bizarre and improbable fabulation, a cover-story about demonic locomotives. Holmes could conceive of the anger growing, amongst the wealthy and powerful of London; the princes of industry and money-men, those heading great trading houses and other investors in the railways – an anger that would strike out, like a cobra, and bite at the ordinary folk of the town. No matter that the witnesses who testified to the Satanic railway train were, almost all of them, labourers in Sir Martins' employ, men with not especial attachment to Camden, no reason to be concerned at the demolition of the borough's houses, and nothing to gain and much to lose if the Middlemarch Grand Congruence Railway Company were damaged – for they would lose their jobs. No matter that most of the ordinary people of Camden had nothing to do with the railway line workings, or with the owner's death. And once the cobra's venom had been delivered, and a quantity of broken bones, and bruised heads, and dead bodies left behind, the true story behind the events of Sir Martin's would remain unresolved.

Perhaps, Holmes told himself, offering a silent prayer to the spirit of his departed friend in supplication, it would be best to throw-over the entire investigation. To devote all his energies once more to his galvanic work. To turn Nelson's blind-eye to the actions of the authorities in the aftermath of Sir Martin's death, and to nod a silent acquiescence when folk mentioned how the mob killed the railway magnate, as if that was all there was to it.

* * *

4

He attended Bryde's funeral: a small affair, held at the New Bunhill Fields burying ground on the New Kent Road – a private speculation recently purchased and established by the Wesleyan church, the grounds walled round and well watched. Holmes had not realized that his friend was Methodistic. He sat through a well-judged burial sermon in the New Bunhill chapel, attached. Barely half a dozen other people were in attendance. After the interment Holmes spoke with each in turn to convey his commiserations: a distant cousin from Yorkshire together with his wife, a colleague from the office of technical drawings, a former schoolfriend. Bryde, it seemed, had never married. Holmes reflected how little he had known the man, as he walked up the steps and away from the vault in which the casket containing Bryde's mortal remains had been deposited. The place smelt not of death or decay, but instead carried a strongly ammoniac pungency that spoke to the attempts at ongoing hygiene undertaken by the place's superintendent.

There was no wake. Holmes, in his mourning dress, rode an omnibus into the centre of town and took a late luncheon at his club.

There was a commotion outside. A political preacher was inciting violence, and two constables had arrived to remove the demagogue. The man's sermon mixed Biblical and socialist-anarchistic elements in a hectic profusion: "Woe unto thee, London! Woe to Chorazin – that is, Albion! Woe unto thee, Bethsaida! For if the mighty labouring men, which were crushed and murdered in you, had been done in Paris and Berlin, they would have repented long ago in sackcloth and ashes! A change is coming! A revolution is coming, comrades, that will bring down rulers from their thrones and lift up the humble! Socialism will fill the hungry

with good things and will send the rich away empty."
The man's words mutated into squawks and shrieks as he
struggled with the officers of the law. His diction altered as
cuffs snapped, crocodile-jaws, onto his wrists and he was
dragged away. "You'll all be sorry!" he howled. "All of you!"

Soon enough tranquility was restored. Holmes smoked a
cigar.

After luncheon he made his way through the crowds in
the centre of town, heading towards his lodgings, where his
wife and child were waiting for him. Then he saw Griffin.

There was no mistaking the fellow: he was, after all,
one of the most distinctive looking men in the country.
His hat (which he never seemed to remove), his purple-
tinted spectacles, his painted pallor and the wide smile that
– unlike Mr Carker's more predatory grin – never displayed
his teeth.

There he was, on the street corner, watching Holmes pass.

Had Griffin been sent to spy on *him*, as he had once been
sent to spy on Bryde? Holmes found the idea insulting.
"Griffin," he called. "Griffin!" Waving his arm, hallooing
across the intervening flow of pedestrians.

There was no question but that Griffin saw him. But
instead of replying, or even waiting for Holmes to reach
him, the fellow slipped away and up the alley. The cheek
of him!

By the time Holmes had shouldered his way through
crush and reached the mouth of the narrow road he saw
only the back of Griffin's overcoat as it turned the corner at
the far end.

Holmes hurried along the cobbles and emerged into a
brick-walled court from which several paths and alleys led
off. He went to the mouth of each in turn, but there was no
sign of Griffin. It was as if the man had vanished into thin
air.

On one side of the space a group of half a dozen people,

all in working-men's clothes, had gathered around one of their own, this latter a young lad who was drawing in chalk on the blank wall. He drew fluently, moving his chalk rapidly over the masonry, and only sometimes pausing to scuff up his hatless head with his free hand, as if searching for the next moment of artistic inspiration in amongst his profusion of curls.

This is what he was drawing: a great snake, from tail – up to the top left, almost as high as his arm could reach – down along its sinuating body to a great, dragon-like head in the bottom right of the wall. The flourishes with which this gape-mouthed serpent were augmented were deftly added: teeth, tentacular whiskers, a feral eye. Then he drew a man, a figure in frock-coat and hat, and a terrified expression upon his face, caught in the jaws of the monstrous dragon. The jaws were about his body, and blood lurched in pear-shaped blobs from his bitten-upon flesh.

"The man is Sir Martin," said Griffin, close behind Holmes. "And the snake is what he called into the world – to his doom!"

Holmes spun on his heel, but there was nobody behind him. There was nobody else in the courtyard save only the knot of workmen gathered around the chalk-artist. He saw no disappearing coat-tails flapping round the corner, heard no heels clattered along the cobbles. Alone! Yet he had most distinctly heard Griffin's voice!

"Griffin?" he called out. "Griffin! Is that you? Where are you, man!"

And then, as with some kind of stage-magic, he heard Griffin once more: laughing. The ghost in Hamlet: swear, swear. Was he under the ground, lurking in the sewers? But no: the fellow's voice was quite distinctive, unmistakable, even when laughing, and Holmes could not tell himself he was imagining it. The laughter mocked him, passing from his left to his right, and then it stopped.

For long moments Holmes stood, only staring. Behind him he could hear the sound of the chalk scraping over the brickwork.

He took an exploratory step forward: there was nothing, and nobody, and only empty air.

He turned back to the knot of men. "You there," he called. "You fellows. What do you draw there?"

The men all turned to look at him, as one, and the artist himself stopped mid-stroke. "Why sir," he replied, smiling unpleasantly, "it's the serpent what devours the unjust, such as is specified most particular in the Book of Saint John's Ending of the World."

"Is that figure you draw there, in the snake's mouth – is that the late Sir Martin Malprelate?" Holmes demanded.

"Why sir," said the artist, putting his head to one side the better to fix Holmes' with his eye. "And if it be?"

"This is most disrespectful. A prominent citizen, a man of wealth and importance, and his funeral not yet conducted. For shame, gentlemen!"

"He was devoured by the same dragon he brought down here from Middlemarch," said one of the workmen.

The others grumbled their assent.

"It was grown there from a basilisk egg," said the artist. "He sowed, and so he reaped. You speak of respect, sir? What respect did he show London Town, tearing it apart with his iron rails."

Another of the workmen, whose lowly station in life had not prevented him from learning some Shakespeare, said: "Unseamed it from the nave to the chaps."

The men were inching forward, and Holmes felt a sudden shock of fear, mixed with a sense of the ludicrousness of his situation. "Gentlemen," he tried, in more conciliatory tones. "I only ask for the common respect due to any man, from whatever station in life, when he meets the grim fate that is common to all."

"And *we* only ask," returned the artist, "that you hurry away to your lair, monster-man – for I see you, with my artist's eye, and you are offspring of the same great snake."

"What's your name?" demanded the man who had previously quoted Shakespeare. He was a tall, ruddy faced fellow with a beard shaped like an apron. "Tell the name, stranger – spit it out."

Holmes took a step back. He discovered his hands were trembling. "I have no desire," he began to say, "no desire to engage in – "and then for the third, and last time in that space, he heard Griffin's voice, loud and strong, filling the little courtyard.

"Holmes is his name," hooted the voice, "and his name is Holmes."

Holmes turned quickly but, as before, there was nobody behind him.

Looking back he saw the group advancing upon him and he turned once again such that they would not seize him from behind. But he had to shuffle backwards, step for step, as they advanced.

He held out his hand, palm vertical, to impel the men to stop, and one of the fellows on the left of the group reached forward with his own hand. For a moment Holmes thought he was reaching out to offer to shake hands – itself a gesture of some impertinence, given the disparity in social class between them – but it wasn't that. The man instead lifted his hand, horizontal, up to his mouth and uncurled the fingers. A heap of chalk dust was sitting in the man's palm.

"Sir!" Holmes objected, as the man pursed his hairy lips and blew hard.

The dust swirled into Holmes's face. He snorted, shut his eyes, coughed and in doing so drew a breath into his lungs, before coughing again.

He wiped his face, roughly, and opened his eyes. "This

is deplorable behaviour, gentlemen!" he sputtered, as the men leered at him. They were no longer advancing, content simply to stand and watch. "Outrageous," Holmes sputtered. Sparkles glittered in the corner of his vision. The man who had quoted Shakespeare, the one with the largest beard, appeared to be swelling. To be growing in girth and stature. The leers widened beyond the point where facial anatomy ought to have permitted them. Holmes thought of Carker, and for an instant he believed he *saw* him, but it wasn't him. It was only the curl-headed artist, holding up one of his sticks of chalk and wagging it, like an admonitory finger.

Discretion asserting itself as valour's better part, Holmes turned and ran, fast as his running feet could carry him. Behind him the men called his name, "Mr Holmes! Holmes! Stay and know us better, man!", the elongation of his surname's vowel being mixed-in with loud laughter. The alley walls slid past Holmes as he sprinted, and he had the sense – it came to him with hallucinatory vividness – that he was a cannon-ball – an artillery shell, passing along the channel of a cannon's tube to burst into the sunlight of Oxford Street's bustle and busy-ness.

He stopped, to recover his breath, and mop his brow, watching the alley from which he had just emerged. But the men were not pursuing him, it seemed. All around him the crowd passed and repassed, all with somewhere to go, and he alone standing still. But there, neat as the answer to a riddle, was the glimpse of something that felt to Holmes like it might provide the solution to the mystery.

He could see it. A serpent, dyed in the colours of hell, large enough to swallow London Town entire, rising from all the chimneys of the country and filling the sky. It opened its smiling jaws. It opened its smiling jaws. It opened its smiling jaws. It opened its smiling jaws.

* * *

5

The next thing he knew Holmes was in Middlemarch. How he got there, and with whom he travelled, returned to him only in the days *after* the fact, and then only in fits and starts. In the moment he was perfectly baffled as to what had happened.

He was in the front room of a dark-panelled hostelry – the place was called, as he discovered when he asked the potboy, *Red Lion* – with a glass of claret before him. This was odd, since he did not drink claret. Still there it was, a glass full of the red fluid, filled indeed to the brim like a giant carved and polished ruby sliced across its top and balanced on a glass stem.

Holmes took a deep breath, and then let it out. "Come again, sir?" asked the potboy?

"Did I ask the name?"

"Of this inn? *Red Lion*, sir, as I said."

"The *Red Lion*, in St James?" Holmes asked. But even as he asked he understood that this was not correct. Flickers of memory were recurring to him, of a lengthy journey – two days and a night in an inn bedroom in the company of some other person. But who?

"James sir?" said the potboy, confused. "But my name is William, sir, after my father."

"What I am asking," Holmes said, with distinctness, "concerns the location of this public house."

"Location, sir? On the Houndsley road." *Row-ad* was his pronunciation of this last word, and the H at the commencement of Houndsley stayed smartly in place.

"I'm not in London."

"London, sir?" The lad's amazement made of his face an arrangement of circles and arcs: mouth, eyes, eyebrows. "No sir – Middlemarch, this is Middlemarch."

Holmes tipped the lad and got to his feet. There was no point in asking *but how did I get here*, for the lad would never have known that. And besides, tessellations in his broken-up memory were recurring to him now: a train out of London to Reading. A coach to Oxford, very bumpy and uncomfortable when in passage, and very tedious when the horses were rested at the top of every hill. On the outskirts of the university-town he *and another* stayed at an inn. Another? Who? Then a brisk morning's walk, and a ride on a carter's dray, descending the downs towards the spread of Middlemarch. The question was not how did I get here? but: *why* did I come here?

And: with whom?

He walked over to the window and looked out. This, presumably, was the Houndsley road. A few people passed along it, though they passed in provincial, rather than London, numbers. It was a bright winter's day, and sunlight marked a trapezoidal shaft of brightness through the window, and through the dust in the room. Holmes looked around. The walls were panelled in dark wood and adorned with some unprepossessing art: a very large-bodied cow seen side-on, whose head looked laughably small in proportion to his blubbery body. A hand-coloured engraving of the young Queen, seated with her hands in the lap of the voluminous gown, looking out at Holmes with chill disinterest.

There was a leaden spittoon for each table. There was straw on the floor.

The potboy put his still-astonished head round the doorway: "Will your companion be returning, do you think sir?" When he said companion he glanced at the untouched glass of wine on the table, and Holmes slotted another piece into the bizarre marquetry-saw-cut puzzle of events.

"I do not believe so," he said.

"In that case, sir, has he left you the distinction and honour of settling the bill?"

Holmes felt for his pocketbook and could not find it. For a moment his heart jittered in alarm, but his wallet was upon his person, just in a different and unusual pocket. Holmes would never place it there! Had it been lifted from him when his attention had been confused? Had the wallet been emptied before being returned? But no: on the contrary, it contained far more money than Holmes usually had about him: silver and gold, and three folded banknotes. Where had they come from? Holmes unfolded one of the notes: £5. MIDDLEMARCH UNION BANKING COMPANY, elaborately curlicued, each letter trailing a ruff pattern of folded swirls. He checked: all notes were drawn on the same establishment. How had they come into Holmes's possession? He tried to recall, but his memories were still shattered and gappy.

"My companion," Holmes asked the potboy, as he put two silver coins on the table. "I must ask you: how did he look?"

"Perfect respectable, like," replied the potboy, looking strangely at him, and adding: "sir" a moment too late.

"I don't mean that. I mean his features, his distinguishing marks, his appearance."

"Sir?"

"I appreciate that it is an unusual question," said Holmes, sensing that the boy might grab the money and bolt. "But be assured, I have my reasons for asking it."

"Yes sir?"

"My memory is affected by... by a certain debility, from time to time," said Holmes. "Oblige me by quickly describing the individual with whom I was sitting?"

"Hat," said the lad. "Eyeglasses of a blue colour, or say, rose-blue."

"Purple, perhaps? Like the heather?"

"Red heather, you mean, sir?" The boy looked confused.

"And his complexion," Holmes prompted. "Was it *very* white?"

"None whiter," said the boy with tremendous emphasis. "White? I should say *so*."

"And he departed?"

"Rushed out! Positively rushed."

"In which direction?"

"Disappeared, he did. When the child stepped in."

"The child? What child?"

"Little boy, youngern me, sir. He was walking up and down the way outside, and you called him in, through the window – do you not remember?"

"Go on."

"Well," said the lad, looking confused, "the white face gentleman, he grew most agitate at this, and then rushed out. Fair disappeared!"

"And the boy?"

"Ran t'other way."

"Very good. Thank you, my lad." Holmes paid him, and the boy was relieved to be able to get away.

Holmes sat down again, attempting to piece together the shards of his memory. But it was no good. He did not doubt he had been present at the scene the potboy just described, but he recalled none of it.

As he made to leave the potboy – hiding behind the doorway, and peeping out – called: "Your wine, sir!"

"Drink it, if you like the stuff," growled Holmes. "Or pour it back in its bottle. I care not."

Vavasour Holmes walked out into the brisk air and wandered the streets of Middlemarch for a time. It was mid-afternoon, and the sky blue as lapis to set, as a jeweller might, the white diamond circlet of the sun. Shadows were watery but distinct. Holmes looked at each passer-by, thinking perhaps to see Griffin, dogging him, spying upon him, but the man was nowhere to be seen.

He had to return home. But it was too late to depart for London now. It was too lengthy a journey to undertake at short notice. The time would come – the reflection made him smile, wryly – when the posthumous project of Sir Martin, the railway line linking Middlemarch and London, would enable a traveller to purchase a ticket, sit for some brisk hours rattling along the grooved rails, and be home before midnight. But such possibility was shrouded in futurity, and for now Holmes had no choice but to rent a room for a night and set out in the morning. He selected the largest hotel he could find, with so much money in his pocket he did not see that he should stint himself. As he waited for the clerk at the reception desk to fetch the ledger from his back room, another shard of memory returned to him: he and another in two narrow truckle beds, in an inn somewhere on the Oxford Road: a tight little room with a single window of ill-fitting panes that snickered like a rattlesnake in the night-time wind. Had this other person been Griffin? Holmes couldn't bring his face to mind, but something told him, no, it had been another.

The room was spacious and soon, with a fire lit in its grate by a coughing, elderly factotum, almost cosy. He ordered an early supper of chops and potatoes, with gravy in a separate jug, and a pewter pot of local ale. As he waited for the establishment cook to provide, he called up pen and paper and wrote a note to his wife, explaining his absence. What must she have thought, when he did not return the previous night? How could he explain himself to her, when he didn't understand what had happened?

My darling – I find myself in Middlemarch. I shall return as soon as practicable. All I know is that I am caught up, in some strange way, with events pursuant to the deaths of Malprelate and Bryde. Know that I love you, and am hurrying home. V.

He wrote a second note, to Inspector Bucket at Scotland Yard.

Dear Bucket – I have been involved in some strange goings-on. Yesterday morning, pursuing Mr Griffin – whom we

*both know and have reason to mistrust – I was waylaid – I
think I must use the word – by a group of some half dozen
workmen, in a courtyard off Oxford Street. One of them was
drawing in chalk upon the wall and another blew a quantity
of the chalk dust into my face where, unable to prevent it,
I breathed a quantity into my lungs. I believe this to have
been some manner of drug, opiate or hallucinatory agent, for
my memory of what happened subsequently is patchy and
unclear. All I know is that I am now in Middlemarch. I will
return tomorrow and hope to reach the capital late in the
evening, but would be much obliged if you would favour me
with an interview. The pharmakon, or whatever this dust is,
may have some part to play in the strange visions reported
by witnesses to Sir Martin's death. As ever, sir, your obedient
servant, Vavasour Holmes.*

When the wheezing hotel servant returned with his supper
upon a tray, the plate, jug and tankard all shivering upon
it, as if in fear that they might be dropped by the feeble old
geezer, Holmes thought to ask what he ought to have asked
before. "My good fellow," he asked. "Today is the second of
December?"

"Third," said the man, without looking at him.

"You're sure?"

The man was focussing prodigies of attentiveness on
the task of lowering the tray to the table beside Holmes's
chair, so much so that it seemed to leave him no mental
capacity for speech. When supper had safely landed upon
the tabletop, he said again: "Third," and departed the room.

Holmes discovered, as if from nowhere, that he was
powerfully hungry. He ate and drank with gusto. Then
he walked down the hotel's creaking main staircase, and
requested a copy of today's newspaper. "Do not fear, I shall
not carry it away. I only wish to glance at the front page."

The clerk fetched it from the smoking room: the

MIDDLEMARCH TRUMPET declared the head banner and beneath it: 3rd December 1848. So the gap in Holmes's memory was longer than he realised. He thanked the clerk, returned the paper and retreated to bed.

6

He slept poorly, his dreams encumbered by snatches of memory, as dreams often are. These, though, were oppressive and strange. He was passing through a great city – London, he presumed, or so his mind rationalised the memory of the dream upon waking. Yet, as dreams themselves are forms of memory, so the waking mind looking back upon the dream is a memory of a memory, and the thing remembered retreats further into haze and incertitude. *Was* it London? It might have been Babylon, or Pandaemonium. He was in a coach, with another person, but the person's face was obscured. Was it Griffin? He thought it was not, but could not catch a glimpse of the features. And when he peered through the windows of the coach, out at the world, it seemed to him the city was a gigantic castle, walls within walls, towers and halls and titanic chimneys built of blocks of granite. The coach turned now this way, now that, and only slackening its pace once – when a gigantic cat, as big as a horse, spotted in ginger and brown, strolled across the road in front of them. Away lurched the coach again, rounding a church the size of Valhalla, its steeple black with dripping ivy, and, with the abruptness of dream-logic, Holmes found himself in the waiting room of a railway station. He thought this might be Reading station but the sign said Brassing – but how could he have passed with such alacrity from London all the way up to Brassing? The walls all around were crowded with glass-doored showcases, and inside each was a profusion of moths and dark-hued butterflies, with a lengthy pin impaling each to the lining of each box. His travelling companion said, "It is good that great beast did not notice us, or it would have eaten us, chewed our bodies and spat out the parts, as it did with Sir Martin." "The cat?" Holmes asked, confused. "The great feline that we saw?" "Cat?" replied his interlocutor, in the dream. "Serpent, rather. Snake. Dragon. And we must track it down to its tail, to locate the basilisk-egg out of which it hatched, to prevent further – "

– and the locomotive's banshee steam-whistle sounded, drowning out his last words.

Holmes looked about, in the dream, and saw that he wasn't in a railway station waiting room after all, but was actually inside the compartment of a railway train. What he had taken for boxes fixed around the walls were windows, and the moths and butterflies within were not pinned but alive, flying through the skies outside like autumn leaves. "Whither goest we?" dream-Holmes asked, as the train plunged into a tunnel. But the tunnel was more like a corridor, for it had a flat roof, and mullioned windows at intervals along its side. The train moved with the languid drift of an oarless boat in a stream, along the dappled passageway of light and fish-grey shadow. Holmes wondered whether he was a ghost, a figure out of time, passing intangibly along the tunnel, before bursting into brightness. They were at the coast – a blur of mud and limpets and a seawall stretching out into a turbulent sea under a swift sunrise.

"Sir! Sir!" There was a light in his face.

It was the hotel clerk, holding a lantern such that the light shone in a beam right in Holmes's face.

"What is it, man?" he croaked, from his pillow.

"A thousand apologies, sir, but there's a fire."

"Fire?"

"Nothing too terrible sir – a fire in the hotel kitchens – contained, sir – but we must, we are obliged, to evacuate the building."

Shreds of his dream still clung to Holmes as he clambered out of bed. His breath took the form of spectral ostrich feathers that expanded into the room. He scooped up his clothes from where he had disposed them across the back of a chair and stumbled and bumbled down the corridor and the stairway. There *was* a smell of smoke, but if he hadn't been told otherwise Holmes might have thought this the preparations for breakfast.

Out through the main entrance, into the chill of the pre-dawn.

Shivering hard, Holmes dressed himself, legs into his breeches, arms into shirt, buttoning his waistcoat and wrapping his jacket around his chilled torso. He had left his hat inside. Would he be permitted to return and retrieve it? There was no obvious sign of conflagration. He checked his jacket: the pocketbook was still there, and his money.

There were a half dozen guests in a similar state of startled disarrangement, half-dressed or still in their night clothes. One big-bellied gentleman, his profile a Þ in his long johns, was noisily insisting he be allowed back inside to fetch his portmanteau, and hotel staff were physically preventing his access. Holmes decided he could do without the hat.

Holmes stood for a while, watching the building, expecting perhaps licking flames, or bales of smoke. But, other than the faint odour of burning which in itself could not definitely be connected with the hotel, there was no sign of the emergency. The sky to the east was beginning to pale and thin with the slow approach of dawn dissolving away the thicker hues of night. The pot-bellied man in long johns was in the process of losing his temper altogether, and soon he had become involved in an unseemly wrestle with one of the hotel porters, in amongst the dirt and mud of the road.

Holmes decided to go.

He walked, first taking a wrong direction, then realising

his mistake and starting back, toward the Inn from which the stagecoaches departed the town. The purple-black of the sky faded, and a deep and glowing crimson seeped up from the eastern horizon, transmuting into the most brilliant of yellows that fizzed higher, drawing behind it, as a train, a sky of apple-green and azure. By the time he arrived at the courtyard from which the coaches left, daily, for Oxford to the south and Brassing to the west, it was light enough to read the notice of fares and rules pinned to the wall.

The ticket office was closed, but after a hearty thumping on the door the ticket man opened and admitted Holmes. There was a hiatus whilst he tidied away his sleeping truckle from the back of the office, stepped outside to draw water from a punch into a bucket in which he then set his head, and finally, after a trip to the privy, settling himself on his stool. He sold Holmes a ticket to Oxford with one hand, whist fiddling, and failing, to tie his cravat with his other.

Holmes located a booth from which he was able to purchase a hot sweetbread and some coffee. Then he sat on the bench in the Post Inn courtyard and watched the busy-ness of the day begin. Boys came and went. Two men backed the coach itself into the yard, one holding each spar tucked under his armpit as though it were a jousting pole. A stout gentleman in a blue surcoat and tricorn hat came and sat next to Holmes. He smoked his pipe, summoning oriental genii of smoke and serpentine splendours out of its bowl. The chill of the dawn air gave the smoke-djinns unusually sharp borders. Holmes, though he was now fully dressed, and though he had a bowl of hot coffee in his lap, could not prevent himself shivering.

Eventually two horses were led into the yard, turned around and backed into harness. Two more waited patiently behind, blowing evanescent wool from their nostrils and watching it float away. Soon enough the vehicle was prepared, all tackle fastened and checked, and the coachman

began the laborious ascent of the west-face of the thing, rung
by rung until he was perched at the Mont Blanc eminence
of the driver's seat.

Holmes got up and waited his turn to clamber up into the
coach. He settled himself, as best he could, in the corner,
as various other characters flourished their tickets and
lumbered in. The cold of the morning meant that most were
muffled up and unrecognisable; but when the coachman
finally snickered his whip and coaxed the drays into motion,
a voice hailed him diagonally across the space.

"Mr Holmes?"

"Is that," Holmes returned, "Mr Aster, is it? Upon my
word!"

"To find you here!" Aster exclaimed. "In Middlemarch! A
coincidence indeed."

"About to leave Middlemarch," said Holmes.

Thereupon there was a confusion of negotiation and
a constrained, awkward dance of strip-the-willow, the
occupants of the cab reorganised themselves, such that Sir
Martin's former secretary was able to situate himself next
to Holmes.

"What a pleasant surprise," said Aster, in a voice that
sounded neither pleased nor surprised. "I did not expect to
see you in Middlemarch, Mr Holmes."

"Nor I you, Mr Aster."

"The business of the London and Middlemarch line
continues," said the secretary, in a bored drawl. "I had to
attend to certain circumstances attendant on the building
of the station terminus in the town. There are – some
particularities, to do with the sourcing of stone, and the
access for workmen across land not purchased by the
company, where a certain diplomatic finesse was required."

"I see," said Holmes. "Since you are returning by the
coach, I presume you have successfully concluded your
business? In which case, I congratulate you."

Aster nodded shallowly. "And you, Mr Holmes? I trust I am not mistaken, but I had heard that you and Sir Persimmon are working together on the creation of a galvanic engine of some kind? Is this why you have visited this," he peered through the window, and ended his question with a voice through which a mournful sigh threaded, "delightful Midlands town?"

"You are correct that Sir Percy and I are working together – Mr Griffin is another party to the group." At the mention of Griffin's name, Aster's demeanour changed. He turned his face and fixed Holmes with a straight look. "Only," Holmes continued, "the specificities are somewhat different. I am working to supply him with an electrical – the term we prefer nowadays – engine; but this is incidental to Sir Percy's main project, which is rather more ambitious in scope."

"Really?"

"It is sub rosa, as yet," Holmes said, "subject to the exigencies of commercial confidentiality."

"Does it have some bearing on the business of railways and locomotives? For if not, I am hardly likely to betray its purpose."

Holmes only smiled. The coach slowed as the gradient of the Southam road increased, and outside the coachman could be heard coaxing his horses with many elongations of the vowels "u" and "e", such that "come up my beauties" chimed through the air as *coo-oo-oo-ume oop umber yoo-oo-oo-tes*. The breath of the steeds rasped and roughened, and the coach shook more slowly.

"Mr Holmes?" Aster asked, abruptly. "I hope I do not trespass upon anything inappropriate if I ask what you were doing in Middlemarch? I have reasons for the question, I assure you."

Holmes looked at Aster. The question was direct enough to touch, almost, on rudeness, but there was something in the man's expression that reached Holmes. It was, he realised, the mention of Griffin's name.

"I do not wish to seem evasive, Mr Aster," he replied, "but before I answer may I ask one question of my own. Do you know Mr Griffin?"

Aster's lips tightened, slightly but perceptibly. "I have encountered him on a small number of occasions," he said, "since he is, as you note, an associate of Sir Persimmon Hawk, who occupies a position on the board of the Middlemarch and London railway company, which, of course, employs me. Until Sir Martin Malprelate's will and testament be proved, Sir Percy is *de facto* the senior officer of the company, the majority shareholder, and will remain so until Sir Martin's shares be released from the purdah of testacy by the court of Chancery."

"His will has not been read?"

"His will, as I understand it Mr Holmes, has not been found. His solicitors are in a state of considerable embarrassment on the matter, although they assure the world that they will locate it soon. But until that happens Sir Martin's controlling share in the company lies intestate, and Sir Percy assumes the mantle."

"The will lost!"

"To answer your question, sir," Aster said, with asperity, as the coach bounced and rattled over the rough road at the crown of the hill, "before you answer *mine*, I know Mr Griffin only a little, and I trust him even less. It is hardly gentlemanly to disparage a man behind his back, but I promise you I would as gladly say these words to his face, were he here."

Holmes had the unaccountable, illogical sensation – an intuition, gut-deep, that Griffin *was* present. But obviously that could not be the case. He looked briefly at all their fellow travellers. Their collective body-heat had warmed the compartment, and all muffles and veils had been removed. None of the sweating faces were Griffin's.

Holmes told himself not to be foolish. "Mr Aster," he said. "I assure you, upon my honour, that my feelings towards

Griffin are no more positive than yours. Though he is an associate of Sir Percy's, as am I, the two of us have no communication whatsoever. What he is adding to Sir Percy's project I could not tell you, nor whence he comes, nor even what he is – I have heard rumours that his training was in the chemical sciences, but I cannot be sure."

"He is a wicked man," said Aster simply.

"Your question, Mr Aster, is: what was I doing in Middlemarch? And the answer is: I am not sure. I am a rational man, Mr Aster, and have dedicated my life to logical pursuits, so I can only say what I remember, and that is not much."

He related his experiences in London, two days prior, leaning-in so as not to share the strange story with the rest of the compartment, and being struck as he spoke with just how strange it was.

"You are sure Griffin was undertaking surveillance upon you?" Aster asked.

"I cannot be certain, but it seems to me likely. There is no question but that he was spying, nosey, upon my friend Bryde, before his unfortunate demise. Sir Percy has many admirable qualities, but he is not a trusting fellow."

"You think Griffin Sir Percy's creature?"

"I suspect so."

"Hmph. I suspect something worse," said Aster.

"But what?"

"That Sir Percy is *Griffin's* creature."

This was so startling a notion that Holmes actually gasped. Aster prompted him to continue his story. Holmes related the strange goings-in in the courtyard off Oxford Street: his conviction that Griffin had been there – his mocking voice, the *sense* somehow of his presence – despite the fact that Holmes could not see him. He talked of the crowd gathered around the chalk-artist, drawing his graffito of Martin Malprelate being devoured by a mighty serpent hatched from a basilisk egg at Middlemarch. And then the chalk dust being blown in his face. And then him staggering out of the courtyard, alarmed by possible pursuit, and then – only a scattered series of broken memories, a journey by coach, by train, and by coach again.

"Most strange," said Aster.

"My coherent consciousness, and the proper functioning of my memory, resumes in a hotel in the town, yesterday, late afternoon. I have, this morning before dawn, come here, to begin my journey home. It is, I agree, very strange. It is moreover an embarrassment to a man such as myself, a scientific man, a man who has hitherto prided myself on my self-control and submission to facts and evidence – an embarrassment that I cannot explain myself."

"The dust blown in your face," said Aster. "I have heard of such things – there are opiates, drugs, poisons that, inhaled, disarrange the proper functioning of the mind. Is it not possible that some new admixture of drugs, powdered, was thrown at you precisely to render you incapable of consecutive rational thought, for a while?"

"Why?"

"I suggest that you were *kidnapped* and brought to Middlemarch."

"But why do that? What would it benefit Griffin, or any man, to drag me all this way – me! Who am I? A nobody. I have no interest, monetary or, frankly, any other in the progress of the Middlemarch London railway. I stand to benefit in no way from the line's success, or failure. I desire only to continue with my researches, and to see my family prosper in the small and provincial ways a family can prosper. I am a threat to nobody, and an asset to nobody."

"You underplay your significance, Mr Holmes," said Aster. "Your friend Mr Bryde was tasked with investigating Sir Martin's death, and now has himself been killed. Tell me: have you taken up the threads of his investigation?"

"I have," Holmes conceded. "But I do not see how that has anything to do with it. Sir Percy is exceptionally keen to have the whole matter resolved."

"Resolved on *his* terms," said Aster.

The coach was picking up speed, finally rolling down the far side of the Southam hill, and the coachman could be heard hooting "he-e-e-y oop" at his horses, and the coach-brake wailed and complained as it was intermittently applied. The compartment began shaking more vigorously.

"You surely do not suspect…" Holmes began, but before he could complete his sentence the coach lurched dangerously, reared up onto the two wheels of its left side, and people in the compartment cried out in panic. There was a bundle, a blur, of motion: legs flew up, handbags bounced from the ceiling and the world hurried past the windows. Then the coach landed, heavily, back on all four wheels, and the coachman reined in his horses with many a "woa" and "ah-woh". Soon enough they stopped.

Everybody climbed out. The horses were standing, puffing noisily, the late morning shining glossily off their wet backs. "Brake's broke," the coachman declared, from his eminence, like a preacher.

"Good gracious!" exclaimed one of the women.

"What will ye do?" demanded the fellow with the portly belly. "What will *we* do?"

"I know what *I* will do," said the coachman. "I'll water th' 'osses. They can graze a peck, o'er yonder."

"How will that get us to Oxford?"

"Won't," replied the laconic coachman.

"My dear fellow," said the burly customer. "I insist you resume. I have appointments. I have appointments I must keep in town!"

"Too," said the coachman, rubbing his nose with his whole hand, "illy."

"Too what, my good man?"

"Ills. Too many ills twixt here and Oxenford."

"What have hills to do with it? We must get on!"

"Brake," repeated the coachman. "Broke."

It transpired that the postillion had been sent, on foot, back to Southam, to fetch the men who could mend the hand-brake – a task beyond the coachman, solus, or so he declared; and the many hills interposing between their location and their destination made progress temporarily impossible. As for the passengers, they might return to Southam, or continue on to Ladbroke. If they pleased they could walk all the way to Oxford, but, as for the coachman, he was going to stay exactly where he was until his coach was made fit for travel.

Southam being the nearer village, several of the passengers mounted Shanks's pony to return, climbing the hill behind them in the hope of finding another conveyance, or failing that at least of refreshment.

Aster and Holmes, however, strode out together, heading south.

The clouds closed, and a thin rain fell. For half an hour the two men took refuge in a tumbledown barn at the side of the road, as the sky filled with myriad parallel grey and black lines like the shading of a book-engraving. The sound of the rain on the leaves outside hushed them as a nurse soothes a baby. "Aster," said Holmes. "When you described Sir Percy as Griffin's creature – what did you mean?"

"I have only suspicions," said Aster. "But I have observed the two of them together. Griffin has some hold over the baronet. He knows something."

"You think he is blackmailing him?"

"I cannot be sure. But there is something secret, and foul, in their relationship."

The rain passed, and the two men resumed their journey, though now the way was much muddier, and country mire spattered their boots and stockings. The clouds thinned overhead and a large patch of sunlight moved across the landscape, over hilltop and down into the river valley, as a man wipes his face with a handkerchief.

"Has this to do," Holmes pressed, "with the Malprelate murder?"

"I have," Aster said, eventually, "no evidence that Sir Percy is guilty in any way in the death of Sir Martin. Indeed, I can tell you, if I attempt to figure out how he might have effected so – strange – an assassination, my mind revolts. It defeats the canons of plausibility, if not outright possibility. And yet, Mr Holmes, I confess to you: if Hawk and Griffin are *not* responsible, I am much deceived."

"This is astonishing. You believe Sir Percy and Griffin together conspired to kill Martin Malprelate? Why?"

"Hawk has benefited, in a pecuniary sense, and in terms of power. Perhaps he and Malprelate quarrelled over how to handle company business, and Hawk decided to remove him."

"But in so elaborate a manner? Why not simply hire a thugee to strangle him in the street – or a footpad to club him to death with a knobstick?"

"I do not know."

"And why, then, be so urgent in commissioning an investigation? It was Sir Percy's motion to hire Bryde, to double-up on the police proceedings?"

"Again, I do not know. Perhaps he believed Bryde would quickly endorse the theory that Malprelate had been killed by a mob of agitators, and the matter would thereby be disposed of."

"Such was not my friend's belief."

"Oh I know. I spoke to him. I know. But perhaps Bryde's reluctance to endorse the mob-theory was why Hawk and Griffin decided to have Mr Bryde assassinated."

"I was a direct witness of my friend's death, Mr Aster."

Aster stopped walking, and put his hand on Holmes's

arm. "I am truly sorry, sir. A grave and terrible thing. My commiserations. I am prone to forget the personal, the human, cost of these matters – to treat them only as a puzzle to be resolved. But I can say, Mr Holmes, that I too suffered. The world believes Sir Martin to have been as wicked as an ogre. But I knew him, I knew him personally, I worked closely with him. He had his quirks, no question. He could be abrasive. He did not suffer fools with any gladness. But he was a deeply good man, with a heart that bled for the suffering of dumb animals – for the victims of society. He was a generous, though secret, dispenser of charity. His death brought me very low, sir, in a personal sense. Very low."

"Mr Aster," Holmes replied. "I believe you. I commiserate. Let us get to Ladbroke, and see if we can hire a gig or perhaps just two horses – for I feel we need to be back in London, as soon as is possible."

Chapter 6

QUEEN LUDD

1

By the time the two men walked over the flintstone bridge into Ladbroke it was time for luncheon, of which they partook at an inn named *The Bell*. Service was not prompt, and the landlady confessed that she rarely saw custom from the stagecoach passage. "Usual, sirs, the coach but rattles through," she announced, as she set two tankards down on the table with such delicacy it seemed she thought the pewter were filigree. "They generally stop at Banbury, as I understand it."

"The coach broke down, upon the road," Holmes told her. "We have had to walk here. But tell me, good woman: where might we hire a gig, or failing that two horses, to continue our journey?"

"It might be Farmer Simpson'll hire you a hoss," said the woman. "But how would he get it back again?"

"I fear one horse would not suffice. We are two men of substantial stature. Is there no carriage?"

"The coach don't stop here," said the woman. "Carts come through."

"Carts?"

"Taking coke stone to the pottery, most."

"If we are to ride on a commercial cart, Aster," said

Holmes, "we might as well walk. How long would it take to walk to Oxford, my good lady?"

"Strong step, long legs," said the lady, eyeing the two of them. "You could be there be nightfall, if you strike out."

"I propose we take refreshment here, and then set out again. If our progress is slow, we can stop at Banbury – there will surely be a greater chance of conveyance there. But if we manage a better lick we could sleep tonight in Oxford and take the gig from there to Reading, where the railway will transport us the rest of the way."

"Railway!" said the landlady, dismissively. "They say they're building a railway-road from Middlemarch, down which those great fire-machines will roll, day and night."

"They say," Aster observed, "correctly."

"It's not coming down *this* way," the woman said, with some emphasis. "I'm glad to say. We don't need it. The line is running full many miles east of here, methinks."

"Youthinks right," said Aster. "Might we have our luncheon?"

"I am fetching it, fetching it," insisted the woman, settling herself into a chair by the door and wiping her face all over with a handkerchief. "They wouldn't dare, you see."

"Who wouldn't?" Holmes asked.

"Dare what?" asked Aster.

"Dare bring that steel turnpike down these parts. We still have Queen Ludd in this shire– though other portions of the land have given her up. But she scares away the railwaymen, at very least, though she couldn't stop them making the pottery, and that has scarred the land somewhat. But at least there's work –work for honest men – in those manufactories."

"Is there, perhaps, work for an honest tap-woman, here, and now?" Holmes suggested. "As it might be, serving us luncheon?"

"Madam," said Aster, his temper aroused. "I must inform

you that I work for the railway company that is driving its line from Middlemarch down to London, and consider your comments insulting."

The pot-woman's eyes grew very wide. "You don't say!" she exclaimed. "Art come here to run your steel rails through the heart of Ladbroke?"

"No, my dear woman, I am not. The railway runs to London, and London does not lie due south of Middlemarch. The path, as you correctly said, goes east. Your village is quite safe from our depredations. Nonetheless – "

Visibly trembling, the woman rose to her feet. "There's no vittles," she declared, in a low and thrumming voice, "for such as the likes of you. I'll thank you to leave my establishment."

"My dear woman," said Holmes, exasperated by this. "Come now: we have walked a long way, and have a long way yet to go. Surely you will not cast us out, upon the highway, with empty bellies?"

"In the name of Ludd," she said. "Go!"

"Is there, at least, another tavern in town? Might another citizen provide us with sustenance, for honest money?"

"I think, Holmes," said Aster, "we had best go."

The two men rose and left the inn, with the landlady following close behind them, informing them that it was Queen Ludd who chased them out, and Queen Ludd who kept the devil train from her door.

"Well," said Holmes as they set off together. "I suppose we had best put on our liveliest speed, and look to refresh our strength at Banbury." Aster, his face gloomy, said nothing.

Clearing the town, they began to feel that they were fairly on their way. For a while the road ran through fields and scrubby patches of heathland. Walking on, they found the ground becoming increasingly parched. The chimneys of the pottery rose over the horizon with their stride, like the lady of the lake lifting Excalibur – though a dirty red-black brick Excalibur, and a lake browned and ill-smelling. The two men passed a long suburb of brick houses: workman's homes, some with patches of garden-ground, where coal dust and factory smoke darkened the shrinking leaves and coarse rank flowers, and where the struggling vegetation sickened and sank under the hot breath of kiln and furnace. The main body of the pottery manufactory lay heavy on the land to their right as they walked, a great slab of brick, its chimneys supplying rainclouds-worth of black smoke.

They passed now through the very heart of a cheerless region, where not a blade of grass grew, where nothing green lived save only the verdant scum on the surface of the pools which here and there lay idly chilly by the black roadside. On mounds of ashes by the wayside, sheltered only by a few rough boards, or rotten pent-house roofs, strange engines spun and writhed like tortured creatures. Dismantled houses here and there appeared, tottering to the earth, propped up by fragments of others that had fallen down, unroofed, windowless, blackened, desolate, but yet inhabited. Men moved slowly, bringing in baskets of chips, or drawing after themselves barrows of coke. A horse, its head down in dejection, inched a cart heaped with slag and ashes out towards a dumping ground. Holmes first, and then Aster, tied their kerchiefs around their mouths, to filter the choking dust.

The two men walked on, passing another mile or so, until they were again in the open countryside. Downwind of the manufactory the shrubs and trees were sugared with ash and smuts, and grew in stunted and unhappy contortions.

During this passage through the wasteland they had picked up a follower, out of the vicinity of the pottery. Holmes noticed her first, walking half a mile behind them along the same road. But though Holmes and Aster stretched their legs to their full stride, this woman seemed to have no trouble in keeping pace with them.

When the road passed over a stream, the two men took the opportunity to wash their faces and hands, and to drink a little water. They sat on the stonework of the bridge for a little while. "There are many such sites," Aster observed. "Scars upon the earth."

Holmes said nothing, but only wrung out his kerchief, which he had rinsed of its dust in the stream.

"You will be surprised, perhaps," said Aster, "to hear *me* say so."

"Why would you think so?"

"Because I work for the railway company, and the construction of railways involves scarring the land. But there is this difference, Mr Holmes: for *we* seal up the work after we are done, leaving only a rapid and convenient new path for the transportation of people and goods. We are the future, and in the future technology will make the land more efficient and more streamlined."

"As the landlady at *The Bell* said," Holmes pointed out, "not everybody in the world sees it so."

"I had thought the Luddites all gone and departed, relicts of the days of our fathers," said Aster. "Tell me, Holmes: what is your background? Where are you from?"

"Hampshire," said Holmes. "My people have lived there for many generations. Country squires and gentleman farmers. You?"

"I am from no such rooted background. My father, I have reason to believe, was of a good family, but although my mother was provided with an income, after my nameless birth – enough to send me to a good school, and provide me with the educative wherewithal to make my own way in the world – there was never such a sense of rootedness in my childhood."

Holmes touched his arm. "You have made a place for yourself in the world, Mr Aster, with determination, assiduity and honour. That is all that matters."

"Not everybody takes so liberal a view of such matters as family, connection, legitimacy," said Aster. "But, you see, Sir Martin did not care about any of that. He employed me, and took me into his confidence. He treated me, always, as a fellow human being. My loyalty to him is predicated upon this commonality – for he too came from no very distinguished or established bloodline."

"He was a Jew, I think?" Holmes said. "Of Polish stock?"

"He believed," said Aster, "that a man should be defined by what he does, and what he makes – the extent to which he makes the world a better place – and not by his family history. What good is a crest won in the wars of the roses nowadays? What does it matter what your great-grandfather achieved, if you yourself do nothing? Sir Martin looked to the future, Mr Holmes, and not to the past. He anticipated a world in which all might have the opportunity to achieve according to their talents."

"You make him sound," said Holmes, "almost like a revolutionary."

"There are many tribes of revolutionary," said Aster, looking away. "Many want to tear down progress, and prevent change – to revolve, in other words, back into the past. Were we not just talking about those Luddites, who set out to smash machinery and trap humankind in medieval primitivism? They worked towards their own revolution, I suppose. Sir Martin always wanted the wheel of history of turn, to revolve, but forward – forward."

As if summoned by his words, a tune, and some words roughly-sung, drifted over the land to where the two men were sitting.

Chant no more your old rhymes about bold Robin Hood
His feats I but little admire
I will sing the Achievements of Honest Queen Ludd
Heroine of all Middleshire

Kind Ludd was to measures of violence unused
Til her suff'rings became so severe
That at last to defend her own Interest she rous'd
And of the great work did prepare.

It was the woman who had been following them along the road, now approaching them, and singing lustily as she did.

She was a person of the lower rank, whose russet kirtle was overlaid with a flowing cotton dress of Middlemarch blue which itself bore a pattern of brown dots, like coffee beans. A red shawl, somewhat ragged, was looped under both arms and tied behind her neck, and upon her head was a black loaf-hat of coarse fabric, itself fastened under her chin with a black ribbon. Instead of stockings she wore breeches, and her shoes were suited to tramping through the countryside rather than the more delicate business of housework. Her clothes, indeed, had been made out of good materials, but this was a long time since and they were but indifferently adjusted and put on. Her size, too, was unusually large; her features swarthy and singularly harsh, and her voice carried a rasp and volume in it. That her chin was supplied with some prominent hairs brought – at least to Holmes's mind – the line in Macbeth, where Banquo declares of the witches:

You should be women,
And yet your beards forbid me to interpret
That you are so.

"Good afternoon, gentleman both," said this Amazonian woman. "I have, as you see, caught you up – though you went off at a brisk enough ramble. Almost one might think ye fleeing from some terror behind."

"Not so, good woman," said Holmes. "We are only in a hurry to find an inn, hungry for a little refreshment on our travels. Why did you hurry to catch us up? Do you have business with us?"

"Gentlemen," said the lady, grinning. "Do you not know me?"

"I do not," said Holmes.

"But *you* do," said the lady, turning to the other: "you recognise me, do you not, Charles Aster?"

Aster growled: "I see you are togged-out in the garb of Queen Ludd – like some mummer in a play, for the Luddites are all grown old and have given-up on their frame-breaking and ruination. But I do not see how you know *my* name."

"I know both your names, gentlemen," said the Queen, turning again to Holmes. "And I know much more besides. I know, Mr Vavasour Holmes, that you are making painful slow progress in undoing your trip to Middlemarch. I would urge you to more haste. What will happen in London will not wait for you."

Aster leapt to his feet. "What is this? Explain yourself! Why have you followed us."

Queen Ludd seemed unconcerned. "Mr Holmes knows."

"Madam," said Holmes, also standing. "I do not."

"Have you forgotten? It is not twenty-four hours since that you dined with Mr Griffin."

"What do you know of *him*?" Holmes demanded. "Griffin – how do you know him? And how do you know I dined with him in Middlemarch?"

"Queen Ludd has her agents everywhere," said the woman, in a low, chuckling voice. "Come now – have you forgotten our prior meeting?"

Holmes pressed his memory, but nothing emerged. "We have met before?"

Queen Ludd laughed.

"I suggest you do not attempt to threaten us," said Aster. "For there are two of us, and only one of you. Madam Ludd, or whatever you are calling yourself. Should you assault us you will find yourself overpowered."

"I think not," said Queen Ludd. "I am stronger than you may think."

Holmes stepped forward. "Wait," he said. "Please, madam. You are alone, and we are two. I will be perfectly frank with you, my memory of the meeting with Griffin is – partial. In truth I hardly remember it at all. I do not know what he was doing there, and, though it sounds a strange note to say so, I do not know what I was doing there either."

"Do not treat with her, Holmes," said Aster, urgently. "Can you not see, she is an agent of anarchy?"

"If by anarchy," laughed Queen Ludd, "you mean revolution, then I gladly accept the title. For revolution is coming, gentlemen. You think the Chartists, and Reformists, the old Luddites and the new Marx-men, can't cooperate in so important a matter? It will happen here, as it is happening across the whole continent of Europe. The barricades are laid in the streets of Paris. The common folk gather in Italy and Spain. Berlin is filled with the new power of the people. This decade has been a hungry one for the ordinary folk, and ordinary folk will endure it no longer."

"You come to smash the machines," said Aster, "as if that will help the poor! It will only immiserate them further."

"You mistake me for my father, General Ludd," said the woman. "He thought small – to organise the working people of the countryside to break a frame here, smash a spinning jenny there, intimidate this squire or that landowner. I am not he. Our movement is more ambitious. There is such a thing as a refiner's fire, gentleman. Not all blazes are mere destruction. We must remake the world. Your old employer, Mr Aster, knew something of that – to tear down the old in order to build the new, and so make the world better."

"Your words have nothing to do with rebirth," said Aster, angrily. "You will conjure the mob – inflame the poor and the simple, prompt them all to desperate actions: preach at them in stern language of their wrongs, urge them on to frightful cries and threats – maddened men, armed with sword and firebrand, spurning the tears and prayers of women who would restrain them, rushing forth on errands of terror and destruction, to work no ruin half so surely as their own – for where will they end, except in the field of fire of companies of troopers? How will they end except shot down and cut with sabres, and filling rude coffins to be carried away in rude carts, as orphans cry, and distracted women shriek and follow in their wake?"

"The world is changing, Mr Aster," said Queen Ludd. "You are right to fear the mob, but wrong to believe they can be dispersed with a little musket fire and a charge of fat troopers on straw-fed nags. Come only to know the mob, sirs, and you'll find it comprised of regular inkle weavers, as thick as."

"They say," said Holmes, "that a mob charged Sir Martin, and beat him to death. Do you believe it?"

Queen Ludd put her head on one side and gave Holmes a shrewd look. "That's the first cute thing either of you have said."

"The old man's death is a mystery," said Holmes, "which has occupied the attention of many of us. *Was* Sir Martin's killing a step on this path – the path to revolution?"

"If Martin Malprelate was slain by a mob," said Queen Ludd, "it was none of mine. Perhaps a mob came from the future to hold him to accompt. Perhaps the ghosts of the dead came revenant from the past, to take revenge upon him. Why do *you* think he was killed?"

"I think he was a notable captain of industry, a man of great wealth, director of a prominent railway company," said Aster. "Such a figure as the mob, in their blind fury, are wont to drag down."

"And I think he was *un*like the other plutocrats of London town," said Queen Ludd, "in his charitable donations and help to the poor. But you know that, Charles Aster, for you knew him well."

Aster scowled. But Holmes took another step forward,

sensing that answers to the mystery were near at hand. "You have followed us, and addressed us, for a reason Madam. What is it?"

"The revolution is coming, dear sirs," said Queen Ludd. "You have had some dealings with the King of Carts. He knows it. You dined with Mr Griffin – and *he* knows it."

"Griffin is no revolutionary," exclaimed Holmes.

"Indeed he is not. You know that much, yet you do not know what he is."

"What is he?" Holmes asked.

"You call me, without politeness Mr Aster, an anarch, a purveyor of chaos. This title better belongs to Griffin. If you do not know what he is, then you must find out, and soon. He deserves to be stopped, and we will stop him." She hoisted her kirtle and made as if to leave.

"Madam," said Holmes, taking yet another step forward. "Wait a moment. I was drugged – rendered unconscious, or at any rate left in a mental condition where consecutive rational thought was impossible. I was ported to Middlemarch and there, you say, you – or one of your followers – saw me dine with Griffin. Believe me when I say I do not remember the encounter, or what he said. Believe me when I say I do not know why he might have wanted me transported to that place. Why was Griffin in that town?"

"It is the town of his birth," said Queen Ludd, simply. "I believe he went to observe the child."

"The child? *His* child?"

"Himself," Queen Ludd said. "And yourself, Mr Holmes." And with no further leave-talking she was away, walking with great unwomanly strides across the fields, calling back, without turning her huge head: "We are everywhere, Holmes! The uprising is upon us!"

* * *

2

Aster was for chasing after the figure, apprehending and if necessary dragging her by main force to Banbury and the police cells. But Holmes prevailed upon his companion to let her go, and to continue their walk.

Aster was not in a mood to talk, and Holmes was content to wrestle with his thoughts, or, rather, with his memory. Presumption number one: Griffin had been behind his abduction (though why? To what end?) Presumption number two: that he had been removed to Middlemarch, from London, spoke to some connection between the two locations – and Sir Martin Malprelate's railway line was the physical manifestation of precisely such a connection. But how did the elements cohere?

Passing through the village of Watergall, Holmes became aware as he had not been before of the looks the working-man cast at the two walkers: not idly curious, but focused and purposive. There were insolent grins, sarcastic nods. A man in a moleskin jacket and patched trousers was mending a flintstone wall; he lolled out his tongue at them as they went, like an overheated dog. Down Watergall high street they passed a Dame School, its mother-hen clucking her charges out of her cabbage-patch front yard and clipping them with expert gestures as they danced around her. The Dame stopped her herding to stare at Holmes and Aster as they walked by, resuming the business of hurrying the youngsters inside her cottage only when they had gone.

In the countryside again Holmes began to notice that they were, again, being followed, although this time by working men in country clothes and flop-brimmed leather hats. None of these men came close enough for Holmes to hail them, or question their intent, but neither did they lose sight of the two men.

Eventually the road brought them down the long slope towards Banbury. The river Cherwell sputtered over stones and flowed through its deeper channels to their left, cottages and hovels on the far side of the water, and more substantial houses on their right. In amongst fields of winter wheat, the locale was well supplied with rhubarb patches: rose-pink stems and green leaves like elephant ears. The more he looked, the more rhubarb Holmes could see being grown.

The sun was low in the sky by the time their feet hit the metalled road of Banbury High Street, and Holmes proposed they take refreshment before doing anything else. He pointed to a milestone, underneath Banbury Cross: "Oxford is yet away thirty miles – even if we hired the fastest horses we would hardly be in the city before midnight. Perhaps we should break our journey here."

Aster went to speak in reply, but his voice broke into coughs. He cleared his throat. "You saw those ruffians following us," he said. "I have no desire to stay longer than I absolutely must – yes, we must eat something, for I am weak with hunger. But let us not loiter."

They called at the *Black Horse*, drank from tankards and shared a large pork pie. But rather than invigorating him, Holmes found the fulness of his stomach to be soporific. "It is possible," he told Aster, tugging on his moustache hairs to keep himself awake, "that my body still suffers the after-effects of the drug – whatever it was – that collapsed my consciousness before."

"I am disinclined to stay here," said Aster. "Can you ride?"

"I fear I would fall from the saddle. We could hire a gig, and take turns driving it," suggested Holmes. "And perhaps, instead of aiming straight at Oxford, we could detour to Bicester? If we are pursued, as you suspect – and if our pursuers have malicious intent – such a destination might throw them off the scent. And we would arrive in Bicester early evening, in time to find lodgings for the night."

"You heard the Luddite Queen," said Aster, grimly. "She has people everywhere. I will not feel comfortable until we are back in London, and can recruit the police to our protection."

"We could approach a magistrate of this town, Aster, if it is protection by the authorities you desire?"

"I would no more trust some tuppence magistrate in a provincial backwater like this than I would trust Queen Ludd herself."

"Are you certain her followers mean us direct harm? She could have summoned them whilst she and we were in conversation, but did not."

"Look through the window, Holmes," Aster instructed. On the far side of the street, lounging against the stone water-trough, were two country-men, dust upon their shoes and breeches. They were chatting and chuckling amongst themselves, showing large mouths with incomplete sets of teeth to the world.

"Perhaps – as with Griffin – they are merely sent to observe us," said Holmes. "Surveillance rather than assault."

"You are too trusting, Holmes," said Aster.

"Perhaps we should split up," said Holmes, struggling to suppress a yawn. He wanted nothing more than to sleep, and yet he knew he could not. "You continue on to Oxford, and thence to Reading and the railway – or perhaps by stagecoach from Oxford to London. I could stay here and make my way tomorrow."

Aster looked at him. "No," he said. "Mr Holmes: it may be that chance has thrown us together – although, recent events have made me doubt my belief in happenstance as mere accident – but thrown together we have been, and I propose we stick together. I do not mind telling you, I feel a bond – a connection. I am used to being shunned, regarded with suspicion and even disdain, known to the world only as Sir Martin's secretary, and he a man libelled by the whole world, presumed to be a very devil. I do not befriend easily, and am not used to being trusted, or to trust. Yet I feel such things with you."

"Your confidence does me honour," replied Holmes. "I, too, feel the mutuality of which you speak. More, I feel that together we have a chance of dissolving away the clouds of unknowing that surround this mystery. Very well: let us not part. I will rouse myself with as much coffee as this establishment may provide, and we shall ride all night if we must, to arrive at Reading by dawn, to catch the earliest railway service into London."

"Yes," exclaimed Aster, grasping the other's hand. "Let us at least try."

"Tired as I am," said Holmes, gesturing to the serving boy to bring them coffee, "I do not fear that you and I would have much difficulty in besting those two rural clowns, presently loitering outside the inn."

"They are but the advance guard, the pickets posted. Once we make our move, I believe an army of Queen Ludd's will seek to hunt us down."

"But – seriously? To what end?"

"To prevent us reaching London," said Aster. "To stop us – perhaps by stopping our mouths forever – from interfering with whatever they have planned."

"You think they might kill us?"

"I do not know. But I feel sure they will capture us, detain us, perhaps beat us."

The coffee arrived: manifestly the morning's brew reheated in a skillet, but welcome for all that. Holmes thanked the serving girl and took a sip. "But this makes no sense, Aster. We don't know what they *do* have planned – or indeed whether they have anything planned at all. And if they do: why, how could we stop it?"

"Holmes," said Aster. "You have observed that we are followed – and spied-upon. Why?"

Holmes stirred sugar into his cup. The teaspoon clinked against the fat porcelain like a tiny clapper striking a muffled bell. "Let us lay out the facts as we know them," he said. "And more: let us augment such hard facts as may be ineluctable with such supposition or hypothesis as does not stray too far from rationality. Sir Martin Malprelate is dead."

"Indubitably so."

"So is my friend Bryde, who was investigating Sir Martin's murder. There may, or there may not be, a connection between the two things. The story goes that Bryde was trampled by an ox, but I, who witnessed it first hand, cannot reconcile what I saw with such explaining-away. I do not know, exactly, what I saw: but if Bryde's death was no accident, and was rather the result of a targeted assassination, it is surely possible that the people responsible for Sir Martin's death intervened to prevent Bryde from reaching the conclusion of his investigation and so unmasking them."

"Possible, certainly," said Aster. "Although the hypothesis lacks proof."

"Yes. Still: the torch, as the phrase goes, having been handed to me – unworthy though I am – events follow which, again, baffle the ratiocinative mind. I am drugged, and my memory and mental capacity is disarranged. In that state I am transported to Middlemarch. Why?"

"We do not know. But it appears to have something to do with Griffin. Or perhaps with the renewed Luddites, the anarchists and revolutionaries Queen Ludd claimed for her cause. Or perhaps both."

"It is hard to see what Griffin gains by allying himself with revolutionary agitators. From the little I know of him it is clear he has no sympathy with anarchy or Chartism or socialism: on the contrary, he would prefer a world in which he is King of All."

"King of All is entirely Griffin's ambition."

"Well then," said Holmes. "Here is one hypothesis. Let us say that Sir Martin was killed by a revolutionary mob – in a preliminary to a more concerted uprising. Call it a proof of concept. A test. A group of men rush Sir Martin and beat him to death."

"That is not what the witnesses reported," noted Aster.

"Indeed not. So add-in this: the organisers have access to an airborne powder that causes a derangement of sensory perception, visions of something that does not exist – a type, perhaps, of mental delirium tremens. A powder, such as I inhaled."

"A delusion," said Aster.

"*Hallucination*, is Thomas Browne's word, and it strikes me as apropos. Imagine it: you puff out this dusty drug, and the various folk present at the assassination – the late-working workmen, the passers-by – see a strange phantasy rather than the reality. Not a group attacking and killing a man, but a demonic locomotive steered by the Devil himself."

"And do they all," said Aster, "see the same thing? The same demonic locomotive? Even granting the hallucinatory nature of the drug – something to which you yourself can attest, I concede – how could it act the same way upon so many disparate folk?"

"This is indeed a key question."

"Could it," Aster pressed, "be in some sense orchestrated by the malefactors? Could they, as stage designers do in the theatre, determine in advance what it is that the witnesses see?"

"I do not see how," Holmes admitted. "But I have been speculating, since the powder was first cast into my face, or more precisely since my shattered consciousness was able to piece itself back together again – speculating whether there might be a simpler explanation. You know Ockham's razor, the venerable philosophical principle?"

"I do."

"So, say this. Posit a group – a dozen people, perhaps: agitators, anarchists, socialists, physical-force Chartists, followers of Queen Ludd, or perhaps of the King of Carts – "

"The two figures perhaps working in concert," Aster put in.

"Perhaps! But stay with our positing: a dozen fellows, muffled up and masked, so as to avoid inhaling the operative chemicals of the drug they are also dispensing. They rush at Sir Martin as he walks away from the meeting, through the fog and the dark, and beat him to death. As they do so they are observed by another dozen folk, witnesses, who then report to the police, genuinely, what they have seen, as they understand it. But these witnesses have all inhaled the drug. Not as intense a dose as I myself ingested, perhaps: for the man who threw the dust into my face was close and I breathed it full, where we must suppose that the powder was more diffusely dispensed on that night. But each of the twelve got some of the drug, and it was enough to derange their capacity for clear sensation and apprehension."

"And so?"

"So they report what they saw. But what did they see? Absent the drug, they saw a group of men, masked, carrying torches or lanterns, perhaps pushing a cart of some kind – yelling and hooting. An unexpected sight even for a sober mind to comprehend! Might a mind whose abilities were compromised by the drug not see this knot of mankind, features deformed by the masks they were working, as devils? Might not all of the witnesses interpret this input similarly? Think of Sir Martin's diabolical reputation..."

At this Aster coloured. "Undeserved reputation," he insisted. "Say rather, the libels that pursued him. The caricature and distortion."

"Quite so, quite so," said Holmes, putting his hand on his fellow's arm. "But recall we are not talking of truth but only of reputation – of the ill-regard in which the common man held him. These associations, unfairly but undeniably, were widely shared. Consider: an ordinary person, out late, sees something extraordinary: devilish faces, lights, noise, a lone man struck down. Consider the location: for everybody there knew the land had been cleared so that a railway could be laid. Consider the rumours that affixed themselves to Sir Martin himself – undeserved, I hear you, but still. Put these things together. Is it not possible that the various witnesses might not, independently, and without need for a centralising coordinator, reach the same, supernatural conclusion?"

Aster considered this. "Possibly, possibly. But why would these revolutionaries bother with the hallucinatory powder at all? We have seen what has happened in the Continent – in Paris, and Hamburg, in Madrid and Rome. Agitators there simply band together and fight: assassinate and intimidate, throw up barricades in the street."

"And so I suppose our revolutionaries plan to do here. I am, as I say, assuming that the attack on Sir Martin was by way of being a test. A mob marching up the Mall, looting the Houses of Parliament or breaking into Newgate to free the prisoners within – that would be terrifying enough. But how much more terrifying if those observing these revolutionary agitations saw them not as disaffected labourers and apprentices, not frame-breakers and carters, but as *demons and monsters*.

"Once on a time," Holmes went on, "popular unrest had been the disorganised milling of a crowd of disaffected individuals. But with the French Revolution of 1789 it became something much more alarming, something collective, something genuinely terrifying because premised upon Terror. Robespierre's Terror is the idiom of revolution, my friend. What I am hypothecating here is the augmentation of terror, using the pharmaceutical resources of modernity. Our present-day Robespierre is, I suggest, aiming not just at collective action and violence, but at instilling a more than mortal terror in the hearts of all who observe it. Honest citizens, police, troopers, anyone who could stand against a mob of their fellow men – infect their minds, overwhelm them with phantasms. For who could stand against a swarm of devils come straight from Hell's mouth?"

"Extraordinary," murmured Aster.

"As it stands, a mere hypothesis," Holmes said. "As you noted earlier, I have no proof of this. But revolutionary fires are sweeping across the Continent. We know the tinderbox that our own land has become. It would be irresponsible to do nothing."

"We must get to London, and alert the authorities," agreed Aster. "We must contact Bucket, and go further – use such influence as we have to speak to the great men of the land. I will see about hiring, or if necessary buying, horses to carry us."

"Accordingly we must decide," Holmes pointed out: "do we ride to Oxford and so on to Reading, to catch the train? Or would it be quicker to ride straight for London from here?"

"The latter is perhaps to be preferred," said Aster.

"We will ride as quick as ever Dick Turpin rode on Black Bess. He came all the way from York, we are only traversing the Chilterns from Banbury to London."

"It's fifty mile and more," Aster cautioned. "But the sooner we depart the sooner we shall arrive. Holmes – "

"Yes?"

"One more thing, before we rouse ourselves. What about Bryde's death?"

"I have of course been revolving precisely that matter."

"Does this hallucinogen perhaps explain the strangeness you reported in *your* own testimony?"

"I was not conscious of any such effect, at the time," said Holmes. "Yet the experience when Griffin's men – if they *were* Griffin's men – tossed the powder in my face was unmistakeable. Still, as you suggest: what I saw certainly did approach the vividness and irrationality of a hallucination!"

"It could be that you inadvertently inhaled a smaller dose, and experienced a smaller but still palpable effect?"

"I had just that minute walked out of the Zoological Gardens," Holmes mused. "A place that contains wild beasts. Then I saw my friend knocked down in front of my eyes, but instead of seeing a man attacking him, or perhaps a carriage running him down, I saw a wild beast."

"As did others," Aster noted. "The maddened ox!"

"But those others had not just exited the zoological space," Holmes said. "What of those others? And who distributed the drug, if drug was indeed dispersed at that scene?"

"Did you not say you saw the King of Carts, on the other side of the road?"

"Bryde said so," Holmes replied. "Never having met the gentleman, I cannot confirm."

"Your mind is a machine of great precision and logic," Aster said, "and you are using it to pry into all the problematic aspects of this hypothesis. But do not ignore the large similarities! Consider the presence of the King of Carts – consider the followers of Queen Ludd now dogging our footsteps – consider the likelihood of a coordinating revolutionary rising, happening soon! And consider, since you invoke Okham's razor, the respective likelihoods. The witnesses at Sir Martin's death saw a demonic locomotive. You actually saw a devilish bull stampeding from Hell's gate."

"Phantasms," said Holmes. "Still, I wonder if…"

"Come," said Aster, getting up. "Hold your wondering-if until we are safely back in London. The Dutch Clock says that it is three hours after noon. Let us go and obtain our transportation."

* * *

3

But obtaining horses proved much harder than either man had anticipated. As they settled their bill and left the inn, the two men who had followed them – on Queen Ludd's orders, as Aster supposed – peeled away from the wall of the building opposite and followed. Holmes wanted to confront them, but Aster suggested they were poorly placed should matters develop into actual conflict.

They made their way round to the back of the inn, and asked the ostler of that place where might they hire a couple of horses. The ostler was a hirsute-faced man with a spine of hair running down the middle of his head, the way some of the more exotic birds have plumes of elaborate feathers crowing their heads – a feature he augmented by rubbing both hands up the vane of hair to primp it up.

"Amos Kirby runs a stable, over on Wroxton Street," he said.

They thanked him and made their way thither. They found Amos Kirby himself asleep, on a bench, lying in the thin sunlight of the winter afternoon.

"Mr Kirby? I apologise for waking you," said Aster. "But we have a pressing need for two horses. We would prefer to hire them, and return them to you within the week, but if necessary we can purchase them outright."

It took Kirby several moments to gather himself. "Bound to?"

"To London."

"That's a moderate distance," said Kirby. "Too late to start today: come back tomorrow morning, early." He lay down on his bench and again closed his eyes.

"I'm afraid that won't serve," said Holmes, who could see the two Luddite spies loitering by the entrance to the stableyard. "We must leave immediately."

Kirby sat up and regarded each of them. "A hurry is it? Why so?"

"That is our business," said Aster, with asperity. "Yours is to take our money, honestly offered, and supply our need. Is that not the business of a stableyard such as this?"

"Tackle too?" said Kirby. "Saddles?"

"We hardly propose to ride bareback into the city!"

"Can't be done," said Kirby, lying down again, and closing his eyes.

"My good man," snapped Aster. "Perhaps you don't understand the urgency of our need."

"I understand," said Kirby, recumbent, and without opening his eyes, "that those two gentleman hanging about by my entrance are attached to you, as a gendarme is to a prisoners. I understand fro whence *they* come, and have no desire to anger her who sent em. Find your oss elsewhere, sirs."

Aster's temper boiled up at this, but Holmes took him aside and endeavoured to calm him.

They made their way back into the centre of town and located the Town Hall. There was no dedicated police station, but they found a mayoral officer and he in turn was able to turn-out the local constable from his home. But though both constable and council officer were sympathetic to Holmes' and Aster's story, and both quite believed the reality of Queen Ludd, neither could help. The former suggested Thomas Gulliver, the latter a man called Holdenby, and gave directions; but the same circumstances obtained in both searches. No horses were to be had for any sum, and neither Gulliver nor Holdenby would be drawn into an action they feared would antagonise Queen Ludd.

"This is absurd," said Aster. "It is now four in the afternoon, and we are no closer to being mounted and away."

"We are going about this wrong," said Holmes. "Come."

Holmes approached a duo of men sitting on the ground with their backs to the wall of a public house. "Gentleman," he opened. "Would you do me the inestimable honour of permitting me to buy you a drink?"

The duo were suspicious, but for some men thirst will always be a greater force than caution, and Holmes' insistence moved them from outside to the saloon where they removed the dust from their gullets, as they styled it, with two sixpennorth's of gin. As the second round of drink was being poured, Holmes confided his requirements to them.

"Do I look," said the first ruffian, "as though I keep a oss?"

"I will be perfectly frank with you, gentleman," said Holmes. "Two men, working for Queen Ludd – whom of course you know – are following us, and her name is enough to prevent reputable horse dealers from meeting our needs."

At this the two ruffians laughed, and the second said, "I should imagine that is so." His laughter was a long, drawn-out syllable of *hoar*, each being distinctly repeated as if he were saying the word rather than just guffawing. "Did you akse Kirby? I should think he'd prefer not to get on her highnesses wrong side, hoar, hoar, hoar."

"My question to you is: imagine yourself in our shoes. What would you do? From where might you obtain two horses, with immediate effect? If you can supply us with such information you will find us grateful."

The two men looked, each at the other. "Stroud'll do it," said the first. "Though he won't go cheap."

"And where might we find Mr Stroud?"

"He's Egyptian," the second said. "Strikes a sharp deal."

"But his horses are good?"

"He knows horseflesh like an Egyptian," said the first. "If you know what you're buying, he won't con you."

"You'll find him on the Chipping road, away out of town."

"He fancies hisself a scholar," said the first. "But you are gentlemen, and know Latin, so that should endear you to him. Only his horses are small."

"So long as they are large enough to carry us," said Holmes. "But will he do business? Is he not afeared of the wrath of Queen Ludd?"

"He?" scoffed the second man. "Her jurisdiction don't extend to Egypt, I think."

Holmes deposited a sum with the landlord of the inn, and left the two men to the business of consuming it in liquid form. And so he and Aster left, and walked as quickly as they could along the Chipping road. They looked behind themselves often, but did not see the two men following them.

The sun was low in the sky by the time they reached the smallholding of Mr Stroud, and it took them a while to convince him that their money was good. "This banknote, see," Stroud told Holmes, turning the paper over and over, "is drawn on a Middlemarch bank. And must I travel all that way so as to redeem it? Res tantum valet quantum vendi potest, you know, gentlemen."

"Here," said Holmes, writing upon the back of the note, "is my London address. If there is any difficulty in redeeming these notes at Banbury, or Oxford, or any other place at which you might do business, you are you contact me and I will reimburse you, plus twenty percent."

Stroud considered this, then folded the notes and tucked them away. He took Aster and Holmes round to the back of his establishment and had a boy bring out two horses.

"You are to give me your word as gentlemen," he said, "that you'll not use these beasts for hunting."

"We do not propose to go chasing any foxes," said Aster, exasperated. "Our business is travel."

"Your words, mind."

Holmes swore, and after an ill-tempered pause, so did Aster.

"It's barbarism and heresy," Stroud declared. "The fox is nature's gipsy, and should be left to his own business. Now, will you be riding these beasts far?"

"Where we ride is our business," Aster declared hotly. But Holmes said: "London."

Stroud nodded. "My cousin is in Southwark, on Coin Street. If you don't propose to keep the beasts, go to him and he'll take them off your hands. They are hardy mounts, though but little to look at. They are what you university gentlemen call multum in parvo."

The deal having been finalised, Stroud then went through a secondary pantomime of beginning to remove the saddles and tackle, acting surprised when Aster angrily demanded they be left in place. A second deal had to be struck for this equipment, which Holmes purchased at what even he – no horse-trader – understood to be an excessive price. But finally the whole was completed, and a toast drunk (Stroud insisted upon this).

"Is this the London road?" Holmes asked, as the two men mounted-up.

"Bicester – Aylesbury – London town," said Stroud, unfolding and refolding the banknotes. "And good riding, my sirs."

Aster and Holmes trotted away. "Were ever such nags purchased for so high a price?" Aster called. "Still, at least we are away."

"It will be a long night," said Holmes.

4

They rode briskly south-east, with the sun sinking behind them, drawing the shadows of their horses longer on the road before them, as a glassblower pulls and extends a stretch of hot glass. The air was brisk. The cold blue sky was filled with prim, white clouds whose edges darkened and purpled as the light began to thicken. Down a shallow valley and up the other side, the horses were already starting to pant.

"This does not bode well," Aster called across, as the two paused at the low summit for their mounts to get their breath back. "We have barely started!"

"I fear we must accelerate," said Holmes, gesturing behind them.

"Oh no!" said Aster, looking back.

Coming across the lower ground, an unofficial *posse comitatus* of five riders was making their way towards them. Even at this distance, it was clear to see that two of the riders were the same men who had dogged the steps of Aster and Holmes down the streets of Banbury. Their three companions were not recognisable, but Holmes had no doubt that all five were pursuing them at the behest of Queen Ludd herself.

"Come," cried Aster, and they spurred their horses.

They rode hard over the brow of the hill, and through the wide woodland that cloaked the downslope on the far side. By the time they emerged into open country again it was dusk. They passed few people: workmen and workwomen making their way home from fields and quarries from foundries – as well as poorer folk returning from the forest clutching their paltry stacks of twigs, with which they planned to heat their hovels as the night closed in. One workman, carrying a great basket on his back filled to the brim with flints, looking like Bunyan's Pilgrim, doffed his cap as Aster and Holmes rode past. There was something sarcastic, even menacing, in the gesture. Holmes spurred his wheezing horse harder.

"We are surrounded by enemies," he exclaimed.

"They mean to prevent us from reaching London in time," called Aster.

As the sky darkened further the few scattered lights of Bicester rose into view. By the time Holmes and Aster reached that town the sky was fully dark. They watered their horses at the town trough, standing in the only street in town to be gaslit.

"We have to get to London," said Aster. "As soon as possible."

"Why?" asked Holmes, although he shared Aster's urgency.

"If only," said Aster, "because Queen Ludd and her anarchist followers are so eager to prevent us from getting there."

"Yes," said Holmes. "Yes."

A few locals opened shutters to look down upon them, but they did not stay long. As the two men remounted, the five pursuing horses came into view at the end of the High Street. "Come on," urged Aster.

They rode on, as fast as they could encourage their mounts to pass and were soon clear of Bicester and travelling the long road, metalled with loose stones under the hooves, towards Aylesbury. Holmes was no habituated rider, and found the constant motion grating and unpleasant. His thighs, unused to the exercise, chafed and raged. But he pressed on. Aster, evidently a more experienced horseman, rode ahead.

But the five chasing riders were relentless, persistent, to the saddle born. It was only by bullying and repeatedly spurring their own horses that they kept ahead of the pursuit. Holmes, looking back, could see that their pursuers were husbanding their energies. "They do not need to force their mounts," he muttered to himself. "For their horses are bigger and stronger than ours. All they need do is keep us in view and follow us until we flag – and then take us, in some remote spot far from any human assistance."

It was not a comfortable thought.

Aster and he galloped through the darkening night. The incessant rhythm of the hooves on the road and the accompanying woodwind of equine puffing and wheezing became the horizon of Holmes's experiences, altogether. There was nothing but that, and his own exhaustion. The temporary elevation of the coffee he had drunk drained away. He became possessed by utter exhaustion, the debt to be paid of days of extraordinary stress. He was rocked by his ride as a baby is rocked into absolute soporism. He clung to the leather reins and grasped a fat bunch of mane-hair in his right hand, and tried to avoid simply sliding, dead-weight, out of the saddle, in a stupor. But it was very hard, very hard. The stars bumped and jolted above him, the road pounded like a drum beneath him, the clear reality of the world around him receded. It was all a dream.

"Ugh!" he called, for his weight had shifted in the saddle and he had almost fallen. He scrabbled to readjust his seat. "Aster!" he yelled. "Aster, wait!"

But Aster was far ahead of him, and out of earshot.

Holmes struggled on, biting the inside of his cheek to try and keep himself awake. After the cold hour of midnight was past, in spite alike of love and of sorrow, the extreme fatigue which Holmes underwent in the preceding days began to have a deeper effect on him. Every now and then, strong consciousness of the risk of falling from or with his horse roused him to exertion and animation, but ere long his eyes again were dimmed by confused shades of all sorts of mingled colours, the moonlight landscape swam before them, and he was so much overcome with fatigue. They were on the outskirts of Aylesbury, and the elevations and obstacle presented by the Chilterns – standing like a colossal defensive dyke between them and their destination – rose up before them, black against the starry sky.

"Do you need rest?" Aster barked, as the two horses stood gasping and frothing at the bit. The beasts were so sweaty that drips fell like a rainfall from their bodies. "Refreshment? Our pursuers are but a quarter hour behind us. If we stop here, for any length, they will be upon us."

"I am struggling, my friend," Holmes returned, slapping his own cheeks with an open hand in an attempt to smarten his wits, to wake himself up. "I drift into sleepfulness, and fear I may simply drop from the saddle."

"We have miles to go, and our pursuers are at our heels!"

"I know, my friend, I know."

"We must strike on – up the hill."

"If our horses survive," gasped Holmes. "Though I may not."

But on they went. When at length they reached the town of Tring, at the top of the mount, Holmes's horse – evidently the weaker of the two – was staggering left and right, and close to collapsing altogether. Aster dismounted briskly and led the two horses, with Holmes atop the other, into the black spaces between the trees. It was a prickly, uncomfortable progress, through a perfect blackness which the moonlight above could not penetrate. They stopped when the horses chanced upon a ditch of water, and drank noisily. Aster hissed angrily at this, since he feared it would give away their location; but soon enough the horses were satiated and simply stood, leaning their rumps against the tree trunks around, and dozing in that upright way in which horses sleep.

Holmes was so exhausted that he was able to curl up amongst the rough brambles at the foot of an oak and sink instantly into deep sleep. He woke, because Aster was kicking him with the toe of his right boot. He had no idea how long had transpired.

"Hsh!" Aster whispered. "They are among the trees, looking for us."

That woke Holmes. He sat up, and rubbed his face. In the middle distance, the bouncing beams of carried torchlight lit one tree, then another. The murmur of voices, pitched too low and too far off for the specific words to be audible.

Behind Holmes and Aster their horses stood, breathing loudly through their nostrils and occasionally shaking their heads. "The steeds will give us away!" Holmes hissed.

"It is my worry," agreed Aster.

"Shall we mount and ride away?"

"We cannot ride them through the trees – we would be captured in moments," whispered Aster. "And if we try to lead them out on foot I fear we would only be signalling our presence."

"Then what?" The lights, moving through the trees, were coming closer. "Shall we leave the horses and simply slip away?"

"We must, I calculate, be near to Watford. Perhaps we can find sanctuary there."

"In a church perhaps?" hissed Holmes. "Come now; let us be sensible." He was, although he did not like to admit it, scared.

"There is a railway," said Aster. "Of course it is my business to know it... "

One of the two horses coughed, explosively, behind them. It was as loud as a shotgun being discharged. The lantern lights stopped, and then grew in brightness, as their bearers turned them in the direction of Holmes and Aster.

"We must go," Holmes hissed. "Right now."

"Let us at least lead the horses with us," said Aster, going over to his mount and starting to untie the reins, where they were looped around a branch. This was harder to do in the dark.

"Leave the horses," urged Holmes.

The lights were more prominent now, and the voices of the men carrying them was growing into audibility. They were not attempting to disguise their speech, so confident were they that they had cornered their prey. "Over here," one said. "See th'steam from their oss's nostrils glinting in thmoonlight."

"Come," hissed Holmes.

"Wait," returned Aster.

"You there," a voice came, loud and imperious through the darkness. "Stop where you are."

"Game's up," called another. "You led us a merry chase, genlmen, but now you must stand, and permit us to take you into our custody."

Aster was making a meal of untying his horse, and his levels of frustration had become elevated. Holmes felt a flush of panic, palpable in his chest, that his friend's temper would betray him – as it had done before. "Come," he hissed, reaching out for his arm. But Aster had stepped away from the horse, and was advancing towards the approaching lights.

"You have no authority to detain us," he boomed. "Cease, desist, retire, or you will face consequences for your illegal pursuit of us."

This defiance was greeted with coarse laughter. "Aster!" Holmes called, abandoning his attempt at muffling his voice. "Come!"

Then the horse coughed again, only much louder, and – Holmes was momently disoriented – before rather than behind him. But the sound couldn't have come from that direction, for Holmes's and Aster's horses were behind them. The cough was accompanied by a starburst, a firework squib that flared and scattered crumbs of light in an oval. Holmes heard the ball sing past his ear, and felt the splinters fly from the tree behind, where the shot struck, before he quite grasped that one of his pursuers had fired a pistol at them.

"Run!" he called.

And ran.

It was a nightmare progress, sprinting, terrified, through the dark, veering away from the black trunks of trees as they loomed up, in the black night, at the last minute, zigging and zagging until, with a hefty collision, he ran straight into a tree, bounced back, staggered and fell. At once, and despite the pain occasioned by the blow, despite the whining in his ears and the sense that blood was coming from his agonised nose, Holmes scrambled quickly to his feet again. As he did so he was aware – he couldn't exactly see in the dark, but felt the brush of air as his companion passed – that Aster had passed him and was running ahead.

He started again, this time in a more moderate jog and with his arms in front of him, passing himself hand by hand around the fatter tree trunks as he encountered them. The pursuers, their way lit by lanterns, came on faster and surer. They were gaining ground.

Holmes didn't know where he was going. The plan – could he still think of a plan? – was to get into Watford and take the train from there. But he was not sure he was going in the right direction. "Aster," he gasped. "Aster – we must stay *together*."

A tree swiped at him, like a giant out of a fairy tale. This was a more glancing blow than the other, and Holmes staggered, span about like a ballerina, and did not quite fall. In his spin, in which he appeared to rotate with bizarre, dreamlike slowness, Holmes saw how close behind him his pursuers were. In a moment, as if illuminated by a flash of lightning, he saw their faces – scarfs around their mouths, hats pulled low, but glinting, wicked eyes. Then, as his rotation continued, he understood the nature of the lightning flash, for one of the men had again fired his pistol. A ruff of light surrounded the circle at the barrel's end, and the flicker of gunpowder brightness fixed the faces of his assailant upon Holmes's retina like a daguerreotype.

Holmes was away again. *They are trying to kill me*, he thought to himself. Those words formed themselves in his mind with perfect distinctness.

Suddenly Holmes was out of the trees. The spaciousness was startling. He was running across an empty frost-filigreed field, beneath a broadcast of stars overhead, the thin moonlight from a sideways arch of crescent moon pasting a meagre light. He looked to his right, and saw Aster. Then to his left and the pursuers burst from the trees, lanterns swinging, tossing shadows like cabers.

The pursuers had emerged some twenty yards further along the open space – it was, Holmes saw, despite the paucity of light, a road.

"Come," yelled Aster, grabbing Holmes as he ran past.

The two rushed along the road, their feet pounding a tattoo upon the surface below them. Holmes, unused to such exertion, felt the air burn in his lungs as he panted, and his legs cramp and seize. He glanced behind. Their pursuers were closing.

"Aster," he gasped. "I can't – we must part – you must get to London with our warning. Revolution! I will detain them as long as possible."

"Vavasour, no," gasped Aster.

"There is no time to discuss!" Holmes gasped. He stopped, and leant his hands on his thighs, his body cantilevered forward, as he breathed deep. Aster stopped too, but Holmes barked at him to fly, to fly, and with that he turned to face their pursuers.

He had scarcely recovered his breath but he found he had breath enough to yell. And so he did, as Aster hurried away: a Holmesian battle cry as he launched himself back along the road and directly at the men pursuing them.

His charge, as bold as any brigade's rushing down an enemy's redoubt, was short lived. Not a man trained in any of the pugilistic or martial arts, Holmes closed the distance between himself and the men very rapidly and then found himself unsure what to do next. On instinct he grasped at one of the men, hooking his arm round the fellow's chest and using his momentum to drag him down, as if playing the "rugby" style of football. But the fellow was quite a bit bigger than Holmes, and quite unalarmed at his assault. All that happened was that the man steadied his foothold and Holmes merely jarred himself against the heftier fellow, collapsing to the left and finding himself, winded, gasping for air, on all fours on the road.

"Jonas," somebody shouted, away to the right and above him, "you attend to that sprat, and we shall chase down tother."

The next thing that Holmes knew, he was hoisted back to

his feet, and his arms were pinioned behind him. He was still struggling with his breathing, and the click of the handcuffs locking resonated through his head.

"Now," said Jonas, in rough tones. "Will you be a nice and conformable gentleman? Or will I be obliged to knock your loaf with the stock of my pistol."

"You have," Holmes gasped, "done me enough violence already, my man."

From further down the road there came another terrifying detonation: a flash of gunpowder and the crack of a pistol being fired that dinned through the night air. A second shot followed.

Jonas, whose features were underlit and ghastly from the lantern he carried in his left hand, grinned at this. "We'll take you alive, if we can," he said. "But will shoot you down like hares if we must, if you insist upon running like hares."

"Murder!" exclaimed Holmes.

"'Tis execution," retorted Jonas, "as, come the revolution, many of your sort will face. But our mistress *will* have words with you, before your neck is stretched – and with tother gentleman too, if George hasn't shot him dead." Jonas laughed. "And George is a deadeye shot!"

"Your mistress – Queen Ludd – "said Holmes, testing the strength of the restraints that pinned his wrists by stretching and wriggling his arms. It was no good: they were fixed and immobile. "I have already had the pleasure of a conversation with her, my good fellow. I am not in need of a second."

"The King and Queen of our folk," growled Jonas, "will determine who they speak to, and when they speak, and you should count yourselves lucky to have their time. Great deeds are afoot, Mr Gentleman. Great deeds that will reform society and take away the parasites and leeches."

"If Queen Ludd thinks I have anything to do with such affairs, either to assist or impede, she is mistaken. I know nothing! I am nobody. This entire business is – for what else *could* it be? – mistaken identity."

Jonas thrust Holmes back a step, and then another. He found himself pressed against the trunk of one of the trees lining the road. Overhead, away to his right, the sky was beginning, very gently, to pale. That at any rate (he told himself) must be the east, and therefore the direction along which he should make his way – if he could only escape this imprisonment – so as to reach Watford.

Not that there was any hope of that.

"You know nothing?" scoffed Jonas. "Walker? You weren't dining with him, in a Middlemarch hostelry, not twenty-four hours since?"

"Him?"

"Griffin," Jonas barked. "Insult me with your pretended ignorance, must you? You tell me you don't know Griffin and I'll knock your pate. Tell *her* you don't know him, and she'll do much worse."

"What's Griffin to her?" Holmes rasped.

"What's Griffin to *her*? Same as he is to *all* who follow our cause, I should think."

"I do not know the man," Holmes insisted. "It is true I dined with him – or so it seems, for I do not remember. I have met him, I have spoken with him, but I know nothing about him."

"The nothing you know will be extracted, as a tooth doctor pulls out a rotten ivory with pliers. Griffin will not thwart us, you can be most assured of that."

"But," said Holmes, and stopped.

Something bizarre was happening. As the thin, chill dawn light began to suffuse the sky to the west, whilst the sun was as yet below the horizon, and with the breath exhaled by the two men glinting white with the cold, Holmes saw something. But what he saw was unclear, and made no sense. For a bar – a spar – a club – perhaps a branch fallen from, or wrenched out of, one of the trees, was floating in the middle of the road.

There was just enough light now for Jonas to see Holmes's face, which is to say to see the direction in which his eyes were pointed. It caused him to look behind himself, and he too saw the floating beam.

"The devil?" he demanded.

Jonas stepped away from Holmes, advancing upon the floating stick. And then the stick flashed, and the end of it connected with Jonas's forehead. The big man sagged and fell, collapsing onto his side.

Holmes, startled, stepped forward. But the stick that had felled Jonas was lying on the road beside his body, and there was nobody else around.

He looked along the road, but there was no sign of the other men, or of Aster either. Perhaps – he could at least hope – his friend had been fleeter of foot than his pursuers.

Then another bizarre moment: the metal cuffs restraining his arms clicked open and fell to the ground.

Holmes span about, looking in all directions. There was nobody there. A faint chittering sound, that so closely resembled teeth clacking together, diminished and died away.

He was alone in the dim predawn. Rubbing his wrists to restore circulation, Holmes crouched down beside the prone figure of Jonas. The man was breathing still, although his forehead was swollen and cut open and a small quantity of blood had pooled onto the frosty surface of the road.

Holmes stood again. He considered the events that had just passed, and tried to construe them in a way that made rational, scientific sense. Then he considered whether he had suffered another hallucinogenic episode, either as a throwback to his earlier debility, or because of a renewed ingestion of the powdered drug.

At any rate, he could not stay where he was. Holmes set off, at as brisk a walk as his tired legs could manage, down the road in the direction of the south-east. He kept to the edge of the road, thinking to duck in amongst the trees if he encountered trouble. But the road was quite deserted. He could not see what had become of Aster.

As the horizon swelled with cool yellow light, and the ruby winter sun began to haul itself over the edge of the world, Holmes emerged from the woodland. Roads branched off to the left and right, and the main thoroughfare passed down a gentle slope through fields and farmhouses. Smoke flowed thin and slow from chimneys as the households roused themselves for the day. Cows stood, still as statues, crowded together and staring at him.

It was not until the outskirts of Watford that he saw another human being: a woman, swaddled up against the cold, carrying two empty milk pails on a beam across her shoulder, hurrying up the road away from town.

The day itself had fairly started as Holmes entered the northward end of the long High Street that almost entirely defines Watford village. The railway station, a tidy little building made of fresh bricks, and supplied with a letter-box and a telegraph office was just opening its doors. Holmes waited, chafing his hands against the cold, as the station master readied his property for the day. When he was satisfied with his preparations, the man stepped behind the ticket counter and sold Holmes a two shilling single to Euston. The man stared pointedly at Holmes's scratched-up face, at the scuffs and derangements of his dress, but he took the money and passed across the ticket.

Holmes took a seat in the waiting room, exhausted, baffled, unsure whether ruffians would appear suddenly to prevent him joining the train. No matter how much he tried to make sense of recent events, a coherent and rational account of them refused to come together in his mind.

The noise of the train woke him from what was – he only realised *as* he woke – a sleep into which he had inadvertently slipped. He leapt to his feet, hurried onto the platform and pulled open the door to the carriage before him. As he clambered up, and hauled the door shut behind him, and settled into the upholstered seat, he saw that he was not alone. It was with the sort of pseudo-logic that occurs in our dreams, and not through any process that made rational, waking sense to Holmes, that he registered the identity of his travelling companion. It was Griffin.

Chapter 7

GRIFFIN

"Mr Vavasour Holmes," said Griffin, smiling broadly (without
showing his teeth). His appearance was the same as ever:
the wide-brimmed hat, the violet-tinted spectacles, the scarf
around his neck, white-kit gloves – and whiter even than
they, the face-paint smeared all upon his visage.

"Mr Griffin," Holmes replied. "Do you know what? I am
afraid I do not know your Christian name."

"It's of no consequence," Griffin assured him.

The locomotive at the head of the train hooted, puffed,
and shook itself into life. The compartment trembled and
then rocked and Holmes felt the slow gathering of motion,
like a knot being tied inside his stomach. Through the
windows Watford station slid to the right and disappeared.

The train passed along the long High Street of the town,
past the backs of many houses, giving Holmes the fleetest
passing glimpses, moments of life: a woman emptying a slop
bucket into a slender back yard; a man smoking a pipe in his
shirt and braces and watching the train pass with a heavy
look of satisfaction; an old woman sat on a stool in her back
yard and peeling onions – holding them underwater, in a
bowl balanced in her lap, to avoid the tearful fumes, and yet
weeping anyway, at some other cause than onions; a dog
leaping and bouncing, barking hard and determined at the
train. Then, with a swerve and a shudder the train passed

beyond the remit of Watford and into the countryside beyond.

The locomotive rumbled slowly as yet, picking up speed in increments, casting red glowing embers upon the ground like rose petals. At every turn, no matter how shallow, the wheels shrieked and groaned and ground, their banshee song hurting the ear, as if they were alive and being tortured. At a level-crossing the locomotive slowed to a walking pace, and Holmes found himself staring directly into the face of a row of cattle, all pressed together in the dawn light, horns entangled, eyes puzzled at the motion they were observing, long icicles of frozen saliva hanging from their lips. The driver deciding the crossing could be navigated without danger, the locomotive trembled and strained, and its small earthquake passed along the whole length of the train.

"I fear," said Griffin, "that I abandoned our last meeting somewhat precipitously."

"If you refer," Holmes replied, still looking through the carriage window, "to our luncheon at Middlemarch, I must inform you, Mr Griffin, that I have no memory – "but he was enough of a natural scientist to abhor imprecision and inaccuracy, so he corrected himself – "*almost* no memory of our Middlemarch encounter."

"Oho!" said Griffin, leaning forward. "That's a curious thing! I'll confess I join ye in that, Mr Holmes, famous father of the other Holmes.'

'What other Holmes?'

Griffin simpered. 'Common-enough name, though, what? And as for me remembering *him*—oh, *I'm* so used to my memory being fragmented, chopped up with a jigsaw, it has become second nature to me. But for you: a shock, I would think!"

"A shock," said Holmes, turning, finally, to face Griffin.

"I am, for reasons that will become apparent, most curious as to your experience. Believe me, despite our radical differences, despite the radical estrangement that exists between us, your experience and mine will not prove *so* different."

"What do you mean, radical estrangement?" Holmes asked.

"So you have forgotten that too? Very well. I see we must proceed from first principles."

"Mr Griffin," said Holmes, sitting up straight and speaking boldly. "Might I suggest you explain exactly who you are?"

Griffin favoured Holmes with another tight-lipped grin. "It is a large request, Mr Holmes."

"You will forgive me," Holmes continued. "I have had a number of days by turns baffling and stressful. I and a friend – Mr Aster, whom I think you have met – were pursued across the downs by men, violent men, with kidnap and even murder in their hearts. I do not know where Mr Aster is, presently, or even if he still lives. I myself was captured, and escaped by only the most extraordinary, and bizarre, circumstances. If I am honest I am not quite sure *how* I escaped. But your name came up, Mr Griffin."

"Did it now," said Griffin.

"These men pursuing us were revolutionaries. A violent revolution – such as is happening across the Continent – is planned, and for soon. Perhaps this very week."

"I know all about this," said Griffin.

"You do?"

"I am here, Mr Holmes, to prevent it."

"To prevent it?"

"Where I come from, Mr Holmes, there *was* a violent revolution in this country, just as there was – is, I should say – in France, Germany, Italy, all across Europe. It had a catastrophic effect upon the development of Britain. It caused the break-up of the Empire, a civil war, huge disruption and human misery. I have set myself the task of preventing it."

"You talk," said Holmes, slowly, "as if these events, yet to happen, are in your past."

"Well," said Griffin. "It is my present *now*, of course. But your intuition is correct. I am from your future."

Holmes considered this extraordinary claim. Eventually he asked: "How?"

"As to that," said Griffin, "it is a curious tale. You may, when you hear it, judge me harshly. That is as nothing. I am here to do good for the world, or for this country at any rate. But I am not motivated by disinterested humanitarianism. On the contrary, I am seeking my own personal ambition. The fact is, Mr Holmes, that moments of great political instability, as this moment is, are times when a canny operator can orchestrate events to their own advantage. I plan to become a man of power, Mr Holmes: a great leader, first of this country and its wide empire, and then of the whole world. Perhaps such ambition shocks you, Mr Holmes. I am merely honest."

"And how, precisely, do you propose to achieve this world-spanning ambition?"

"With your help," smiled Griffin.

"I think not," said Holmes.

"Surely you will not permit *bloody revolution* to overtake this country? No, no, I think you will *help* me."

Holmes stared at the man. "I have had," he said, "some issues with a toxin that was blown into my face, some days ago."

"I was there," said Griffin. "I saw!"

"I thought I heard you – though I did not see you."

"I can avoid being seen, when it pleases me."

"You can?"

"Indeed. Observe." Griffin pulled off the glove from his left hand. There was no hand inside the glove. The hand had been, Holmes thought, amputated, and the glove was actually a prosthesis: but no, the glove was a piece of tailored cloth, and hung limply. It was being held between finger and thumb, but Holmes could not see either digit.

"What I mean to say," said Holmes, "is that I am currently unable entirely to trust my perceptions. Your presence here may be real, or it may be a kind of dream. You may be nothing but a phantom."

"I am real," returned Griffin. "You can see with your own eyes my condition. Or rather – you can't."

"You are... invisible?"

"I worked for years on the technology to render my living body's diffraction equivalent to the air around me. I was a medical student, you know – or, from where we sit now, I *will be*. But I dropped medicine and took up physics, because I was fascinated by light. Optical density! I vowed to find a solution and I went to work. Prodigies of work, heroisms of effort. In doing so I found a general principle of pigments and refraction – a formula, a geometrical expression by which it would be possible, without changing any other property of matter – except, in some instances colours – to lower the refractive index of a substance, solid or liquid, to that of air."

"Astonishing!"

"You are a man of science yourself, of course. And so you do understand the principle. Visibility depends on the action of the opaque bodies on light. Either a body absorbs light, or it reflects light or it refracts it – most objects, in fact, do all these things in varying proportions. If it neither reflects nor refracts nor absorbs light, it cannot of itself be visible. You see an opaque red box, for instance, because the colour absorbs some of the light and reflects only the red part of the light, to you. If it did not absorb any particular part of the light, but reflected it all, then it would be a shining white box. A glass box would not be so brilliant, nor so clearly visible, as a diamond box, because there would be less refraction and reflection. Yes? From certain points of view you would see quite clearly through it. Some kinds of glass would be more visible than others. A box of very thin common glass would be hard to see in a bad light, because it would absorb hardly any light and refract and reflect very little. And if you put a sheet of common white glass in water, still more if you put it in some denser liquid than water, it would vanish almost altogether, because light passing from water to glass is only slightly refracted or reflected or indeed affected in any way. It is almost as invisible as hydrogen is in air. And for precisely the same reason!"

"I understand."

"The technique I developed – well, it is not an absolute. I must walk about in air, I cannot exist entirely underwater. If a sheet of glass is smashed, Holmes, into a powder, it becomes much more visible: an opaque white powder. This is because the powdering multiplies the surfaces of the glass at which refraction and reflection occur. And you can see, as I flex my hand..." Griffin took hold of his empty glove with his other gloved hand. Holmes stared at the invisible limb. "I am waggling my fingers, and if you concentrate you will see – "Griffin said.

It was true: there was the vaguest, ghostliest sense of something, an intimation of something shifting or moving.

"My fingers are a complex shape, and their edges interfere with the refraction dynamic. But it is only partially visible, and then only in good light, direct sunshine. In darker, or mistier environments, I am impossible to see. I pick my moments, unless I am obliged to come out in bright sunlight, as I sometimes am. But I prefer to work in other lights."

"This is extraordinary."

"I am the Invisible Man," said Griffin. "My name – Hawley Griffin – is what I was Christened. Under it I grew up, a lad in Middlemarch, the town you and I have recently left. But I grow beyond that name. I am a new being. I am the Invisible Man."

"The boy – in Middlemarch?"

"Come now, Holmes. Where I come from, your son is famous for his intellectual powers. He surely inherited his abilities from *someone*. Don't tell me it was only from your wife?"

"My son? Mycroft?"

"Not he," said Griffin, obscurely. "But you have the data now to deduce the truth. I am here, a full-grown man, though invisible, before you right now. I am also a small boy, growing up – as I did – in Middlemarch. How can I be both?"

"It is as if," Holmes said, "as if you come from – "

"Go on: complete the thought."

"The future?"

"Bravo. You *are* capable of intellectual agility, after all."

"How can that be? How can invisibility confer upon you the ability to travel through time?"

"No, no," said the Invisible Man, pulling the glove back onto his invisible left hand. "Nothing like that. How could it? Invisibility is a matter of refractive index. Time travel is a much more profound scientific intervention – one beyond my scope as a researcher, I am sorry to say. I don't say I *couldn't* have cracked that nut, if I had chosen to make it my goal. I believe I could. There is no merit in false modesty."

"Another scientist developed it?"

"Indeed. As a technology. A machine. His name was William Reynolds. My contemporary."

"When?"

"The last decade of this century. The 1890s. I am in my fifties, though my skin of course displays no wrinkles, no blotches. I live a healthy life. I plan to live into my hundreds. When I have consolidated my position here – in this year of our lord 1848 – I intend to open a new avenue of scientific research: longevity. I see no reason why my lifespan could not be very markedly extended. Perhaps I could render myself immortal."

"I cannot believe," said Holmes, "the things I am hearing."

"And I cannot believe," returned the Invisible Man, "that we must go through all this again!"

"Again?"

"We have conversed for hours. I have explained – for hours. Have you truly forgotten our long luncheon in Middlemarch?"

"My memory – "said Holmes. But then he decided he did not wish to stoop to explaining himself to Griffin. "Pray continue," he said.

"With my explanations? Very well. If we must go through all this again, we must," said the Invisible Man. "Reynolds developed a machine that could travel through time. A remarkable piece of equipment. Then he used it to travel into the further reaches of the future – the year eight hundred thousand, or thereabouts. He saw some sights there!"

"And you travelled with him?"

"Not I. Frankly there developed a certain professional jealousy – on his part, I should specify – that occasioned a breach between us. I was willing to collaborate, but he took against me. No, no, I heard about his adventures when he related them, to his friends: me standing, invisible, eavesdropping! It was a fanciful narration, and to be frank with you, I am not sure how much of it I believe. Reynolds was never too exact when it came to truth." At this, the Invisible Man laughed, and Holmes understood why he smiled with his mouth closed and lips tight: for opening his mouth revealed teeth whited with paint, and beyond them a void, a vacancy. It was most unnerving to see.

"I do not see the occasion for hilarity," said Holmes.

"Oh, it is just that I am talking about an event in the future, but using the past tense. It strikes me as comical."

"The future pluperfect is always available to you."

"Reynolds was a young man. He is not yet born, as we sit here, you and I, gaily conversing in 1848. I do not know his exact birthday, but when I knew him in the 1890s he was, I would say, thirty years of age. So he *will be* born some-time in the 1860s I suppose. It is odd to think that though he roamed England in the year 800,000, he will never see the year 1900."

Holmes grasped what the Invisible Man was saying. "He is dead. In the 1890s, he is dead." Then, as realisation sank further in: "You killed him, and stole his machine."

"I could have developed my own machine," said the Invisible Man, haughtily. "Had I enough time, and resources – the wealth at Reynolds's disposal was prodigious. It's no wonder he beat me to the pip. But I do not have time. And I did not have wealth: I was a poor chemist, and trained only in chemistry." He waved his hand, dismissively. "As a chemist I am a genius. I *could* be a genius in engineering, and technology, and the manipulation of time – of course I could. If I chose to. But I have other aims. Yes, I took his machine. He would not simply give it to me, after all; and my need was greater than his. What... he, gallivanting through the far distant future with leprechaun men and women, and trolls out of caves, indulging himself? No, no. I had a better use for it."

"You killed him, stole his machine for travelling in time, and came – here."

"Unfortunately," the Invisible Man said, "the machine had malfunctioned. Sir Percy Hawk thinks I broke it, by using it incorrectly."

"Sir Percy *knows* of this?"

"Of course. It took me a while to convince him of the veracity of my tale, but he believes now. He and I are working to repair the machine. Today's electrical piles are feeble things, only able to activate parts, and then only in a very limited way. We need the machine as a whole to operate at full potency. It is in need of a more powerful electrical source than can be obtained in the 1840s, and so we have approached your good self, to develop precisely such a motor."

"I am flabbergasted," said Holmes. "To think I have been working towards such an aim!"

"We need the motor," shrugged the Invisible Man. "Obviously we could not explain to you *why* we need it; but fortunately you were incurious on the matter. It was enough that we requested it, and that we paid you."

"I did not wish to pry into your private affairs."

"I make it a matter of principle," said Griffin, "*always* to pry."

"Are such electrical motors commonplace in the 1890s? If so, could you not have instructed me in the advances in technology from this year to then?"

"Chemical advances, certainly," said the Invisible Man. "But electricity is a different magisteria. I am not a physicist, and have little interest in that discipline. It matters not: with influence – with money – one can always buy the expertise one requires."

"With Sir Percy Hawk's money."

"Since I have none of my own, why: yes! And it is not truly his money. It is the London and Middlemarch Grand Congruence Railway Company's money, to which Sir Percy has access, and from which he is not inhibited by petty moralities or legalities from availing himself. We have grander aims than keeping a railway company profitable. Come now! Can't you think a little bigger?"

"What you have said is as extraordinary as it is terrifying," said Holmes. "If you repair this device – this temporal displacement machine – you will be able to move freely along the tracks of time, as the locomotive currently pulling his carriage can move freely up and down these railway tracks."

"Reynolds, the inventor, the time traveller, did not understand what he had wrought. He thought only as a tourist does, to visit exotic locations and enjoy himself. He did not see how the machine could be used as a tool – to leverage power for its owner."

"To turn you into a tyrant?"

"First things first, Mr Holmes. And that first thing is: we can use the machine to avert the revolution currently simmering in our country. That is the first order of business. Observe the ringleaders, the organisers, the pinch-points and key moments. Step back in time a week, a day, perhaps even an hour, and prevent them from leading, organizing, agitating."

"You mean to kill them?"

"It is one of the options at our disposal. But we need not be so absolutist. There are other ways."

"This is appalling!"

"You forget, Vavasour, that I know – as you do not, yet – the consequences of the successful revolution. If you did, what price would you set upon peace and stability, and the continuation of Britain as an Imperial power?"

"You set yourself arbiter over us all," snapped Holmes. "You oppose Providence, and pretend to know what is best for the entire nation – for the world. It is monstrous, man! Monstrous!"

"Hark," drawled the Invisible Man. "The bleating of the lamb."

The train shook itself, and began to decelerate, gathering slowness to itself like a kind of consummation. They were rolling in towards its final destination. Through the windows of the carriage he saw the tall backs of town-houses slide past, and then, with a change in the timbre of the sound of their chuntering onrolling to a more echoey and reverberatory clang, the train slid into the great wrought-iron shed at Euston.

"Mr Griffin," Holmes said. "Did you kill Sir Martin Malprelate?"

"I?" returned the Invisible Man, smiling his old smile: lips tight together. "No, my dear fellow. Not I. You're barking up the wrong tree there."

"You *were* there, at the London Zoological Gardens," Holmes persisted. "With Sir Percy. Just before Bryde died."

"Was I?" He seemed uninterested in this. "I often meet with Hawk. He's as keen to get the machine up and running again as I, and is constantly badgering me for this and that – stock investment advice (as if I know anything about the stock market in the 1840s!) and engineering advances and specifics relating to the time machine – though he only half-believes its potential. Where I have first-hand experience."

"Did you kill Bryde?"

"No, my *dear* fellow. I did not. That harmless drudge? Why would I kill him?"

"I don't know. But you could have done it."

"By metamorphosing into – what was it? A maddened ox? Such is not within my powers. I am no different to you, in most respects... except that I have altered the refractive index of my flesh. Come now! Holmes, my friend. Come with me now. Great events are afoot! We can change the course of history."

The train had halted. Holmes got to his feet and grasped the compartment doorhandle. He stopped.

"Griffin," he said, turning his head to look at the still-seated man. "What *were* we doing in Middlemarch?"

"We went there to meet me of course," said Griffin.

"You went to meet you?" The truth broke in upon Holmes in a rush. "Your younger self?"

"Yes."

"You drugged me – gave me a hallucinogenic powder, shattered my memory... for that?"

"There was no hallucinogenic powder, my dear fellow. It was a simple soporific. I only needed to get you to Reading, which I and my hired help did by bundling you into a cab to Paddington. From there we shot up the railway line."

"To Reading."

"We needed to be out of town for a day. And I wanted time to talk to you. It was *you* who insisted on hiring a carriage and running up to Middlemarch. Have you truly forgotten?"

"Because of the drug you dealt me!"

"No, no. You have again misunderstood. *You* wanted to see the young me. I was curious, but wary – for I believed, and now am certain, that to meet yourself is a dangerous matter. It is what we, in my era, call a feedback loop: a shriek, a destructive wrench to the matter of existence. You took this as proof that I was a liar, about the time travel story. So I agreed we should go, provided only that my child-self and my adult-self should not be in the same room at the same time. And I'll confess I was curious too... curious to see myself from the outside. For that is something few people ever manage to do. And, I will make another confession: though Reynolds had warned me, I did not understand the depths of the danger. But you proved it!"

"I proved it?"

"Indeed. You paid my younger self a sixpence to walk up and down the street outside the inn – the very hostelry in which we were having luncheon. The strange thing, or so I said, was that *I* had no memory of this incident, of being paid the sum as a lad, and of parading in that manner. But I'm sure there is some explanation, folded into the world of physical sciences, as to why this might be. My younger self, though, did not stay where he was supposed to: out on the road. No, he – I – crept into the room, unbeknownst to us. I suppose I – he – wanted to know who these strange gentlemen were, and insinuated his way into our conversation."

As he said this, Holmes had a sharp moment of clarity. He *had* been there! He remembered now: conversing with Griffin over lunch. And then, a growing sense of unease, something awry in the nature of things, a fizz in his stomach and a migraine slapping across his brain pan, and at that precise moment, the boy's face, from the doorway.

Then Griffin reeling back, overturning his chair, rushing for the other exit. And Holmes caught in the explosion of –

Of – whatever it was.

"*That* was what shattered your memory," said the Invisible Man. "Not the simple soporific I administered. Memory is of course very sensitively calibrated to time, and that encounter was a rip, a wrench, in time itself."

"Did it shatter your memory too?"

"To some degree. To a lesser degree than yours, it seems. I remember most of our conversation. I had won you round, I think. I was explaining to you the strategy when... a sound like a screech inside my head, a devastating pain, and I staggered away. By the time I had recovered myself you had gone."

"A shock," said Holmes.

"And now here we are again. Having to start from first principles. Do you still have the money I gave you?"

"I," said Holmes, unnerved, discombobulated. More memories were recurring to him.

"Come with me, Vavasour," said the Invisible Man. "We must save the world, you and I."

But Holmes's hand turned the handle, almost without conscious instruction from his mind. The door opened and he stumbled through it, down the steep step and onto the platform. People were milling, walking up and down, waiting for the train. Overhead the complect of iron spars and lines, woven into the pattern that upheld the roof. Holmes hurried along the stone platform. Behind him he heard Griffin call out: "Holmes! Holmes!" – but he was away, and through the giant stone arch at Euston entrance and onto the concourse beyond.

Chapter 8

THE MIGHTY MEETING

1

The concourse outside Euston was a place where cabriolets assembled, to carry new arrivals to their various destinations. It was somewhere in Holmes's scattered thoughts to mount one and return home – to greet his wife and babe, and from there to coordinate with Bucket, and the authorities, to report the strange events that had happened, and set the instruments of the law upon the apprehension of the criminals who had threatened and assaulted him.

But, on this day, instead of ranked carriages there was only a great crowd of people, most dressed in their working clothes, milling and wandering.

With some difficulty, Holmes pushed his way through the crowd to the road beyond, where he found one hackney carriage parked, an island in the sea of people. "Can you take me to Baker Street?" he called up, but the driver, his whip tucked into his back pocket like a fishing rod, only glowered at him. "Force a way through this mob?" he returned. "Not bloody likely, my good sir. I'm a-sitting it out."

"Sitting what out? What is going on?"

"You haven't heard? Them Chartists are gathered. They have a prodigious petition, five million names have signed they say. They intend to force open the doors of Parliament, drag the speaker from his woolsack and set up the petition in his place."

"Good grief," said Holmes, and set off on foot.

It was a slow business working his way south from the station. The main thoroughfares were clogged with folk, and a steady stream of people kept emerging from the side-alleys. There was some mockery of his gentlemanly clothes: women hooting and yelling, men threatening to box "Lord Ponsonby here" in the eye, or calling him "his Duke-ship" and "No-Cheese".

He worked his way up Marylebone, against the direction of human flow: for most people were swarming into town, to join the mighty meeting: south of the river, at Kennington, is what Holmes overheard. He saw, too, some strange goings-on. As he peered through the crush of folk, trying to spy-out a way of proceeding, he sometimes chanced to see an arm stretched out – sometimes the arms reached *under* his own perhaps, or perhaps across him – to thrust some paper into the hand or pocket of another person in the crowd, then be withdrawn so suddenly that it was impossible to tell from whom it came. Nor could he see in any face, on glancing quickly round, the least confusion or surprise.

Many people were carrying bottles and billy-cans which they frequently fitted to their lips. The murmur was good natured, augmented by occasional bursts of song. Holmes struggled further on.

He turned down Luxborough Street, hoping to cut through to Baker Street from the side. But the crush was as great down there. The stream of life was all pouring one way, joining the throng of persons looking to cross the river from the Middlesex to the Surrey shore, all in unusual haste and evident excitement. Nearly every man and woman – a human stream which still came pouring past, without slackening – wore in their hat a red cockade.

It was strange for Holmes to feel, in his heart, an acute

sense of his solitude, a strange and novel thing to feel considering the size and press of the great crowd all around him.

His train journey with Griffin had, in his memory, the feverish quality of a strange dream. And yet it had taken place.

Had he not, then, been dosed with an hallucinogen? Griffin claimed so, but he was hardly a trustworthy source. And the alternative was much more fantastical – that bringing two *temporal iterations* of the same man into proximity each with the other would lead to such a mental derangement. Yet, as he dismissed the very possibility, a voice in his head confirmed it. Holmes had worked with electrical equipment. He knew that touching two live wires together, without an object of galvanic resistance to mediate the flow, would cause a short-spark explosion in which the entire circuit collapsed. Might there be a similar logic in the world of time-voyaging?

It was too bizarre. And then, with a jolt not unlike a galvanic shock, a great rush of memory returned to Holmes. The carriage ride to Middlemarch. Meeting Griffin in the inn. Their conversation. It all fell back into place.

What he said on the train was correct: he had – he had explained the whole extraordinary state of affairs. He had given Holmes money, drawn on a local bank, and encouraged him to avert the danger of the mob. Had Griffin fully grasped the imminency of the uprising?

But if he *hadn't* been dosed with an hallucinogen... perhaps there was no such substance. His explanation for the bizarre visions that had accompanied the deaths of Sir Martin and Bryde was exploded.

"This," Holmes burst out, as he wriggled and squeezed through the crowd, "is ridiculous! Ridiculous!"

He found himself at the side of the street. All the shops and businesses had closed for the day, and many had taken the precaution of boarding-up their windows. Holmes clambered up a brick wall and over the top into a private garden.

He dashed across this space and climbed over the far wall. Now he was in a back-yard court of miniature size, in which an elderly woman was seated, on a stool, peeling potatoes into a bucket.

"I apologise for this intrusion, ma'am," Holmes said. He reached to tip her his hat and then remembered that he had lost it, in Middlemarch. "I am only passing through."

He ran down the side of this house and wrenched open a rude gate, emerging into Baker Street at last. But here the crowd was even thicker.

The houses here were taller, and the shops again all shut up – the passage of so great a crowd having alarmed the tradesmen for their goods and windows. Holmes saw, in the upper stories, various inhabitants congregated, looking down into the street below. A few applauded, and others hissed; but regardless of these commentaries upon their action the vast congregation of people continued their tidal flow southwards.

It took Holmes a long time, and it cost him a hard physical labour before he reached the front door of his London lodgings. He fumbled the key, jostled and shoved by passers-by, and finally made his way inside to the temporary sanctuary of his hallway.

"Gwendolin?" he called, leaping up the stairs in threes. "Gwendolin!"

But his wife was not there. "Mrs Holmes departed yesterday sir," said his landlady. "When she received your letter."

"Departed where?" Holmes demanded, gasping.

"She didn't tell me sir; only she took her baby, and her maid, and they all got into a cabriolet outside. Mayhap she was returning to your house in the countryside, sir? I can only commend her foresight, to get out before today, for now the whole of London has been possessed by a mob as

shocking and alarming as ever chopped off a king's head, or
set out barricades in the road!"

"Stay here," Holmes instructed her.

The usual deliveries of food having been interrupted by
the mob, there was little to eat in the apartment. This was
unfortunate, since Holmes was fiercely hungry. Mrs Hudson
found a heel of bread, and some cheese, and uncorked a
bottle of good beer, which Holmes devoured. Then he
washed and changed his tattered, grimy clothes. Peering at
his own face in the mirror he examined the contusion on
it that ran from the bridge of his nose to the top of his left
cheek. He had almost forgotten it, but dabbing it with a wet
cloth to clean the wound brought it stingingly back into his
consciousness.

He thought of himself looking upon himself. Then he
thought of older Griffin looking at himself, younger, in a
different way. Could it be true?

"Is the world going mad, Mr Holmes?" Mrs Hudson asked,
plaintively.

"The city certainly seems to be doing so," Holmes replied.

"They are all off to Kennington Green," said Mrs Hudson.

"Is that so?"

"The Boots was saying, yesterday. Don't dismiss him, sir:
he's young."

"You're young yourself, Mrs Hudson."

"But I've been married and widowed, and so I'm older
than my years. He's only a foolish lad."

"What did he say?"

"It's the Chartists, sir. They are orchestrating, they say,
a mighty meeting, at Kennington Green south of the river.
They have a – what is the word? I would say list, but that
ain't the proper term."

"A list of demands?"

"A list of names. Millions upon millions of names, signed,
and ready to present to Parliament."

"A petition," said Holmes.

"That's the word! They will gather and march as one upon the Houses of Parliament, and present the petition. The Boots says he's not cleaning any boots today, for he's off down to the river, and across it, to join the mighty meeting."

"Mrs Hudson," said Holmes. "I must get to Scotland Yard – though I fear I may already be too late."

From the window, looking down, it seemed as though the crowd was beginning to thin. "I think the majority have moved on, down to their destination. There are still many people in the streets, but the numbers are fewer. Mrs Hudson: I must go out."

He went to his writing table and scribbled a note.

"When the crowd has died down, I'd be grateful if you would post this – to my wife, addressed to where I hope and trust she has gone... home."

"Where else would she be, sir?"

"I wrote to her from Middlemarch yesterday, and it's possible she has gone there hoping to find me. But if so I would not expect her to have taken the baby – and her maid. No, I trust she has gone home, where she will be safe."

Holmes handed his landlady the note, put on his overcoat, retrieved another hat, and went out again to face the crowd.

2

There were still enough people milling along the streets to make passage difficult, a strenuous and continuous effort to force a way. Holmes began, as English people tend to, by voicing a string of "excuse me's and "I beg your pardon's, but the crowd was so focused on its own designs, on singing revolutionary songs, waving scarlet flags and bottles, that there was no merit in politeness. By shoving and pushing Holmes made his way to the new Square, with its minaret-like Trafalgar monument.

This open space gave him an easier pass, and he moved to the head of the Mall, so as to cut through to Scotland Yard.

"Holmes!" cried a voice, hoarse but recognisable. "Vavasour Holmes!"

It was Aster.

The two men embraced, Holmes joyful. "My friend," he cried, as the passing press of people jostled and jarred them. "I had thought you lost – perhaps dead. The last I saw, Queen Ludd's men were shooting their flintlocks at you."

"Their aim was as poor as their morality," Aster replied. "I was fortunate to chance upon a team of horses, being brought into town under police orders, and was able to persuade the mounted constable of my urgent need. I rode one such straight to Scotland Yard, arriving as the dawn was breaking – and just as this monstrous crowd was beginning to assemble all around."

"I am on my way to Scotland Yard now," said Holmes. "My progress has been slower – but I have had the most illuminating, or perhaps the most unimaginable, conversation with Mr Griffin on the way."

"If you are going to find Bucket, then he has already left the Yard. The dragoons have been mustered, and cannons are being readied outside Buckingham Palace. But what did Griffin tell you?"

"Too much to compress into speech in such a place," said Holmes, shoved so hard by a passing labourer that he almost fell. "When leisure is ours I will tell you all."

"The urgent task is to contain this uprising," called Aster. A gush of new people pushed their way between the two men. Holmes felt himself being carried away from his friend, as a swimmer is borne against his will by a strong current.

"Aster," he called. "The protestors are assembling in Kennington. They plan to march on Parliament!"

"Yes," Aster called back. "The mob must be stopped – contained, as I say, south of the river!"

"Aster!" Holmes called again, lifting his arm. But the crush of people was too overwhelming, and he was shoved away, and bundled down Whitehall.

It was beyond Holmes's power to resist: an influx of new people, all eager and hurrying to cross the stone arches of Westminster Bridge to arrive at the meeting place in time. Holmes struggled to avoid slipping and falling between the urgent bodies – a fearful effort at times, for to fall would surely to be trampled underfoot.

The crowd flowed over the bridge and Holmes was carried along. The force of it moved not only his physical form, but swept through him, penetrating his interiority. Perhaps it was some remnant of the hallucinogen (though, he recalled, Griffin had denied that there had ever been such a drug) but he felt his individuality dissipate, his distinctness as a separable human being erode, washed away grain by grain with each wave of the pulse of the crowd. *Was* he, in the fullest sense, an individual? Are any of us? Here, as a molecule in the great flow, he became aware of a different perspective. This stampede rumble of many feet on the stony floor, this sense of continual motion, this heat and press and smell and sound of so many other folk. The flags and banners red as cherry, red as blood, red as sunset, red as poppies, red as the breast of a robin or the stippling of a trout, was his blood, his tongue, his sky. As certain adepts in the skills of witchcraft speak of departing their corporeal form and floating through the sky as a mere spirit, so Holmes felt himself somehow looking down upon the progress of which he was a part. It was no longer a gathering of separates; it was instead a giant organism, in which each man and woman was a cellular component. He saw it pulse and slide along the channels carved into the fabric of the city by its streets and bridges – a serpent, the brown and tan and black and green of the various clothes and hats blending into a moleskin taupe colour, spotted with dots of red.

The creature drew itself into Kennington Common, and Holmes was a cell of it. Here this immense multitude was collected, bearing flags of various kinds and sizes, but all of the same colour – red, like the cockades – some sections marching to and fro in military array, and others drawn up in circles, squares, and lines. A large portion, both of the bodies which paraded the ground, and of those which remained stationary, were occupied in singing revolutionary hymns and songs. With whomsoever this originated, it was well done, for the sound of so many thousand voices in the air must have stirred the heart of any man within him, and could not fail to have a wonderful effect upon enthusiasts, however mistaken.

Holmes struggled, inwardly, to shake himself out of this mass-identity. He shook himself physically, and returned, with a jolt, to his individuation. He was a single man, though surrounded by a vast number of single women and single men.

"Come now," he told himself. "It won't do to stay here."

Struggling through the outer area of the crowd, he began the process of zagging and zigging, wriggling and pushing to extricate himself from the main crush of the gathering. The mass had fallen quiet, such that the fluttering of a banner struck the ear, and caught the eyes. Holmes looked back. A platform had been erected in the middest of the common, and various folk stood there, awaiting the arrival of the governing figures of this assemblage.

The quiet, and motionless, enabled Holmes to move more quickly. Soon enough he was at the edge of the common, where the press of people was thinner. He stopped for a moment, and turned back, just as the entire crowd burst into a tremendous shout, into another, and another; and the air seemed rent and shaken, as by the discharge of cannon.

Two figures had mounted the central platform. Even from this great distance Holmes could see who they were:

the King and Queen themselves – Carts, Ludd, the peoples' appointed monarchy of revolution. They were speaking, although the distance and the murmur and chatter of the crowd made it impossible for Holmes, at the very edge, to make-out what was being said. But he didn't need to hear the specific words: the import was clear. March, they were saying. Move this mighty serpent to the Houses of Parliament, and Buckingham Palace. They were saying: the tongue of this serpent is a vast petition, signed by five million and more, which will unroll between the fangs of the dragon's head and lick at the great door of the House of Commons. They were saying: the bite of this serpent's jaws will break the walls of power asunder, crash it to rubble, and slither across the ruins. They were saying: we shall build a new land from the detritus of the old. Liberty, and Justice; Fairness and Equality; Work for all and Play for all; Love the Belovèd Republic.

Holmes couldn't hear the words, but he understood them.

3

He turned back and hurried up the streets, where now only a few stragglers were coming the other way. At Westminster Bridge he crossed to the Middlesex shore, and on that northern side of the river he met Mr Bucket, a dozen police constables, and Aster. Some few curious passers-by, idlers and dallying servants interrupted such errands as their masters and mistresses had sent them on to see what this small group of Peelers was about.

"Mr Bucket," Holmes cried, somewhat out of breath. "I cannot say how pleased I am to see you here."

"Mr Holmes," said Bucket, nodding.

"I have travelled – Aster and I have travelled – far, as fast as we could, to reach you."

"And here we have both arrived," said Aster. "Though I fear we come too late."

Aster and Holmes both shook hands with Bucket. "I have this very moment run up from Kennington Common," said Holmes. "The crowd there is very large – very large indeed. It is currently being addressed by the King of Carts – and by Queen Ludd as well. It is clear what they will do next."

"They plan to march on Parliament," said Aster, "no doubt."

"And we are here to stop 'em," said Bucket, firmly.

Holmes looked at the twelve constables. Ten of them were young – extremely young, or so they seemed to Holmes's glance – and thin. Two older policemen, with the triple-lambda of sergeants' stripes on their shoulders, looked more substantial and more experienced.

"Forgive me," said Holmes. "I have no wish to impugn the integrity or courage of your officers, Bucket. But will – will a dozen men be enough?"

"As Mr Aster notes," said Bucket with his characteristic imperturbability, "we have been apprized of the danger reasonably late in the day. Had I known a day or two earlier we might have brought in extra bodies to swell the ranks, here. As it is, the force is stretched thin across the centre of town. Dragoons have been mustered, and cannon set and loaded outside Buckingham House. But as to the present redoubt, we will have to make do with what we can."

"A dozen is a small number," said Holmes. He rubbed his face with both hands and turned to look back across the bridge. "But then again, having seen – having experienced – the magnitude of the crowd, I fear even a hundred men would not be enough."

A carriage came rattling down Saint George Street, and rolled to a stop, across the northward side of the bridge. Holmes was surprised to see the crest of Sir Persimmon Hawk on the side of the vehicle, and more surprised when Sir Percy himself stepped through the carriage door.

"Would have been here sooner," the baronet barked, "but there was a shocking press of paupers through the streets. Only now are the roads clear enough for my cart to come through. Chartists, what?"

"Quite correct, Sir Percy," said Bucket, calmly. "A large gathering of agitators south of the river. We believe they will soon be marching on Parliament, so as to present their petition for political reform."

"Petition my eye," cried Sir Percy, crossly. "Petition my belt and breeches. They mean nothing so mild. They're revolutionaries – anarchists and smashers. The Luddites are back, I hear? It's upheaval on a dreadful scale."

"That's as may be, Sir Percy," said Bucket. "But I must ask you to remove yourself from this scene. I cannot undertake for your safety once the mob start coming across this bridge. They will, it is only too likely, be no respecters of rank or seniority. They may outrage your person, destroy your carriage – it would be best for you to return to your house, and barricade the door."

"Nonsense!" said Hawk. "I'm a justice of the peace, what?"

"Notwithstanding your civic responsibilities and roles," Bucket continued, in the same measured, unaggressive, irresistible tone, " which nobody respects more than I, Sir Percy, I must ask you to take a withdraw from this particular arena."

"You think I'm *scared*," barked the baronet, "of a rabble of geese?"

"Sir Percy," Holmes inserted. "I don't mean to presume, for you and I are hardly intimates. But I am obliged to report that I have just myself fled from the nexus of this great gathering – tens of thousands, and possibly hundreds of thousands, of folk, all fired-up with revolutionary fervour, presently having the fires in their engines stoked and heated by incendiary rhetoric from their revolutionary leaders. They will march here, and soon."

This appeared to catch Sir Percy by surprise. "Thousands?" he said. "Tens of thousands, ye say? Surely it is but a gaggle of excitable geese, nothing more?"

"I fear," Inspector Bucket said, gravely, "it is considerably more. I entirely believe Mr Holmes's estimations, as regards numbers."

"Damnation!" ejaculated Sir Percy. "So many? How could you permit such a large body of agitators to assemble, Bucket?"

The Inspector was unflappable: "With a little more advance warning, Sir Percy, it might have been possible to intervene and prevent so dangerous a build-up. However, we must deal with the situation with which we are presented."

"I'll not believe there are so many malcontents and socialists in all London!" Sir Percy declared, loudly. But, as he spoke, Holmes could see that his attention was not upon the Inspector, nor directly at Aster – the secretary of his former partner – nor Holmes. He was instead looking past them at the southern reach of the bridge.

Holmes turned to look. On the surrey shore, a huge milling crowd was apparent. Heads and shoulders, banners carried aloft, spread across the southern bank of the Thames and the first of what was, evidently, a vast army of revolutionary foot soldiers was stepping out onto the southern reach of the bridge.

"Gracious," said Sir Percy, in quite another tone of voice. "Perhaps, Inspector, you are correct. A modicum of discretion, here, might be the better strategy."

"I am pleased, Sir Percy, that you," Bucket began. But the baronet had already shown his back, and then, as he clambered into his carriage, his heels. The door slammed shut, and the sound of Sir Percy knocking his walking stick on the roof of his compartment, to tell his driver to hurry away, was clearly audible.

But there was no driver.

Holmes, afterwards, tried to remember if he had actually seen the carriage driver slip away – alarmed at the size and ferocity of the approaching crowd – or only filled-in that detail after the fact. Either way there they were: with nobody to stir-up the horses, the carriage sat where it had been parked.

"Do you think...?" Holmes asked Aster.

"... that one of us should clamber up there and drive Sir Percy's carriage?" completed Aster. "But, Holmes, I don't know how."

"Nor I."

"Gentlemen," said Bucket, standing foresquare to meet the advancing crowd. "The time for such shifts is behind us."

There was no more time. The cheering throng was pouring across the bridge. Poles and pikes jabbed at the air in amongst the scarlet banners. It came to Holmes that so vast a press of people would simply sweep them away, as a mountain avalanche blasts though fences made of stick. It was perfectly useless simply to stand there. And yet neither he nor Aster moved.

"Mr Holmes," said Bucket, imperturbably. "If you cannot drive Sir Percy's carriage, perhaps you could at least lead the horses by their bridles, and so move it out of the immediate path of this advancing crowd. Otherwise I fear it will be upended, and trampled."

"Yes," said Holmes, breaking from his reverie. "Yes of course." As he stepped over towards the horses he heard Bucket order his small detachment of policemen into a line. It seemed so extraordinarily futile a thing to do that Holmes almost laughed. He put his hand on the rein where it dangled from the bit of the nearest horse and clucked at the beast. "Come along. Let's be on our way."

But he did not move, for, looking back at the bridge, he was arrested by an unprecedented sight. There was Bucket, and his dozen men, forming a thin line across the bridge's egress. Aster stood behind this line, his right hand in his jacket pocket. Holmes for a moment wondered if he had a pistol in there, although he also considered the perfect uselessness of such a weapon against so multifarious an adversary.

The petitioners formed a solid phalanx and advanced determinedly until they were so close that Holmes could make out the individual teeth in their grinning mouths and could see the wrinkles at the side of their eyes. The cheering grew in volume. Staffs were being waved. A stone flew, hurled out of the mob. It clattered onto the ground, before Holmes. Then another was thrown – and another. One of the policemen was struck on the chest, but the fellow didn't flinch. Half a brick soared, came down – half a brick, half a brick onwards – and caught Holmes on the side of his head. Holmes staggered backwards, more startled than stunned. He rubbed his cranium, stepped forward again.

The bridge was empty. Or was it? Holmes looked again. The crowd was there, coming from the far end. And they were still coming, marching aggressively straight towards him.

They came in noise and tumult, the sound swelling again like a crashing sea, the poles and banners bouncing and waving over their heads. Why had he thought the bridge was empty? Was it the knock on his head?

Again the crowd advanced across the bridge, a more confused crush, a mass. Holmes walked forward to get a better look at what was happening. On the far bank the crush of people, coming up from Kennington, continued to grow. It was as if the advance party crossing the bridge reached the Middlesex bank, and somehow returned again to the Surrey shore, where they found themselves in a more crowded place, and fewer of them could fight through the mass to get back onto the bridge. But how were they returning so rapidly? Why were they retreating in such a fashion? How had they not crossed over the bridge entirely? Holmes could not comprehend.

It was baffling. The men at the front of the advancing group lowered their pikes and broke into a run – and just before they broke against the line of policemen they were gone.

The group started across the bridge, but the crowd upon the way was smaller, somehow, diminished in numbers, and from their expressions as they approached a degree of confusion had passed through their ranks. On the far bank the crowd had become an effective log jam, preventing the many people behind from coming any closer. The advanced guard reached the line of policemen and, straight away, were back on the far side again.

By now it was not possible to co-ordinate a march over the bridge: there were simply too many people crowded into the space on the Surrey side. Indeed Holmes watched as people were shoved, or squeezed, over the balustrade to fall into the Thames, and splash their way unhappily back to shore; others spilled out along the bankside, or were lifted and carried over the heads of people. It was a mess – a crush – a blockage comprised of raw humanity.

For long minutes, Bucket stood, his hands behind his back, as the crowd slowly disintegrated on the far bank. Some made their way northwards, to hurry round the bend of the river and cross at the Strand Bridge – the tollbooths were empty, and the bridge was unguarded. But too few made their way to be a threat, and those that crossed dissipated into the centre of town. More simply retreated back to the Common at Kennington. Over the course of the next hour, the whole gathering melted away.

Holmes came back over to Bucket. "What happened?" he asked. "What did I just witness?"

"Commendations, men," Bucket told his officers. "You held firm, and rebuffed them."

"But," Holmes said. "You surely saw the same thing I saw, Bucket! You saw the crowd approach and then, as if whisked away by a genie from the Arabian lamp, return instantly to the far shore – did you not see that?"

Bucket turned his face, slowly, to Holmes. "Mr Holmes," he said, in a deliberate and measured tone. "I can tell you what I saw. I saw my men hold firm, and the rioters returned to the far side of the river. That is what I saw."

"But the *manner* of their return!" Holmes insisted. "It was not a regular retreat on foot."

"Of course it was," said Bucket. "How else could it have been?"

"Inspector, I implore you – ask yourself – is that truly what you saw?"

"I can hardly have seen anything else, Mr Holmes."

"It is not what I saw!"

"Come now," said Bucket. "Be reasonable. Surely you do not mean to impugn the courage of my men? Standing firm as the mob advanced, their steadfastness deterred the riotous assemblage from proceeding."

"I mean no disrespect, no disrespect at all, Inspector. I only appeal to the evidence of your own eyes."

"My eyes can hardly have observed an impossible thing, Mr Holmes."

"Aster!" Holmes cried. "You saw it – didn't you?"

"I'm not entirely sure what I saw," said Aster, uncertainly. "Though, like the Inspector, I commend the courage of these police constables."

"Mr Holmes, forgive me," said Bucket, all uncertainty now banished from his expression. "I must advert to the strain under which you have been labouring: you suffered a trauma, seeing your friend killed in front of you, mere feet away, some few weeks ago. A horrible and destabilising thing to see. Your account of that accident was, as we must be honest with one another, bizarre, improbable – a vision of nightmare, occasioned by the shock you had suffered. Since then you have been hither and yon, and suffered more stresses and strains. Might you accept that your sensorium has been, for understandable reasons, disarranged by all you have been through?"

"Aster –" Holmes pressed. "You know it is not so simple. You know!"

"I'm honestly not sure," said Aster, looking distressed.

At this juncture the door to Sir Percy Hawk's carriage smacked open, and the baronet's head emerged. "Have they gone then?" he boomed. "I knew it – mere geese. Scotch mist. Cowards!"

"I am pleased to report, Sir Percy, that my men stood firm."

"Turned and ran, did they?" the baronet called. "I daresay the sight of my carriage, blocking their way, dissuaded them! Not just a cart, but a fine carriage bearing a baronet's device on its side – that surely cowed them into retreating."

"No doubt," Bucket said, diplomatically.

"No question. Mere geese! Fools." The baronetal head withdrew into the carriage and shut the door. There was the sound of Sir Percy banging on the roof of his compartment with his walking stick, for he seemed to have forgotten that his driver had absented himself. There was a pause, and then the door opened again. "Inspector, might I trouble you – perhaps one of your men could drive my carriage back to my house? My driver seems to have run off."

"Of course, Sir Percy," said Bucket. "Armstrong: you can drive the carriage, I think?"

"Yes Inspector."

Holmes watched all this with an increasing feeling of unreality: a corrosive sensation that the world was not cohering after the logic of common sense the way it should. Bucket's certainty, and Aster's refusal to back him up, were causing him to doubt what he had just seen. But he *had* seen it! – hadn't he?

"Come Mr Holmes," said Bucket, approaching him. "I suggest you return home. I am no doctor, but surely a period of rest and recuperation would be advisable, to restore the balance of your mind."

"Perhaps," said Holmes. "Perhaps you are correct."

Chapter 9

THE SOLUTION THAT IS NO SOLUTION

1

Holmes walked, or staggered, back through town until he again reached his lodgings. Young Mrs Hudson, opening the door, wept with sheer relief to see him again. "Oh Mr Holmes! I was sure you were to be swallowed up by that mob!"

"The mob has dissipated, Mrs Hudson," Holmes said. "It seems – though I can hardly believe it myself – that the authorities mustered enough men to dissuade the crowd from becoming a mob, and now the various individual people are scattering, back to their homes, or workplaces, or wherever it was from whence they came."

"That's very good news Mr Holmes!"

"Indeed. And now, my dear woman, I am exhausted – perfectly exhausted. I am going to sleep."

He removed his hat and jacket and sat on the bed to push each shoe off with the toe of the other foot. Then he slumped, and slept for twelve hours in his remaining clothes.

When he awoke he was in a dark, silent space. The two windows of his room – he had omitted to draw the curtains – were starting to thin the darkness into pre-dawn gleam. He fumbled to where he had hung his jacket, on the back of a chair, and pulled out his half-hunter: still ticking, but it was hard to read the face in the dimness. It was some time before dawn.

Holmes lay back. His thoughts reverted to all that had happened over the preceding days. Twenty-four hours earlier he had been in the woodland, to the north-west of the city, pursued by violent agitators – revolutionaries, followers of Queen Ludd. Had it really happened? How had he escaped? He recalled the train ride into town, and Griffin's elaborate and improbable account of himself. Was he truly an invisible man? Or had it been a mere mode of magic-trick, a theatrical routine – perhaps Griffin lacked a left hand, amputated following an accident. Had he removed his prosthesis in order to trick Holmes into believing he was invisible? Which was more likely: that he *was* invisible, or that he was visible flesh-and-blood like everyone else, and was trying to confuse and baffle Holmes? Put aside for a moment the question as to *why* he would do such a thing, and ask only this: *which was the more probable eventuality*? As a man of science, as a man of common sense – and as a man keen to hold on to his sanity – he had to choose the second.

What Holmes knew is that, during that train ride, in that moment, he had believed Griffin's improbable story. What followed? Only that there had been moments, during the previous twenty-four hours, when Holmes had found his sheer credulity stretching, when he had come to believe impossible things. Ergo, the events of the last few days had compromised his rigid good sense and capacity for clear observation and logical deduction. He had been exhausted!

Three things, then. One – he had observed Bryde struck down and trampled by a demonic monster, a bull from hell upon whose back a faceless, glistening, leathery demon had ridden. The rest of the world was certain Bryde had been the victim of an unlucky accident, in which a common-or-garden bull, of the kind which drovers march into London every single day, got loose and ran him down. Which of these two things was more likely?

Two – he had sat in a railway compartment, travelling in toward central London, and observed a man peel off his glove to reveal a hand invisible to sight. Or perhaps this man, by his own confession a man unconstrained by conventional morality, a man who delighted in mocking, fooling and exploiting others, had performed a simple conjurer's trick upon Holmes. Which was more likely?

Three – he had stood at the northern end of Westminster Bridge and watched a marching mob of revolutionaries plucked from their position and transferred, as by the magic hands of genii, back to their starting point on the bridge's far side. Or perhaps the marchers, advancing upon the line of policemen waiting there, had been discouraged, or persuaded to retreat, and had returned to the south bank on their own feet. Which?

Holmes had not *seen* the rioters walk back across the bridge. If he was to trust his eyes, he must find himself in some uncharted territories of scientific possibility. But before he made such a reckless leap, he had to be sure: *could* he trust his own eyes? Were his eyes seeing events as they actually happened? Or were his eyes exhausted, confused, baffled, prone to distorting or even inventing inexistent things?

The last time he had been in town, some ruffians had blown a powder in his face. This powder had certainly had an effect upon him. It was a mere soporific, according to Griffin. But Aster had agreed with Holmes that it might have possessed hallucinogenic characteristics.

The light at the windows was stronger now, though still the dim of pre-dawn. Holmes rose, fetched himself a bowl of water from the pump, and lit a candle next to the mirror so as to shave. Then he washed. By the time he had dressed in fresh clothes, Mrs Hudson was awake. He could hear her moving about downstairs.

From then on, events slipped back into their usual groove, and Holmes found the strangenesses he had witnessed – which he *believed*, perhaps erroneously, he had seen – recede into further dubiety. Holmes descended and ate the breakfast which Mrs Hudson served him. She brought him the morning paper, and he sat and smoked a cigar in his parlour whilst reading it. The shift was palpable, as if something had reordered itself in the logic of the cosmos.

The newspaper gave a detailed account of the Chartist meeting and subsequent events.

CHARTIST AGITATION. A large and determined crowd assembled yesterday on the unenclosed portion of Kennington Common, on the south side of the city. Their declared aim was to present a large petition to the House of Commons demanding their Charter be implemented, though there is little doubt, from the military order with which the crowd marched, and the fact that many were carrying poles, pike and other implements of belligerent intention, that their true aim was violence. The object undoubtedly was to make such a parade of physical force as should overawe the Legislature and the Government, and demonstrate the impossibility of refusing a demand backed by such a reserve of power. This procession on Parliament was declared illegal, and all peaceful and loyal subjects were warned not to take any part in it. The advance of this mob was arrested on the northern portion of Westminster Bridge by the firm and immoveable opposition of a squad of London policemen, and the crowd, repulsed, returned to Kennington and there largely dispersed. The coolness and presence of mind of these officers of the law was commended by the Duke of Wellington. The petition was eventually delivered to the main entrance of the House of Commons, although carried there by one man, William Cuffay, also known as the King of Carts, rather than

by the entire gathering; Mr Cuffay was accompanied by half
a dozen co-conspirators, and afterwards evaded the attentions
of the police and is presently believed to be in Essex. Of the
purported six million signatures upon this petition, officers of
Parliament report that fewer than two million are genuine,
with many pages written in the same hand throughout, and
including such signatories as Her Royal Highness the Queen,
the Duke of Wellington, Pugnose and No-Cheese.

There was no intimation, in any part of the paper, of the
strangeness Holmes had seen on the bridge – the strangeness
he had *believed himself* to have witnessed. Had it only been the
confusion of being struck by that projectile upon the head?

"To think," Mrs Hudson said, bringing through the post,
which had just been delivered, "that I was so alarmed
yesterday! It seems the authorities have very swiftly dealt
with the dangers of popular uprising."

"It does seem so," Holmes agreed, stubbing out his cigar
and looking through the correspondence. There was a note
from Gwendolin which, of course, he opened immediately.

Dearest – I am so relieved to hear from you! I've taken Mycroft
home, for the capital no longer seemed safe, and will wait for
you here. Yours, Gwendolin.

He leapt up. "Mrs Hudson, I must immediately leave for the
country."

"Very good, Mr Holmes."

Holmes gathered a travelling bag, and hurried out to the
Post Inn, where he bought passage in a stagecoach heading
down to Hampshire that very morning. By sunset he was
embracing his wife, and dandling his son upon his knee, and
the world shifted further in the direction of normality. Of
the ordinary, the common-sensical, the regular.

That night, with a full belly, and contentment in his

heart, Holmes slept a deep and refreshing sleep. When he awoke the next day all the bizarreness he had experienced in the previous week seemed nothing more than the memory of a dream. Perhaps, as Bucket had intimated, he had suffered so traumatic an experience, witnessing Bryde's death, that the balance of his mind had been disturbed. After all: everything strange seemed to stem from that event, when he looked back at it. And here, home again, surrounded by the people he loved most in the world, reinhabiting the old routines of life, eating, reading, fishing, playing backgammon with Gwendolin – here the nonsense of the previous week receded almost to the point of invisibility.

He could not, however, stay in the countryside forever. His work was waiting, and his work was in London. And so, although the prospect filled him with a quantity of dread, Holmes packed up a travelling bag, kissed his son and his sphere-bellied wife farewell and travelled back into the metropolis.

2

Upon returning to the capital, Holmes made three calls. The first was a visit to Inspector Bucket, at Scotland Yard.

He found the Inspector at his desk, working a pen slowly but unstintingly across successive sheets of paper. "Good day, Mr Holmes," he said, looking up.

"Inspector, I apologise for intruding."

"Please: take a seat."

Holmes, arranging his coat tails, sat down. "I promise not to take up too much of your time. In point of fact, I have come to discover the state of the official investigation."

"You mean, the investigation into the death of Sir Martin Malprelate?"

"And also Bryde."

"Of course."

"Bryde was my friend. I regard the investigation into Sir Martin's death as a continuation of his incomplete work, a task taken up in his honour, if you see what I mean," added Holmes.

"The official status of the case is that we have our suspect in view."

"The case is effectively closed?"

"It is the view of Her Majesty's metropolitan police that the murder of Sir Martin Malprelate was an assassination, motivated by political and terroristical aims. Subsequent events at Kennington Common, and on Westminster Bridge, were, we believe, merely the continuation of the events that resulted in the death of Sir Martin, the propinquity of the one and the other being no mere coincidence."

"And so your suspect is William Cuffay? The Cart-King?"

"We believe him to be in Essex, fomenting further disorder. But we believe we shall have him, soon, in custody. His trial will at the least lead to an order for transportation to Australia. Possibly he will hang, for if we can gather enough evidence, we may yet charge him with orchestrating Sir Martin's murder."

"I see," said Holmes. "And those reports of a demonic locomotive...?"

"Those reports have only grown more outlandish and incredible over time. That in itself is the operation of gossip, and fevered speculation, and it points to the fundamental exaggeration of the original story. Witnesses saw an armed gang, shouting and swinging lanterns, perhaps riding on board a cart, running Sir Martin down and beating him to death. The lateness of the hour, the fog, the suddenness and ghastliness of the crime, and above all Sir Martin's reputation, the prior rumours of diabolic association, all contributed to a phantasm: an interpretation of the ordinary as supernatural."

"It is," Holmes was forced to concede, "a persuasive explanation."

"It does not diminish the horror of the crime," said Bucket. "On the contrary, it intensifies it. Not painted devils cavorting, like mummers from a medieval miracle play, but actual men, human beings, destroying the life of a fellow man."

"And this investigation is regarded as separate to the inquiry into Bryde's death?"

"I am sorry, Mr Holmes," said the Inspector. "I know he was your friend, and I appreciate that you are yourself a material witness to that tragic demise. But the official line is that Mr Bryde was crushed by a bull, run rampant. Several other witnesses reported as much, and though your own account was more – ornate, shall we say – you were, at base, reporting the same thing. You saw a something, of the size and ferocity of an angry bull, and you saw it collide with Mr Bryde and crush him. That you insist it was *not* a bull, but something much more phantastical, speaks, I suggest, less to the identity of the agent, and more to the state of your own mind: – the sudden and unexpected shock, the profundity of grief. I do not seek to contradict you, Mr Holmes; and certainly I would not give you the lie. But I would suggest you consider whether such a derangement of the senses and the fertility and adaptability of memory, might not have generated the more interesting, less insultingly mundane and accidental, account?"

Holmes nodded. "Believe me, Inspector: recent events have caused me to question the veracity of my own sensorium: my senses, my memory. It is an alarming thing for a man of science to confess, but there is, after all, all the difference in the world between an improbable and an impossible thing. And it would be arrogance to insist upon my own absolute infallibility."

"This is wisdom, Mr Holmes."

"Have you tracked down the bull?"

"We have questioned a number of Smithfield drovers, and they report that bulls and cows do sometimes break free and run through the streets. No-one confesses that *their* bull broke free, for to do so would be to admit liability in Mr Bryde's tragic demise, and lead to prosecution. But there we have it. For an animal habituated to the countryside, the noise and confinement and strangeness of the city can be an upsetting experience."

"It seems," said Holmes, "that the mysteries have mundane solutions. Perhaps the time for my investigative endeavours has passed. I am only sorry that I was not able to uncover information of use to you. Before I go, though: might I press you?"

"Concerning what?"

"The events at the bridge? We were both there, after all. I saw, or believed I saw, something impossible. You did not."

"No," said Bucket.

"What did you see? Precisely?"

For a moment there was an uncertain look in Bucket's eye. But he smiled, and folded his hands together, and said, in his usual, level tone: "I saw the rioters approach, then turn back and retreat, discouraged from further advance by the line of policemen standing there."

"Forgive me, Inspector: but for absolute clarity. Did you see – do you distinctly remember seeing – those men walking back across the bridge?"

"They must have walked," Bucket said. "Lacking wings, they can hardly have flown."

"Without wishing to be offensive Inspector, I must, as I say, press you. Did you see, do you have the memory of distinctly *seeing* those people retreating on foot across that bridge?"

Bucket looked at him. "Mr Holmes," he said. "As you yourself said, it would be arrogance to pretend that I have an absolutely objective or godlike perspective on the universe.

To be a detective is to work with witness statements, and to do that requires understanding how subjective any perception or observation is. It would assist my work if such things were guaranteed objective and true, but such is not the nature of sublunary humanity. Accordingly we must parse statements by witnesses by coordinating them with *other* evidence: not only physical specifics but, as you say, the constraints of both possibility and probability. Certainly, on that day, a mob advanced across the bridge towards us. We both saw that. We also saw that they went no further, but rather retreated to the far side of the river. That is enough."

"Thank you for your time, Inspector," said Holmes. "I bid you good day."

Holmes made his way out of Scotland Yard and walked up Whitehall towards the city. He walked slowly, allowing his mind to run-on. Frost sparkled on the stonework. His breath fluttered in the air like spectral feathers. Putting on his gloves as he walked, he thought again of his train ride with Griffin. It had been in his mind to report the whole conversation to Bucket, as something germane to the larger investigation. But he could not think of how to frame it in any way except that it sounded insane. And since the investigation was, in effect, concluded, to the satisfaction of the authorities, Holmes did not see how his report would benefit the Inspector.

It was unsatisfactory. But life is not obliged to supply us with satisfaction. Not every mystery has a neat and logical solution.

Holmes came, in time, to the main gate of Sir Percy Hawk's London residence – for this was his second appointment in the capital.

The butler showed Holmes through to a room in which a fire was dining brightly upon its meal of coal. He stood, slipping out of his overcoat and plucking off his gloves, thinking once again of Griffin. How *had* he played his trick?

To make it appear he was an Invisible Man? Perhaps, Holmes told himself, he ought to seek out a stage magician, some expert in prestidigitation, obtain a professional opinion on such things. He handed his coat and gloves to the butler, and stood with his back to the fire.

Sir Percy came striding through some minutes later. "Holmes!" he barked. "Good news that this business of Malprelate's demise has been cleared-up, what?"

"I have just come from an interview with Inspector Bucket," said Holmes. "He certainly believes it to be only a matter of time before Cuffay, the King of Carts, is arrested. And with that the investigation will be officially concluded."

"Not before time," the baronet declared. "What a load of stuff, what a heap of nonsense, the aftermath of that grisly business threw up! But it was as I always said: of course – some political agitator, socialist, vegetarians, anarchists. Trouble makers. When they apprehend this Cuffay fellow, I hope they hang him in Parliament Square, as a warning to the others."

"I am, I must say, less sanguinary in my desires. And I cannot entirely believe that the arrest of Mr Cuffay will draw a line underneath the entire affair."

"Nonsense, nonsense," said Sir Percy, tetchily. "Let it go, man. That's your problem: always poking and squirrelling into things. It's your nature, I know: it's part of your process as a technician and scientist. But on *this* matter – the less said the better. The purpose of Malprelate's assassination was to rile up the common folk, to agitate the mob, to terrorise the ruling caste. It is our duty to resist such a programme, and feeding the wider speculation only keeps it alive."

"As for my process – as, in your words, a technician and scientist – I am here to report that I have made very little progress."

"Process?" Sir Percy barked. "Progress?"

"I have just returned from Hampshire, where my wife is very close to term."

"Ah, yes! Your second child, I think?"

"Just so. I have spent a week doing nothing. And before that, certain events occurred that have taken the wind from my sails."

"Events? What d'ye mean?"

"It is concerning that that I wished to speak with you, Sir Percy."

"You're telling me you're no closer to supplying the galvanic device? That's disappointing, disappointing, but if you've hit a brick wall then it's best to be honest. Perhaps we can find somebody else to manufacture the machine. You can surely recommend a fellow toiler in the electrical fields?"

"I can certainly proffer the names of some very able men. But that is not what I am here to discuss, Sir Percy."

"No?"

"I am here to ask after Mr Griffin."

At the mention of that name, the baronet's visage darkened visibly. The corners of his mouth drove down, and his brow contracted. "That rascal," he boomed. "Have you seen him?"

"Do I take it, you haven't?"

"Point him out and I'll take a horsewhip to him. The scoundrel! Gone – cleared out, God knows where. And taken some of my most valuable equipment with him! Absconded with all his geegaws, and some of mine too."

"Dear me. Have you informed the police?"

"And have to detail all the pieces that are stolen? How can I do that without betraying their secrecy. No, no, I've employed my own agent to hunt the fellow down. And when we find him, I shall administer justice myself, by my own hand."

"Sir Percy," said Holmes. "I must report a conversation that Mr Griffin had with me, a week since."

"Aye? What did he say?"

"I am in the difficult position of, perhaps, seeming to violate a confidence – I don't mean Griffin's, but yours. You and he have been building a particular machine of your own, and you have always been clear that you do not wish to share the nature or identity of that device with me, or for me to say anything at all regarding it to the rest of the world. Naturally I respect your privacy, and have kept your confidence. All I know is what you have told me: that it must receive a certain, large quantum of galvanic power, and that I, having worked for years in that field, were to construct a generator capable of supplying that. Beyond such specification, I am wholly ignorant as to the nature or purpose of the machine you and Griffin are building."

"Go on," growled Sir Percy. He was looking ferociously at his interlocutor.

"I will not weary you with an over-long narrative. Suffice to say that Mr Aster, Sir Martin's former secretary, and I came to suspect that Griffin was spying upon us."

"I wouldn't put it past him! He's a blackguard."

"Did you not request he check-up on Bryde?"

"What? No no – just go along, encourage him in his investigations. But that's ancient history now, since the fellow died. And I never set him to spy on you!"

"He did, though. I saw him, and followed him through certain streets and then lost him. Here I was drugged, as I believe: a powder blown in my face that certainly had a soporific effect upon me, and perhaps worked in other ways upon my brain as well. At any rate I have a lacuna in my memory. The next thing: I was in Middlemarch."

"Extraordinary! You think Griffin did this to you?"

"He all but confessed as much, Sir Percy. Then, returning from the midlands to London, I was pursued by agents of the same upheaval we witnessed in Kennington Common. I managed to evade them, and caught a train at Watford.

Upon this journey I shared a compartment with Griffin, and he said a number of things to me."

"I see," said the baronet, coldly. "What did he say? Pray, in your relation, bear in mind that the man is a scoundrel, a liar and a defamer."

"This is my difficulty, Sir Percy. By relating what he said it may appear that I am asking you to confirm or deny his claims, which in turn would be to trespass upon the confidentiality which you have made the basis of our working relations."

"Oh spit it out, Holmes! Enough of this over-nice equivocation. We are men, are we not? Can we not speak straight to one another."

"There is another consideration," Holmes said. "Much of what he said was, frankly, incredible."

"Ah. Did he show himself to you? His actual self?"

"He removed one of his gloves," said Holmes.

"Startling, what? It took me a while to get used to it, I don't mind telling you. Invisibility!"

Holmes's heart galloped. "So it's true? He actually is transparent?"

"As glass," said the baronet. He took a step, and pulled the servant bell. "Will ye have a drink, Holmes? I feel this to be a conversation best lubricated with some brandy."

"It is a cold day, Sir Percy, this roaring fire notwithstanding. A little spirit would be most agreeable."

The butler returned and left again with this order for potation. The baronet sat himself in an easy chair, and, at his invitation, Holmes sat on the other side of the fireplace.

"It's the damnedest thing," said Sir Percy. "When *he* drinks, or eats, you see the matter slide down his invisible gullet and pool in his invisible guts. I've watched with my own eyes! Then, over time, it is absorbed into his flesh and so disappears from sight."

"He is wholly invisible?" Holmes asked.

"Not wholly. His retinas are only semi-transparent."

"The retinas of his eyes?"

"Oh yes. If the backs of his eyes were clear like the rest of him, he'd be blind. You see? Which is to say: *he* wouldn't." At this, Sir Percy chuckled. "The light wouldn't strike the retinas, what? He tells me that he didn't anticipate this, and the original treatment he gave himself left him sightless! He had to fumble around concocting a remedy for that, which he then injected into his own eyeballs. Can you imagine it! Sliding the needle up the tear-duct, he said. It's a kind of permanent dye, of a violet colour, that brings some functionality back to his eyes. The way he described it to me is: he can see, though not with the clarity or precision with which he used to, when he was The Visible Man. And it seems, two violet patches, not much bigger than a thumbnail, are not often noticed by other folk, when he chooses to go about naked and invisible. It's not the sort of thing a person would expect to see, hanging six feet above the ground, is it. And that's the really crucial thing: people mostly see what they *expect* to see. And if they see something that they don't expect, that doesn't make sense or which they can't compute, why then in nine cases out of ten they don't see it at all."

The butler returned, with a tray, two glasses and a bottle of Burgundian Brandy, and set them down on the low table beside the fireplace. Toasting "good health" Sir Percy downed his in a single swig, and immediately poured himself another.

"And what of his other claim, Sir Percy?" Holmes asked, sipping his own.

"Other claim?"

"He spoke of time travel."

"Oho," said the baronet, in a very low growl indeed. "He spilled *those* beans, did he?"

"That was why we went to Middlemarch, it seems. He

wished to meet his younger self. Although the meeting appears to have occasioned what electrical engineers call a short-circuit."

"He was trying to recruit you," said Sir Percy. "He was trying to get you to supply him with the galvanic engine, and to cut me out of the process altogether. The dog! Horsewhipping is too good for him."

"My memory of our conversation is very gappy. I do not recall exactly what we talked of."

"Trust me. That will have been his purpose."

"Now that you say so, it makes sense."

"I'll flay him!" Sir Percy bellowed. "But you *didn't* supply him with what he wanted, what?"

"As I mentioned, Sir Percy, I have made no progress on my generator over these last several weeks."

"That's right," the baronet returned, calmer. "You said so. Well that must have been a disappointment to the rat."

"Sir Percy I confess to you, I have effectively discarded these things from my mind. I told myself I only *thought* I remembered them – that my memory was in some sense contaminated by phantasy. But now it seems that all is true."

"The invisibility is true," said the baronet. "That I will affirm. As for the rest: I am not so sure."

"There is no time travel?"

"Mr Holmes, my disinclination to broadcast the nature of my researches was, in part, a selfish desire to keep its fruits to myself. This I confess. But it was also motivated by a desire that posterity not take me for a fool. Griffin gave me reasons to believe his story. He told me he had travelled here from the year 1900, backwards through time, in a machine built by another man."

"He told me the same."

"Well, I believed him! Or at least I was prepared to give him the benefit of the doubt. He told me the machine was broken by his transit – he declared himself unsure what he had done wrong. But there was no complete, functioning machine. There were only components. Some of these displayed remarkable properties, to be sure. But Griffin was not able to present me with a functioning machine for travelling in time, though he promised me – if only I supplied enough money, and we worked together, and could attach a suitable galvanic power source – that he would."

"And you joined him, in the work? You supplied the funds needful and partnered his work?"

"A sensible man would doubt so extraordinary a story – but then again, what if it be true? Only think of it, Holmes! A machine in which I could pass forwards and backwards in time, as I wished! I could travel into the future and learn the secrets of their advances! Or I could step back in time, a year, a week, even a day, and intervene to alter things to my advantage." Sir Percy caught Holmes's eye. "To *our* advantage, I mean. To make the world better."

"Griffin told me," Holmes said, "that the Chartist uprising was inevitable, but that we could ameliorate it, if we intervened. He spoke of terrors to come: bloody revolution, civil war. Perhaps we have averted such a fate?"

"Or perhaps Mr Griffin is a mere fraud? Perhaps he spins a beguiling story without regard to the truth? Invisible he may be – but chancing upon the chemicals to render himself invisible in the year of our lord 1900? Why not in the year of our lord 1840? Sweeping you up to Middlemarch, of all places, to meet his so-called younger self? Bunkum. Gammon. I say it with a grim expression upon my grim face, Mr Holmes, for it paints me as a fool – a plain fool – an old-fashioned fool – for believing him in the first place. But does one marvel, his transparency of flesh, truly licence another marvel: a machine for passing through time?" Sir Percy shook his heavy head. "I chose to believe his story and now that he has robbed me and disappeared I am revealed as the old fool I am."

"His time-travel story," Holmes said, "mere fiction?"

"The broken-up components of what he claimed was a time machine: it did not work. It was, as a whole, dysfunctional. With my help – and money – we could repair it, he said. And then once it was remade, we would share it. Now, I am not an *absolute* fool. I examined the components he carried, in detail. They looked like no other engineering I have seen. Some of those components manifested peculiar and fascinating properties: of course, they could only operate when fed a galvanic charge, and such batteries as I was able to obtain were not enough to power it fully."

"Hence you approached me."

"I suppose I allowed my hopes to overcome my caution. But perhaps the way to think of it was: if you could provide the power source that Griffin insisted the machine required, then we would be able to see if it worked, as Griffin swore it could. If not, then the question would be settled."

"You now think the machine a hoax?"

"One extraordinary thing – Griffin's invisibility – does not guarantee another extraordinary thing. Griffin is a freak, a man transparent to visible light. But he is a man, and greedy, and ruthless, unconstrained by the trappings of morality. Of course he would lie, to access my money. It is a confidence trick, pure and simple."

"Yet he took the equipment with him when he decamped? You mentioned that those pieces, fragments of the whole machine – "

" – What he claimed were fragments of the whole machine – "Sir Percy put in.

" – but you mentioned that they did exhibit certain properties. Might there be something of worth in them?"

"I think not. They were Griffin's props, his stage-set. I daresay there are some fancy clockwork inside, or something similar. But they were there to fool me. He is welcome to them, to port them over to his next victim. But..." and here,

Sir Percy gritted his teeth, "I will horsewhip him, nonetheless, when I find him. What do you think, Holmes? When the blood flows from his lacerated back, will it come visible? Once it has left his corpus, d'ye think it'll retain the transparency?"

Holmes shook his head, not wanting to be drawn into the baronet's more bloodthirsty speculations. He put his glass down. "Thank you for your time, Sir Percy."

"Onward," said Sir Percy. "I still have the railway company to run. And without Sir Martin getting in my way, I think I'll be able to run it rather better."

"I suppose you have no further need for my galvanic generator?"

"What-what? No, I suppose not. You say you haven't worked on it for a number of weeks? I suppose you haven't incurred any further expense, then."

"I don't believe I have."

"A shame. It would have been glorious – if only the time machine had been a real thing. If ye do find extraneous expense, as you wrap-up your workshop, send an invoice to my estate accountant. As you've been doing."

"I do not anticipate any need to draw upon your generous emolumentary support, Sir Percy."

"Yes, yes," said the baronet, draining a third glass of brandy in one go, as if it were an oyster. "A damnable shame. But there we are."

"There," Holmes agreed, "we are."

"If you come across information as to where the rascal is," was Sir Percy's parting shot, "Or if he contacts you again – tell me, will ye? I have, as I said, men out looking for him. But it would be a service to humanity to capture and punish the beggar. What?"

Holmes walked out and, as he reached the street corner, he stopped. For a moment he dallied, putting on his gloves, fixing his scarf in place, looking around. What if Griffin were there with him, right now? Truly an Invisible Man? But in weather so cold, how would he avoid freezing to death? "No," Holmes said to himself. "I think only extreme need would compel him to come out, clothesless, in weather such as this."

Confident that he was not being observed, or at least confident that the balance of probabilities indicated as much, Holmes walked on. As he went he pondered further. For such a being, invisible to sight but only when he went naked, life would assume seasonal rhythms. He might walk about a great deal in the summer, but loiter indoors in the cold of the winter. "Or," Holmes thought to himself, "he might migrate to the tropics, where the weather is clement all year round."

Holmes considered other constraints. The Invisible Man could not go abroad when it rained, for the falling droplets would indicate by their absence and splash precisely where he was. The same would be true of snow, and indeed fog – for surely, even an invisible man would disturb and stir up the fog as he walked, and so betray his position. And his breath would be visible, in the cold. The more Holmes thought, the more constrained he realised Griffin's life must be. There was, perhaps, some comfort in that thought.

3

Holmes's third social call was an agreement to dine, at his club, with Aster.

"My dear friend!" Aster exclaimed, leaping up as Holmes came in. "How are things at home? Are you a father for a second time?"

"Not yet," said Holmes, shaking his friend's hand; "but it will not be long now."

The two went through to the dining room and took their table. As the courses were brought and removed, Aster talked about the events of that memorable day, escaping Queen Ludd's men and making it eventually to Westminster Bridge. Holmes did not press his friend on exactly what he had seen, although he did mention that he had asked Bucket precisely that question.

"And what did the Inspector say?"

"I feel his mind is too rational and common-sensical to digest the sight of something that is – I must confess it – strictly impossible. He insists he saw the Chartists retreating on foot back across the bridge."

"As you say, Vavasour," Aster replied. "If we are to live our lives in sanity, we must, when faced with a choice between the probable and the impossible, choose the former."

"I shall not quiz you on what exactly you saw," said Holmes, blowing some of the heat away from the coin of hot soup cradled in his soup spoon. "It does a kind of violence, I fear, to compel people to admit impossibilities. Mm! The leek is excellent."

Aster tasted his, nodding. "Inspector Bucket is satisfied, then, that Sir Martin's death is down to probable, not impossible, causes?"

"The investigation is in effect concluded. Political agitators assassinated the railway magnate, as one of what are, I am assured, a spread of violent acts and vandalisms that prefaced the big gathering at Kennington. The ringleaders – and the King of Carts in particular – hoped to generate revolutionary momentum, culminating in their rush on Parliament and seizing control of the country."

"We must be thankful," said Aster, "that their hopes were dashed."

Aster then went on to fill Holmes in on the specifics of his journey from outside Watford, into town. "I escaped my pursuers more by luck than skill. I would make but a poor fox, when the hounds are on my scent. Yet I chanced upon reinforcements making their way into the capital and was able to persuade them to lend me a horse. I arrived at Scotland Yard just as Bucket, and his squad, were leaving the building."

The waiters took away the soup dishes, and brought the main course: fillets de snarke, in raspberry and mustard sauce with turnips and boiled cabbage. The turnips were a little spongy, having been stored since the early autumn, but the tender flesh of the snarkebird had been perfectly roasted, and there was a delicious sweet-savoury *jus de vin rouge* to add moisture and flavour to the dish.

"As for me," said Holmes, "I took the train. And as I mentioned, I had an interview with Mr Griffin – who has now run away, it seems."

"Run away?"

"He was working with Sir Percy Hawk, having assured him that he knew the secret to – "but here Holmes paused, considering himself still bound to the confidentiality he had promised to Sir Percy, even though the machine in question had revealed itself a mere hoax: " – a certain device that interested Sir Percy. But it seems, and I have recently come from Sir Percy's house where we discussed this matter, all to have been a hoax."

"A hoax!"

"Though a strange one – one of the strangest. You see, as I intimated before, Griffin is an invisible man."

"Truly?" Aster asked, wide-eyed.

"I believe so. Hawk considers him a freak of nature – though it seems it was his own scientific endeavours, and not a mere accident of birth, that resulted in him acquiring a transpicuous corpus. At any rate, what I have seen with my own eyes, and what Sir Percy tells me, incline me to believe that Griffin is indeed a man with those unusual properties. But a false fellow, a liar, and fraud!"

"Dear me," said Aster. "And he has robbed Sir Percy?"

"So it seems. Who knows where this Invisible Man is

now? As he and I rode the train into town those weeks ago, he made some large and strange claims."

"Such as?"

"Concerning the coming revolution, and how to avert it. Offering me, like Satan tempting Jesus to turn stones into bread, riches and power if I assisted him in his plans."

"And, like Jesus, you told him to get behind thee?"

"Of course. You understand, he was visible all this time. For he paints his face, and wears glasses and a hat – a scarf and gloves. But at one point he removed his glove and I saw his hand – or rather, I didn't."

"You believe he truly is invisible?"

"I do," said Holmes. "Though I accept it is a strange thing to concede."

"Well," said Aster. "I suppose there are more things in heaven and earth, Horatio – or Holmesatio – than are dreamt of in my philosophy…"

Dessert, and brandy, were brought through. Holmes asked after Aster's own plans.

"Did you know that I have lost my position in the Middlemarch and London Railway Company?"

"I did not!" said Holmes. "I am sorry to hear it."

"Sir Percy plans on running the company in a rather different way to that embraced by my former employer," said Aster, excavating a trench down the middle of his *mousse au chocolat*, unconsciously replicating in miniature the work the labourers were doing in Camden Town. "And he sees no place in his organisation for one such as me."

"What will you do?"

"I was thinking of going abroad. There is talk of building a railway in Egypt – Abbas Pasha has just acceded to the throne, following the death of Ibrahim Pasha earlier this year. Ibrahim was dissuaded from adding railways lines to his country, but his son is much more enthusiastic about progress."

"Egypt!" exclaimed Holmes. "An adventure!"

"I have yet to confirm it – the official announcement has not yet been made. And I daresay the place will be hot and unpleasant. But I will confess to you, Holmes, that I am looking forward to leaving this town. My memories here are mostly painful ones. And you? What will you do, now that Sir Percy no longer requires you to develop your galvanic generator?"

"I might continue the work myself, if I had the funds," said Holmes. "As it is, I will return to my pure research. Something will turn up."

"In a manner of speaking, Sir Percy had dismissed both of us from our employment!"

Holmes laughed. "It has been a strange few weeks, no question about that, my friend. Strange and often upsetting."

"I lost, in Sir Martin, a good man and a humane employer. I would not call him friend, but my heart was sorely bruised at the loss of him. And you – I know Bryde *was* a friend, to you."

"There have been grave losses," Holmes said. "And I cannot pretend I am satisfied with the solution to the mystery, as consensus and the authorities have determined it. But there have been consolations too: meeting you, my friend, in particular. And marvels: imagine, a truly invisible man!"

"To think such a thing is real!"

"I believe so. Sir Percy certainly believes so."

"But do we believe Sir Percy?"

"Why would he lie? How would it benefit him so to do?"

"Holmes, I am aware that my opinion of Sir Percy risks expressing a merely private crotchet of animadversion, for he has always been hostile and unpleasant to me, and now has relieved me of my employment. But I submit to you that, irrespective of my individual experience, he is not a good man – not a virtuous or truthful man."

"He is certainly bad-tempered and short, and sometimes cruel. But do you actually consider him dishonest?"

"He claims he employed Griffin," said Aster. "As you know, I question whether Griffin was his creature, or he Griffin's. He says that Griffin is an Invisible Man – very well. Now he says Griffin was a confidence-man, pretending to offer him some special technology, with the aim of defrauding Hawk of his money."

"Just so."

"But if Griffin truly is an invisible man, why go to such lengths? Why not simply slip out of his visible clothes, sneak into Sir Percy's study – or into his bank – and steal the money directly? Why so circumlocutionary a method of taking the baronet's wealth?"

This had not occurred to Holmes before, but now that Aster had said it, he found himself considering its likelihood. "You think Griffin not likely to be invisible? And that Sir Percy is lying about him?"

"I know that Griffin goes about with his face strangely painted, wearing those glasses, and that he never takes off his gloves. This is equally what an actually invisible man would do, and what a man who wished to give the impression he was invisible would do as well. As to where the truth lies, I cannot say with certainty."

"Griffin might be truly an invisible man, and not truly the owner of the advanced technology he promised Sir Percy."

"If Griffin was a fraud, and the equipment he promised Hawk was just pasteboard, then why would Hawk be upset that it had been stolen?"

This was hard to counter. Holmes asked: "But if the technology is real, and needs the galvanic generator I have been developing in order to operate, why would Sir Percy cancel my work?"

"Perhaps he worries that your work might be completed only for it to fall into the hands of Griffin. If Griffin has the power of invisibility, like a character from Arabian Nights, then surely he would be able to steal your device from you? He might dismiss you merely to prevent such an eventuality."

"I suppose so," Holmes conceded. "But in fact what we are saying is: if Griffin's technology is fake, then Sir Percy would tell me to discontinue my work, for there would be no point in it; but that if Griffin's technology is real, then Sir Percy would also tell me to discontinue my work, to prevent it falling into Griffin's hands. The only thing we can be sure of, in his situation, is that Sir Percy and Griffin have experienced a breach, and are now disposed to one another with hostility."

The two men repaired to the smoking room, to take a cigar each and continue the conversation. Afterwards they walked out together and hailed a cab on the Strand. "Goodnight, Holmes," said Aster. "Goodnight Aster," said Holmes.

4

The reality, or otherwise, of Griffin's invisibility, and the reason why Sir Percy Hawk had instructed Holmes to discontinue work on his generator, was made plain that very night.

Holmes paid his cabbie, and climbed down to his door on a quiet, dark Baker Street. As he stepped towards it he glimpsed, in the coign of his eye, a shark-grey triangle, small as a bat, turn and catch the moonlight, gleaming dimly for a moment a half dozen feet above the ground. Had his brain not been a little stupefied with brandy he might have realised what this meant, but as it was he was only confused.

Then he was struck from behind, a hefty weight pushed hard into him and crashed him up against the door itself. The

triangle whipped around and showed itself to be a knife –
showed itself in the moonlight, and by the pressure it now
exerted against the skin of Holmes's neck.

"Hawk told you to stop work on the generator?" Griffin
hissed, in his ear.

"I," Holmes gasped. "Griffin! – what are you doing?"

"I am making a *demonstration*," said Griffin, his voice
unpleasantly close to Holmes's right ear. "And I am
performing a threat. By these actions I prove to you that I
can find you at any time, in any place, and that you will not
see me coming. I demonstrate that I have no compunction
about cutting your throat. And with this fate I threaten you
– unless you continue manufacturing the generator."

"The time machine," Holmes gasped. "Is real!"

"It needs power to operate fully. And you will supply that
power. If you do, I shall leave you and your family alive. But
if you deny me my power source, or try to thwart me in any
other way, I shall kill you. Am I clear?"

"Clear," said Holmes, "as glass – clear as you yourself are
now."

The knife tightened against Holmes's neck for a moment,
and then Griffin began to laugh. "Very good," he whispered.
"Very funny."

And then the knife was gone – and though Holmes spun
about, and looked, there was no sign of his assailant. He
cocked his head, hoping to hear the sound of Griffin's
footsteps retreating, but the man must have the tread of a
panther. Breathing hard, his heart thundering in his chest,
his hands trembling with the shock and fear of it all, Holmes
turned the key in his doorway and made his way inside.

Chapter 10

NO SOLUTION THAT IS A SOLUTION

1

Though he locked the door, Holmes did not feel safe. He settled his nerves with another drink, and then sat up until after midnight contemplating what next to do. Could he persuade Inspector Bucket of the reality of this threat? Would Bucket not dismiss his bizarre tale of a man invisible to sight, compelling Holmes to work on pain of violence and even death?

He wrote a note to Aster and left it on the table by the door for the boy to take in the morning. Then he went to bed, although sleep was fitful and shallow. What is it Thomas Browne wrote? *It is delivered as an emblem of vigilancy that the hare and lion do sleep with one eye open.* He was hare, not lion, in this case, and the slightest noise or creak in his room, the merest dream-thought of attack, made him jerk awake.

Should he do as Griffin demanded? *Could* he? Say it was all true, and Holmes's work gifted the Invisible Man with the needful to operate a fully-working time-machine: what then? Griffin was a man without morals or scruples, a dangerous, violent man: it could not be right to give him the wherewithal to travel wheresoever he chose in history – the past, the future. What terrible damage might he do? What harm might he inflict?

On the other hand, how could Holmes refuse him? To prevent his own murder, and perhaps violence enacted against his family too? Was such a price not too terrible to pay, merely to thwart one man's desire?

And then Holmes found himself engaged in what he recognised, even as he thought it, motivated reasoning. For whom (he asked himself) would he harm, if he provided Griffin with the power-source he required? Say Griffin used his time machine to go into the past and commit atrocity: he could not *add* to the historical record in that particular, the historical record being fixed. So in what way would Holmes be making the world worse? And what if Griffin chose to go into the future and do the same? From where Holmes sat, these future people were inexistent, not-yet-born, spectral possibilities rather than actual individuals. But he could not satisfy himself that this Pilate-style washing of hands actually absolved him of complicity.

Come now, Vavasour, he told himself. Harm is harm, wherever and whenever it happens. *It is my duty not to facilitate it, under any circumstances.*

Before dawn he rose from his bed, and, rather than disturb Mrs Hudson, made himself some coffee. He sent the boy running off with a note to Aster, and he soon returned with a reply. But then the postman delivered another letter, and this occupied Holmes's attention, for it was a notification from Hampshire that Gwendolin had gone into labour.

So he roused Mrs Hudson after all, and quickly dressed and packed his travelling bag. "I will return, Mrs Hudson, within the week, unless events detain me. During that time there is a man – name of Griffin – of interest to the police, and a danger to others. You will recognise him, if you see him, by his strange visage: for he paints his face with white powder and paste, and it resembles nothing so much as a mask. He wears tinted spectacles and never removes his gloves. If he comes to the house, Mrs Hudson, do not admit him – indeed, if he appears at all, contact the police."

Mrs Hudson, though alarmed by this instruction, was cognizant and capable. "Very good, Mr Holmes. And convey all the best wishes and love and hopefulness to your lady wife."

With that, Holmes rushed from the house. The coachman at the *Nag and Bailey* wanted to wait for further travellers, but Holmes persuaded him to depart ahead of time with a gold coin chinked into his waistcoat pocket. He climbed into a carriage and settled himself on the seat. And then: away, rattling and swaying and shaking through the city streets, as dawn's light began to tremble into the sky, and the stone valleys formed by the tall buildings of London eased their deeper darkness and began to broaden the light into morning.

Holmes could not think to any purpose. He tried to consider the situation in which he found himself, with Griffin's threat, but he found himself unable to separate speculation from anxious and excited reflection of his wife's expectancy. A hurry and contradiction pervaded all his thoughts.

He slid down the carriage window and put out his head. The fresh morning air washed all thoughts, of whatever kind, from his mind. He could make out the driver's right leg, and the equipage further up, looped into the leather entanglements of their harness, clouds passing out from the horses' nostrils. They went on slowly through the city streets, and then sped-up as they left the metropolis behind and rattled along the turnpike. They slowed again as they mounted the incline, and then they were hurtling through the wilderness of Chobham Common as the sun fully showed his face over the eastern horizon, and the morning dew glittered like constellations upon the bushes and long grass, and the driver put a new lash to his whip, calling out "hallo, whoop! Hallo, hi!"

And soon it was broad day, and the carriage rolled down into the richer lands of the south, and the sun shone on cornfields and hopfields and pasturage where cows stood, chewing meditatively, and watching the ratcheting, rattling, rolling equipage go past; and solitary labourers, risen from little temporary huts by heaps of stones upon the road, were, here and there, at work repairing the highway, or eating bread, and farm-workers could be seen going to their daily labour, or lounging at the doors of poor cottages, gazing idly at the passing car. And then there was a postyard, ankle-deep in mud, with steaming dunghills and vast outhouses half ruined; and the horses were swapped about for fresh mounts, and they were away again.

Finally Holmes, clutching his travelling bag to his chest as if it were a baby, hollered to the driver to pull up, and jumped down from the conveyance, shouting his thanks over his shoulder. Then it was half a mile along a road supplied with an honour-guard of lime-tree soldiers, the winter sun shining as strenuously as it could manage, and then he was home, and Molly the housemaid was shrieking with joy, and he flung his bag and hurried up the stairs to the bedroom.

There was the doctor, and Gwendolin's maid Janey, and Gwendolin herself in the big bed, attempting, as it seemed, to blow a hole in the ceiling from where she lay, and gasping in-between her puffs.

"Mr Holmes," said the doctor, without looking round. He had taken off his jacket, which was neatly hung over the back of the dressing-table chair and had rolled up his sleeves. "You're just in time."

"Vavasour!" gasped Gwendolin. Holmes ran round to the head of the bed, sat down and took his wife's hand in his. "My darling!"

"They're coming in waves," she said, in a low voice. And then, on a crescendo: "oh, oh, oh, oh!"

"Push, Mrs Holmes," said the doctor. And with a mighty effort, Gwendolin pushed, and pushed. Time stretched, as the pushing ceased, and then started up again. She pushed, straining with all her might, and then there was a pause, perhaps one second, perhaps long enough to include eons, and then a thin wailing warble started up, and the doctor was snipping the umbilicus and wrapping the new human in a soft blanket and passing the bundle up to the bright-faced, panting mother. "Oh my!" said Janey, over and over. "Mistress, oh my! Oh my!"

"A boy," said the doctor. "Congratulations!"

2

For three days Holmes forgot all about the danger of Griffin, forgot all about the strange and murderous business in the capital, forgot about everything that was not his home: his wife: his son Mycroft and his new baby Sherlock. The days were a whirl of experiences, familiar in one sense from when Mycroft had been new-born, and yet somehow new and fresh all over again. The nights were repeatedly interrupted by the stutter of indignant baby-squalling that aggregated into a rising cry. Gwendolin and Vavasour were perfectly modern and progressive in their attitudes, and took a Rousseauian view of feeding: no wet-nurse, since Gwendolin could suckle the baby perfectly well herself. But it meant she was up throughout the night, and that she drifted through the days in a half-somnolent state.

Little Sherlock was, Holmes thought, the single most beautiful thing he had ever seen. Holmes senior stumbled through the days, sat at breakfast trying to read the newspaper only for the printed words to blur into exhaustion, he came upon himself (as it were) staring thoughtlessly at the wall. And then his wife would hand him the baby and he would cradle the little creature in his arms. He had never been happier.

But the outside world could not be kept at bay indefinitely. On the fourth day a letter arrived from Aster, having been sent initially to his London place, and clumsily redirected. *Your reports of Griffin are alarming indeed*, it read.

I never trusted him, and do not doubt his capacity for violence – whether or not he is, as you now believe, literally invisible. We must go to Bucket and involve the police. We will have a better chance of convincing him of the urgency of this matter if we approach him together.

Have you heard the news? It seems that Carker, the managerial secretary at Dombey and Son, has absconded. Run off with Dombey's own wife, no less! The pair have, rumour says, fled to France: but they'll find a hot reception there, if reports of the ongoing revolution are anything to go by. Dombey himself is inconsolable, and it seems his firm will go down – Carker has run-up debts, hidden the fact from his employer, wasted or speculated the money. A thoroughly bad sort. The collapse of the firm will upset the stock exchange, although I daresay it will please Sir Percy, who regards all forms of transport not railways as direct competitors.

Holmes read the note twice. Then he wrote a quick reply, agreeing to come up to town at the next opportunity. He did not mention the birth of his new son, not wishing to put Aster under any uncomfortable sensation of having imposed upon Holmes, or having compelled him to act in ways counter to the good of his family. In fact, brought back from his idyll to the bald fact of Griffin's threat, Holmes saw that dealing with him *was* the good of his family.

He explained to Gwendolin that he had to return to

London – "but only for a few days. My heart is here with you". Then he packed his travelling bag again and made his way to the main road.

3

It was not until he was walking up Baker Street that Holmes began to feel, once again, a sense of dread. Griffin could be watching him right now – could be walking right behind him. He cast his eye all around, looking for the slightest shimmer of unusualness in the air, or perhaps for two semi-transparent violet-coloured dots, hanging in the air at head-height.

He saw nothing. But that was no reassurance.

Holmes made it through his front door and upstairs. There was a note from Aster, suggesting the two men meet at Holmes's club to confer. *Events*, Aster said, *have been so extraordinary, and are set fair to become even more so. Let us talk and establish our plan of action.*

It was early afternoon.

Holmes turned into Marylebone Road and fell. A passer-by helped him up. "Have a care, my friend," said this person. "Is the ground icy?"

"I do not think it is," said Holmes, resuming his feet. His elbow had been jarred in the fall, and in the moment it had seemed a trivial thing, a tumble of the sort to which young children are prone. But when he was upright again, a sense of alarm rose-up in his chest. Why had he fallen? He put out his foot and the next thing he knew, he was on the ground again.

This time there was no Good Samaritan to help him. He picked himself up. His trousers had torn over the knee and it hurt to put weight upon it.

He had fallen twice. It was disconcerting. Before he

took another step he looked down, but the ground looked normal. There were no potholes or ridges. There was no ice.

Then, quickly, he looked up, and turned to look all around him. Did he see two extremely pale small circles, hovering in the air at head height? It was not clear. Perhaps he imagined it. But then he heard a perfectly familiar, low-pitched, grim laugh and he knew he was not alone.

He broke into a run, darting across the road, up York Gate and over the bridge into The Regent's Park. He thought to himself: I am a taller man than Griffin, and I am shod where he is barefoot. Surely I can outrun him?

But as he circled the centre of the park, he found himself unable to continue the sprint. Panting, and cursing his lack of fitness, he stopped to regain his breath. Had he evaded the Invisible Man?

Two promenaders, walking arm in arm, passed him without giving him a second look. He inhaled deep, and deep again, his breathing returning to normal. There was no question: his knee had been ripped. He ought to return home and change his trousers before meeting Aster at his club. But the diabolic tricks Griffin had just played upon him kindled a sense of urgency. He must get to his club and immediately inform Aster of Griffin's game.

But as he put his best foot forward he again unbalanced, toppled and sprawled on the ground. He landed this time on grass, and so was not so badly shocked as the first two times, but this fall was accompanied by Griffin's voice, very close to Holmes's head: "You see what I can do, whenever I choose? Will you do what I demand of you now?"

"Damn your eyes, Griffin," Holmes cried.

"Go back to your laboratory and complete your work," Griffin snarled. "Or it will be the worse for you – and for your family too."

Holmes scrambled to his feet. His clothes were muddied, and he was panting – not from exertion, but from fear. A crazy bravado overwhelmed him. "I'll never complete that device for you, monster that you are! Never!"

"Then," came Griffin's voice out of the empty air, "I shall find someone who will – and have no further need of you."

The voice seemed to come from Holmes's left, but it was out of the corner of his right eye that he saw something moving. He turned to see better and just had time to observe a fist-sized rock, plucked from the Park's grounds, hurrying towards him at head-height, supported, it seemed, by nothing but air.

He did not even have time to flinch. The rock caught Holmes hard on the right cheek, and he staggered back. The Invisible Man had swung it right at him. A second rock, smaller, was – it seemed – thrown, and hit Holmes's forehead.

The other people in the park saw a strange sight – a man seemingly leaping and falling for no reason, as if performing a mad dance. They steered their paths away from the lunatic.

Griffin's voice was close by Holmes's ear. "Better to die in a garden," he mocked, "than in a sick-bed, surely! Better to die in your prime than after years of slow decline and misery. I am doing you a favour."

Holmes saw from where the Invisible Man had been sourcing these stones: a flower bed ringed by a border of large stones. He lunged at this, picked up a rock, and span about.

"Aha!" cried the Invisible Man. "But *where* will you strike, with your weapon? You cannot hit what you cannot see!"

Holmes lunged at where he thought the voice was coming from, met only empty air, and then howled as nails scratched at his face. He flailed away, and felt one, two, three pugilist's blows to his body.

He dropped the useless rock and set off running, a low-slung, hunched-over lope forced upon him by the pains in his body. He thought he felt a presence on his right, and veered left, but he miscalculated and ran into a tree. The collision was such as to knock him right over, and he fell onto his back.

At this, the Invisible Man's laughter was immoderate. "How foolish you look, Holmes! Why struggle? You cannot escape me."

Holmes struggled up again. "I know what I am doing," he gasped, and launched forward. The sound of the Invisible Man's laughter went past him, from in front to behind, and he knew for a moment where his adversary was. But though he looked for the pale-violet disembodied retinas, he could not see them.

He ran on, his chest humming with pain on every breath. Blood was trickling from his face.

And here, with seeming ease, and not even challenged for breath, was the Invisible Man's voice, beside him. "Run on, little hare. The chase is intensely entertaining for me – and like any good huntsman I know how it will end."

Holmes launched himself at a hedge, and scrambled through. From the far side he scrambled over a fence, but then fell ... stumbled over his own feet, rather than pushed over by Griffin. As he looked back he saw the leaves of the hedge shudder around nothingness and, just for that moment, knew where the Invisible Man was. But he had no weapon!

He got to his feet and ran on.

There were fewer people here, but they seemed more incommoded by the sight of this dishevelled fellow scrambling along. Holmes reached a low wall, and could go no further.

"Is this it?" came Griffin's voice? "The chase over so soon? Ah well. I tell you what I shall do. Do you see that gentleman over there?"

Holmes looked around. The low wall against which he was resting circled round on itself; in the middle of the ground it marked out was a declivity, with a tall poll rising from its midst. There were several gentlemen visible about the grounds, and if the Invisible Man was pointing a finger, of course Holmes could not see it.

"Which?"

"It hardly matters," said Griffin. "Any. I shall walk over to them, and they will not see me. I shall steal their walking stick and they won't know what is happening. Then I shall beat you to death with it, and, when I return it to them, *they* will be blamed. Delicious!"

"Monstrous!" Holmes yelled. The other denizens of the gardens looked at him: a strange man, yelling at the air. And yet he was not yelling at the air, nor at Griffin neither. "You monstrous man!"

He was shouting for the benefit of quite another.

A stout, elderly fellow some twenty yards away yelped with surprise, and fell backwards. As he foundered on the ground, his silver-headed walking stick zipped through the air. Holmes watched its approach and tried to dodge it, but all Griffin needed to do was wait until he had moved, and then swing the stick. It caught Holmes a blow on the side of his head that made his ears shriek.

"Is that how you killed Martin Malprelate?" Holmes cried. He began backing away, keeping the wall to his right. There was the sound like snoring from below, but whatever was making it was not asleep.

"You silly fellow," Griffin laughed. "I told you before it was not I who killed him. Have you not deciphered that riddle yet? Must you go to your grave never having solved the mystery? What a *pity* that is."

Holmes took another step backwards, and another. Griffin's voice was coming from somewhere at his front.

"I cannot see you," Holmes said. "And so I cannot fight you."

"At last you understand," said the Invisible Man.

"But," Holmes said, as a mass rose slowly to block the light to the right, "not everything in this world hunts by sight. Do you not see where we *are*?"

"We are in the Park of – "Griffin began. But then the hefty paw of the great bear, roused from his time at the bottom of the pit, reached across from the pole its ursine owner had climbed, and smote Griffin hard. The Invisible Man screamed, Holmes darted forward and snatched the stick from him.

Spatters of blood – visible blood – fell upon the wall.

At this Griffin moved back. Holmes could not see where, but he could see where the bear, twitching its mighty nostrils, was turning his head. The bear, chained to its pole, could not leave its enclosure. It reached with a hefty paw, and connected only with air, as Griffin darted back. But Holmes watched where the ursine head angled itself, smelling the scent of its prey, and with that he swung the stick and – connected.

The blow unbalanced Griffin, and he fell against the wall, back within the reach of the bear. There was a massive stroke from the bear's paw, and another, and this latter broke the skull of the Invisible Man and turned him, as he fell, naked and scratched and blue-tinged at the extremities, into the Visible Corpse, on the ground of the London Zoological Gardens.

Holmes dropped the walking stick, and staggered back, away from the bear pit. People were screaming. One of the keepers was running across the park towards him. "Stay away from the bear, ladies, gentlemen!" the park keeper was calling. "It is not a tame animal, ladies, gentlemen!" But Holmes could hardly hear him. The whole mystery had fallen at last into place. Not Griffin, but another – and as he stood there, gasping, bleeding, Holmes finally understood who it was who had killed Martin Malprelate.

* * *

4

At the Hawk Mansion, Sir Persimmon was just that moment stepping through his front door and coming out into the wider world.

He wore a dark purple suit with orange lapels. A black overcoat flapped crowishly around his legs. He was still affixing his hat to his head, with his walking stick tucked under his arm, as Holmes approached. Aster was only a few steps behind.

"Sir Percy," said Holmes, walking up to him.

The baronet looked surprised. "Holmes? What d'ye do here? I thought you were out of town."

"I returned last night."

"Did you! Oho. And are you – are you well, man? There's blood on your face."

"Sir Percy," said Holmes. "I have hard words to speak to you. But they must be spoken. You lied to me."

Hawk's face darkened. "How dare you, sir!" he growled. "Give me the lie? I'll horsewhip you, sir! How dare you!"

He took a step towards Holmes and raised his walking stick, to bring it down across the younger man's pate. Holmes did not flinch: he only stood there, awaiting the blow. But rather than strike, Hawk paused. He had noticed that there was somebody else present.

"You sir! Who are you?"

"It is I, Sir Percy. It is Aster."

"Oh – I didn't recognise you, sir. What do *you* do, here? I thought I had dismissed you from my employ."

"What I do here is – well, Sir Percy, in truth: I attend upon the pleasure of Mr Holmes."

"No, let *me* tell you what you do here, Aster," said the Baronet, stepping towards him aggressively. "You are here as a witness."

"A witness?" said Aster.

Sir Percy lowered his stick. "Do not think, Holmes, that I can permit so foul a calumny to pass unnoticed. Call me a liar? I would fight a duel with you, sir, if my responsibilities – to the railway – were not so pressing. And in this day and age such behaviour has been superseded. But I'll have you in court, sir – you, Aster, are a witness to the slander. You heard him say it! I'll have you in court too, and you'll swear under oath as to what you heard Holmes say just now. Here! In this public space!" Hawk stepped back. "I'll sue, Holmes. You dare to say such a thing to me? I'll have you for your every penny. I'll make your wife a beggar and send your family to the workhouse. I will ruin you."

"I have called you a liar, Sir Percy," said Holmes, mildly. "I will not deny it court. But there is a worse word for you which I shall use. Shall we truly wrangle it out in court?"

"Worse word?" blustered the baronet. "What-what?"

"Are we, gentleman, to stand in the street, like brawlers?" Holmes asked. "As you noted Sir Percy, there are certain cuts upon my face. I do not flatter myself that you have any kindness of feeling towards me, but perhaps, out of simple common-humanity, you may permit me to go into your house and wash?"

Sir Percy looked up and down the street. There were various people perambulating to and fro. A coal-cart rattled past, dropping stray coals upon the road like a horse relieving itself of dung. The baronet put his head back and looked at the sky.

It was clear to Holmes that he was weighing his options. A difficult interview was about to happen. Would it not be better to hold it in his house, upon his own territory? Could he risk passers-by hearing these accusations?

Could he run the greater risk of allowing Holmes simply to depart and tell his story to who knew howevermany others?

Because, Holmes realised, Sir Percy already knew what Holmes was going to tell him. A sense of chill crawled through his gut. He already knew. This, more than anything else, was the confirmation that Holmes was correct.

And that meant that Sir Percy was dangerous.

"I've half a mind," said the baronet, "to tell ye both to retreat, to depart, to run along, to 'sling your hooks' as the sailors say. The impertinence! But – "and a strange smile grew across his face, " – it would be cruelty to send a wounded man away. You appear to have suffered some injurious blow to the head Mr Holmes, and perhaps it has unsettled your sanity – such at least would explain why you have approached me in the street and called me so calumnious a name! Come in, come in."

He gestured for Holmes to go in through the main door, but when Aster stepped forward to follow him he turned his body to block the second man's access.

"I trust you will not deny Mr Aster the hospitality you have so generously offered myself," said Holmes in a warning voice.

Sir Percy glowered at him, and then looked back at Aster. Again, that options were being weighed, and possible lines of action assessed, was only too obvious in the baronet's face.

He stepped aside. "By all means, by *all* means," he said. "Mr Aster too, why not. Let's have a regular ball, shall we not? I'll have the kitchen cook the fatted calf and gild its ears and rear with gold leaf, why not?"

Holmes walked up the steps. The big door swung open as he approached, and a skeletal-faced butler scowled at him as he walked inside.

"Thompson," Sir Percy called up. "Mr Holmes needs to wash his face. Will ye provide him with a bowl of water, and all necessaries for his ablutions?" He pointed at Holmes's face.

"Very good sir," replied the butler, in a voice like a tomb door creaking shut.

"I will await you in the snug," Sir Percy added. "Thompson, be so good as to direct Mr Holmes and his friend there, when he's done. The snug, yes? Snug!"

"Very good sir," the butler repeated, almost an octave lower.

Holmes followed the old retainer to some room towards the back of the house. A bowl of water, soap, a cloth, a towel, and a mirror were brought to him and he examined his own face in the bright circle. The marks looked like the actions of a wild animal, careless with its claws. Holmes washed the majority of the blood away, dabbed at the cuts. Several had stopped bleeding, but a long stripe across his cheek still oozed red.

"Taken the liberty," croaked the butler, coming up behind, "of conveying, hither, this plaister." He sounded as though his voice was powered not by a regular breath from the lungs, but his very death-rattle.

"Thank you," said Holmes, manoeuvring the patch to his cheek. The butler nodded.

Holmes dabbed the rest of his face dry, and then followed the butler back along corridors and across the hall to the snug.

Inside Sir Percy had taken a seat in one of the room's several leather-upholstered chairs and was pouring himself a brandy. Aster was standing with his back to the window, his arms crossed, looking down upon him. A fire was burning heartily in the grate, and though it was evidently but newly lit it was already warming the book-lined space.

"I understand Mr Aster here," the baronet was saying, "having lost his position, is in a blue funk about it. Too proud, and angry, to take a seat. I hope you won't be so haughty, Holmes."

Holmes sat.

"Your face looks better," the baronet observed, genially. "A drink?"

"Thank you."

"Now," said Sir Percy, pouring a second glass. "Shall we resolve this awkward matter? I am willing to overlook the foul language you used of me, Holmes – to put it down to the hurt you suffered to your head. But you must withdraw it, you know. You cannot use such a word to describe me."

"The word being liar," said Holmes.

The baronet scowled. "Repeating the slander is only to deepen the offence and therefore the sanction. Recall, I have a witness – Mr Aster is standing right there."

"I must inquire," said Aster, "for since I may have to give testimony in a courthouse I would like to be as well-informed as possible – in what respect, Mr Holmes, do you consider Sir Percy has lied?"

"It is a strange thing," Holmes said. "And may strike you as merely bizarre. The facts of the case are this: a third party brought Sir Percy the components to a certain machine – a machine unlike any other. Sir Percy told me these pieces of technology were mere chaff, stage-props, brought to him as part of a confidence-game to defraud him of his money. But they were not. They were genuine, and the machine in question genuinely could do what was claimed for it."

"Which was?" asked Aster.

"It was a time machine, Mr Aster," said Holmes. "Or I should say, it *is* a time machine – and indeed, for completion's sake, it *will be* a time machine, for the machine in question is not to be invented and perfected until the year 1900."

"And it has," said Aster, speaking slowly, "been directed back in time, to this year of 1848? Do I understand what you are saying correctly?"

"Say rather, piloted. But yes, you have grasped it."

"It's stuff and nonsense!" barked Sir Percy. "Listen Holmes. You must stop this. If you withdraw this absurd claim, and your offensive language, then we may perhaps come to an arrangement. Perhaps I terminated your contract of work on the galvanic engine too abruptly – if any financial embarrassment has ensued, we could certainly talk of a suitable sum in reparation."

Holmes took a glug of the burning liquid in his glass. "I am not interested in your money, Sir Percy."

At this, the baronet glowered harder. "But I shall have yours, Holmes – the court will award me such damages as to bankrupt you utterly!"

"Forgive me, gentlemen," said Aster. "But I am still unaware of the nature of the lie."

"It is simple, Mr Aster. Sir Percy told me this machine did not work, despite knowing perfectly well that it did. I should say: knowing that it *does*. That was his lie."

"Absurd," said the baronet. "You have no shame, Holmes – and once the court has finished with you, you'll have no money."

"You *know* the machinery works," said Holmes. "Because you have used it. And more than once."

"Travelled in time, did I?" scoffed Sir Percy. "Yet here I am, standing in front of you, in the year of our Lord eighteen hundred and forty-eight."

He chuckled at this absurdity. The fire in the grate chuckled along with him.

"I did not say you travelled, Sir Percy. I say you *used* the machinery. And that brings me to the worse term of which I spoke earlier. For you are not merely a liar. You are a murderer."

At this Sir Percy opened his mouth very wide, and then closed it again. "I'm almost sorry," he said, "to take you to court, for I see now that you are quite insane. That won't save you – I'll have you confined to an asylum. I'll have you picketed in Bedlam for strangers to gawk at."

"Mr Aster," said Holmes, turning to his friend. "Permit me

to explain. Of course you remember the fantastical stories – diabolical locomotives, devils from hell – that circulated concerning the lamentable death of your former employer, Sir Martin Malprelate?"

"The death was as mysterious," said Aster, "as it was grievous."

"For a long time I laboured without a solution to that mystery. But I have the solution now."

"Really?" Sir Percy's voice creaked with contempt.

"Somewhere in the year 1900 a scientist will invent a machine that can carry a passenger backwards, or forwards, in time. He himself will use it to explore the future. But then he will meet another man, Griffin by name, who will kill him and steal his machine. It seems strange, perhaps, to talk of something that has yet to happen as over and done with – and yet here we are. Fleeing not just the scene but the *time* of his crime, Griffin will pilot the craft back here – but he will do so incompetently, unskilled with the equipment, not knowing its dirigible or accelerative tolerances. He will, in temporal terms, *crash* – just as a runaway horse and carriage might crash in physical terms. The machine will – or now we must shift tenses, the machine did – break. This stranded Griffin in this year, which was an inconvenience and irritation to him. So he gathered the pieces of the machine together and sought people more expert in technological matters to help him repair it. He found Sir Percy, who was excited at the thought of owning such a device. But of course, there is only one device, and only one person can own it. Of course Griffin and Sir Percy were doomed to fall out, as the repairs continued – for one or other would seize it, and so deprive the other. There would come a time where one, or the other, would ride the completed device away: into the past, or into the future."

"This is your solution?" mocked Sir Percy. "Madness."

"What I did not grasp until now," Holmes explained, "is

that the components were not in themselves inert. Permit me to inform you, Mr Aster, that Sir Percy approached me, on account of my work with galvanic generators, to construct for him a generator of unprecedented power. The time machine runs upon electricity, you see, and what is commonplace in the year 1900 is hard to access in 1848. And for months now I have been doing just that. Then, a few days ago, Griffin took the various components of the machine and absconded. Sir Percy told me his story – his lie – about it: that the machine was a fraud and Griffin a mere confidence-man. He told me to stop work upon my generator. But he knew the machine was real, and only wanted to deprive Griffin of the ability to power it and so carry it away. His hope was to locate Griffin and retrieve the machine."

"It is," said Aster, looking from Holmes to Hawk and back, "certainly an extraordinary story."

"Indeed! But this is what I had not understood: *how did Sir Percy know the machine was real*? It cannot function in the way it was first built to function, or else either he or Griffin would have ridden away on it. Sir Percy now claims it is a mere stage-prop, pasteboard and paint and brass trimmings. But if he thinks it a hoax now why did he ever think it real? You see, I had in my head, I suppose, that the machine's component parts were all *in themselves* inert, like the cogs and chambers, the piston-shafts and sheet metal of a disassembled steam locomotive. But this was clumsy thinking on my part. I am ashamed! Because had Griffin brought mere useless bits and pieces of metal and wire to Sir Percy, he would have sent him away as the charlatan he now claims he is. No: Griffin must have been able to show Sir Percy proof of concept – as the technicians call it. He *must have been able to show Sir Percy that time travel was possible*. Or Sir Percy would have shown him the door! I may call you a liar, Sir Percy; I may call you a murderer; but I do not call you an idiot. No: Griffin showed you something that persuaded you."

"You expect me to reply to these absurdities, Holmes?" growled Sir Percy. "You have twined your own rope – quite a long spool of it now – and it will hang you. You shall be hearing from my lawyers."

"Wait a moment, Sir Percy, if you please," said Holmes. "I have an inkling of what it was that Griffin showed you. It would be a single kindness to me if you would be so good as to confirm it."

"Go to hell!"

Holmes smiled. "I do not pretend to understand exactly how a time machine might actually operate, but I believe I can speculate within the parameters of the constraints of physics. This machine first opens a portal, or doorway, in the medium of time – and then propels itself and its passenger through – to a new time, past or present. Is that correct?"

"The machine is mere bunkum," barked Sir Percy. "It *don't* work."

"But we both know it does, Sir Percy! I suspect that, though broken to such an extent that it can not, at present, move passengers through time, the machine is still capable of opening the portal in that medium. Perhaps unsteadily, presumably unpredictably – for I suppose the proper operation of such an action would require the complete and repaired control panel, or equivalent. But predictability is not necessarily what you required."

"Nonsense!"

"I believe that one portion of the device *is* operational. I think it opens the portal I mentioned – an aperture in time that manifests, in our space, as … let us say: a trench, some hundreds of feet long. Let us say eight hundred feet."

"Eight hundred feet?" asked Aster. "That seems a very precise measurement, Mr Holmes, given that you are only speculating as to the operation of this – this machine?"

"Indeed. But I have a reason for it. Westminster Bridge is 800 feet long."

"Westminster bridge," said Aster, in a tone that suggested he was beginning not only to understand, but to believe.

The expression of barely-suppressed wrath melted from Hawk's face. He drained his glass, poured himself another dose of brandy, and held it to his face. It was apparent to Holmes that a change had occurred in his manner. He was now deciding to abandon his bluster and threats, and try a different approach.

Holmes was well aware that this increased the danger.

"It means nothing. Can you imagine a jury of twelve ordinary men accepting such outlandishness? But where the bridge is concerned, I should be given a medal. Were your ridiculous story true, why: then I should be acclaimed the saviour of society!"

"You have changed your tone, Sir Percy!"

"Oh nonsense. You can prove nothing. Nothing! Go to the police with your fairy-tale, by all means. They will laugh in your face."

"You remember that day Aster: the great Chartist gathering in Kennington. We both hurried into the centre of town. At the northern end of Westminster Bridge we stood – the police were there, but not in great numbers, and the mob that was intent upon storming Parliament was very large. I was surprised, at the time, that Sir Percy's carriage happened to arrive at just that moment. It seemed – what shall I say? Out of character for you, sir, to put your own life in danger, with such recklessness. I see now that was not what you were doing at all."

"Out of character to act selflessly?" Sir Percy laughed. "I suppose I did have a personal interest in crushing the serpent-head of revolution before it could sink its fangs into our crown and state – but my action was more than mere self-interest. I was protecting my country!"

"Horatius at the bridge?" said Aster.

"It is a most unusual circumstance, more strange even that that old Roman story" said Holmes. "You see: Sir Percy had with him, in his carriage, the component of the time machine of which we are talking."

The baronet saw no reason to dissemble further. He drained his brandy again. Holmes was prepared to believe that a sense of actual pride in what he had achieved that day swelled his heart.

"Horatius at the bridge," he said. "That's well said, Mr Aster. Well said! As for the component: it must be *charged* – that was the word Griffin used. And once *charged*, it is ready to be *discharged* – one must aim, and press certain levers within the device." Sir Percy was grinning now. "The effect is remarkable. It lasts between thirty seconds and three minutes: it is not possible to predict, or so Griffin said. And it opens a portal – you're right there, Holmes, though how you guessed it I *don't* know. Opens a portal into the past or the present. How far you depress the lever, and which direction, determines it. When it is part of the complete machine, according to Griffin, it connects with a system of motors and dirigibilities. At the bridge I was able to aim it and, with the slightest motion, send the mob backwards in time: mere minutes, but enough to deposit them back on the far side of the bridge."

"I saw it with my own eyes," said Holmes, "and yet did not believe it."

At this, the baronet put his head back and laughed. Evidently he had decided there was no peril to him in confessing: for after all, whom else would believe a story so outlandish? "I cannot tell you how much *fun* it was. The look on their faces, as they laboured and laboured across the bridge! And of course, each time I sent the mob's advance guard, the space into which they arrived had filled up further with people coming up from behind. In the end it became a perfect log-jam. The fools were tumbling off the edge and into the river! Confusion midst their ranks!" The smile slipped from his face. "I saved our nation. The queen should grant me the order of the garter! But of course I can never claim the credit I deserve."

"Once I understood what had happened at Westminster Bridge," said Holmes, "everything else fell into place. For if a man – and who else but Sir Percy, inside his carriage, could have effected the transformation? – if a man could open a chasm in time itself that placed a whole crowd of people under the iron law of the past, he could surely do so with the future. And then I thought of Bryde."

"I didn't see Bryde properly," said Sir Percy. "I needed to peek through my carriage window to aim the device, but we were moving away, and the road was busy. And I wasn't sure what it *was*, exactly, that emerged from futurity – that made its apparition in our time, for those few fatal seconds, before roaring away back to its own time. But Griffin was there too and he claimed to recognise it. He called it a *motor-sickle*."

"What on earth...?" asked Aster.

"He had to explain it to me. It seems he had seen them himself, in the future. You'll have heard of these new velocipedes, I think? In Germany they call them *Laufmaschine*, running machines: a two wheeled conveyance where you run along the ground with your legs, and steer the front wheel. Griffin says the time will come when they put an engine to that device."

"A steam engine? Like a locomotive?"

"He seemed unsure exactly how the engine is to be powered. But it propels the rider, the fellow who bestrides the motor-velocipede, with tremendous celerity."

"And you," Holmes asked, "were able to summon such a device?"

"I had no idea what would come out! Only he was on the street – and the streets of London are much the same, in their lay-out, two hundred years hence, I suppose. All I did was create a little cleavage through which our future motor-velocipede could slip. It might have been some other kind of rapid vehicle. It might have been nothing, and Bryde would have crossed the road unharmed! It happened to be this particular vehicle. I often think how surprised the future-fellow must have been, to see a man appear in front of him, in nineteenth-century clothes! But his surprise can't have lasted long, for he struck and killed Bryde in an instant, and then was gone."

"Gone back to his futurity," said Holmes.

"I could only partially encharge the device," said Sir Percy, "lacking the new design of galvanic pile."

"How *was* the machine powered?" Holmes asked.

"The machine, as a whole, was not. I have not been in a position to be able to power the whole machine – not the full device, capable of carrying a passenger backwards or forwards in time. That would require the development of a device capable of delivering more galvanic potency than can be generated with today's piles. It is only the operative temporal circuit. I do not have the power to navigate myself through past and future, but I can encharge the circuit sufficiently to produce bubbles of temporal disturbance."

"You have wrought great damage with these bubbles," said Holmes. Then: "Bryde was my friend."

"He was a damn nuisance," snapped Sir Percy.

"But good God man!" exclaimed Aster. "Being a nuisance is no reason to murder a person!"

"Bryde contacted me, and asked me to meet him at the London Zoological Gardens," said Holmes. "He had uncovered something important. We met, but he was inhibited from telling me what he had uncovered whilst Sir Percy was also present. As soon as Sir Percy left he was killed. It is not difficult to link together the causality here."

"*Damn* nuisance."

"What puzzled me," Holmes conceded, "is that you hired Bryde in the first place."

"He was a company man! I expected him to expedite the company line – swiftly to conclude that agitators and anarchists had murdered Martin Malprelate, and draw a line underneath the affair. At the very least, since *I* was the man employing him, he would not suspect me of being involved in the death – for why would I hire a man to investigate and expose my own guilt? I genuinely thought he would close down all the crazy speculation, not open it up. But there you go."

"What had he uncovered?"

"He discovered that Malprelate and I quarrelled, bitterly. I used my influence, and expended a very large sum of money indeed, obtaining the necessary senior figures and parliamentarians to have the Zoological Gardens shut down. Malprelate blocked me."

"But – why close down the gardens?"

"For the line, man! Obviously for the line! That ground is the perfect path for the Middlemarch line to come into Euston – perfect terrain, perfect path from northwest to southeast, and no need to plot a big detouring loop, and demolish a gaggle of houses. Which is to say no need to pay a gaggle of folk inflated sums for their hovels, by the compulsory purchase laws! But Malprelate wasn't having it. The most ridiculous thing about him was his excessive sentimentality for animals. Damnable animals! It took precedence even over his thirst for money. You know, he kept a menagerie in his own house? Not just a dog or two, but cats and birds – a bear he had rescued from bear baiting. The fellow was unhinged."

"The line has been laid now: those compulsory orders have been paid for. The excavations are going ahead."

"Tearing the heart out of Camden Town, yes indeed. Too late to change that, more's the pity."

"Too late?" Holmes queried. "For a man with a time machine."

"I did think of that," agreed Sir Percy. "I did wonder if

I might complete Griffin's machine and use it to reverse Malprelate's foolish decision. But it transpires such a thing is not possible."

"No?"

"Griffin was insistent. I had to accept it was too late to change that decision."

"But if it was too late, why did you kill Sir Martin?"

"Why sir?" Sir Percy was suddenly bellowing, at top volume. "To damn him, sir! To damn his bones! To pay him back! He? He dare to twit *me*? He dare dismiss all the work I had done? All my labour insinuating my way with the bigwigs and honourable members, to get the garden's charter revoked? All the money I had spent, cast down the sewer? To sneer at me, and dismiss me, and mock me?" The fury drained away, and Sir Percy looked again blithe. "The company was certainly better off without him. He'd never sell his shares. Not to me. But he might be – inched – out of the way."

"Knocked out of the way. Murdered, in short."

"Not that it matters. Let me inform you, Holmes: none of this matters. It is a great truth, and one that time travel reveals to you. It is all the same. Past, present, future, all the same. Why weep for Malprelate? You do not weep for Alexander the Great, for he died millennia since. You would not weep for some greater Alexander, to be born a thousand years hence, for he is a mere phantom of futurity. And yet you weep for Sir Martin Malprelate! Why? Because he is flesh and blood? So were and will be these others – and Sir Martin's blood flows no more, and his flesh is turning to dust as we speak. Life is not a fixity, gentlemen. It is a flux, a flow, an endless passing-away, and endless yet-to-come. The only *real* person is he who can *master* the flux. Griffin is too paltry of soul to be that man, for all that chance threw this mighty machine his way. But destiny has another in mind, I fancy!"

"Good grief man," said Aster, in disgust. "Do you hear yourself?"

"You followed Malprelate," said Holmes, keeping his eye carefully on the baronet. "You followed him to his public meeting in Camden, that night. As he walked away, down the course of the excavation, you used your device – which had been *charged*, to use your word – to open a portal to futurity. But as with Bryde, you could not be sure that the pocket of futurity, eight hundred yards long, the device summoned forth would be fatal to him! With Bryde perhaps it mattered less, for he was, in your eyes, a petty target. But what if you had missed your chance to assassinate your rival? Your colleague, I should say. What then?"

"Then I would have tried at some other time. I did try before, in fact – before he was able to rescue his precious Zoological Gardens. By the time of the public meeting that cause was lost to me, although my fury had only intensified over those weeks. You are, however, missing one crucial matter – you do not understand the nature of this city, as it shall be. Griffin told me and I didn't believe him at first. But he had seen it with his own eyes."

Sir Percy gestured at the window.

"Behind you, Mr Aster, is the largest metropolis in the world. To you, I daresay, it seems busy, bustling, even restless and exhausting. But I tell you this, Mr Aster. This metropolis, our city of 1848? It is a positively pastoral garden compared with the city two centuries hence. In that city there are hordes of folk – great crowds of people shuffling the pavements and through the courtyards and across the bridges. Enormous migrations of people to and fro! But there are also machines, motile machines, trains and motorized carriages, self-propelled carts and wagons. There are many, many thousands of these, and they pass at ferocious, impossible speeds, up and down all the roads, all through the day and all through the night."

Sir Percy poured himself a third, full glass of brandy. He was, Holmes deduced, steeling himself prior to enacting some enormity.

Be ready, he told himself. *Be ready to act quickly*.

"The roads of that London to-come are, mostly, laid upon the same grid as *our* roads. But they are also vastly busier. Vastly! Open a door from our time to theirs and it will, like as not, be possessed by some roaring, hurtling, metal engine. There were times when, experimenting with the device, I opened portals of futurity that chanced to be empty. But those times were rare."

Putting his now empty glass down, Sir Percy got to his feet, his knees popping with a sound like two pebbles falling in a pond. "Earlier I told you I realised I could not use the machine to return in time to alter the course of the railway. The reason I know that is simply this: the railway runs, in that future London, along the same track that it does now."

Sir Percy stepped over to a bureau and angled back its lid.

"I was at the top of the excavation, looking down upon Martin as he stomped along the bottom of the works. There was just enough moonlight, reflecting off the roiling mist, to see how disaffected he was. It amused me. So I opened a door into futurity, and instead of a contemporary locomotive rolling down that space came *a giant engine of the future time*, passing faster than could be imagined, twice as tall as the biggest train-engine built today, twice as long, lit on both flanks with galvanic light, screeching like a banshee. There were giant portholes on either side, and the faces of the folk of the future could be seen. They looked like ordinary folk! Though not a one, I saw, was hatted. What did they see? Rolling from futurity, through a few hundred yards of our time, and back into futurity?"

"But that can not be what happened," said Holmes, ever the rational man. "There were no train tracks, so the future-train cannot have travelled along that road. You did not summon that train back into our time – instead you did what you did on Westminster Bridge: you moved an object from *our* time into the past or, as here, the future. Sir Martin Malprelate was briefly superposed on our time and that time as well, and in that time his body was smashed to atoms."

"Parts of him were still falling through the air after the train had returned to its proper time. Or perhaps you are correct: perhaps the train never left its proper time, and Malprelate was briefly sent to the future to encounter his doom, as we all watched. It little matters, for he was dead."

When Sir Percy turned to face Holmes and Aster he was holding in his hands two pistols.

"Constructed for me by Joseph Child of Birmingham," he announced. "Large bore Damascus steel barrel, chequered walnut stock. I keep them always armed and loaded."

"You're mad, man! Your manservant will hear the blast!"

"He?" Hawk laughed. "He couldn't hear the last trumpet if Archangel Gabriel blew it straight in his ear."

"Sir Mulberry – "Holmes began, reaching out a hand.

The pistol in Sir Percy's right hand, pointed at Aster, discharged with a cacophonous crack.

Aster yelped and banged hard against the window behind him. But the frame held, and the glass did not break. Aster sagged to his knees, a great sheep's-wool excrescence of white smoke hanging in the air. Pungencies of saltpetre and sulphur assaulted Holmes's nostrils.

Holmes afterwards reflected on Sir Percy's choice of target. He could have chosen either man to shoot first. Perhaps it was mere chance that he selected Aster; or perhaps his decision was influenced by the fact that Aster, standing, seemed to him a greater threat than Holmes, sitting. Either way the moment it took the baronet to pivot, raise his weaker, left hand and aim the pistol at Holmes was long enough.

Holmes snatched the poker from the fireplace to his right and rose to his feet, in one movement. As Sir Percy aimed, Holmes struck his wrist with the metal pole.

The baronet grunted with pain, and the pistol slipped from his grip. The weapon flew from his hand, struck the side of the fireplace and bounced into the fire. The baronet turned his head in dismay to watch it land, where the flames intemperately ignited its gunpowder, sending its bullet speeding instantly out again to strike Sir Percy Hawk directly between the eyes.

He took a step back, looking immensely surprised. His gaze did not move from Holmes's face. Then, as the fire flared, he took another step back. His heel struck the leg of his leather chair, and, as a sack is deposited, he slumped down into it. He was still clutching the other pistol in his right hand.

Holmes's immediate concern was for Aster, who was kneeling before the window. He replaced the poker by the fireside and stepped over to his friend.

"Are you badly wounded?"

"There is pain," said Aster, in a constricted voice, "but not, I think, blood." He moved his right hand to his chest and moved it around. "I believe," he gasped, "the ball struck a rib."

"We must remove you to a hospital," Holmes urged. At that moment it was all that was in his mind. He put his arm around his friend and helped him rise. Then, together, they made their halting way to the door of the snug, out into the hallway and to the front door. The ageing butler emerged from the back of the house and began shuffling along the hall towards them. Very slowly.

"It's alright," Holmes called. "We can let ourselves out."

The old man did not hear them. He continued his shuffling, extraordinarily slowly. "Come on," said Holmes, taking Aster's hand.

Outside, they soon hailed a cab. But although Holmes managed to help his friend up into the carriage, it took only moments of rattling passage over the uneven road surface for Aster to call out that he couldn't bear the motion. The distance to the Royal London Hospital was excessive, so instead Holmes instructed the driver to turn down into Baker Street. Here he and Mrs Hudson carefully encouraged and levered Aster up the stairs and into the parlour, where he collapsed on the sofa.

It was still hard for Holmes to comprehend the suddenness with which things happened. Young Mrs Hudson was unbuttoning Aster's jacket. Beneath was a shirt, with an oval hole in it, and when this was lifted Aster's near hairless chest was revealed. A bruise the size of a cabbage-leaf extended across the right portion of this, and at its centre was a puckered circle of skin, a miniature crater of flesh.

"The bullet is visible," said Holmes. "It has struck the rib-bone, and gone no further."

"It hurts to breathe," Aster reported.

"I suppose the bone itself, underneath, is cracked. But I can remove the ball, I think." He rummaged through drawers in the room he used as his laboratory, and returned with fat brass tweezers. Mrs Hudson supplied a wooden spoon, upon the handle of which Aster bit. In a moment, and with an audible sucking-sound, the bullet was out.

Holmes deposited it in his ashtray, which was adjacent, and then helped Mrs Hudson lead Aster through to the bathroom. She washed the wound and wrapped a bandage around his chest. Holmes leant his friend one of his shirts, and, as if nothing had happened, the two men sat down in the parlour of Holmes's apartment and took tea.

5

Aster was breathing shallowly, and wincing visibly on several breaths. "I fear my rib is broken," he said.

"I cracked a rib falling from an apple tree when I was a

lad," Holmes told him. "It took weeks to heal – I'm sorry to say it, but it was many weeks."

"Hawk tried to slay me. An eighth of an inch further up and he would have shot me through my heart. I am grateful to be alive, my friend."

"You have suffered a shock, Aster."

"So have you, Holmes."

"Indeed. I would not normally put so much sugar into my tea. But on this occasion…" He stirred another spoonful into each cup. "To be honest, I am still computing – still processing – the experience. It does not seem real."

"It is real enough," said Aster, "for us to have to answer for it."

"To the police?"

"Aye." Aster picked up his tea-cup with his usual, right hand, and then brought his left hand across and took the cup in that. "You struck Hawk? With a poker, I think? I couldn't see clearly, on account of the pain, and being on my knees."

"He was aiming the second pistol at me," said Holmes. "I struck his hand with the poker."

"Then he dropped it? You picked it up?"

"No – it flew from his hand, into the fireplace, and discharged there by accident. You did not observe this?"

"I did not," said Aster. "Naturally I believe you, but I could not, in good conscience, testify in court that I had actually witnessed it. I was in too much pain. You acted in self-defence, however."

"Of course. But I can see, without your testimony, it might look as though I shot Sir Percy and tossed the gun into the fireplace afterwards."

"Even with my testimony," said Aster, "we might not be believed. What can we say? That we had entered the baronet's house because we suspected him of the murder of Sir Martin Malprelate? Who would believe us – it is, after all, a story of unusual improbability. We cannot produce the time machine."

"We could produce that one working component, the one Hawk used to commit his crimes," Holmes points out. "By demonstrating that it worked, and how it worked, we would be bolstering our story considerably."

"Forgive me," said Aster. "But it is your story, not ours. I cannot be certain it is true, and I have certainly not observed any such thing."

"But – "said Holmes, eagerly. "You were *at* Westminster Bridge!"

"I do not know *what* I saw at that bridge that day," said Aster, wearily. He really did look very grey and exhausted. "It may have been what you say it was. But Bucket was there too, remember, and he is adamant he saw the men retreat on foot to the south bank."

"People only see what they believe it is possible for them to see."

"Very likely. But you would be asking me to swear, in court, to something concerning which I am not certain. The element you speak of, the portion of the machine, or whatever it is: this must be somewhere in Sir Percy Hawk's house, most likely locked away securely. How could we obtain it? We could not even enter the property without a search warrant, and what justice of the peace would grant one on such – forgive me, again – outlandish premises? No Holmes: without the machine, we have no proof. Now consider the other perspective. How will it look to the police? We entered Sir Percy's house. We leave. He is found dead. If we go to the police accusing *him* of being Sir Martin's murderer, that will only convince the authorities of our animosity towards him, and make it more likely they arrest, try, imprison, perhaps hang *us*."

"But what can we do?" asked Holmes.

"I do not know," said Aster, his eyes drooping. "Though I

am devilish tired. Might I sleep here, Holmes? I am not sure I can face the journey back to my own lodgings."

"Of course," said Holmes. "You must have my bed. I can sleep in the maid's room – it is vacant."

"I am content with the maid's room."

"But I am not content you should lie there. You are injured, and need recuperation in a proper bed."

Holmes summoned Mrs Hudson to make the bedroom ready. He helped Aster out of his clothes and into a borrowed night-shirt. Then, though it was barely six o'clock, the wounded man lay carefully down, pulled the eider over him, and fell fast asleep.

In the morning, Holmes was awake before Aster. He took some coffee, and wrote a note to Bucket, care of Scotland Yard, begging the honour of a visit from the Inspector at his Baker Street rooms as soon after breakfast as was convenient.

When Aster rose he still looked ill, but declared himself somewhat refreshed. He moved gingerly, breathed shallowly, and was prone to clutch his side; but having omitted to take any supper the previous evening he ate heartily of the breakfast Mrs Hudson served.

Holmes explained what he had done. "Perhaps I should have waited until you were up, and consulted with you. But the way I see it, informing the Inspector, and facing the consequences, is not only the right thing to do – it is the only thing."

Aster nodded slowly. "I suppose we cannot hope to hide what happened in that room."

"Indeed not. The butler, Thompson, is very deaf – but even he, surely, must have heard something. To say nothing of the other servants in the house. The police, when called, would surely search the fireplace – and though the wooden stock of the pistol must have burnt away, the iron barrel would be discernible among the cinders and ashes. If we lie to the police, our lie will be uncovered."

"My worry," said Aster, in a thin voice, "is that the truth is so strange it will not be believed."

"We must say that Sir Percy attacked us and that, in defending ourselves, he was killed. Your wound is prima facie evidence that he did so!"

"Or that *we* attacked *him*, and in defending *himself* he shot me. How are the police to know which way around events passed? We invaded his house, after all. And what motive would he have for trying to kill us?" Seeing the expression on Holmes's face, Aster quickly added: "Of course I know what happened in that room. I know he did. But now, my friend, I am speaking from the perspective of a police officer, wholly new to the circumstances. If we start babbling about time machines and invisible men, we will be thought lunatics."

Holmes shook his head. "It is a most unfortunate set of events, no question."

"And for you, Vavasour," said Aster. "More so than for me! I have already lost my position. I have no dependents. If I am sent to gaol, or transported, or even – God forbid – hanged, then nobody suffers but I. You, though, have an adoring wife, and two children. You have responsibilities, and a position in society, and prospects, and research that fascinates you. To lose all that, through no fault of your own! It is heartbreaking."

Holmes stared gloomily down at his toast. "It is," he conceded, "a most despondency-provoking circumstance."

For a while the two men continued their breakfast in silence. Eventually Aster spoke: "At what time did you ask the Inspector to call?"

"I only specified after breakfast. But Bucket is a prompt fellow. I would imagine he will come earlier rather than later."

"And I imagine he will arrive with some constables, in order to take us under arrest."

"Yes," said Holmes. "That is likely. Well, excuse me, Aster. I must write a note to my wife, explaining my position. She is hardly in a position to travel, having so recently given birth, but I can ask her to send one of the servants up with some necessaries. What does a fellow need, in prison, do you think?"

"She will be shocked," said Aster, delicately. "To receive such a note."

"It is not ideal timing, no," Holmes agreed. "But she would be more shocked, and indeed more angry, if I hid the truth from her using her recent labour, and exertions, as an excuse to shy from my painful duty."

Holmes went directly to his study and began writing a letter to Gwendolin. But as he wrote, the full enormity of what he was describing – depriving a loving wife of her husband, abandoning two young children to grow up fatherless – grew more and more pressing to him. How could he do it? "Say rather," he told himself, "how can it be avoided? The police doubtless already know everything. To attempt flat denial would be to add the ignominy and dishonour of being a liar to the judgment of society." *But*, retorted his inner voice, *you* are *innocent! Hawk attacked you. It was mere mischance that he died.* "I will of course attempt to explain so much to the Inspector," said Holmes, resuming his writing. "Though I do not know if he will believe me."

He had just finished his note when he heard the bell sound, through the wall, in Mrs Hudson's room. With a sigh, he folded his note, got up from his desk, and went through to meet his fate.

6

Inspector Bucket stepped into the parlour, removing his hat as he came, and Holmes shook his other hand. As he did so he was struck by the fundamental disproportion of what was about to happen: this pleasant man, with whom Holmes had always been on the best of terms, this modest-mannered man, quietly professional, not of the same social class as Holmes but, in his way, a gentleman – was about entirely to upend Holmes's life, destroy his reputation, remove his freedom. And he would do it courteously, with impeccable manners.

He would, Holmes thought, believe his victim's professions of innocency: but what could he do? There must be an arrest, for a man of wealth and status had been shot dead, and for that a price must be paid. Holmes and his legal team might, in court, raise, perhaps, a reasonable doubt, or enough of a shred of one to acquit him: but the trial itself would annihilate Holmes's social reputation and standing. He would go either to gaol, or the gallows, or have to retreat into a hermit's life in the country. And all this was because of events over which Holmes himself had no control. But here they were.

The first surprise was that Bucket came alone. But, Holmes thought, of course he trusted the decency of his quarry: a fellow who would come when requested, who would not need to be strong-armed.

Aster, on the sofa, was looking paler than he had. His breath came shallowly, and he winced when he reached up to shake the Inspector's hand.

"I am pleased to find you both here, gentleman," said Bucket, holding his hat before his stomach like a buckler.

"Will you take some tea, Inspector?" Holmes asked. "There is breakfast, if you haven't eaten yet."

"I won't, if it's all the same, though I thank you for the offer."

"Please do sit, though."

"Thank you." Bucket sat and placed his hat on the side-table. "Gentlemen, I must inform you I am here on official business."

"Of course you are," said Holmes. "Sir Percy Hawk?"

At this Bucket looked mildly surprised and, registering this fact, a tiny ember of hope in Holmes's heart glowed dimly red. "You have heard, then?"

"Heard?" asked Holmes.

"Of his death? It has been kept out of the papers, but will appear in the evening editions."

Aster, a fraction quicker on the uptake, said: "He is dead?"

"He committed suicide in his own home, last night."

Holmes and Aster looked at one another.

"Good gracious," said Aster, without conviction. "Really?"

"I'm afraid so. Mr Aster, I know you had no love for the man, and that he dismissed you from your employ following Sir Martin Malprelate's death. But I am sure you are grieved, as am I, by so tragic an end to the man's life."

"Suicide?"

"He shot himself."

"Good gracious," said Aster.

"But," Holmes offered, tentatively: "why?"

"Remorse, perhaps," said Bucket. "We did not find a final testament, explaining his action, but we found a memoir, of sorts. According to his butler Thompson – a decent fellow, but very deaf, and rather too unobservant to satisfy a police inspector's more exacting desires, a man came to call upon Sir Percy yesterday afternoon. Thompson did not recognise the man, and all my sergeant could extract from him by way of description is that he was a ruffian. Ugly and low class. And who had a cut upon his face. Much as you do, Mr Holmes!"

"Holmes and I spent the afternoon and evening yesterday together," said Aster, a little too eagerly.

Bucket looked at him somewhat quizzically.

"Did you, sir? Very well. Anyway, as I was saying: this low-born stranger had an interview in Sir Percy's study. When it was concluded, and the stranger had departed, Sir Percy opened his escritoire, took out the pistol he kept there, sat in his chair before his fire and shot himself in his forehead."

"Oh my," said Holmes.

"Very grim," agreed Bucket. "Might I smoke?"

"By all means," said Holmes, automatically. Only when he had spoken did he remember that he had placed the bullet, pulled from Aster's chest, in his ashtray. But it was too late to rescind the offer.

Bucket brought out his pipe, packed it with tobacco from a small pouch, and accepted a lit lucifer from Holmes. He puffed meditatively for a moment, and then breathed out.

It took all of Holmes's willpower to prevent himself staring at the ashtray. He forced himself to meet Bucket's eyes. He smiled.

"None of the staff were aware he possessed this pistol," Bucket said. "But there it was, still clutched in his right hand when the body was discovered."

"Do you know what time the act was," asked Holmes, "uh – enacted?"

"We cannot be sure. The body was discovered at about eleven pm, when a servant came through to see about Sir Percy's desires for supper. It was still warm, which perhaps meant he had taken his life but recently; but the chair in which he committed the deed was near the fire which may have meant he died hours earlier. It had burned down by the time the servants found the body, but there was still warmth coming from the embers."

"Somebody must have heard the shot, surely?"

"Nobody did. The butler swears he heard nothing, although, as I said, he himself is very deaf. The rest of the servants were in the far wing all afternoon and evening. Some talked of bangs and crashes in the early evening, but could not be sure: it may have been noises from the road, carts and carriages banging across the cobbles, workman working and so on. But shot there certainly was, for the pistol Sir Percy was holding had been discharged, and the bullet was in his forehead. Of course," Bucket added, looking shrewdly at Holmes. "There is another possibility."

"There is?"

"We must consider everything, no matter how unlikely. Could Sir Percy have been killed somewhere else, and moved back to his house? A risky procedure, for a servant or other onlooker would be likely to observe it. No, it is not likely. And it does not account for the other evidence."

Bucket took his pipe from his mouth and, without looking, reached over and tapped out the ashes into Holmes's tray.

"Other evidence?" Holmes prompted. When Bucket reached into his jacket for his tobacco pouch, Holmes cast a quick look at the ashtray. The bullet was only half-covered in grey soot.

"Inside his escritoire," said Bucket, refilling his pipe, "was an account Sir Percy had been keeping. A diary of sorts. I was up late into the night reading it, Mr Holmes, and it is strange stuff. Might I trouble you for another lucifer, Mr Holmes?"

"Of course."

"It is clear – ppff – that the dead man – ppff – blamed himself for the death of Sir Martin. Thank you, Mr Holmes. In the diary, in several places, he actually accuses himself of complicity in the death, although in phantasmagoric terms: claimed he could summon devil machines from the future and cast Sir Martin into their path. It's nothing a court would accept, you see. Nothing a judge would permit to be entered into evidence, for they would say it only speaks to Sir Percy not being in his right mind. As he manifestly wasn't, for he killed himself! But at the least we must accept that it evidences a degree of guilt that weighed upon Sir Percy's conscience. Now, how *justified* that guilt was – well: I don't know if we will ever know how far it was. Perhaps he did play some part in orchestrating the mob that rushed Sir Martin and beat him down..."

"The mob," Holmes repeated.

"... or perhaps he felt he could have done more to prevent it. Perhaps he had the chance to dissuade Sir Martin from going out that evening, and did not – I do not know. But guilt can be a powerful force, deforming the soul to the point where the supporting pillars shatter, and the crossbeams splinter, and the self collapses into self-murder. I pity Sir Percy. For though he presented an uncharitable and angry version of himself to the outer world, clearly there was a place inside him that suffered. I have sometimes seen guilt chew out a healthy human soul, like a grub inside a sailor's apple. Whatever we may think of Sir Percy, we must, in simple common humanity and charity, pray for him that, at the very least, he finds peace now."

Bucket stopped speaking and puffed at his pipe for a while. Holmes had to restrain himself from goggling at the man, after so uncharacteristic a stretch of eloquence. He caught Aster's eye, and saw, with a flash of insight, that his wounded friend was worried – worried that Holmes might blurt out a confession.

"I did not realise, Inspector," he said, "that you possessed such depths of insight into the human soul."

"It is a necessary skill for a policeman," Bucket replied.

Holmes experienced a giddy rush, as of blood gushing through his head; a knot of what might have been either excitement or terror – he couldn't say what – in his chest. "But," he said, "can you be sure Sir Percy's death *was* suicide? If there was no note?"

"Holmes," said Aster, in a warning tone.

"It is not in the strict sense a note," the inspector replied. "But his diary, or memorandum book, or – I know not what, exactly, to call it – amounts to such. Truly, Mr Holmes, it is the record of a disordered mind."

"But – "Holmes began, prepared to take the plunge.

"It is why I have come to see you, in fact."

This brought Holmes up short. "Sir Percy's memorandum book? Does it mention me?"

This puzzled Bucket. "Why would it mention you, Mr Holmes?"

"Holmes only means," Aster put in, from the sofa, "that he was working on a galvanic device, which had been commissioned by Sir Percy for some project of his own."

"Ah!" said Bucket. "Yes, I think I had heard something of the sort. No, Mr Holmes, he does not mention you. And I fear your contribution to his larger project would not have prospered. I asked an engineer friend of mine to take a look at those portions of the notebook and he assures me it's gibberish, Hurdy-gurdy terminology, impossible equations."

"And this made you wish to come speak to me?" Holmes asked. His buzzing excitement of anticipation was shifting in a deeper, more heady sense of liberation. The light gleamed as the train-tunnel's exit neared. Did it?

"Not the gibberish, of course, Mr Holmes – I do not mean to be insulting! No. It is Sir Percy's account of that memorable day, on the north bank of Westminster Bridge." Bucket looked over at Aster. "You were there as well, of course."

"An important bridgehead," said Aster.

"As you know, Mr Holmes, you have pressed upon me a – shall we say: counter-intuitive account of what happened that day."

"An account you did not endorse from your own memories of events."

"I am not sure *what* I saw, Mr Holmes. I can be that honest. But my sense is that I saw … shall we say, that I saw only what it was possible to see. Mr Aster: what did you see?"

"You mean," said Aster, in a pained voice, cradling the right side of his chest with his left hand: "the mob? There must have been a reason why they advanced to the northern side of the bridge but went no further."

"My men were lined-up, let us not forget," said the Inspector.

"But they were few, and the demonstrators were very many. Why did they turn back?"

"They either chose of their own will, *en masse*, to retreat," said Holmes, his stomach fizzing, "or they were compelled to turn back against their will. The problem with the latter explanation is that you, Inspector, simply lacked the numbers of constables to achieve it by force. The problem with the former explanation is – well, human nature, Inspector! Exactly what you were talking about a moment ago. One man might be discouraged, or have a change of heart. Two or three might. But every single man jack of them?"

"I do take the force of your argument, Mr Holmes," Bucket said. He took his pipe from his mouth and reached over to empty it, again, into the ashtray.

"As you know, Inspector," Holmes began, but then stopped – for he saw that Bucket was looking for the ashtray, to be sure he tapped out his pipe cleanly into it. He located it, and then he stared at it.

Had he seen the bullet? It was plainly visible, poking through the ash. Or did Bucket merely see an unusually large, silver-grey cinder?

The policeman reached over, tapped out his pipe, and put it away in his jacket. "You were saying?"

"As you know," Holmes continued, his heart burbling. "I have a different view of the second option. You think the crowd was forced back across the bridge by the intimidating sight of your twelve officers. I saw – or think I saw – something more unusual: a passage, as though acted upon by Arabian Nights genii, that transported the whole crowd back in one swift movement."

"Exactly," said Bucket, getting to his feet. "And that is why I came to see you. Reading Sir Percy's book of memoranda, I came across an account of that day from his perspective.

You'll remember he arrived, shortly before the crowd advanced, in his carriage."

"Inside which he hid," Aster recalled, testily, "for his driver had fled like a coward and he could not move it."

"Just so – though coward seems to me, if you'll forgive the observation sir, a touch uncharitable. But Sir Percy's account accords, Mr Holmes, with yours."

"Really!"

"Indeed, it goes further. Sir Percy claims credit for the dissolution of the mob. He says he himself projected – his word, gentlemen, *projected* – the marchers instantaneously back across the bridge. It is not clear from his account how he believes himself to have achieved this. The sheer power of his mind perhaps? Some aspects of the magical machinery he elsewhere boasts about? At any rate: during our previous conversation, Mr Holmes, I suggested that all the witnesses at that event agreed with me, in terms of what we saw, and you were alone in your more unusual testimony. But now, in all policemanly good-conscience, I am come to inform you: there was another witness at that event whose account tallies with yours."

"It is a poor sort of confirmation," Aster noted, "if the man's balance-of-mind was so disordered. You are quite right to rebuke me for uncharity – I confess it, I have no great love for Sir Percy, but a gentleman and a Christian ought not to speak ill of another, least of all the dead. So I will not use the word insanity. Nevertheless!"

Bucket nodded at Aster, and then bobbed his head again at Holmes. "As for me, sir, I must remain within the bounds of plausibility. But I am here to tell you sir, if I implied that your account lapsed into mere impossibility, I apologise. Say rather, it is im*plausible*. But if two witnesses agree in reporting an implausible thing, it becomes less implausible. Perhaps other witnesses will come forward – men from the mob, it may be – who add further support, and I might have to reopen the matter."

"It is not likely such lawbreakers will voluntarily approach the police," Aster noted.

"I do not disagree, Mr Aster. And until such time, Mr Holmes, I am here to tell you, the authorities consider the matter closed."

For a moment – only a brief moment – Bucket's steady gaze met Holmes's, and held it. Holmes was visited by a moment of surety: *Bucket knew all.* He was cognizant of everything that had happened. This entire exchange was his way of speaking the "official" truth in order to communicate, as in in code, this fact to Holmes. But then the Inspector was walking smoothly out of the parlour and down the stairs, and as soon as the mutual gaze was broken, Holmes doubted that Bucket knew anything at all. Such is the incertitude of embodied existence.

Once he had gone, Holmes found himself trembling. He stepped past the breakfast table, opened the *armoire à boissons* and poured himself a brandy.

"Good god man," said Aster, laughing and wincing from the pain that the laughter was causing him. "You thought he had come to arrest you!"

"I did," said Holmes. He downed his drink, and gasped, and then took a seat opposite his friend. "By God, Aster, so I did!"

"We are in the clear," said Aster. "For which I thank providence! And yet it is nothing more than natural justice. We did *not* murder Hawk, Vavasour – he attempted to murder us, and was hoist on his own petard. Guilt for this is not our portion."

"No," said Holmes. "I suppose not."

"For a moment there I thought you were going to confess to the Inspector!" Aster laughed, again flinching from the pain of the laughter.

"For a moment," said Holmes. "So did I."

"And so the matter is tied-up. There is an official solution, which is no solution. And there is another solution, a no-solution, that will never be official."

"Tied-up and shuffled away," said Holmes. "I tell you, my friend: it has quite discouraged me from pursuing any further investigations into mysteries, of any kind whatsoever."

AUTHOR'S NOTE

Some of the names in this story, of places (Middlemarch, Barsetshire) and people (Scrooge, Copperfield) are famous enough not to need explanation. The character of Sir Persimmon Hawk is my invention, but in my headcanon he is the brother of savage old Sir Mulberry Hawk from *Nicholas Nickleby*, whose baronetcy he inherits when the old rake dies in disgrace, childless, in France. Mr Wittiterly, the senior clerk, is a character from the same novel. The incident with the hairless bear is adapted, though considerably altered, from Scott's *Redgauntlet*. I have taken the name William Reynolds – he is unnamed in H G Wells's novel – from Christopher Priest's fine novel *The Space Machine* (1976). James Carker running away with his employer's wife is from *Dombey and Son*. Those curious as to Carker's eventual fate can, by reading that novel, discover it.

I have taken the liberty of moving the celebrated Chartist mass meeting at Kennington Common from its actual date, of April 10th, 1848, to a place nearer the end of the year. But it was, as I notate in this novel, widely feared that this gathering was the first stage in revolution. The real-life William Cuffay was a tailor, not a carter, but he was a leading figure in the movement, later transported to Tasmania for his political activities.